TEN SIGMA

THE TEN SIGMA SERIES BOOK 1

A. W. WANG

*To all those who fight the good fight
and never give up…*

ONE

In the dying rays of daylight, the old man leaning on a cane and huddling inside a black cloak watches me through the frosted bay window. Although he stands across the street and the shadow from his broad-brimmed hat rests over his face, I can see his electric blue eyes and ugly speckled-gray mustache. The icy temperature coupled with the swirling gusts of winter should dissuade him from looking into my bedroom, but he's been rooted in the unpleasant environment for the past five minutes. I don't know who he is or why he's there, but I'm annoyed at the intrusion in my life.

"Mary, are you okay?"

I turn my head.

Just beyond the footboard of the bed, the ancient hologram projector displays my younger sister Emily in her kitchen outfit, hair pulled into a tight bun, a white apron cinched around her narrow waist, and a mixing bowl and spoon in either hand. Although she's harried and the spotty communications channel runs static over her body, the figurines sitting in the bookcase behind her 3D image form a heavenly halo around her angelic face.

Emily is the first in a small parade of well-wishing friends and family expecting to digitally visit me this afternoon.

"One second." I pluck at my thick sweater. Underneath, my sweat-soaked shirt clings to my itchy skin while a pool of nausea lingers in my stomach and bile pushes up my throat.

When my husband, Nick, who's been seated in the alcove of the bay window, rises to help, I wave him back to his chair.

After another minute of clenching my teeth and taking steady breaths to quiet the side-effects of my newest cancer treatment, I nod.

Emily continues speaking about her preparations for our family's traditional holiday dinner. As the words spill from her mouth in a jovial tone, her sad eyes betray the somberness of my situation.

My indignation rises at the world and the invasion of privacy. I don't need pity. My gaze flicks past Nick and outside to the street.

Holding the wide hat and still propped on his cane, my unwanted intruder hunches as a fierce wind swirls through his cloak.

How can I be that interesting?

Before I complain, a squeaky voice comes over the channel. "Hi, Mommy!"

My spirits lift at the thought of my niece. "Let me see her."

Relieved to spread the burden of the conversation, Emily says to her seven-year-old, "Darla!" She waves the spoon in a come here gesture and says with more urgency, "Darla, it's your aunt Mary."

"I'm playing," replies the high-pitched voice.

The hologram empties as Emily leaves the frame to chase her reticent daughter. There is a groan, and she returns carrying an adorable girl of seven with long brunette pigtails hanging down a messy red and green dress. Although the youngster has my sister's cute nose and the darker traits of her father, her uncommon violet eyes are her best feature.

I smile for my niece and give her a hello by splaying my fingers and twisting my elbow in a giant wave.

Darla opens and closes her small hand as a response. "What happened with your hair?"

Blowing out a breath, I send my fingertips through the remnants of my once luxurious red hair. I should have worn a cap, but my scalp is on fire, and it's all I can do not to claw at it. "Your aunt is a little sick, but I'll be better soon."

The girl returns a toothy smile. A life-threatening illness is beyond her understanding. "Ugh, you are getting too heavy," Emily says as she deposits her load to the floor.

Before Darla runs out of the hologram, she sends a goodbye kiss.

Emily brushes imaginary strands of strawberry hair from her forehead and smooths her apron. "Sorry, you know how fussy kids are."

Although I can't have any children, I understand their motivations, and considering the circumstances, the tiny stretch of time has gone as well as could be expected. "No, it's great to see her. And it gives me another reason to get healthy."

Emily's tightening lips betray her worries about the failure of my first four treatments.

Because she thinks the odds are stacked against me.

My throat scratches from dryness, and I let out a weak cough.

Leather crinkles as Nick gets off his chair. He steps to the nightstand and grabs a bottle of water. When he offers me the straw with a big smile, the musky scent of his old bomber jacket flows over the bed.

Embraced by the reassuring odor, I relax as I sip the tepid liquid.

The hologram glitters as Emily changes the subject. "Mom and Dad are trying to get over to you. There are riots and a high terror alert in St. Louis, so they'll be a day late."

Nick says, "We'll be on the lookout. If any other issues come up, just let me know."

Although he's only trying to shield me from the world's problems so I can concentrate on my own, I frown at the over-protectiveness.

A crash of pans comes from the hologram. Emily throws her hands to the sky. "Damn. Sorry, I have to cut this short."

"It's okay," I say.

She clasps her fingers in front of her chest. "Don't get discouraged. Things are always darkest before the dawn. We're a family and we'll get through this together. If you need money for more treatments, just ask."

Nick leans over me. "Don't worry, Em. We'll be fine. We have investments."

"Great. We'll arrive next Sunday. See you then."

After the hologram dissolves in a sparkle of static, my calm mood evaporates, and I glare at my husband. We've liquidated our stocks and bonds over the past year.

"I took out a second mortgage on the house," he explains.

An angry breath leaves my lips. Every painstaking detail of this place matches my antiquated tastes. I love every part of our two-bedroom cottage, from the oiled wood-molding framing the white-and-red-flowered wallpaper, to the vintage furniture and adorable trinkets found from years of wandering through flea markets and estate sales. I'm even fond of the old smell hanging in the hallway. Everything feels comfortable and right.

And now all will be sacrificed at the altar of my sickness.

"How much is left?"

"Enough."

Knowing my husband of eleven years, the answer means we spent the funds on my last failed cancer therapy.

I chew on a dirty fingernail, a habit he's been trying to get me to break since college.

When he frowns, I pull the digit from my mouth and waggle it at him. "I wish you would consult with me before you do these things."

"Why?" he says with innocence. "The price of a house is nothing compared to your health."

Glancing away, I shake my head. Nick doesn't consider the debts, only the potential cures. "If the worst happens, you'll have nothing."

A confident grin creases his face, the expression saying he will make sure everything is okay. It's one of the many reasons I love him. "When you're better, we'll make everything back. Who's a better team than us?"

That is my husband, Nick—always taking charge and dreaming the big dream. His optimism keeps us charging forward. My healthy skepticism keeps us grounded and sane. The combination is why we work so well together.

I let his cheerfulness win and say with a conviction I don't feel, "Fine, my college friends are next."

"No."

"No? I really want to see them."

"For today, no more guests. Unless you need more pity."

I curl my lips to show lots of teeth and wrinkle my face into an "Only a Mother Could Love" expression.

Laughing, he marches to the bookcase and unplugs the hologram machine. "Today is a day for fresh air, exercise, and happy spirits. We'll bundle you up and go for a walk and check out the holiday decorations. Maybe even get a bite at your favorite waffle house."

Although my stomach mounts a mini-rebellion at the notion of eating, his mood infects the rest of my body. I push myself to the edge of the bed, letting my feet touch the hardwood floor. "Fine, but this year for the festivities, you do all the cooking."

He steps in front of me, holding my custom walking shoes, and pumps his head in a vigorous nod. "Damn straight."

As he kneels and puts on the heavy one with the large heel, I add, "And all the dishes."

"Damn straight again." The winning smile reappears, wider than ever.

Even though Nick's lying about the money and Emily has her worries, I know with their help and support everything will get better. We always beat the odds, and I can't imagine that in this case, the sickness will win against all of our efforts.

"Before we go, one thing first," I say, pointing to the bay window.

Nick looks outside and then gives me a questioning expression. "What?"

Only a gusting wind blows down the empty street.

TWO

THE CLOMPING OF a cane on the hardwood floor interrupts the night. In the center of the bookcase, the glowing hands of the vintage clock point to midnight. Despite tingles I imagine are tiny spiders roaming across the back of my neck, I strangely have no fear.

An uneasy moment passes before the figure of the man in black slips into my bedroom and quietly closes the door. Framed by the dim slats of the streetlight seeping through gaps in the curtains, he tips his broad-brimmed hat.

Although an inevitability surrounds this visit, I slap my cheeks to make sure it's not a dream or hallucination.

The intruding form is neither.

Leaking a foul mist, he hovers at the footboard. Then with his free hand trailing over the polished wood, he hobbles past the bookcase. A greasy film spreads from anywhere his fingertips linger while oil drips off his cloak with every labored step.

I shiver from revulsion.

After passing the bedpost, pausing only to smooth a wrinkle in the comforter, he completes the journey by plopping into the alcove chair. As he removes the broad-brimmed hat, the odor of mothballs invades my personal space.

Wrinkling my nose, I push myself upright against the headboard. When a momentary dizziness passes, I turn on the small lamp centered on the nightstand.

The golden-hued light spilling through the lampshade reveals the tired face of an old man under wild tufts of scraggly white hair. His brows are bushy. Deep smile lines crease his cheeks while worry wrinkles crisscross his forehead. Unruly gray hairs form a thin mustache under his prominent nose. Except for a spark of youth in his blue eyes, he exudes the weariness of someone who has traveled too many long journeys. No oily smoke surrounds him, nor is anything greasy; his winter cloak is only wet from melted snow.

Angry with the side-effects of my latest treatment, I scowl.

Instead of reacting to my disdain, he pulls an inhaler from his breast pocket and gulps a mouthful.

I glance at the doorway. Where is Nick? In our PR consulting business, he handles the people stuff while I take care of the practical matters—meaning everything else. It's why we make a great team.

My visitor says, "Your poor husband is getting some much-needed rest."

"Who are you?"

He attempts a welcoming smile and is clearly not used to the gesture. It comes out as squarish, both too wide and toothy, as if he read an instruction manual on how to put a person at ease. When I arch my eyebrow, he sighs. "Forgive my intrusion. This is new to me."

"Breaking into other people's homes?"

His lips curl into a sarcastic expression, which fits his wrinkled face perfectly. "I'm from the government."

I loop my finger over the surroundings. "Yeah, because I'm so special." The sarcasm undercutting my tone feels exactly right.

Sighing again, he sets his cane against the side of the chair and pulls out a leather wallet. When he flips it open, a hologram of DARPA, the Defense Advanced Research Projects Agency glitters.

I shrug, deciding the expense of forging something that intricate would outweigh anything a conman could get from our drained bank accounts. While not penniless, we're close to it. "Okay, you're from the government."

After putting the identification away, he says, "First, let me congratulate you. Your potential is extremely high, and I wanted to make the offer myself." He pauses for dramatic effect. "We've been watching you for quite some time."

I snort mucus bubbles from my nose. Another reason not to like him. While the childish reaction is satisfying, I quickly wipe my face clean.

"If you would refrain from uncouth behavior, you'll find that my proposal may be beneficial to both of us."

"I need my husband."

"The poor man is asleep in that garishly decorated man-cave. In the morning, he'll feel better than he has in a long time."

"He's allowed his tastes."

"I trust you can speak for yourself?"

Annoyed by the rhetorical question, I reply, "Of course, I can make my own decisions. Why are you here?"

As his electric blue eyes study me as if I'm a biology experiment, I resist shrinking from the unwanted attention.

"I represent a group of scientists who have created a military program called Ten Sigma. It requires exceptional volunteers."

"And this concerns me in what way?" I say, loving sarcasm more than ever.

He takes a wheezy breath. "Everything discussed here has the highest classification. Nothing may be repeated to anyone under any circumstances. Do you agree?"

Somehow curiosity wins over dislike, and I nod.

"The United States as we know it is finished."

"That can't be true."

"Why? All the great empires have fallen over the course of history. Even Rome."

"We would have heard something in the news."

"Would you feel better if society ended because of an atomic bomb or some computer hack? Perhaps a wave of zombies?

"No. This catastrophe won't begin with anything that obvious. It will be something small like a missed bond payment or a pension fund missing an obligation. Maybe an entitlement program will be curtailed. Then the contagion will spread and the house of cards will crumble. This is the result of the empty promises of too many politicians for too many years. The bill for all the free stuff is coming due."

"The Ten Sigma Program is supposed to stop this?"

"No, the tipping point has passed. The program is meant to help pick up the pieces."

I frown, resisting the prognostication. "I still don't understand why I'm so special that you're sitting in my bedroom in the middle of the night."

He smirks. "I'm here sitting in your bedroom in the middle of the night to offer you an escape from this existence."

Despite the discomfort, I lean forward.

"We can remove your consciousness from your body and place it into a virtual world that will seem as real as this room. There, you will never go hungry, never be thirsty, never be sick. Never even have to go to the bathroom if you don't want to." He chuckles at the last perk.

The technology is past the cutting edge of science fiction, yet I see no reason to doubt him. "I have mixed feelings from my one computer programming class."

"You will only be required to function within the world."

"Given the problems you just mentioned, you need some sort of master magician. Aside from doing well in math, I'm not sure how I qualify as special."

He pinches his chin, saying, "Your life is rather unremarkable—"

"That's very kind."

"Let me finish," he says, raising his hand. "While you live a nondescript existence, your test scores are very interesting."

"Test scores?" Before he can answer, I put it together. "You mean the unnecessary body and brain scan that we spent our remaining healthcare ration on?"

He flicks his fingers, diminishing the importance of my question. "Yes, yes. The very same. They indicate you have exceptional situational awareness which is a highly desirable trait for our program."

"That tells me nothing."

"Do you enjoy driving?"

"Nobody drives."

His fingers repeat the same grating movements. "Of course, but when the self-driver program on your car malfunctioned and tried to career through a guardrail, you saved the car. And your sister Emily."

"That was when I was eleven. Everyone would have done that."

"Everyone would have tried, but you succeeded."

"My leg still got mangled in the accident."

His eyes bore into me. "You survived and that makes you special, because under times of stress, almost all people become myopic, while you expand your field of attention. In the worst predicaments, time slows down for you. And we know of three other cases where this exceptional trait of yours came into play. This type of intuition cannot be taught."

I think of the tingling sensations that run over my nape whenever something isn't right. "I can't even eat without making a mess."

"Poor table manners are irrelevant. We're not producing English aristocrats."

The joke on top of the flattery almost makes me laugh. Almost.

"I'm a glorified accountant with a gimpy leg and nothing more."

"Please don't be so hasty. For your potential, the compensation would be quite generous. All of your external medical debts nullified and two years of standard salary for your husband. We've only made this offer in one other case."

"What would I have to do?"

"The exact details are only available in the virtual universe. However, to make an over-generalization, you would give us your soul."

"Will I see my family again?"

"That is not the purpose of the program."

"Then, no."

He frowns. "We are maximizing the potential of people who can change the world. But you want to waste your talents. You allowed one physical injury to turn you into a stay-at-home bookworm."

This lecture seems to be coming from my father. "Did your stalking include learning precisely how to get under my skin?"

"Forgive my bluntness. My passion for this program sometimes gets the better of my temperament. Please think of this offer as a second chance to realize your potential. Your situation is terminal."

"This is 2050 and cancer has been curable for years."

"Most forms are. But yours is a newly discovered type. It's a cancer that produces other forms of cancer."

"You expect me to believe that?"

"Research papers will be released in the coming months, and there aren't any cures. Any treatments work only temporarily, then the hostile cells send out a mutated pathogen to produce a different form of cancer. The current remedies only handle the symptoms, not the actual cause.

"You can spend money you don't have on one of the clinics that have sprouted up in the hinterlands. But, they'll only prolong your agony and each cycle will weaken your body until one of them finally kills you."

I take a few deep breaths, not knowing what to believe. Then my dislike for the government and love for my family makes the decision for me.

"While the offer is interesting, I'll get through this with my support group. You'll have to find another perfect person."

"As a person, you are certainly not perfect. Far from it. At best, you're an incomplete human being, using your family and friends to cover up for all of your shortcomings instead of growing by facing your insecurities."

My anger rises. "You've never had a family."

"No," he admits. "I've never been coddled and allowed my potential to be stifled."

"Well, the answer is still no."

He pretends not to hear. "Your poor husband does love you."

"Did you figure this out by yourself?"

"No, the profiler did. He concluded that your husband will destroy himself to save you. Is this what you want?"

"We will beat this," I say, chewing a nail.

When he scowls at my nervous habit, I feel better. A little petty but definitely better.

"The poor man will kill himself before allowing you to die because he truly loves you. Will you allow that to happen? And destroy the rest of your family in a pointless endeavor?"

I don't have an answer, but I've had enough of my midnight visitor. "This is my home, and it's time for you to leave."

"You're an unusual case. You follow the rules but hate authority."

"Did your profiler tell you that?"

"No, your unruly attitude did."

I slam my palms on the sheets. Unsurprisingly, kowtowing to government flunkies in the middle of the night in my bedroom brings out the worst in me. "You want unruly? Get out. If what you say is true about a coming apocalypse, then what type of person would I be to leave my family?"

He takes a gulp from the inhaler and, grimacing, pushes on the cane. The floor squeaks as he shakily rises. After finding steady footing, he replaces the broad-brimmed hat. "The world is getting worse and now is the time for bold thought and sacrifice. The program needs superior individuals."

From inside his sleeve, he produces an electronic pad, the size of a business card, and places it on the bed. "This contains the pertinent information for the Ten Sigma Program. It's coded to your DNA. When you're ready, just press your thumb in the lower right corner."

My reply comes in a deliberate tone. "I will not leave my family. And I never want to see you again."

"I shall honor your wish. You shall never see me again. Please understand that while the coming disaster is inevitable, your mediocrity is not." With a tip of the broad-brimmed hat, he hobbles past the bed.

After opening the door, he draws another breath from the inhaler. "Remember, this conversation should remain confidential, especially anything regarding any incidental surveillance by the government. Any disclosure will null the terms on the card and open you to charges of espionage."

Without waiting for a response, he slips out of the room.

As the clomps of the cane fade into the night, my fingers touch the silky surface of the device.

I should smash it.
I really should.

THREE

UNDER THE LAST glows of the sun streaming past distant mountains, Nick carefully negotiates the rickety handcart down a rocky ridge. The jostles and hairpin turns of the narrow, winding foot trail—which my healthy self would love—send waves of queasiness into my stomach.

Pushing down a surge of bile, I take a deep breath of the thin spring air and try not to fall from my overly inclined seat.

Mercifully, after a few minutes of nothing worse than pebbles tumbling down the treacherous slope, the creaking wheels roll onto level ground as the last of the sunset surrenders to twilight.

I sigh with relief and appreciate the beauty in the streaks of pink and violet painting the stretched clouds near the horizon.

Ahead of us lies our exit from this sea of desolation, a dusty airfield with a single dirt runway, while behind and beyond the ridge resides a dingy two-bed clinic, another disappointment in our ends of the Earth search for my cure.

The worst part of the fruitless journey is the resignation seeping into my psyche. As predicted, increasing fevers, nausea, and dizziness have accompanied each new treatment cycle. The sickness is going to win. Sometimes, I wish it would just score a decisive victory and end my life before killing everyone around me.

You are terminal. Your husband will destroy himself trying to save you.

True to his promise, the man in the broad-brimmed hat hasn't returned. But after these months, he never strays far from my thoughts, especially after failures like the last three clinics.

This insanity has to end.

"Stop."

Nick sets down the handles of the wooden cart and removes his sun hat. As he stuffs the floppy material into his back pocket, his pearly teeth flash in a wide smile. The confident expression only adds to my annoyance.

"Okay, so that didn't exactly work," he says.

"That specialist was a quack. And we're running out of quacks to visit and the money to visit them."

"At least he pinpointed the cause. That's something."

While Nick's thrilled about the discovery, I place the win squarely under the ledger of the man in the broad-brimmed hat, who correctly predicted the diagnosis.

I squirm under my thick blanket. Despite the chill settling from the coming night, my body is pouring out beads of sweat.

"We can't keep doing this."

Nick fiddles with his scruffy hair, considering a delicate response to my despair. Thinking of the last vestiges of hair under my headscarf doesn't help my mood.

The parched air tickles my throat. I grab the squirt bottle from the sidewall and spill water into my mouth. The warm liquid tastes stale but serves its purpose while giving Nick a chance to complete his thoughts.

After I finish, he takes a deliberate step toward the carriage. Although his smile tightens into a straight line, his eyes twinkle in the gloom.

My mood softens even as I want to frown. "Nick…"

"This is the first step toward a cure." With gentleness, he kneels before me, grasping my hands much as he did on the night he proposed.

Even in the diminished light, I see he believes every word.

"This is the last one. I'm done," I reply. Given my terminal prognosis and its costs, his life would have been far better if I had said *"No."*

"Now, we know what we're dealing with and someplace on this green Earth is the cure. We'll find it." He brings my hands to his chin. "You think if I let you go quietly, I'll have enough left so I can pick up the pieces and have a life."

After eleven years of marriage, he knows my thoughts very well. "That's what you deserve."

"Mary, without you, my life is over. So, if you die, I'll die too."

While his death would be metaphorical, I get his point because I would do the same for him. "You'll find someone else."

He gently squeezes my fingers. "Listen to me. We're a team. No matter what. You can't quit. No matter how hard it gets, you don't stop until you're whole and healthy."

"We can't keep going like this."

He returns an understanding stare. "This is just a temporary thing. After you're cured, we'll have the rest of our lives together. That's a long time."

My lips quiver as the big dreamer optimism weakens my resolve. The man in the broad-brimmed hat can't be right about everything. But even if he is, I'd rather face the coming calamity with my family rather than as part of some stupid program.

Nick pulls out his wallet and flips it open. "I have a new credit line, and this last doctor said a lot of research is happening near the Canadian border. So promise."

I sigh. Although the other credit lines are fully drawn, I can't stand in the way of his faith. "I promise," I whisper.

Satisfied, he rises and grabs the cart handles. The gravel crunches under his boots as he runs us to the tiny airport with a newfound pep in his stride.

As I gnaw on a dirty fingernail to pass the time, a nagging thought pesters my mind.

You'll wind up killing your husband.

FOUR

From the middle of the ceiling, a slowly flickering bulb casts a pall over my ratty bed while shadows shroud the rest of the tall cubicle. Beneath the dark panel of a flat screen TV, happy "Get Well" cards stand amongst shriveled arrangements of flowers on a corner table. The spoiled food from my untouched breakfast sits on a plastic tray at my side.

Death, with its chilly touch and sickly stench, lingers everywhere.

The makeshift medical center is located in a failed warehouse and all we can afford. Although the level of care is more than nothing, with only five doctors and thirty staff serving a thousand patients, it's barely enough.

I force out an angry sigh.

2051 has rolled past with the backdrop of chaos growing larger and the promises of politicians becoming more hollow. Now, with the return of the holiday season, the man in the broad-brimmed hat and his offer occupy most of my thoughts. Too many of his prognostications for the country and my health have come to fruition.

While my mind is still sharp, my frail body, battered from the unrelenting assault of the sickness, rests under a loose smock sandwiched between sheets stinking of dried sweat. With each breath, my lungs labor while every twitch causes my flaming skin to itch from bedsores. I shift my legs, willing the movements to remain silent.

Visiting hours are long past, but my exhausted husband sits just beyond the siderail of the bed with his eyes closed.

Although he still keeps his big dream optimism, I wish he would complain. Something, any tirade about the unfairness of life would be welcome. Instead, he only gives sympathetic understanding. He only wants me to live.

And I only have guilt. I blink back tears of frustration.

While I'm the nerdy one, he's got the charisma and winning smile. Together, as a team, we've conquered everything.

Except for this sickness.

The disease and the medical bills have won. Our wonderful cottage has three mortgages and our twenty-four percent interest credit lines are full. Emily and her husband have given us Darla's college money. We have no more resources.

But Nick won't stop trying even if it kills him and destroys everyone we hold dear.

A tear spills down my cheek.

I'm thirty-three and that's too young to die.

As I come to terms with the lack of options, I listen to the faint chirps of the obsolete EKG machine and watch clear fluid drip into my IV tube.

The dirty sheets rustle when a persistent itch forces me to scratch at my gimpy leg.

Nick's head pops up. "Are you okay?"

As I nod, the tips of my breathing cannula tickle the hairs inside my nostrils. I wrinkle my nose.

After smiling at the funny expression, he stands and grabs a tissue. As he lovingly wipes the tear from my face, I frown at my inadequacies. I'm supposed to be the steady one.

When he fumbles with the TV control, I shake my head. The thought of watching National Guardsmen battling food rioters in southern California or what new Draconian measures are being used to quell the disturbances along the East Coast turns my stomach.

"Do you want dinner?"

"No," I whisper. Speaking is painful. "Go home and rest."

He removes his glasses and pinches the top of his nose. Under his speckled hair, fine lines of worry etch his forehead while fresh wrinkles crease the sides of his bleary eyes. He wants to stay, but there are more bills to pay and more negotiations to have with collection agents.

After a moment's deliberation, he plants a goodnight kiss on my cheek.

I force a smile.

He returns to the edge of the bed and gazes at me with the look. It's the one he had during our first date, after we first made love, and throughout our wedding day. It's the one that says, "You're my one and only love." And on this of all nights, the expression that makes me feel I can do anything is here again.

I will myself not to break down or betray my plans. Instead of meeting his gaze and crying, my eyes wander over my emaciated body.

"Remember your promise to never give up. You don't quit until you're whole and healthy again," he says in a tender voice. Then, his fingers gently tilt my head until he fills my sight.

Although I return a shallow nod, my heart wells with sadness.

"Mary, promise," he says with urgency.

My lips squeeze together before I whisper, "Promise."

He holds the stare for an uncomfortable moment then puts on his glasses and grabs his leather bomber jacket. At the doorway, he stops. "There's another lead in the Andes. This will be the one. So keep your head high and stay strong. I'll see you bright and early tomorrow."

While the flickers of light play over his glasses, I bite my lip. Never have I uttered a lie to my husband and I won't start now. Staying silent, I lift my palm and wiggle my bony fingers in a goodbye wave.

When the door shuts, I reach below the sheets and pull out the electronic card from my midnight visitor. As my thumb hovers over the silky surface, I hesitate. Committing to the decision is harder than I expected.

I gaze at the ceiling, wishing I could talk with someone without nullifying the offer.

In the best case, Nick is right, and the final remedy lies at the end of this trip. Then we'll pay off the debts and survive the coming disaster together.

More likely, the cure fails or I die in the process. And if I die, then only the debts will remain.

My eyes drift back to the card.

Besides receiving a healthy body, I have no idea of what will happen in the Ten Sigma Program, and I hate the idea of being alone.

A few seconds lapse before I sigh at the selfish thoughts. This isn't about me. This is only about doing what's best for my loved ones. It's time for Nick and me to diverge from our life plan. While I'll hopefully survive like he wants, we're going to be separated, and the thought tears at my insides.

After taking a sorrowful breath, I blank my mind and force my thumb onto the lower right corner.

The device chirps in acknowledgment and displays my enrollment information.

Test Subject: #30578A.

When my arm flops to the sheets, the damning thing slips through my fingers and tumbles off the bed, hitting the floor with a lonely clatter.

FIVE

THE REPRESENTATIVES of the Ten Sigma Program time their arrival with midnight. Instead of using names, they introduce themselves by their function. Mr. Leader, a workout warrior, dresses in a gray suit complete with a bold red tie. A taller woman, Ms. Lawyer, sports a professional haircut and conceals her femininity under a loose blue top covered by a conservative gray jacket. The last member of the team, Mr. Scientist, drapes a white lab coat over his pudgy frame.

Not wanting to stare up at the guests of necessary evil, I use a surge of adrenaline to grab the bed control and push myself into a sitting position.

As my torso rises, the leader ensures our privacy by locking the door. With crisp motions, Ms. Lawyer pulls a large glass tablet from her briefcase while Mr. Scientist sets a square black container on the EKG machine.

My heart thumps, and my nails crease my palms. Clenching my stomach and taking shallow breaths, I force aside the nausea; it's important not to show weakness to these people.

"There are a few legalities to attend to before we begin," Mr. Leader announces.

Sporting a professional smile, Ms. Lawyer holds the screen in front of me. While her wedding ring glimmers under the flickering light, a sexy perfume overpowers my ever-present odor of sickness. I wonder which of the gentlemen she fancies. My single healthy self would have picked the nerdy scientist, but I suspect she prefers the powerful official.

Glowing yellow text appears on the tablet, seeming to float over the clear surface.

"You'll find everything as stipulated," she says in a practiced tone that omits any softness. I make tiny bobs of my head as she swipes through various pages, the fine print blurring past my tired eyes. It's only when she reaches the last section that I focus.

"In return for your cooperation, our organization shall pay all the medical bills you have accrued during your illness. In addition, your husband shall receive the equivalent of two years of salary from a new life insurance policy."

She brings up the final page which requires a thumb and voice signature.

I shake my head. It hurts to form words, but I croak out, "And all liens on our home and lines of credit. Also, any loans from my sister Emily." My husband will be alone, but I'll make sure he gets a fresh start.

"You may think the recommendation from this program's lead scientist entitles you to special dispensations, but we do not renegotiate our agreements."

It's torture, but I speak louder. "No. The debts too."

"Nobody else entering this program gets anything."

"Valerie, we need her," Mr. Leader interrupts. His fingers gently touch the inside of her arm, which to me confirms their illicit affair.

"The family loans can be made up," she replies with measured anger.

The muscular man considers then asks, "The rest of the documented debts and a year of salary for your sister?"

I dip my head.

"Fine, three years and debts," the disgusted woman says. A moment passes before her face recovers a professional demeanor and with irritated flicks of her fingers, she alters the agreement.

This time, when she presents the acceptance form, I press my thumb onto the tablet and say, "I agree to abide by these terms."

"Because of the secrecy of the program, you shall be declared dead ten minutes after the transfer of your consciousness. Your husband will receive the death certificate within three days. Upon completion of a seven-day waiting period, the life insurance policy will be paid to the appropriate parties and your debts zeroed. You are now the property of the United States of America."

Although she is speaking on behalf of governmental responsibilities, the details are important because my husband must be one hundred percent certain I'm gone or he'll never go on with his life. "Thank you," I whisper.

With a huff, she passes the tablet to her lover.

He presses his thumb onto the glass, saying, "The United States of America accepts this contract."

A moment later, the device beeps and a mechanical voice replies with a confirmation code.

The ordeal is finished, and I sigh in relief. Except for keeping my last promise to never give up, this reset is all I can do for my husband and family.

Now, there is only eternity to deal with the consequences.

The slim tablet disappears into the briefcase, and with the legal portion of the festivities complete, Ms. Lawyer steps aside.

Mr. Scientist takes her place. When he pulls the cover from the cube-shaped container, the black sides fall to reveal a glassy sphere crowned by a ring of gold. Attached wires lead to a silvery headband. The entire contraption looks completely innocent and incredibly fragile.

A proud smile crosses his face. "This is the download machine."

As I push out the words, my throat burns. "I'll be stored in that?"

"Yes, this is an electro-magnetic containment field for your consciousness, until we can get you into the virtual environment."

"What happens in there?"

Ms. Lawyer steps forward. "Whatever we deem necessary, which is stipulated in the agreement."

I roll my eyes at both my question and her answer.

What does it matter and what difference does it make?

Regardless of the program's secrecy, I will have no opportunity to divulge any information.

And regardless of knowing what will happen, my body is going to waste away.

Whatever will be, will be...

Mr. Leader quietly says, "This is a special access project to create a specific type of warrior."

His lover shoots daggers at him. He'll need a week of perfect behavior to return to her good graces.

He ignores her anger. "We are creating fighters who will be essentially impossible to kill. The virtual environment is a proving ground to hone your skills."

I get my husband to kill insects and mice. I'm not even sure I could hit another person. If they want a fighter, they have their work cut out for them. However, I'm too tired to tell them the flaw in their plan.

"So, I can come back?"

"Not to that body. But yes, the goal is to create warriors in this world."

It's all I need to know. I made a promise to my husband, and when I return whole and healthy from the virtual universe, that pledge will be kept.

"Okay."

Wearing a curious look of reverence, Mr. Scientist places the cold metal band snugly around the wisps of hair remaining on my scalp.

In a final goodbye, my eyes wander down the filthy sheets, trailing the flatness of my form. Besides ridding myself of the sickness and fixing the finances of my family, I have one other reason to commit to such a drastic unknown.

I can't stand losing, especially to the hanging gloom of death.

"Whenever you're ready?" Mr. Leader asks.

With these people, I don't feel the need for last words or fanfare. "Just do it."

He nods and Mr. Scientist touches a switch on the device, giving an unnecessary countdown.

"Three."

I relax by closing my eyes and enjoying the salty taste of my thumbnail. As my final sensory input, it's oddly satisfying.

"Two, one…"

Instead of zero, a jolt ripples through my reality.

My eyes fly open.

The dreary surroundings have flattened into a picture, as if it had originally been a two-dimensional cutout folded to create a 3D room. Cracks extend from the floor, crawling over the flat surface, and follow the outlines of my IV tubes, the rails of my bed, the visitor's chair, and the EKG machine, extending up and past the darkened TV and into the ceiling. When they reach the flickering light at the apex, the material shatters into long geometric shapes that spin as they fall into the distance and disappear.

Next, the center of the gray backdrop behind my splintering reality pulls away with an awful shredding sound, stretching the fabric of space and creating an endless tunnel that darkens into infinity.

My arms flail as my existence tilts, and suddenly I'm above the passage, slipping forward and then tumbling into the virtual universe, accompanied only by my pointless screams.

SIX

SURROUNDED by shrieking echoes of hysteria, my sickened, naked form falls faster, even as the dark end of the tunnel rockets into the distance.

What mystery awaits there, I have no idea.

"This can't be real, this is a virtual computer simulation," I repeat, fighting the fear consuming my insides.

The meaning of the words dies when a new force arrives and buffets me, penetrating my skin and softening my tissues and bones.

Quaking with panic, I scream louder when my flesh starts stretching into goo.

The incoherent sound leaks past my mushy lips, slowly joining all the other notes of my previous screams, which somehow are matching pace with my descent.

Rationality abandons my thoughts as everything from the toes of my gimpy leg to the wisps of hair on my head liquefy and drift apart, the streaked droplets riding alongside the accompanying chorus of fear.

The unseen forces continue shredding the elongating blobs of flesh until I'm only a streaking rain of dust accelerating down an ever-lengthening tunnel.

My self-control disintegrates, but when I cry out, nothing comes out of my now nonexistent mouth.

Then, even the dust disappears, leaving only my consciousness riding on the crazy journey.

To keep a sliver of my sanity, I focus on my husband and my promise to him.

I will never quit until I return whole and healthy.

The passage meets a glassy sphere and stops stretching.

My speed rockets higher.

Engulfed by terror, I cling to the image of my husband sleeping next to my hospital bed and brace for the collision.

At the final instant, a tiny aperture appears in the curved surface.

As I flash through it, the invisible forces leave, and an abrupt halt jars my consciousness, ending the awful descent.

While I wail in mute horror, the accompanying chorus of fright withers into silence. Then the aperture shuts, sealing me alone without form or substance in an icy blackness.

———

When rational thought returns, I toss choice curses at the representatives of the Ten Sigma Program—the man in the broad-brimmed hat, Mr. Leader, Ms. Lawyer, and Mr. Scientist. Especially Ms. Lawyer, for her irrational devotion to secrecy.

Time stretches in the nothingness. Perhaps a minute passes, perhaps a century, until suddenly, I'm no longer alone.

Looming from the edge of my perception, giant presences hover like hazy shadows. They are the masters of this universe, the virtual overlords. Why that knowledge arrives, I have no idea.

As they trade indistinguishable whispers, I sense curiosity, anticipation, and surprisingly, twinges of envy, anger, and hate.

What have I gotten myself into?

Before I can consider the question, the ether of my form coalesces into a vortex of golden sparks. While the glittering dots swirl, they lengthen and become fine golden threads weaving into a tight lattice until I'm a glowing tapestry of memories and essence.

A vast dome of the most perfect blue appears.

I'm awestruck, and the fabric of my being trembles at its beauty.

The invisible vortex returns and shreds my woven form.

My mind shrieks as I struggle to hold the material together.

As the golden scraps tumble into the cyclone, I abandon the effort to preserve my physical self and fight to retain my sanity, concentrating on my husband Nick and my family—all the good things from my life.

Agony twists through my core as the decaying pieces whip around the whirlwind's center and dissolve into their individual threads. Many of the shimmering strands split and regrow. A few crumble into dust.

Sparks of red and specks of black materialize, instantly getting swept into the maelstrom. When they stretch into filaments matching the length of my gold threads, a shock hits me.

They are altering my essence.

Before I can resist, a black filament slams against my consciousness, wrapping and tugging at my perception until my world alters into …

Salty air tainted with sulfur under a cloud-streaked sky. I blink to fight the sting in my eyes as my combat boots dig into loose sand and I sprint up a blackened shoreline. Nearby, friends fall in thick splashes of red while bullets spray dirt and whiz past my face. I lurch from an explosion spraying sand over my helmet then plow through puffs of greasy smoke, reaching the cusp of the beach. The wooden stock of my rifle pounds into my shoulder as I fire at the nearest enemy, whose head bursts into bits of blood and bone. Quickly reloading, I charge over a slit trench and fire again.

Shocked by the ferocity, I wrench myself from the clutches of the foreign memory, spinning back into the black and red blizzard.

A red filament instantly grabs me and hijacks my reality.

The heavy weight of a short sword rests in my grip. Despite seeing quite a few Roman movies, I never knew it was called a gladius. I take a tentative swing and then a thrust. Moving faster, my hand and body practice combinations of attack and defense. The pace increases and soon, the parries, thrusts, dodges, swings, and footwork blur into a long smear of motion. When the dizzying training finally stops, I understand everything I didn't want to know about fighting with a short sword.

I'm ripped back into the whirling threads. Helpless against the mysterious forces, I grasp at the memories of my loved ones to combat the militaristic knowledge flooding into my being.

A black strand engulfs my mind.

I thud up and down inside the confines of a suit of armor, the heavy air stinking of fermented sweat. Resisting the urge to heave, I aim my lance at an escaping swordsman. The tip punches past his flimsy leather protection. Impaled, he drops in a puddle of blood as screams pour through his contorted lips. After yanking the lance from his twitching body, I twist my stallion to pursue another fleeing enemy. Elation spreads throughout my being as the distance shrinks.

The savage emotion drives me back to sanity. Blood makes me squeamish.

I am not a fighter.

A tangle of red slashes across my mind.

Under a cone of illumination in a black space, a .22 semi-automatic pistol rests on a table in front of me. I disassemble and reassemble the weapon in twenty-six seconds. Not fast enough. I try again and again, continuing until my speed is acceptable. Another pistol, this one a .45, appears. I repeat the same process, my fingers blurring under the bright light.

After each success, a different gun, one of every type of rifle and pistol, materializes for a new round of learning.

When the firearm instruction finishes, more red threads overrun my consciousness.

Dressed in a white karategi, I stand under the midday sun in a dirt square. After assuming a horse stance, my body flows into the different positions, practicing the dance of a martial arts form. Like everything else, the speed increases until my motions blur. When I stop, my mind overflows with every nuance of Karate. An instant later, my body resets and repeats the exhausting process for Kendo. Jujutsu follows. Then another one. Seemingly lasting forever, the session covers every variation of moving and punching and kicking in everything from Aikido to Wing Chun Kung Fu.

When the last of the empty-handed techniques concludes, other red threads pound knife fighting lessons into me. Having only rudimentary culinary skills in the real world, the sheer number of ways a sharp edge can be used to kill or maim is amazing.

After I'm kicked back into the tempest, I understand. The red threads contain martial knowledge and the black ones hold combat experiences.

The understanding vanishes as more of them claw at my consciousness. Ugly skirmishes from trench warfare in WWI fill my mind. Surrounded by the hordes of Genghis Khan, I help destroy a long-lost civilization. Pens, glasses, rulers, cards—every mundane item becomes a deadly weapon in my hands. The lessons move into all forms of street fighting. Then techniques for every bladed weapon. Guns. Explosives. Moving in all possible terrains. Combat in jungle, deserts, ice, steppes, and forests become second nature.

And I kill in every conceivable way. Hundreds of thousands of people fall under my hands or feet or whatever exotic weapon is available.

Mercifully, I maintain my sense of self by focusing on my husband and family as I lose count of the number of times the process repeats.

The maelstrom abruptly stops.

Wind gusts down a lonely, frost-covered avenue while a dusting of snow swirls around my huddled, shivering body. The jagged ruins of a large factory surround me. Ice covers my matted hair and inside my frozen boots, my toes tingle from frostbite.

This isn't the product of a thread.

My reality is Christmas day, 1942, during the siege of Stalingrad. I'm exhausted and starving from over thirty straight days of fighting in the fierce Russian winter. There would be no shame in resting my eyes and letting the cold take me.

I won't succumb.

Surprised to find my body responding to my commands, I push my frozen fingers into my ammo pouch and then after forcing them around a clip, reload my old rifle with shaky hands.

The clink of metal treads heralds a fresh German attack. At the far edge of the street, white-clad stormtroopers fan out behind a gray tank with a prominent swastika painted on its side.

Although we cannot surrender a millimeter of ground, in face of the disparity of numbers, my few remaining comrades scuttle away.

Bullets zip past.

Crusts of snow fall from my winter coat as I force my frozen body to move, hunkering down, my eyes flicking from the irresistible German attack to the safety of retreat.

"What will you do?"

I pause, not knowing the source of the strange question. In my prior safe life, depending on my husband, the answer would be easy. But with the numbness, the shaking ground from the unstoppable tank rattling my frozen bones, and the projectiles whizzing past my helmet, this is utterly different.

Each icy breath scorching down my throat magnifies the fear tugging at my psyche. My husband is the brave one while I'm the back-office person.

The question reverberates as the tank swivels its long gun at me.

Having to act but not wanting to make a decision, my panic explodes. But before I can take action, everything warps and drops away, and a new situation arises.

The clash of swords rings between burning stone buildings as Greek hoplites, the bronze circles of their heavy armor rattling, rush down the haze-infested streets.

While I lie in a darkened hollow between two high walls, the screams of the terrified citizenry echo in my ears. My leg throbs from the gash of a spear wound.

I'm a Trojan, and the Greeks are sacking Troy.

Children hide in a dark staircase across the street while another Trojan beckons me to escape in the other direction.

Ignoring the pain in my leg and wishing I could be anywhere else, I rise and consider my options, wondering what my husband would do.

Nothing comes to mind when the bearded faces of a phalanx of Greek warriors approach, their short bladed xiphos at the ready. Coughing from the smoke, I waffle in indecision.

"What will you do?"

Again, I'm transported to another hopeless place before the answer comes.

The hot Pacific sun beats on my wrinkled and emaciated body, the white sand of an atoll burning my bare feet. Huge warriors from a neighboring tribe, blood-painted cannibals displaying macabre necklaces decorated with human body parts, advance behind a wall of shields, ready to destroy the thatched huts and innocent people from my fishing village. We're outnumbered ten to one.

Others from my island paddle away in dugout canoes. It would be so easy to join them in the safety of the ocean.

The woman and children cry as the enemy nears.

"What will you do?"

As I hesitate, I fly into another desperate scene in a jungle and then the process repeats in an 18th century city. Each time, the same two choices are presented: charge into an unwinnable battle against an implacable foe or give into fear. And each time, reality warps into a different situation before I can force myself to choose.

What would I do?

I have no idea, and I don't want to know.

Finally, the cycle of desperate realities stops.

I'm back in the indeterminate place, my mind stretched like taffy. After the shock fades, I'm only left with my fright, embedded in an exploded consciousness.

The vortex is gone.

Uncountable red and black threads are woven throughout my golden form. While not a violent person, the power of the knowledge sends a thrill into my being.

It shouldn't be that way.

I retreat into my essence and panic. In place of my name, there is only a designation, B243-R9860-000I-74N.

What else is missing?

Alarmed by the depth of the changes, I look for memories. Scattered images appear. The first ones are broken. I frantically search for something intact. A low, one-story home of red brick means nothing. Nor does a purple ribbon looped through a shiny medal. Children play but I never had any.

A vivid image of a man sitting by a hospital bed surfaces.

He is my husband, Nick, and I love him.

My other memories bind around his steadying influence. Besides my loving husband, I had parents and a sibling. Also, a niece with beautiful violet eyes.

The main elements of my life are intact.

I will not quit until I'm whole and healthy again.

The promise offers a flicker of hope. No amount of training can alter who I am as a person.

With that bravado, I confront my biggest remaining problem.

B243-R9860-000I-74N.

The sanitary designation is not a name, and I won't accept it as my identity.

The man in the broad-brimmed hat said I would be forfeiting my soul to the government, but I won't surrender that easily.

After a moment's consideration, I return to my memories. My husband is Nick, my sister is Emily, and my niece is Darla.

Nick, Emily, Darla...

For as long as I can hold on to their love, I will keep my essence. For every trial I have to endure, for everything that will happen in this weird place, so long as I retain a grasp on my family, the virtual world won't change who I am.

No matter what happens.

After a moment, I silently repeat with less confidence, *No matter what happens.*

SEVEN

THE DOWNSTAIRS COMPUTER science lab rarely gets visitors. It's in the basement, there are no windows, and the company is just us geeks. Fifteen guys and four gals, including me, are stuffed into the dingy room. One of them is my future husband, Nick. The other three girls and at least four of the guys are in love with him.

I don't care. My stupid program isn't working, my last shower was two days ago, and spilled portions of my dinner salad lie over my lap. I'm an overworked mathematician, pretending to be a computer scientist because it will help my job prospects. I curse at the person who recommended the course.

As I chew on my ratty nails and stare at the screen, willing the lines of code to function, laughter erupts. My frustration boils, and I slam my hands on the table.

A few curious glances come my way.

The unwanted attention overcomes my anger, and I return to my work, putting my head down and not saying anything.

Snickers come from the rabble-rousers, who look ready to begin again, but the ringleader, my future husband, rises and shushes everyone. Then he walks to my workstation.

Before he sits next to me, I hurriedly brush my dinner off my jeans.

"Hi," he says in a friendly voice and with a winning smile. "Sorry about the loudness."

"I'm not angry at you. I'm angry with my idiotic programming."

He laughs.

His good nature is infectious and despite my mood, I discard my frown.

"You, you're the smart one in the class. I'm just trying to get my communications degree. But one of my friends said I needed to take this class to get a job."

After moving a lock of red hair over my ear, I smile with him. He is cute, and I like the smell of his leather bomber jacket.

Shaking his head, he says, "I really hate that person now."

"Me too."

We laugh together.

While not love at first sight, it's a start.

———

Air expands my lungs to bursting, and the dream ends. My eyelids flutter open.

I have a body!

Better yet, I have a healthy body. Even better than that, my formerly gimpy leg is symmetrical with the other one. And they're longer. A lot longer.

I'm tall.

My urge to dance a jig wanes as I examine the new me. The only thing matching old me is the luxurious mane of red hair pouring over my shoulders.

The rest is seriously upgraded. Unblemished, smooth skin covers perfectly toned muscles that run the length of my body. There are more curves than I remember, especially around my breasts and thighs.

Feeling conspicuous and uncomfortable with my new stature, I slouch.

This form is something for you to become.

Not sure of the origins of the faint thought, I move onto more important things and survey the immediate area.

While I've always been observant, my perception is astounding. In an instant, I take in every detail of the environment.

A naked man with bulging muscles stands in front of me. Reminding me of someone I can't recollect, he sports a cleft chin. Ten meters away, a nude woman has a striking mane of blonde hair. Beyond her, another woman—model pretty and also naked—sways on muscular legs. From my high school or college? Should I recognize them?

Perhaps, I'm layering familiar traits onto the different people to feel more comfortable. Or maybe it's a desperate attempt to cling to my past. I'm not sure.

Scattered behind them are one hundred and fifty-eight other nude men and women.

Although I lack clothing too, nothing about the bizarre circumstances is arousing.

We stand under a cloudless gray sky on a tacky, rust-colored platform. Except for a slow rise that peaks in the center, the large circular structure is featureless. Beyond the edge, a translucent-red ocean stretches to the horizon. Despite the mild acidic breeze, its surface remains flat.

Welcome to the virtual universe.

The sea rises, and the crowd ripples. I hold my breath as the liquid oozes over the lip of the platform with a hiss.

Acid!

A directive appears in my mind: *"This is a primordial test—be the final one."*

Everyone else must die.

Before I can react to the horrible notion, the man with the cleft chin bares his teeth and charges.

Panicked, I step backward.

He launches a vicious sidekick.

While the blow is expertly delivered, I easily slide past it, amazed by my coordination.

Off balance, he fires a lethal follow-up punch that I parry and guide past my cheek. I use my other hand to slip under his guard and jam him in the throat.

He gags.

Before he recovers, I twist his arm aside and snap his neck with a jolt from my hands.

His limp body collapses at my feet.

Horror wells inside me as I stare at his broken form. He had equal training to myself, yet without thought, I defeated him easily.

I'm supposed to be klutzy, and now he's dead because I killed him.

Trying to come to grips with the disparate thoughts, I tear my eyes from the awful sight.

Across the platform, chaos reigns. Mad, naked strangers battle, wounding, maiming, and killing each other as far as the eye can see.

A crunch of cartilage comes from the closest fight as a man pummels the face of his smaller opponent.

Shying from the carnage, I circle toward the edge of the rising ocean.

A huge man with dark curly hair singles me out, but a pretty woman with full lips shrieks and jumps on his back, trying to claw his eyes out.

Pain sears the side of my foot.

I yelp, jumping from the acid and up the slope. When I check, the skin is melted an angry red. As if emphasizing the danger, hisses come from the bodies being consumed by the advancing sea.

It's die by acid or fight to be the sole survivor. Hating both choices, I pause, wishing to be anywhere else.

What will you do?

I made a promise and getting eaten by a corrosive liquid would get in the way of keeping it. Steeling my nerves, I edge toward the battle.

Before I complete my third tentative step, a muscular-legged woman leaps and hurls a punch at my face.

With a snap of an elbow, I break her fist then drive a stomp-kick into her knee as she lands.

Her leg crumples.

As she staggers forward, I smash my other knee into her bare chest, shattering her rib cage.

She flops onto her back with blood spewing from her mouth. She could be someone from a ladies' night out. A moment passes before I can rip my attention from her dead body.

Because I have trouble killing insects…

I force away the revulsion and focus on completing the gory task.

Across the dwindling landmass, tangled combatants fight a confused battle. The nauseating sounds of bones cracking and devastating blows pummeling flesh fill the air. At most, half remain standing, while the broken forms of the rest lie scattered in hideous poses over the platform.

Although people grunt from exertions, nobody cries for mercy or shows any other manifestation of fear.

Very strange.

With the corrosive sea rising behind me, there's no time to waste.

Nearby, a man knocks the woman with the lovely blonde hair to the ground and pounds on her face.

I leap at him and drive my fist through his temple.

He succumbs instantly, blood leaking from his eyes, and his limp body collapses in a heap.

When the bloody mess of the woman I saved rises and attacks me, I kill her too.

What's happening? What am I becoming?

There is no time to ponder. Another man with bloodied genitals hanging by a flap of skin singles me out. The victor of several fights, this combatant moves with intelligence, and thankfully, reminds me of nobody.

Disregarding the other battles, we cautiously circle each other. As we search for weakness, no words are spoken, nor am I surprised. What would be the point? Only one of us is leaving this island alive.

And that person will be me.

He charges behind a slick Savate combination.

I yield ground then reply with lightning punches and kicks from three different martial arts to keep him off-balanced.

As the fight lengthens, his strategy changes. He wanted a quick kill but has realized that won't happen. From lessons taught by the black threads, I know he's planning to feint a lethal attack and then try to damage something to limit my fighting ability.

We exchange strikes with no effect, then he launches a roundhouse at my head. It's the decoy.

After I dodge, he brings his leg back for a heel kick aimed to destroy my front knee. As he delivers the blow, I loop the leg backward then lunge inside his foot. Slipping past his guard, I grapple with his arms and drive my forehead through his nose with a disgusting crunch.

As his eyes roll into his head, I twist and fling him down the incline and into the acid.

After filling my lungs with mouthfuls of tainted air, I walk higher and survey what's left. Of the original one hundred and sixty-two, only two women and five men remain besides me.

One is a charismatic girl with striking violet eyes circled by a heart-shaped face. She is unhurt. Even though there are six others, my instincts say this person will be my last opponent.

A breeze bearing the scent of death ends the momentary truce.

All must die.

While the girl with the amazing eyes duels a taller man protecting a broken arm, a woman with a torn nose jumps at me.

Because blood clouds her vision, and she has trouble breathing, I easily dispatch her after I destroy her elbow with a Jujutsu technique.

My next opponent hobbles with an injured shin.

I crush his other leg using a Thai kick and before he hits the tacky surface, I plow my kneecap through his nose.

It makes an appalling noise.

When I look up the slope, only the girl with the violet eyes is standing. Everyone else lies dead. In an unspoken accord, we edge toward the peak, getting away from the gruesome bodies and sizzles of the rising acid.

After we stop, her eyes study me. Unlike everyone else, this girl is cautious and not relying on her newfound abilities. And that makes her far more dangerous than anyone else.

The lull ends when she opens the contest using an Eastern boxing style.

I counter with a flurry of kicks and punches.

When we separate, I'm nursing a fractured foot while she shakes a broken hand.

Long hisses arrive as the rising ocean meets some fresh meat.

The fight has to end quickly. Because she has more mobility, but her wounded hand carries no punching power and weakens her defense, I abandon any sophistication and lunge at her, grabbing the fingers of her injured hand and crushing them.

She grunts in pain and smashes me in the face with her free palm.

Stars cloud my vision as my nose breaks, but I return a punch that wrecks a couple of her ribs.

She staggers then closes, sending a knee into my thigh, which deadens the already wounded leg.

As I stumble backward, she leaps and uppercuts the flat of her forearm to shatter my cheekbone.

While spikes of pain stab into my face, my fist blasts into her chin, breaking two of my knuckles.

Her head rocks back and before she can recover, I launch the base of my hand in a sword strike at her throat.

She twists away but my fingers catch enough tissue to cripple her breathing. While she gulps for air, I destroy another two knuckles punching her nose. Ignoring the pain stabbing up my arm, I follow with a shot to her chest. The blow drops her, and while she lies on her back, I snap her neck with a vicious stomp of my heel.

I rest my weight on my good leg, my lungs struggling to supply oxygen to my exhausted body. Although my face screams in pain, and my injured hand dangles from my wrist, I am the only one alive.

The last one standing.

Since I've never had a shred of athletic talent or physical ability, the result is unexpected to say the least.

"What will you do?"

The carnage below isn't the answer to the strange, yet familiar question. All my actions were based on self-preservation, not any noble sense of self-sacrifice. The fighting has only proven that combat seems to agree with me.

Except…

From next to my foot, the stunning violet eyes of my last victim stare skyward.

The part of me that was appalled by the violence lies mute. Perhaps my callousness derives from using the threads and allowing uncountable experiences of war to pollute my mind. Or perhaps my lack of morality results from the fractures spread across my memories.

However, regardless of the reason, I respond to her unspoken recriminations with blankness, which is more troubling than the number of people I've just killed. Even though I had to keep my promise, the dead deserve better than a hollow stare.

A savage howl cuts through my melancholy. A brutish man—bald, a head taller and half again heavier than myself—strides to the apex of the platform. His powerful arms flex as they raise a broken body over his gleaming head.

I couldn't have missed such an opponent.

After the giant fixes his beady eyes on me, he bares his teeth and tosses his victim in my direction. The tumbling mass of flesh lands with a thump and slides down the shallow slope.

When the macabre trophy stops short of my toes, I roar in defiance. Although severely injured, I limp forward to meet his challenge. It doesn't matter where he came from, he's going to die too.

He's upon me before I can react. A lightning punch cracks three ribs and punctures a lung.

Wheezing, I lower my elbow to protect my damaged midsection.

A hook arrives and obliterates my broken cheekbone, collapsing shredded flesh and bone splinters into my mouth.

Hands covering my face, I give a pitiful moan. The huge man is incredibly strong and much faster.

My leg cracks from a kick, and I'm lying on the platform. Agony screams from every part of my body. Dazed, I helplessly stare as his heel crashes into my broken ribs, shattering bones and shredding internal organs.

As I tremble from the fresh injuries, he kneels next to me, grabbing my hair.

Another weak moan pours from my lips as he yanks my head up.

Then in quick succession, his meaty fist mashes twice into my broken face.

The hand holding my hair releases its grip, and stunned by the brutality, I do nothing as my torso flops to the platform.

Disoriented and blinking from the shock, I wait for my end, unable to move, only seeing the gray sky high above me.

The hissing sounds of flesh being consumed by the rising acid grow louder.

My eyes search wildly for the bald giant. He's nowhere in sight, but shockingly, I'm more afraid of his return than I am of being horribly dissolved by a corrosive fluid.

Long seconds pass and then my destroyed mouth emits a wail as the acid trickles under me, searing skin and tissue.

I'm going to die.

EIGHT

My consciousness returns to electric tingles running over quivering muscles. My knees press into my breasts while my arms wrap around my ankles. I'm curled into a ball.

After the strange sensation evaporates, a moment lapses before I realize the air is devoid of acidic undertones and nobody is stomping my life away.

I brush my fingertips over my face, finding only smooth skin and intact bones. Miraculously, the gruesome injuries to my mouth and nose have been healed. Amazed but disbelieving the news, I move my hands down my pain-free body, verifying that everything is in a perfect state.

I died.

No, that isn't right. I didn't die. I was wounded and on the verge of dying, but just as the acid touched me, a wave of golden sparks filled my vision.

And now, I'm here.

Straightening my limbs, I roll onto my back and open my eyes to the same long, accentuated form.

This is going to take getting used to...

While I'm not naked, I'm not happy with what passes for clothing.

It's like underwear, only less. The band over my breasts resembles a strapless bra except thinner, showing too much over and under and made from a sheer black material so stretched it enhances the shape of everything underneath. The garment covering my bottom is similar although perhaps covering proportionately less area.

I sigh. The style is minimalist to be sure.

Beyond my feet, the new surroundings are different, peaceful. Instead of a coarse representation of a circular island, the new place is a cheery representation of a military barracks.

I lie on the bottom mattress of a beige-colored bunk bed. Rows of the same indistinguishable and featureless metal frames sit to either side. Further away, mostly dull earth tones cover the curving wall and domed ceiling of the gigantic circular space. The overhead lights are off and the only illumination arrives from rectangles of sunlight pouring from small square openings cut into the top of the wall.

A broken image of my cottage, painstakingly adorned with vintage furniture and exquisite antiques collected throughout the years with my husband comes to mind. When I examine things closer, my memory is still fractured and the label B243-R9860-000I-74N resides where my name should be.

Silently, I recite the names of my loved ones.

"Nick, Darla, Emily—"

Hums fill the air while the other beds shake. When the rattling stops, every one of them holds a new individual.

Terrified, I desperately search for the bald giant, whom I'm expecting to jump out and kill me at any moment.

What have I gotten myself into?

But none of the newcomers threaten, instead most rub their hands over their bodies like I did, probably checking for wounds that are now healed.

I force aside the irrational fears. Part of me doesn't believe the bald giant even existed because he certainly was far stronger than humanly possible.

"Hello! My name is Haiku," says a happy voice as a strawberry aroma cascades over the bed.

Above me, a small girl floats in the aisle. Her glimmering silver hair stretches to her lower back, complimenting the sparkle in her silver eyes. Draped over her thin body is a simple dress woven from a fine silver material, the loose hem hanging below her knees. Streaks of dirt stain the bottoms of her bare feet, conforming to the earthy feel of the rest of the place.

Her pleasant appearance juxtaposed with everything that happened on the island and all the lethal knowledge stuffed into my mind is weird at best and downright insane at worst.

I arch an eyebrow.

"Have you acclimated to your new body?"

Involuntarily, my hands again travel over my face and torso, double checking the healing power of the virtual overlords. "So, every wound can be healed?"

Her smile brightens the immediate area. "Of course, no matter how badly you are wounded we can always repair it."

"Then, I can't die?"

The smile returns, impossibly wider. "I wouldn't say that."

"What does that mean?"

"All will be explained in due time. Meanwhile, don't do anything to get yourself killed."

I once again look for the bald giant, who I was sure had already murdered me. The question of his identity forms in my mind, but no matter how hard I try, my mouth refuses to ask it.

What the hell is wrong with this place?

Haiku breaks my forced silence. "Congratulations on passing your first test."

I imagine the revolting sounds of breaking bones and the haunting stares of the dead in the middle of the sea of red acid. The remorse that should be exploding from my conscious is nowhere to be found.

"What is wrong with me?"

"Nothing. You are better than you were before and will become better still. All will be explained at the appropriate times.

"For now, please accept that I am an artificial intelligence programmed to be your guide, friend, and confidante. This is Home, your place of rest. If you call my name, I will appear anytime you are within this sanctuary."

She doesn't tell me the magic word to make her disappear.

The pillow crinkles when I flop my head back onto the bed and glare at the beige underside of the upper bunk.

"Come with me, your body is restored and there is much to learn."

Her too-cheery mood is grating on my nerves. Expelling a long breath, I close my eyes. Normally, I'm the type who sarcastically quips while staying in the background and not rocking the boat, but listening to a twelve-year-old therapist while almost naked in a room full of similarly clad people after a bloodbath is going too far. "I am not moving until I get something decent to wear."

Tingles of static leech onto my skin. As my orientation changes, my frustration builds until a long curse spews from my lips.

———

When my lungs empty, the curse ends, and I open my eyes. I'm sitting as part of a semicircle in a windowless room with bright, colorful geometric shapes glowing from the wall and cloying scents of honey and citrus filling the air.

A therapist's wet dream...

The four women and five men occupying the other cushioned chairs send me questioning looks.

I sheepishly slouch into my seat.

They are all fit, looking like the "After" photo of a health magazine, and wearing the same ribbons of clothing as myself except for the men being bare-chested. Similar to the deathmatch, the atmosphere strangely lacks any sexuality. At least, it mostly does.

Sitting farthest to my right, a lean, plain-faced man whose most distinguishing feature is spiky brown hair leaves his dark, unblinking eyes focused on my body.

I fold my arms and angle myself away from the unwanted attention, the legs of my chair squeaking on the hardwood floor.

Dirty feet and all, Haiku appears with a pop and floats in the center of the group.

"Congratulations on passing your first test, and welcome to the Ten Sigma Program," she announces in too bright a voice. Then sweeping her hands over us, she continues, "All of you will comprise a team." She pauses, expecting some positive reaction.

A few ragged claps fill the void.

"Are there any questions?"

Two seats to my left, a large, attractive man with perfect ebony skin raises his hand. He has a square face that's strong and somber eyes fused with certainty. "Excuse me, but you don't seem to be a typical drill sergeant."

Happiness flashes through her expression. "The red fibers are your weapons training. The black threads give you the experiences of thousands of soldiers. That is all you need. My function is to accustom you to the new environment and then guide you through the next series of trials. This appearance is designed to put you at ease. No mean taskmasters here!"

Troubled smiles appear across the semicircle.

I shift, uncomfortable as well, wondering if anyone else feels the disconnect between her unabashed joy and the horrific killing in the middle of the sea of acid.

Characters and numbers forming the designations of my teammates enter my mind.

Sitting on my right, a woman of Indian descent raises her hand. Her shiny black hair is braided into a ponytail while long bangs frame her roundish face. She's pretty in a welcoming sort of way, which softens the appearance of her well-toned figure.

"I've shortened my designation to Suri. Instead of that sixteen-digit alphanumeric monstrosity, maybe we can go around the group and have everybody make up a simple name for themselves and explain from what's left of their personal history why they decided to enter this wonderful program?"

The sarcasm underlying her statement elicits nervous chuckles. I guess when everyone was stuffed with the threads, they went through the same hell I did, and judging from the dour expressions, nobody is happy with the results.

Haiku speaks over the unrest. "That is an excellent idea to help create informal bonds. Let's begin on my right and go through the semicircle in order."

The third person to my left, a slender brunette sitting in a closed posture, shyly rubs behind her ear. Her dark hair lies in a loose bun atop her head. She has a handsome face and looks in her mid-twenties. "Vela, I like that name," she says in a flat voice. "An animal attack disfigured me. After a few years of bad bone and skin grafts, I decided not to stay home for the rest of my life."

She stops and a few seconds pass before the next person, the attractive man with the drill sergeant question, speaks. "Jock. Football quadriplegic." He taps an unblemished arm. "I used to have a tattoo here. A screaming eagle that lit up in the dark. I'll have to adjust to this bare look."

A surprising number of nods come from around the group. I wonder how many piercings and other works of body art were left behind.

"Don't get too bummed if you lost one," Jock says with a grin. "Not having a glowing signpost in a night fight is probably for the best."

Genuine laughter greets the remark. Despite never having body ornaments, I laugh too.

Jock finishes with a flourish. "I wanted to enlist straight out of college, so this is a fresh chance to help my country."

When Haiku gleefully applauds, I roll my eyes.

Suri notices my reaction with a faint smirk.

A young-looking teen with flaxen shoulder-length hair follows. Surprisingly, residing amongst his delicate features, is a pimple in the middle of his chin. He purses his full lips. "Walt. To celebrate my eighteenth birthday, I committed suicide," he says, glancing at his arms. "Or at least, I got myself most of the way there. I suppose this is better than what I left."

After the last word trails off, he rubs his chin hard enough to erase the pimple and gazes at his feet.

Guess he doesn't want to add any specific details.

When nothing else is forthcoming, the attention shifts to me.

My identifier is B243-R9860-000I-74N. By using only the letters, it reduces to B-R-I-N.

"Brin—I suppose that works as well as anything."

I pause, surveying the semicircle. I can understand Walt's point of limiting personal history. While there are many good things left in my memories, I did abandon my loved ones, even if it was to save them. These people are strangers and I really have no incentive to share more than necessary, especially with the creepy glances coming from the spiky-haired man. "Terminal illness."

When I tighten my lips, Suri gathers my introduction is finished.

"Suri. Old age. I was ninety-two when my spouse died, so I didn't have much time left. Then the riots happened, and I took the risk." She gestures down at her young and flawless body. "And now I look like this, so except for the killing and the absence of libido, it's a pretty good trade-off."

I snort while the others laugh. At least I'm not the only one who's noticed the dearth of sexual tension. Vela touches her cheek as if still not believing her virtual appearance. I guess the disfigurement was horrible.

The three people after Suri add their stories. A chunky-bodied ex-politician calling himself Simon, Ally who is a cute, engaging girl with freckles, and Carol anxiously twirling her long blond hair—victims of old age, alcoholism, and arson.

Sitting with a perfect posture in the second to last position is a balding man with a wide face dominated by a flattish nose and square chin. "Rick. I was in the army."

From the rod I imagine stuck up his back, it figures. I decide Sergeant Rick has a nice ring to it.

He continues. "I was a captain and in charge of the Thirty-Third Rangers."

Still calling you Sergeant Rick.

Although he speaks quietly, an undertone of strength accompanies his words. "I got hit in a firefight after an airdrop in the Himalayas. Shot in the gut and bleeding out. Got lucky, when my master sergeant dragged me to the medics, they had one of those quantum things and pulled my consciousness out. I want you to know I take teamwork very seriously. I will assist anyone who needs it. I have your backs."

In the few seconds of speaking, his blue eyes connect with everyone in the semicircle. While overly polished, Sergeant Rick's straightforwardness reeks of honesty. I'm not sure if he's likable, but I trust him.

At least more than I trust anyone else in this crazy place.

The ex-ranger looks to the last person, the man with the lecherous stares, whose dark eyes flick across the semicircle with suspicion. Then of everyone, his gaze locks on me.

A queasiness puddles in my stomach.

"Call me Syd. I'm here because I want to be here."

Suri snorts while Ally snickers loudly. Even Sergeant Rick widens his eyes in surprise. Judging by the varied expressions around the rest of the group, nobody believes anyone would want to be here, because given any alternatives, nobody would have left the physical world and given their soul to the government for this second chance. Or in my case, a clean start for my husband and family.

Syd replies to the incredulity with an unsettling grin.

Haiku claps. "Now, it's time to choose a leader!"

I suck down an impatient breath, wanting to be a team player but finding her gleefulness tiresome.

Syd raises his hand. "Why is a command structure so important?"

"Because we're a team and we need a commander," Rick says.

When nobody else objects, we move to a simple selection process. Everyone votes for Rick except Syd, who annoyingly names me as his choice. Then Simon, the former politician, wrangles his way into the second-in-command position, which I was sure didn't exist until he opened his mouth.

While everyone congratulates Rick, and Haiku applauds, I slink into my chair. The stories, or non-stories, of my new teammates fill me with dread. We are like the island of misfit toys—if the toys were qualified in every last deadly skill known to mankind.

After Rick returns to his seat, he asks, "What's next?"

"Nothing," Haiku replies.

"Nothing?" Suri says suspiciously.

"You've each been through a lot to reach this point," Haiku explains. "This is a time of acclimation. Your minds will optimize themselves to maximize your chances of passing the program. Since each mind adjusts at its own pace, this period has no set time limit. But rest assured, once everyone reaches a certain level, the next phase will begin."

While a chorus of questions erupt concerning the meaning of "adjustments" and "next phase", I rub my nape.

The cheery avatar raises her voice. "In order to smooth your transition, the answers will be given at their appropriate times. Now, let's visit the facilities and the rest of Home. Come, there are many fun things to do!"

As the familiar tingle of static flows over my body, Syd slyly winks.

While the queasiness twists my stomach into a knot, I grind my teeth and look away.

Then everyone dematerializes and we head to our next location.

NINE

"THE MOVEMENT of the sun and the phases of the moon keep pace with their counterparts in the physical world," Haiku says as we stroll through the place she calls Home and I've secretly named "Gigantic Game Map."

Our path has taken us to a spacious patio near the four-leaf clover-shaped perimeter. Outside the three-meter boundary wall, a stunning mountain range with snow-capped peaks rises majestically through a cloud bank. It seems unnaturally high until I realize the virtual world isn't curved like the Earth. As a computer creation, it's flat.

Overhead, the splendor of the blue dome stretches, and my eyes glimpse skyward to catch all its glory. This type of spiritualism is completely out of my character, but I can't help the feelings bubbling inside me.

"The home of our virtual overlords," says Syd.

For the entire tour, I've been working to avoid him, but he keeps finding his way to my side.

Frowning at the unwanted friendliness, I tug at the band over my breasts, trying to cover more skin. Then, determined to escape any further conversation, I sidle away from him and across the group, studying the massive buildings ringing the interior of the sanctuary.

Unlike the impressive outward scenery, these objects don't pretend they could exist in reality. Giant in scale and constructed of impossible architectures, each of them is a testament to the 'big, bigger, biggest' philosophy, a complete sellout to the religion of over the top extravagance.

Although conceptually beautiful, the towering structures lack any function. Among their many useless features are grand walkways leading to nowhere, colorful spirals resembling antenna communicating with nothing, and tall, empty towers capable of housing ballistic missiles. Only their massive doors, which are always locked, seem to serve any purpose.

Noticing my gaze, Haiku launches into a history of the closest tower despite it only being a software construct created from a few million bytes of code and data.

I feign enthusiasm. It's as real as she is. The disquieting thing about the entire experience is that the more Haiku tries to make us feel comfortable, the more anxious I become. The happiness she layers onto everything is too much when paired with the lethal knowledge embedded in the threads and the gorefest of the island. And there's the warning not to get killed, which has to mean more than not leaping head-first off a tall building.

A shadow from the dipping sun crosses my face as a team led by a floating teddy bear walks past our lecture. Although Home is large, close to the size of a small city, occasionally we see one of the other hundred groups of ten wandering the grounds.

Like a tick embedded into my subconscious, my first instinct is to search in terror for the bald giant, who I know is always right around the corner. Beside me, several others flick wild glances. I'm not crazy—everyone seems to have some muted fear burrowed into their mind.

When it's clear he isn't one of the intruding group, which, like us, consists of five men and five women in identical minimalist outfits, I relax.

As they pass, I try not to blush from the abundance of skin while the others on my team react differently. Jock and Sergeant Rick obliviously strut about in their rigid postures. Vela gains more confidence with each passing glance, while on the other side of the spectrum, Ally chats, friendly to all. Carol ignores everyone, choosing instead to play with her long blond hair.

Suri returns each bit of attention by manufacturing a sultry gaze of her own. While her meaning is obvious, I'm not sure I understand why she's doing it. Besides simple curiosity, none of the men exhibit any interest.

And except for making creepy glances at my rear, the plain-faced Syd shows no inclination toward any of the new females.

While my main goal is to stay anonymous, I garner the most platonic leers of everyone. Among the attention thrown my way is a protracted stare from a large man with a civil war era beard and thick hair creeping down his back and over his broad chest.

I roll my shoulders, tugging at my elbows and ribs, trying to fit my new body to my personality. When it doesn't work, more uncomfortable than ever, I shy away and resort to walking in front of Suri and Rick to use them as shields.

The other group soon curves behind a massive column with a final gander from the hairy man and a mean stare from the beady eyes of their teddy bear leader.

Although the notion's crazy, I'm beginning to think the avatars dislike me.

Suri leans, ogling at the retreating forms.

"Why are you doing that?" I ask.

She quickly checks the immediate area before replying in a conspiratorial tone, "I'm not happy about losing my name or having my memories ripped apart. The overlords want my soul, but I won't surrender without a fight. Killing is so simple now, but the simple act of making love impossible?"

And I thought I was the rebellious one. "The idea of sex does nothing for me."

"Me either. But that won't stop me from trying."

"You shouldn't worry about such things," says Haiku.

Startled, I twist my head. While a floating software construct sneaking up on someone shouldn't be surprising, it's still disconcerting.

"Any lingering desires you have for sex will disappear as part of the acclimation process. It's for your own good," Haiku says in her happy voice. Then, she smiles before zipping away to answer a question from Rick.

Suri steps close. "I was afraid of that. The longer we're here, the less like ourselves we'll become. I already feel bad enough for not caring about anyone I killed on that island."

"Me too."

"I'm not giving up that easily. Besides, if I succeed, I might have fun too."

After I wish her the best in her sexual rebellion, we proceed from the giant buildings and into an enclave situated a ten-minute walk from the barracks. Haiku's voice rises in excitement. "This is the play area," she says, sweeping her arms. "These places offer wonderful activities. Bowling, archery, sauna, swimming, volleyball, and an opera-styled theater. We have a movie night every week!"

I roll my eyes. Although lacking a beach, the diversions cover everything else one would discover in a tourist resort.

Haiku points. "That's the museum for anyone with sophisticated tastes."

While the rest of the group remains uninterested, I peer in the direction of her finger. It's a delightful one-story 17th-century brick-work with loving touches of wooden window frames and wrought iron grilles surrounding classical artwork, reminding me of my two-bedroom cottage.

I take tentative steps from the group toward my new favorite place in the virtual world.

Loud grating static floods my ears. Suddenly, I'm knocked to the ground.

A red-bearded, red-haired leprechaun hovers above me with an angry stare poking from under his shamrock hat. A moment later, his team of ten materializes behind him.

More stares.

I puff stray hairs from my face and twist myself into a sitting position, hunching to be as small as possible.

Syd steps in front of me, presenting a full-frontal view of his body. He offers me his hand. "Milady."

"I don't need your help," I hiss, wanting to dig a deep hole and hide. When his hand doesn't move, I slap it away.

"It was merely an attempt to be chivalrous," he says in a hurt voice.

I shove myself upright and twist my body from his reach. "I beat hundreds of trained people to get here, and I don't need a protector. Go bother someone else."

As the other team walks away, the leprechaun sends one final glance. It's not anger. It's hate.

I rub the back of my neck.

"What's wrong?" Suri asks.

"The leprechaun," I whisper through gritted teeth.

"What about it?"

When I point, he's leading his team past the swimming facility with a wide smile plastered across his ruddy face.

Just dandy.

I groan and walk toward Haiku while my mind avoids asking more questions about my sanity.

Even better, as I reach my group, the teddy bear arrives with his ten charges in tow. More curious gazes flood over me.

Wishing to be in my former cute, petite body—minus the gimpy leg —I brush my red mane over my shoulder and sidle next to Suri. While I chew a nail, the large hairy man stops and stares. Although the gaze is more from ingrained habit than any lewdness, I fold my arms and face away from his attention.

There is a snap and a crunch of cartilage.

I whirl in time to see Syd deliver a vicious kick to the hairy man, who lies in a heap on the rubbery walkway. Ribs crack as the poor man grunts.

Team Teddy Bear jumps to their teammate's defense. Jock and Rick rush to help Syd.

Partly from astonishment, but mostly in embarrassment, I cup my hands over my cheeks.

Before anyone can strike a blow, a barrier of air materializes between the combatants.

"Stop," yells Haiku, zipping between the two parties. The teddy bear mimics her efforts, except his commands come in high-pitched shrieks. "Everyone behave."

Syd points at me. "I was protecting her."

"Yes, that man was being lewd," Jock adds in a loud voice.

As the object of their protection, I blow out an angry breath. I didn't think the bearded man exhibited anything more than a past habit, and with my skills, I can defend my own honor.

Haiku raises her hands to stop any further babble. "This place is a sanctuary from violence. No fighting is allowed."

"We can't let people disrespect us," Syd protests.

"I can take care of myself, and he didn't mean anything," I say, throwing my hands to the sky. The long stare was less annoying than the clandestine glances I've been getting all day from Syd.

Mercifully, the shimmering barrier limits attacks to only angry gazes and mean comments.

After glaring at me, the teddy bear snaps his fingers. The blood spilling from the nose of Syd's victim disappears. The hairy man puts his hands on the ground and stands.

"Now that's fixed," the floating stuffed animal says in his squeaky voice. "Apologize."

The large man faces me and bows his head. "I'm sorry ma'am. No disrespect intended."

"This isn't necessary," I say to the virtual universe.

Haiku says, "Syd, don't you have something to add?"

A contrite expression falls over Syd's face. "My humblest apologies. Perhaps I overreacted."

The words exude sincerity, and the hostility between the groups diffuses.

Shocked by the reactions, I try to figure out where the gentleman persona came from, because it matches nothing I've seen while dodging him all afternoon.

Am I the only one he creeps out?

After the other team leaves, Haiku calls us together. Her small hands rub over her cheeks until they turn a bright red. In her serious voice, she says, "This is a place of sanctuary. Whatever the reason, conflict is not allowed here. If you have an issue with another group, let me handle it. If you have an issue with a teammate, let me find a solution. If I cannot find a solution, I will break up the team and place everyone in new sanctuaries. Harmony is very important in this world. Does anyone have any issues?"

This is news. Although I'm sorely tempted to get away from Syd, the prospect of winding up in a worse situation causes me to hold my tongue.

The grass isn't always greener.

Syd points at the retreating group. "What if those people harbor resentment?"

"This is a place of sanctuary. No team you see in this location will ever be in a scenario with you," Haiku replies.

"What's a scenario?" Rick asks.

Haiku gasps. "Something I shouldn't have said."

"Can you tell us anything else?" Suri asks.

After a moment, Haiku blows out a breath. "You are all sworn to secrecy."

Everyone nods.

"In the coming phase, scenarios are the tests you must pass to graduate the Ten Sigma Program. Now, no more questions concerning that subject," she says and turns away, heading for the next destination.

Although the answer is innocuous, a chill spreads over me as I rub my nape.

TEN

After the tour of Home, we have a tedious session in the shooting range as part of a team-building exercise courtesy of our illustrious leader, Sergeant Rick.

Our downtime comes when daylight ends.

While we aren't truly flesh and blood, basic rules govern our physical state, and in most aspects, our bodies operate as they ordinarily would in order to mimic fighting in real life. Air is a requirement. Inside, our hearts beat and blood flows through our arteries. We tire and have adrenaline bursts. There is sweat. Sleep too is a necessity. And according to Haiku's ominous warning, we shouldn't do anything to get ourselves killed.

On the other hand, our muscles and coordination stay in perfect shape regardless of physical activity. Also, no personal grooming is necessary. And true to the man in the black broad-brimmed hat's promise, we don't even need to pee.

However, the one thing superfluous to combat, but deemed indispensable to the human condition, is the act of eating. Although I have no idea why, I suspect the virtual overlords want to establish the normalcy of a daily routine to ease our transition into the virtual universe. Or it could be something totally nefarious, but in the interest of team harmony, I abstain from asking obnoxious questions as we sit down for our first meal.

A wide, off-white room with drab brown frames around its windows and metal doors serves as the cafeteria. Arranged in ten rows, laid end-to-end from the guard rails of the food service area to the opposite wall, are long foldout tables with brightly speckled, laminated surfaces. The molded chairs lined on each side are cheap. In every way possible, this facility feels like an afterthought compared to the spectacles outside the plastic windows.

Tonight, the place bustles with unwinding people who were strangers in the morning, now trying to share a bond forged from an afternoon's orientation. Occasionally, the air pops when one of the avatars appears.

We occupy a table near a bank of windows, with five of us on each side. I'm in a center position with Suri—whom I find myself liking more and more—on my left. Sergeant Rick sits on my right, his ramrod-straight posture stiffer than humanly possible. From across the table, Jock gives Walt a good-natured headlock as Ally contorts her too cute face by letting out a series of chortles at a horrible joke from Simon. Carol wrestles with a tangle in her long hair, while, furthest from me, Vela shyly touches her cheek.

A loose plastic sack filled with a syrupy blue liquid, the central ingredient of the activity, rests in my palm. The other members of the team hold identical packs. While growing accustomed to virtual eating will require suspending more than a handful of disbelief, at least I can't make a mess. I hope.

Below the bag, I spot Syd, who has somehow wrangled the seat across from me, leering at my breasts.

I let my hand fall to the table. Syd's smugness is ruining everything about my newfound friends.

As he notices my stare, his dark eyes narrow and his thin lips form a wry smile.

Unwilling to give him further attention, I angle myself to Suri and try to immerse myself in a conversation about the spiciness of Indian cooking. However, I can't concentrate because my peripheral vision catches Syd making quick glances at my chest. If it wouldn't be ridiculously obvious, he probably would be sneaking peeks under the table.

Enough.

"Why do you keep staring at me? Do I excite you?"

He huffs and lifts his gaze to my eye level. "Don't flatter yourself."

Teenage chin pimple and all, Walt leans into our budding disagreement. "Well, you are super-duper hot," he says innocently.

"Everyone looks good," I reply, crossing my fingers.

Except for Syd.

Walt presses on. "No, you're in a different league. You have those long legs and perfect boobs, along with that thick red hair. Nobody else is close."

My glare silences him.

At least for a moment. The teen adds in a murmur, "I'm just being honest. Don't worry, I used to get excited by any bare skin or crappy hologram, but my parents beat it out of me. Now, I guess I'm glad not to have to worry about it anymore." He titters at an unseen joke.

"Good," I blurt, feeling guilty the instant the word leaves my mouth. I know he had a terrible childhood, but this excess attention is killing me. My sister was always the "hot" one. I was the girl who needed special shoes to correct a gimp and was happy to become a nerd.

On top of being a hypocrite.

Being short with Walt triggers remorse, yet I can't muster a sliver of emotion for killing people with my bare hands?

Suri interrupts my self-loathing. "You are pleasingly perfect. I love your eyes. They're an amazing shade of blue and they sparkle. And you have sensual lips."

Vela nods. "She's right. You have a distinctive and intimidating look."

I hunch, my face burning from embarrassment. "You're both not helping."

"Maybe you should fret about them, not me," Syd says.

Suri chuckles. "Keep your fantasies to yourself, Syd. I'm attracted to men. A lot." She straightens and raises her head to reinforce the point by checking out different men wandering around the cafeteria.

After manufacturing a few sultry gazes, she sighs disgustedly. "Not that it matters here."

I shouldn't, but my mouth opens before I can resist. "How about you Syd? You looking for a girlfriend?"

He takes a short breath and casts angry eyes at the ceiling.

As I wait for a witty retort, I purse my lips.

A moment passes before he leans back and raises his hands in surrender. "This place is like bathing in saltpeter. I got nothing."

Suri and Vela laugh. Syd can be a charmer when he wants, which is something I find more disconcerting than his covert glances.

Fingers wrapped around the end of her long blond hair, Carol asks the table, "I wonder why they hate sex so much?"

"It's the Garden of Eden," Ally cheerfully says.

I snort at the reference. "Right, this is the Garden of Eden, except that we have all the knowledge of killing and every other sin besides sex."

"We can ask Haiku," Walt says.

Plastic scrapes over the cheap floor tiles as Sergeant Rick adjusts his chair. "I know the answer," he says with focused blue eyes.

When everyone stops to listen, I give him props for having a commanding presence.

"It's about simplicity."

I tilt my head. "Simplicity?"

Rick's crooked teeth show when he smiles. "We're warriors, and in war, the less going on in your head besides surviving and accomplishing your mission, the better. With men and women together, having sex or relationships would cloud the thought process. Removing sexual tension is the best thing that could have been done to save your lives."

Although Rick's words work at an intellectual level, Ally bites her lip while Jock grumbles. Suri sends me a clandestine eye roll.

Except for a shy nod from the teenaged Walt, mostly embarrassed smiles complete the remaining reactions. My guess is that bodily pleasures are more important to the rest of us. At least until the virtual overlords wipe those desires from our minds.

Pretending not to notice the dissent, I tighten my cheeks and tug at the thin material covering my breasts. "Well, I still don't understand why we're dressed like this."

Rick thumps his chest. "The bare skin is refreshing. This is the finest uniform you can wear. It's natural, honest, and never leaves you. As a matter of fact, it would be better if everyone was completely naked."

I grimace at the thought of Syd staring at my completely naked body.

No matter the situation, things can always be worse.

"That is brilliant," Syd says with an enthralled expression, his gaze flickering over my chest.

I groan at the lewd image involving me that is almost certainly dancing in his imagination.

Rick adds in a commanding tone, "Now I know some of you are suspicious of our virtual overlords. But give them a chance. Everything has a purpose. Not worrying about sex or clothing is for the best, people. It might seem funny now, but we'll get used to it."

Scrunching my lips, I suppress the urge to say something obnoxious. Sex is the creating life part of the human existence, and I'm not sure that eradicating any feelings toward it is in everyone's best interests.

Jock leans forward, saying, "Remember, this program wasn't created on a whim. The real world needs us."

A nodding Rick holds his blue pouch over the table. "That's right. So suck it up and let's have a toast to the greatest team this program will ever see!"

Syd matches our leader's enthusiasm, and when everyone else joins the happy parade, I force away a pang of guilt from leaving my loved ones and reluctantly add my bag to the mix.

"Cheers!" Rick bellows, lifting his arm.

Elbows rise, the inexpensive chairs squeak, and the team echoes Rick's toast with shakes of their blue food. Then copying his lead, we each puncture the plastic seal of our meal with a sharpened straw.

Weird views of sex aside, whatever Rick's reasoning, his straightforward attitude has me the most at-ease since they put the contraption on my head in the hospital room. I relax, watching the others sip the blue liquid.

Their faces express contentment while satisfied moans drift over the cheap surroundings.

"Hey, what's it like?" I ask.

Suri scrutinizes her blue pouch. "Like the most wonderful food my mother made."

"Better than anything I ever ate," Walt timidly says.

"Back when I was the mayor of Seattle, we had this expensive banquet —" Simon announces as an introduction to a long self-aggrandizing story.

I give a silent thank you when Rick shakes the table with a massive fist thump. "Christmas dinner after you survive a dangerous mission."

Syd stays mum, his forehead wrinkled in concentration.

Vela smiles. "Just imagine any food you want. It's awesome."

Somewhat nervous, I run through the remains of my culinary history. There was the waffle house I loved.

I take a sip of the gooey substance.

Buttery waffles smothered in thick maple syrup cascade over my taste buds. My lips twist in delight.

"Wow," I say, my mouth dripping syrupy liquid.

Suri laughs when I wipe blue drops from my chin. If she only knew the truth about my eating habits.

While everyone else continues, I take another gulp and swish it around with my tongue. The stuff could be anything I want, but when I blank my mind, the flavor evaporates, leaving only a tasteless, gloppy substance. The effect is purely psychosomatic.

Syd yelps. From anyone else, the spontaneity would be funny, but coming from him, it's disturbing.

"What? No remembrances of anything yummy?" Suri asks good-naturedly.

His plain face holds a bemused expression as he says to nobody, "The most decadent thing one can imagine."

"Well, that was a fine meal," Rick announces, squishing the empty pouch in his hand.

I snort bubbles of blue before I embarrassingly swallow the tasteless portion in my mouth.

"Come on everyone, finish up," he says.

Sergeant Rick is the type of person who doesn't need three cups of coffee to power up for the day, which automatically makes him a better person than me. For my own sanity, I hope the gung-ho attitude is contagious.

After wiping the wetness from under my nose, an action that feels all too natural, I put the straw back to my lips and close my eyes, thinking of the holiday dinner right before I met the man in the broad-brimmed hat.

When I concentrate, my memories produce a blank.

I drop the pack, accidentally spilling blue droplets on the table. Tensing the muscles across my face, I try harder. After a moment, the delectable flavor of prime rib and the creamy texture of mashed potatoes smothered in gravy roam over my tongue.

Mission accomplished!

I pause. Not accomplished. When I attempt to recall the seating positions and guests, there are only featureless mannequins around a featureless kitchen as if painted by an insane impressionist. Worse, as I focus, pieces of people break off and evaporate while parts of the furniture wither and turn gray. When the form at the head of the table blackens and crumbles into its body, I flinch.

"What's wrong?" Suri asks.

The thought of losing my past, the sole remaining link to my loved ones, is more terrifying than my fear of the bald giant. It's my one pillar of support, the one decent thing I need to keep my sense of self in this crazy place.

"Haiku!"

Everyone stares in surprise, but I'm not sure what volume I need to get her attention.

She pops above the table with her dirt-streaked feet across from my eyes.

I look up. "I have a memory disintegrating into literal ash. Can you explain that?"

"Of course." Her eyes deepen, and her smile flattens. "The memories specific to your prior life can interfere with the threads. They are being erased to increase your effectiveness. This is a perfectly natural part of the optimization process. Please don't be alarmed; this is for your own good."

"The longer we're here, the more our memories fade?"

She bobs her head.

"Until when?"

"Until you are your own essence," she replies with perfect innocence.

I shudder.

It's another way of saying 'until nothing is left.'

ELEVEN

THREE DAYS PASS. Besides panic rising from our fading memories and the rest of the acclimation process, the specter of what the next phase will bring hovers over everything.

To increase our readiness for anything that might happen in a scenario, Sergeant Rick has scheduled four two-hour training periods per day. Since nobody has any idea of what might happen in a scenario, we tediously practice everything imaginable from our threads.

A large, multi-purpose room overlooking the fun district holds our current session. Eight of us, and one angry Rick, practice empty-handed fighting inside the glass cube-shaped space. Missing is Syd, who participated in the first boring session about firearm safety but has since gone off to do whatever Syd does when we prepare. Although the behavior is a flagrant rejection of all Rick's pleas for unity and teamwork, he's not AWOL because technically, there isn't a formal military command structure.

While nobody mentions Syd's absence, occasional glances sneak beyond the glass walls, looking for our missing teammate.

Vela fires a punch at the bridge of my nose. The fist comes slightly high with too much committed action.

With a quick half-step, I lower my head and guide her attack past my face. Then, seizing her arm and twisting into her body, I flip her over my shoulder.

She lands on a foam practice mat with a terrific thump. Before turning, she slams her fists.

"You'll get it," I say with encouragement.

"Sorry, it's just that you're not even sweaty. Can you at least pretend to be breathing hard?"

I shrug and help her to her feet.

As she steadies herself, adjusting the ribbons of her clothing, she says, "You said you were a pencil pusher in real life. Not some superhero, right?"

Letting my fingers brush through my hair, I reply, "Just a nerd with a superb head of red hair."

She glances at my body with suspicion. "I don't understand why you look like that. Sorry, I mean, everyone else looks great too, like at the best point in their lives but in better shape. But it's an extension of their original appearance. Why are you different?"

"The hair is the same."

"You know what I mean." Shyly rubbing her cheek, she adds, "Sorry, I don't mean to be so distrustful."

While Ally is the most outgoing of the group, Vela falls to the opposite end of the social spectrum, being more awkward than even Walt. Although I'm the one she's opened to, she keeps quiet about her past except for her love of animals. But the attack that disfigured her face erased that love and now she has to fight against her mistrust of all things. I hope one day before her memories die she'll talk about it because I know she has a good heart.

"There's nothing to apologize for," I say. "Let's do it again."

"Just go easy."

"I'll go hard to make you better."

She responds to the tough love with a tense smile and resumes a combat stance.

We run another bout of hand-to-hand combat. When I focus, it's as if I'm in her mind and can see which thread she's using for her next attack.

In seconds, she's awkwardly sprawled on the mat.

Rubbing her bottom, she faces me with an expression that's more bewildered than annoyed. "I just can't understand how you keep winning so easily. We have the same training and experiences. You had to be some kind of superhero in real life."

"No," I say, stretching the word into a long syllable, more from embarrassment than anything else.

While her words are true, I have no explanation for why I'm better at fighting than anyone else. Especially since everyone passed the test of "Acid Island." Maybe I'm improving because I'm gaining confidence in my new body. Or it could be that the credit belongs with Rick's extensive training regimen.

Or perhaps I've received a gift from the overlords.

However, no matter the reason, even though we all have identical threads, I react faster and with more precision than any of the others.

Except for the bald giant, I remind myself, irritated I still can't mention him to anyone else.

Rick claps and everyone stops sparring. "Okay, people. That was a great session. Gather around."

Carol frowns as Suri helps her up. Besides myself, Suri has excelled too. With a grin, she tussles Carol's hair and then points at me, mouthing, "You're next."

I reply with a wink.

As everyone meanders to Rick, Ally lets out a good-natured laugh while chatting in a loud voice with Simon and Jock.

"Come on people. Let's act like we're real soldiers. Have a little urgency," Rick says.

After we crowd around him, Rick focuses on Walt. "Keep at it. You're improving."

Unsure of how to handle compliments, Walt giggles nervously and rubs his chin. Although lethal by real-world standards, he's by far the worst of the group. For the virtual world, he's only one step above hopeless.

I frown at Simon, who stands next to the thin teen. The former politician always partners with Walt and thinks he is tougher than he is.

Jock wipes his sweaty forehead and gazes at my clean appearance with a playful look of disgust. From across the group, Suri sends me an accusing smirk.

I raise an eyebrow and mouth, "Married."

In addition to having zero libido running through my virtual body.

Suri breaks eye contact when Rick continues, "I appreciate all of your perseverance. With this type of effort, we'll accomplish stupendous things."

"Where's Syd?" Simon asks. "We can only win with discipline. He'll wind up getting one of us killed."

Nervous heads bob in agreement.

I clench my teeth and say nothing. Although Syd's stares at my body have subsided, his unnatural focus and strange mood swings are just as bad. I'm happier without his company.

As if my thoughts have power, I see him through the glass wall as he saunters on the path below the facility.

Walt naively points. "There he is."

Simon flies out the door and runs down the slope with a frumpy gait.

So much for military discipline.

As we follow the ex-politician, Rick sprints past us.

When Simon cuts him off, Syd stops, his plain face expressing surprise. He's playing coy because it isn't possible he didn't notice the gaggle of us running after him, especially with Simon's heavy thumping steps.

A furious Rick plants himself next to Simon while I outrace the others, arriving as Syd says with nonchalance, "What?"

When the rest of the team catches up a moment later, I feel Jock's large shoulders at my side.

"We're a team," Rick says.

Syd shrugs. "So?"

Simon cuts across Rick and gets in Syd's face. "We rely on each other to stay alive." Although pretending to be levelheaded, Simon's more on edge than any of us. My theory is politicians don't get shot at too often. But the knowledge of the threads and the power in his virtual body have put a whole new veneer of bravado over his mindset.

The physical threat does nothing to Syd's demeanor. Without blinking, he states, "We're ten random people thrown together as a unit. That is all. Haiku said we all have the threads of combat." His voice rises higher to parody our avatar. "The red threads are your weapons training. The black threads give you the experiences of thousands of soldiers. That is all you need. No mean taskmasters here!" He finishes with a loud clap.

A vein pops out on Rick's forehead. His ranger cool vanishes, and pushing Simon aside, he jabs his index finger into Syd's chest. "For better or worse, we're stuck with each other. And that means we've got to have each other's backs."

"Says who?"

"Says the man who's seen combat and who knows what can happen."

"Oh, so you know what's going to happen when the scenarios start?"

Rick pauses at Syd's point. A scenario could be a knitting demonstration or a mass parade in skirts. Nobody knows. He recovers and replies, "That's why we prepare."

"Okay," Syd says. "Make me. If practicing is so grand, you shouldn't have a problem beating me in a fight."

Used to pounding on Walt, Simon steps forward. "Fine."

"Nobody fights except me," Rick says. "Until someone taps out?"

Syd nods.

We form a loose circle around the two men as they assume combat postures.

Vela whispers, "Rick's got army experience. Real training. He'll win, right?"

I bite my lip. Sergeant Rick is bigger and more muscled. Syd is thin and only average height. "It'll be closer than you think," I whisper back.

Suri nods. "Agree."

Ally claps. "Get him, Rick!"

Others yell encouragement for our team leader.

My thoughts stay sober. While I'd love to see Syd go down in a humiliating defeat, I'm smart enough to know encouragement won't make the slightest difference. Given the military makeup of the threads, everyone is an expert. And if Rick loses…

Neither man is stupid, and the fight starts with a feeling out period. They circle, probing for weak points. While Rick exudes a sure competence, Syd moves with feet light enough to make his wiry form appear to float.

When they finish a semicircle, Rick attacks, snapping a jab into Syd's face. It's perfectly executed, the entire weight of Rick's shoulder behind the punch, and Syd's head snaps backward.

Of the ensuing cheers, Ally's voice rings the loudest.

I refrain from celebrating, keeping silent and chewing on a thumbnail.

Eyes focused, Syd straightens and side-steps a jab. He takes a step and plows straight into a devastating right cross from Rick, the violence of the impact cutting through the shouts of the team.

As Syd staggers with a blank expression and regains his balance, I'm frightened. The punch would have dropped most people, but despite the force hitting his face, Syd didn't blink.

While everyone else leans forward, anticipating Rick's imminent victory, Syd licks blood from his split lip and grins.

The familiar spiders of doom tingle on my nape.

Oblivious to the clues, Rick shuffles his feet, looking for an opening.

I'm surprised when I glean his intentions. Rick will launch the same left-jab right-cross combination, intending to open Syd's defense, and then execute a quick lunge to grapple and take his opponent out with elbows and knees. I hold my breath and wait for the disaster.

Rick advances with a two-step and, lightning fast, fires the jab.

Syd reacts with shocking speed and power. He dodges the fist, and slipping under Rick's guard, strikes the inside of his bicep, deadening the brachial nerve plexus.

The pain from the wounds have made Syd stronger.

Realizing something isn't right, Rick backs away, but Syd's quicker, closing and hitting the former army captain with powerful jabs to the chin and solar plexus. A dazed Rick swings his fist in desperation. Syd slips under the punch and plows into Rick's armpit, jamming the arm into a useless position. Wrapping his forearm on the other side of Rick's neck, Syd locks him into a stranglehold. Rick struggles, his arms flailing over his head.

The cheers from the circle turn into gasps as Syd squeezes and Rick gurgles for air.

Unsurprised, I frown in disappointment.

Rick taps out as his face turns purple. Instead of releasing him, Syd applies more pressure. Rick sinks to his knees, his eyes rolling into their sockets.

"He's going to kill him," Ally screams.

"Do something," Simon shouts.

I glare. Simon had no problem fighting when he thought he might win.

While I hesitate, hating my inaction because I'm used to my husband dealing with confrontation, Jock, the best athlete and biggest among us, leaps into the circle and covers the distance to the two combatants in a flash. He grabs Syd's arms and twists them apart. Rick crumples to the ground.

Instead of trying to break the grapple and separate from a larger opponent, Syd reverses his grip and digging in his heels and using leverage, drives into Jock.

After a trio of stumbling steps backward, Jock gets angry and tries to use sheer physical strength to win. It's a gigantic mistake.

I ball my hand and bite on a knuckle. To my knowledgeable eye and heightened senses, the new disaster unfolds in slow motion.

Using Jock's power, Syd shifts slightly to unbalance him. With that advantage, he twists, breaking Jock's grip, and tosses him through the circle. Ally and Walt jump aside just in time to avoid the huge tumbling form.

One of my black threads whispers, *"The meaner person usually wins."*

This I know without being told.

"Haiku," I say.

Nothing happens.

Catlike, Jock leaps to his feet and side-steps a flying kick from Syd.

He follows with a vicious punch at the back of Syd's head. The tremendous blow carries his entire weight and meets nothing, Syd angling himself just enough to allow the fist to pass a millimeter from his ear.

Pivoting with amazing speed and before Jock can recover his balance, Syd leaps, firing a blur of strikes past Jock's feeble blocks, a staccato of violence erupting from the impacts.

"Haiku," I scream.

Where the hell is that avatar?

Two seconds later, Jock collapses from a broken kneecap, busted nose, and fractured ribs.

Syd's in a frenzy and lines up a death blow at Jock's temple.

Without realizing how, I'm next to them. My hand flicks out and deflects the punch from the killing zone.

The blow still clips Jock in the head and knocks him out. Syd's arm moves a touch to reverse and slam his elbow into my chest.

I twist, barely dodging the strike, which carries enough power to break my ribs.

Quicker than I thought possible, Syd swivels and, like a malevolent force, comes at me.

I surrender ground, terrified.

So much for not doing anything to get myself killed.

While his outside demeanor stays icy, rage and hate swirl in his unnatural, unblinking eyes. He fires attacks that are faster, cleaner, and more ferocious than anything I've witnessed.

My awareness expands through my fear, and I elude or block everything he throws at me.

I'm better at using the black threads, Syd the red threads.

The thought is startling, but there's no arguing that I'm still alive and unharmed.

Maybe I do have special skills.

My confidence rises as I escape a flurry of attacks with only a glancing blow on my shoulder. Then, from his posture and position of his feet, I anticipate a snap kick and slip inside his guard.

He's off balance but resets himself with the light feet of a dancer.

Shifting to my right for protection, I launch a right-cross at his face an instant before he fires a murderous stiff hand at my throat.

My attack is quicker, and I hope it's enough because his strike rips past my hasty block.

An unseen force seizes us. My fist stops a hair from his chin while his motionless hand sits a finger's length from ripping out my trachea.

From the awkward position, I catch Syd's stare. Instead of swirling malice and hate, his eyes show respect.

I'm stunned. Given the raw emotions I saw during the fight, the calculating stare is more than a little unexpected.

Haiku appears and shrieks over our frozen bodies, "Is there a problem?"

Rick staggers upright in spite of his injuries and says in a raspy voice, "No, the team's fine. It was just a training exercise."

With Ally's help, Jock groggily sits up.

The force holding us vanishes, and Syd and I unceremoniously flop onto the soft ground.

Taking advantage of my unfrozen muscles, I push myself into a sitting position and use a moment to shake off chills from the near-death experience. It reminds me too much of my confrontation with the bald giant on the island.

Vela kneels next to me, whispering, "Wow, that was amazing."

Hating the adulation, I glare past her and yell at the avatar. "Where the hell were you?"

Haiku slowly faces me. "I have other responsibilities."

I return her silver-eyed stare without believing the statement. Although Haiku's always been honest, the exact timing of her arrival was too coincidental. But, what could be gained by allowing things to get so serious? I rub my neck, confused by the unknown motivations.

Haiku breaks the mini-showdown by saying to the others, "If you cannot act as adults and need constant supervision, then I will break up the team."

"No, that shall not be necessary," Syd says in his gentleman persona. If I hadn't seen the fight and the rage in his eyes, I'd believe him to be the most delightful human being who ever lived. He rises and, tucking a hand over the small of his back, bows with the grace of a nobleman. "My sincerest apologies to everyone. At times, I get carried away. It won't happen again."

I stand with a ready retort but refrain from protesting when Suri shakes her head.

The grass isn't always greener.

A relieved smile comes over Haiku's face. She snaps her fingers.

Although everyone's wounds heal instantly, angry glances still find Syd, who seems oblivious to the hatred.

Or doesn't care.

Haiku pops away, and a grim silence settles over the group.

Rick and Suri are wrong. I didn't trust Syd before fighting him. I thought he was just lewd, but now that I've glimpsed into his base nature and seen his talent firsthand, I understand how dangerous he is. The best choice would be to get away from him, but until I discover his secret, I decide to keep quiet.

Syd smiles pleasantly.

"So when's the next training session?

TWELVE

TAKING a long sip of the gloppy blue liquid, I let my gaze trail to Syd, who is outlined by the early morning sunshine filtering through the cafeteria windows.

Good as his word, the plain-faced man has stayed on his best behavior and no further incidents have occurred. As an appeasement for the brawl that almost became a deathmatch, he arrives early to every training session and leaves late, even spending extra time with Walt. At mealtime, he adds his presence and makes witty conversation, and except for an ever-present grin of stupidity that sticks to his face when he sucks down the blue liquid, he's a charming companion.

Syd's not what he appears to be.

At least beyond the lecherous looks and covert glances, which are the least annoying of his traits.

Partially, I'm bothered by his wild mood swings that encompass everything from lashing out at all enemies to his agreeable gentleman persona. Also, there are his eyes and their unnatural focus. I've never seen him blink. Not to mention, the malice they radiated during the fight. He would have killed Rick and Jock. Even in his current placid state, I can sense the simmering rage threatening to emerge. He enjoys pain, and worse, loves inflicting it onto others.

And somehow, everything I've noticed is a symptom of something deeper, and something I'm missing.

Trying to ignore loud snickering from Ally, I blow out a breath.

Given the fixation Syd has for me, I wonder for a crazy moment if he's my husband, following from the real world.

I hold back a smile at the silly notion. One condition of my enrollment was that Nick would one hundred percent believe I was dead. While they both have paid me the same level of attention, Nick was loving and nurturing, while Syd is different—possessive, jealous, and dark.

Definitely not my husband, but perhaps the bald giant?

Although more likely, the idea is also ludicrous. While I fought Syd to a draw, my fight with the bald giant wasn't even close. And when I look at Syd, all I see are riddles, but when I think of the bald giant, all I have is fear.

They're both malevolent but in different ways.

But then, who is Syd?

Somehow, he's something less than everyone, yet at the same time, something more.

Syd catches my gaze, and his thin lips return a bright smile. While similar to Haiku's vapid expression, considering my current train of thought, the whole picture only adds to his creepiness.

I tactfully nod and look away, pretending to be interested in a conversation between Suri, Vela, and Carol.

Suri winks at me and then continues telling a crude joke, the sexual innuendo generating embarrassed snickers from Carol and Vela. After she delivers the punchline, I throw out a pained smile amid the forced laughter.

While Suri's means of rebellion is the pursuit of sex, I'm more practical. Ally was right when she compared Home to a weird Garden of Eden. But given the dystopian nature of our existence, the snake has already polluted the surroundings. Something is wrong with this world and Syd is somehow part of it.

Although the line of thinking is harsh and paranoid, at least in my mind, Syd represents the greatest threat to everyone despite the looming specter of the next phase.

Even if it kills me, my rebellion will be solving this mystery.

Rick proposes a toast, and the idle banter stops long enough for everyone to sip from their pouches.

Watching the others delight in their food fantasies, I keep my mind clear, letting the blue liquid swish around my mouth as I plan my next actions.

Courtesy of a Haiku discussion with Rick, today is a free day to acclimate ourselves to the virtual surroundings. For different people, free time means different things. Some want to wander around the vast space of Home while others want to hang around with everyone else in a normal setting.

I'm trailing after Syd to discover his secrets.

When his breakfast pouch is empty, Syd takes a moment to remove the stupid eating expression from his face, and then after rising and saying polite goodbyes, he walks from the cafeteria.

As he reaches the door, I excuse myself from the table and slip past a row of food-slurping zombies, chasing after him. When I get outside, Syd is strolling toward the early morning sun and the shaded eastern skyline. I follow in stealth, using the cover skills provided by the threads.

During the next hour, Syd meanders, doing nothing of interest while being more uninteresting than anything I could have imagined. He speaks with no one and interacts with nothing. Walking with the focus of a gnat, he randomly changes direction, his attention moving from one fleeting thing to another.

As he continues, his movements become more erratic, forcing me to jump in and out of cover, acting nonchalantly to the platonic leers of curious passers-by, and then running and catching up to him to only again repeat the same process when he flitters in another direction.

Bewildered by his actions, my patience evaporates, and I gnaw on a thumbnail, battling the urge to run from hiding and scream at him to do something, anything different.

Finally, after enough time elapses for the long morning shadows to shrink and blacken under the midday sun, and right before I'm about to give up the hunt in order to preserve my sanity, Syd quits his direction-less path and saunters to a broad soaring walkway. He follows the alien symbols embossed over its surface to an elliptical platform sprouting from a sky-high building weighted by a spiraled crown.

When Syd disappears around a wide support column, I leap from my hiding spot and sprint after him. As the platform comes into view, the cap of the leprechaun floats from the opposite side.

I duck behind a shallow wall.

There are whispers and then a faint tremor rattles the ramp.

After a few silent moments, I peek.

Only broken shadows from the overhangs rest on the empty platform. The hateful avatar and my quarry have vanished.

Perplexed, I march up the walkway and stop in the middle of the elliptical area. Except for the stale scent of cut grass, nothing breaks from the ordinary. I dash to the opposite walkway and then circle the enveloping walls.

They've vanished.

Frustrated by the finish of the morning search, I throw up my hands and frantically look for any clue as to their whereabouts.

There is nothing, except a blinking green light by the main doors. It's odd because the indicators always glow red, signifying a locked status.

I take wary steps to the side panel, and pushing through some indecision, press the circular button in its center.

Hidden machinery whirs and the massive doors separate, letting a breath of musty air roll past me.

Wrinkling my nose, I peer into a star-shaped room. Sunshine pours through long single-panel windows crawling to the barely visible ceiling. Overhead, a broad balcony under a pair of cascading blue banners spans the wide space. Except for rectangular control stations, the rest of the place is deserted.

Because it's an afterthought; nobody should be here.

Before my mind can think of reasons not to enter, I step past the threshold.

The doors close with a metallic thud.

Afraid to advance but unable to retreat, I surrender to my curiosity and edge into the building, not knowing where to go.

Although no marks are on the shiny floor, avatars leave distinctive odors. After a moment of sniffing, I detect a grassy scent and follow it to a concrete staircase leading into the lower levels.

None of the threads offer any experience for detective work, but overriding my worries, I tread down the stairs to a narrow landing, which serves as the entrance to a confined hallway lit by dull ceiling panels. Still trailing the leprechaun's odor, I turn to my right and head down the long empty space.

The passage soon leads into another winding staircase and following more sniffing, I slip further into the bowels of the building. The trail descends past many landings with each level becoming progressively darker and less detailed. Finally, I reach the bottom and follow a pathway illuminated only by sparks of red light. However, the grassy smell is stronger, and not wanting to miss my chance to discover Syd's secrets, I hurry.

Before long, the dots fade in number and intensity, and to continue, I slow, feeling with my hands for each step.

Total darkness soon surrounds me.

Even worse, the scent fades.

I stop, attempting to orient myself and control my growing fear. I'm on a narrow path confined by guardrails. Guarding what, I have no idea.

While there aren't any reference points, the volume below feels huge and foreboding while the ceiling seems an infinite distance away. When I stretch my hands past the metal rails, they meet emptiness.

What have I gotten myself into?

Sweat trickles down my body. While everything is light and overly happy above the surface, down here in the darkness, the mood is the opposite. My inflated imagination conjures hordes of oppressive things floating nearby. Swathes of misery, hate, fear, anger, even murder, as well as every other dark part of the human psyche feels like they're seeping into my being.

When I was dying, volunteering to go into the great unknown was easy. But now, because of my health, I have more to lose. And while I have a terror of the bald giant, this is far worse.

None of which matters.

Determined to solve the mystery, I push further on the path, becoming more disoriented with every step. The nausea rising inside my body reminds me of the worst of the treatments during the worst of the sickness.

Although the scent of the leprechaun vanishes, I still sense Syd. But in my current confusion, he seems scattered like sunlight cast through a prism, except instead of colors, the spectrum of his being is splayed across the neighboring space. While the differing aspects represent mostly shades of hate and sadism, surprisingly, there are pockets of humanity.

It's all nuts, and even though I'm close to losing my grip on sanity, I haven't come this far to quit. Whatever the riddle is, I'm close to the answer.

After a few more plodding steps, I sink to a knee, overcome with faintness. My mind disconnects from my body, which strangely seems rubbery and soft. The feelings remind me of my entry into the virtual universe, of being shredded, the threads threatening to rip apart my being.

The bizarreness has to be a hallucination, but when I scream, my lungs won't function. I fold my arms tight over my knees, willing myself not to disintegrate, but somehow my skin gives way into spongy tissue and hazy bones.

The sadistic parts of Syd quake with laughter.

Shudders run through my tissues as I gnash my wilting teeth, and then, steeling my nerves, I force myself upright and lean over the railing, preparing to jump into the blackness.

The aroma of sage mixed with rosemary floods the area.

"You're not supposed to be here," a girlish voice says.

Slowly twisting my head as if it's disconnected from my neck, I pivot to the sound. The darkness is too heavy to discern any details, but the new presence seems gigantic. "Who are you?"

A disquieting moment passes before there is a pop and a spark flares. I squint, adjusting to the brightness, my mind suddenly clearing. When I glance down, my body is back to being healthy, long, and perfect.

Strange.

Holding a lit wand, an avatar-sized witch with jet black hair floats on a short broomstick. She has a cute face under her pointed hat.

"Why are you here?" she asks.

"I'm looking for a plain-faced man accompanied by a leprechaun," I say, realizing exactly how stupid the words sound as they leave my mouth.

"Nobody is down here. Since the initial construction, this place has been empty."

I wave my arms at the black space. "Are you sure?"

She closes her eyes and flicks her wand.

Illumination arrives from wide ceiling panels.

We're on a narrow suspension bridge, which isn't as high as I expected. About a meter below the railing lies a lattice of glass containers with smoke swirling under their thick tops. A malevolence seems to emanate from mysterious substances.

"As I said, nobody is here. You've made a mistake. It's not uncommon for people imported from the outside. Perhaps you are experiencing dementia from the acclimation."

"I am not imagining things."

"Of course not. Yet, there isn't anyone here. I give you my word."

"What's in the glass boxes?"

"Nothing that should concern you."

Of course the witch won't answer the question. The avatars are never forthcoming with any information. I turn and walk away.

There is another pop, and she floats in front of me, her shallow eyes staring placidly.

"There's something very, very wrong with this place, and I will figure it out if it kills me," I say, my tone exaggerating my hyperbole.

I wait for the hatred that arises from every avatar not named Haiku. Instead, her face remains stoic as she says, "You should be more concerned with succeeding in the coming phase of the program."

"What can you tell me about it?"

"Nothing."

I put my hands on the railing. "I'm leaving."

She makes the teleport gesture, and I find myself standing in the sunshine and fresh air of the elliptical platform outside the building.

Although relieved to be free of the dark, evil place, I'm angry about the lack of truth amongst all the innuendo.

"I promise, I will figure out what you're hiding."

As I step toward the massive doors, the witch zips around and blocks my path and the indicator panel switches to a bright red.

"You should beware of traps."

"Traps?"

"There are those that would induce you to bend the rules, so the rules can be bent against you."

"What?" I answer my own question. "You mean the leprechaun and other avatars that have been giving me the stares."

"My meaning is for you to follow the rules and not try to discover things that are none of your business. Do not allow yourself to be provoked."

"But why would they single me out? Is it this body?" I ask, pointing to myself.

She examines me like a biology experiment. "While aesthetically perfect, that form is ordinary. It serves only as a shell to hold your true essence."

"You mean I haven't been given any special powers?"

"No. That would defeat the entire purpose of the program."

The words are stated so matter-of-factly and with such obvious logic I feel stupid not only for asking the question but for even thinking of it in the first place.

"It's just that everyone else resembles their real-world selves, except for me."

"Everyone receives an appearance conducive to maximizing their success in the Ten Sigma Program. There is nothing special about your body. Perhaps it's meant as something you should grow into."

I raise my hands. "Grow into? Who wants all this attention?"

"Exactly my point."

Clasping my cheeks, I knead my temples with my fingers. I'm losing an argument to a software construct that looks like a five-year-old dressed for Halloween. Worse, I'm surprised to find myself liking and trusting her. "Why are you being so helpful? Nobody else is."

"No more questions. Please, have a great rest of your free day," she replies.

"How do you know I'm having a free day?"

Blankness covers her face while her body remains motionless, her clothing still in the soft breeze.

As I turn away, she begins the hand motion to leave. Although I spent the morning following Syd, my real purpose was finding out more about the virtual world. And I was close to solving the riddle.

I reach for her.

She stops. "That would be a mistake. There are things you should not know and consequences for every action."

This time, when she gestures, I let her leave.

Afterward, I stay lost in thought, contemplating without resolution the entire weird experience, until two people walk onto the empty platform.

They stare at my aesthetically perfect form.

Rolling my shoulders and wishing I was dressed in a long trench coat instead of something better suited for an S&M party, I try to hold my ground against their attention, but after a few moments, my resolve wilts. Defeated, I gnaw on a thumbnail as I slink away and return to the barracks.

THIRTEEN

FRAZZLED BY THE MORNING ENCOUNTER, which only succeeded in creating more riddles than answers, I salvage the remainder of the free day by taking an afternoon walk with Suri, Jock, Vela, and Walt, my best friends in this world. Suri plays the role of a close sister while Vela acts as the critic. Walt is the teenager everyone needs to protect. Jock is…

I'm not sure what Jock is.

"Hey everyone," Suri says. "Let's go catch the sunset."

"Lead on," Jock says to me.

As I step on a winding path to the western wall, Suri calls out, "It'll be romantic!"

I respond with a faint smile, the most romantic reaction I can force upon my face. True to Haiku's word, our residual desires for sex have faded as our minds optimize for what comes next.

As we wend our way amongst the tall buildings of the western skyline, my anxieties increase. Despite the witch's bland explanations, I know a dysfunction underlies everything in sight. With each step, the urge to mention the morning's adventure wells in my throat.

I sigh, not wanting to involve my friends in some unwinnable conspiracy.

Jock glances curiously at me but oblivious to the dangers, marches ahead, appreciating the beauty of the architecture. And he's not wrong. Here on the surface of this imitation Garden of Eden, we're safe. Nothing would be allowed to disturb the harmony of our acclimation.

While I wrestle with the dilemma, Suri acts as a mother hen to Walt and Vela, slowing their pace to allow a sizable gap to open between us.

I roll my eyes at her rebellious fantasies of romance.

After a few tranquil minutes, Jock and I are wandering alone.

"When I lived near the Shenandoah Valley, I used to love nature," he says and takes a deep breath. "This reminds me of an October evening hiking up a hillside."

The futuristic buildings towering over us bear no resemblance to anything I remember of Western Virginia. "That sounds a little weird. None of this looks natural in the slightest."

"It's the clean air, distant mountains, and sunshine."

I gesture at nearby sights, snickering. "Look at the size and shape of these things. That building is all giant buttresses. How about that looped overhang? Those struts can't possibly be holding up that block. What's up with that pudgy obelisk?"

"It looks cool."

"Ha. That's the point. Everything has some feature that's matched to the golden ratio or pi or the square root of two. It's just a hurried design to be cool rather than a construct emphasizing realistic details." Thinking of the interiors and creepy avatars, my voice rises. "None of this can exist in the real world."

Then, to emphasize the spoken and unspoken, I flourish my arms at everything.

Shaking his head at either my math knowledge or overwrought attempt of persuasion, he veers off the path. When he reaches the edge of a terrace, he stops and rests his large hands on a railing overlooking the boundary wall.

"And what about the food?" I say, catching up.

"There's something in the air, but I can't put my finger on it," he replies, ignoring the logic of my arguments. He gazes into my eyes. "And the company."

I bite my lip. Jock's alluded to his nature walks with his high school sweetheart in previous conversations. She left for college after the terrible accident paralyzed him. While I remember his romantic stories, I'm uncertain if he has any remembrances of his first love. I want to mention her, but the breakup was painful and maybe he doesn't need me bringing back any haunting memories of their relationship.

Instead of replying, I step next to him and place my hands on the railing.

His fingers tense, but otherwise, he makes no response to my intrusion.

As we stand close, his musky scent fills my nostrils while the warmth of his body tingles my skin. I wonder if my gimpy real-world self would have interested him. Or if I would have stayed with him after the horrible accident.

A breeze rises and he shifts, his arm brushing against my elbow.

Although my physical desires are absent, I hold my breath, waiting for his next action. Perhaps if something happens, he can provide a spark.

As the moment stretches, I try getting excited by imagining his large arms cradling me against his muscular chest and his hand reaching between my thighs.

I could kick his ass.

The bizarre thought breaks my reverie. Even if Jock shows affection, then what? Any libido still buried inside me is crumbling in deference to the will of the virtual overlords. Besides, my loving husband Nick still dwells in my disintegrating past. I miss his big smile and confident attitude.

Leaving the sexual rebellion to Suri, I create space between us with a half-step. While my memories remain, I won't taint them with an affair, regardless of my affection for Jock. Our relationship will never progress beyond a simple friendship.

Blowing out a breath, Jock squeezes the metal guardrail and straightens.

I tilt my head as he faces me.

"There's no place for love here," he says.

Although anger underlies the statement, his eyes waver, allowing an opening to prove him wrong.

My decision's final. "It certainly won't win any fights," I reply, returning my gaze beyond the mountain peaks and to the wonders of the blue dome.

An uncomfortable silence falls between us.

Finally, Jock recovers, saying, "When you look at the sky, what do you see?"

"Our virtual overlords."

He laughs. "Don't be such a downer."

"What's it to you?"

"The dome is the way to get home."

"Ha. Were you a poet?"

"Hopefully not," he says with a straight face. "I might have dabbled in it to be romantic, but judging by that last line, I probably had no talent." He shrugs. "Either way, who knows?"

I frown because a time will come when I'll have the same sense of loss trying to recollect my husband and family.

"Hey, no unhappy faces."

Rather than making a remark, I express my sarcasm via widening my lips into a squarish smile which shows lots of teeth—the "Only a Mother Could Love" expression.

"You won't be so beautiful when your face freezes like that."

Not taking the bait, I quickly reply, "What do you mean by way to get home?"

He purses his lips, perhaps regretting the lost moment between us, then he points skyward. "Beyond that is your true home. Never forget it. Your way back is past whatever is up there. Past that gigantic blue monstrosity."

My sarcastic thoughts evaporate as I consider his words. They're a bit more profound than I've given him credit for, and ironically, sound like something my husband would say. No wonder I enjoy the huge man's company. The blue dome is important but only as a reminder; the ultimate goal lies far beyond it.

No matter what's left of my memories.

"So, you're saying: don't get used to this wonderful place?"

He laughs. "I'd be worried if you ever got comfortable here."

It's a perfect moment to express my worst fears. "Speaking of comfortable, have you noticed anything strange about this place?"

"That's where you went off to," Walt says with Suri and Vela in tow.

As they near, Suri glances between Jock and myself. Flashing a look of disappointment, she asks, "What intimate things were you two just discussing?"

"Brin was just mentioning how strange this place is," Jock replies.

Suri says, "You mean stuff like being dressed in something less than lingerie without any desires?"

"Or the avatars materializing out of thin air?" Walt adds.

Raising both hands, I forestall the other thousand things they could mention. "No, none of those things."

Vela says, "I've noticed something truly weird."

Because she's always suspicious, Vela notices more than most. "What?" I ask.

After her wide eyes circle the empty terrace, she says, "We're in the military right?"

"Yeah, so?" I reply. With the knowledge of a million soldiers residing in each of us, there's no argument there.

"Doesn't anyone find it funny we haven't bothered trying to create a spree du corpis?"

"Esprit de corps," Jock says. "It means to build up pride and loyalty."

"Rick's doing that," Walt says.

"But nobody else is," Vela replies. "Everything I've ever read or seen has the military indoctrinating people through drills and mass formations. To stamp out individuality and set people into a group mentality. We do nothing like that.

"No drills. No marching. No parades. Nothing. What's more suspicious is none of the threads hold any knowledge of those things.

"I can kill in a thousand different ways with a thousand different weapons, but I don't know how to march in unison with anyone. If Rick didn't have that overly upright posture, I wouldn't have the foggiest idea of how to stand at attention. And forget about doing a proper salute."

"What are you getting at?" I say.

She shrugs. "I don't know. I'm probably being paranoid."

Jock scrunches his brows while Walt splits his attention between Suri and me, waiting for either of us to produce a reaction he can imitate.

Suri says, "It's okay to be anxious."

I chew on a nail. Although Vela's overly skeptical because of her past, she's not paranoid. That kind of coordination takes practice, and while we've received metaphorical mountains of knowledge and skills, we have no threads devoted to esprit de corps. This sanctuary is closer to a giant meditation resort than a military base, but while odd, I don't understand how it's an issue, especially compared to everything else.

Vela rubs her cheek. "Who can you trust around here?"

"Haiku?" Suri whispers.

I'm not sure I trust her, but it can't hurt to ask. "Haiku!"

After a gentle pop, her strawberry scent rolls past us. "Yes," she says in a cheery voice.

Uncertain of how to begin, I take a moment to appreciate her silver hair and matching outfit, which shimmers in the fading orange sunlight. "We have questions about this place. About some of the people."

"And some missing army training," Vela says.

Jock adds, "Specifically about esprit—"

"There is plenty of time for questions," Haiku interrupts. Her eyes glaze for a moment before she continues. "But, you should enjoy your remaining free time without worrying about things that needn't concern you."

"What does that mean?" I ask.

"Your acclimation period has ended."

"But...I still have some of my memories," Walt says.

For some reason, Haiku glances at me before replying. "Each person adjusts at a different rate, which not only depends on what's best for them, but how accepting they are of the changes. Rest assured, you have all reached the level required for the next phase of the Ten Sigma Program."

While her smile brightens, my stomach sinks as I wonder what will be left of me when the adjustments end.

"Can you tell us more?" Suri says.

"Tonight, there is a fun event for your send-off. I hope you enjoy yourselves."

And with that vapid statement, the avatar vanishes.

I exchange an uneasy glance with Suri. There are so many unanswered questions and so many unknowns.

She says, "Brin, did you want to say something else? You guys were talking about something strange?"

I think of my morning adventure and all the riddles. Given the upcoming uncertainty, I can't burden my friends with extra worries.

"No, it's nothing."

"Even though we can't march as a unit, I know we'll be ready for anything in the scenarios," Jock says, straightening with self-assurance.

Vela rolls her eyes but stays silent, lost in her suspicions.

And she's right to be.

Walt murmurs, "I'm just glad to be part of this team. This is a lot better than what I was used to."

Suri warmly smiles. "It's good you're here with us. Right, Brin?"

I reply to their expectant stares by dipping my head. It's not my place to tell everyone things will be okay. The next phase is barreling toward us and while nobody knows what will happen, I do know that only actions, not confident words, will get us through any dangers.

Avoiding further conversation, I turn to the last glows of sunlight outlining the snow-capped peaks and lift my gaze to the darkening blue dome, thinking of Nick and wishing to be with him in the real world.

I sigh.

That life is a long, long way away.

FOURTEEN

IN MY DAYDREAM, balloons float past my face as one of many falling streamers catches in my hair. When I brush it aside, a cloud of graying confetti spills over my summer dress.

The birthday celebration is not as colorful, loud, or detailed as it should be.

A fading caricature of my husband, wearing a blackened and decomposing paper hat, leans and delivers a huge kiss. Instead of having the flavor of cake and champagne and everything wonderful from my prior life, his mouth and tongue taste like polished stone.

As the whiskers of his budding goatee tickle my chin, I break away. With a smirk, I trace my finger over the offending hair.

A bashful smile crinkles his crumbling face. "I'll get rid of it tomorrow."

The scene deteriorates into swirling dust and piles of ash and then reality returns.

I'm seated in a plush chair near the orchestra pit inside the opera house. Overhead, elegant horseshoe balconies stack high into the dark recesses of the vast space, while in front of us, a motion picture flickers on a towering screen.

It's the special event Haiku promised: "Movie Night."

The G-rated entertainment keeps with the suppression of sex drive, and except for all the killing, the innocence of the virtual universe. My leftover sarcasm from the real world makes me smile.

Sitting on my left, Suri misinterprets the expression. "Do you like this?"

The animation features a princess, a villain, and a love interest. Although well-crafted, I'm sure I've seen dozens of movies involving the same plot. I just can't remember any of them. "What's not to like?"

"I love this activity—"

"Quiet," interrupts Simon in his crotchety elder statesman voice. He's terrified of what tomorrow will bring.

Suri flashes an apologetic expression and returns to the movie.

I roll my eyes.

Vela shifts in the seat to my right, subconsciously rubbing her fingers against her cheek. While I'm saddened by every memory I've watched disintegrate into nothingness, I'm sure she's thrilled to be losing the memories of the assault that disfigured her.

The rest of the team sits either to the front or behind us, and without looking, I can sense Syd stealing glances at the back of my head.

Remembering the morning's misadventures, I clench my jaw. The plain-faced man arrived for the special event in a joyous mood and not a whit wiser about my detective work.

If he was even in the building, and I wasn't crazy imagining things.

Forcing away all thoughts of Syd, avatars, and malignant spaces beneath Home, I return to staring at the predictable movie, struggling to recollect other details from my real-world life.

I don't know if I'm being paranoid, but the memory loss seems to be accelerating.

However, on occasion, a long-forgotten event emerges, which throws everything into confusion. And while I flail away, hunting for things in my fractured mind, the unknown looms in the morning.

On top of all the other issues.

As the crowd laughs at a joke, I blow out a breath of disgust.

Instead of fretting about what will happen, I'm mired in chaotic thought, trying to figure out what memories are gone and which are going, as well as trying to answer unfathomable riddles about the Ten Sigma Program.

None of which matters.

After a sigh, I focus on what the next phase might bring.

Besides dying, I'm hoping not to be gruesomely killing anyone else, because my lack of remorse continues to be a sore topic with my conscience.

Sinking into my seat, I close my eyes, trying to imagine what else could go wrong.

By the time the end credits roll, I've reconciled my myriad of competing worries into a single feeling of dread.

As I tap Suri to leave, a tear trickles down her cheek.

"I used to see these movies with my grandchildren," she explains.

"Do you want me to stay?"

She shakes her head. "No, I need to be alone with my memories while I still have them."

Respecting the request, I stand and skirt my way around slow-moving people, mercifully getting to the exit without suffering any interaction with Syd.

Outside, on the smooth marble of the grand lobby, the team disperses with even Sergeant Rick understanding everyone's need for alone time before the big day.

Unhappy with the continuing glances at my figure, and more disappointed in not having any special gift or superpower for my troubles, I decide to clear my conscience and head away from the crowd that's returning to the barracks.

As I trudge into the fun district, the up-lighting casts an unusual magnificence on the impossible structures while the rubbery material of the path seems more springy than usual. Although the stars of the computer-generated night sky have no familiar patterns, the view is pleasing, and coupled with a pleasant breeze laden with citrus scents, my head clears and my mood improves.

Regardless of its flaws, living in the virtual world is better than the nausea and frailty of the sickness.

I pause. Those memories have faded as well.

With lighter steps, I wander until I spy the cultural museum, the place most suiting my personality in this universe. Given the rah-rah team building, my impromptu detective work, and the final night's entertainment, I haven't had the chance to visit.

Happy with the empty surroundings, I march past a tall row of conical ferns to the elegant building. Amazed by the thought and detail put into the construction, I trail my fingers over differing shades of red bricks, each littered with unique imperfections. At an iron-barred window framed by wood panels carved with twigs and butterflies, I stop to appreciate a neoclassical sculpture of a Greek king. From what I can view, the other statues in the hall are exquisite too.

I putter out a breath and make a note to return on my next free day. The museum's tasteful-yet-antiquated feel brings back memories of the cottage I shared with my husband.

When I step away from the window, my skin prickles.

Wonderful.

The phrase "No Upside," enters my mind as I face Syd.

He says, "Please, can we speak for a moment in private?"

Although he stands in a passive posture and has been on his best behavior, I flat out don't trust the man. However, given the upcoming scenarios, I don't want to get on his vindictive side either.

"Okay," I say as a heavy sigh.

He smiles and leads me to the entrance where we pass under a raised portcullis and through wooden doors with thick glass panes. In the lovingly detailed foyer, a single light floating in a wrought iron cage casts a dappled pattern on the oiled wood paneling and water-cut stone floor.

Impatient to start and finish the conversation, I stop him at the arch of the main hallway. "What?"

His eyes wander to the exhibits. "This is a beautiful place. I can see why you like it."

"What did you want to talk about?" I ask louder and more annoyed.

A pleasant countenance falls over his face, and I prepare for the gentleman persona.

He doesn't disappoint, saying in his most charming voice, "For some reason, we got off on the wrong foot. But, I'm not a horrible person. I wish to apologize for anything I've done."

Although the statement is pleasant enough, I rub my nape. He's blocking the exit when all I want to do is leave. "Tomorrow will be a long day. Get to the point."

Unhappy with the results of the opening salvo, his eyes lose focus as he searches for another tack. He blurts, "I think you're special, and we would be a great team."

"We are part of a great team."

"I'm being serious. We should form a pact to watch out for each other." He pauses when I arch an eyebrow. "You were correct, I have been looking at you this entire time, but it's mostly not from any attraction. It's because you're going to do exceedingly well in the trials. As will I."

I laugh, remembering the witch's words. "Why would any of us be special? You never told anyone about your past, and I'm not sure who you've conned, but it won't happen with me."

"I am not a conman," he says with indignation. "Your battle awareness is unique. You anticipate things."

"So what?"

"While everyone has the same threads, the others aren't like you and me. They're slow and inefficient. You've practiced with them. You know this."

"They'll catch up."

"Stop," he says, holding up his hand. "You and I are fully integrated with the threads, and we instinctively understand what to do and do it well. The others need to think about what the best action is and have irregularities in their execution. Even if their indecision only lasts for a millisecond or their movements are off by a millimeter, it's plenty."

"Who told you that?"

"I'm not allowed to say, but it's called a thread optimization issue."

I want to throttle him, all the stupid avatars, and the stupid secrecy surrounding everything. However, the empirical evidence backs up his statement. Both of us, for whatever reason, are far better than anyone on the team even if I haven't received any special power.

But that doesn't mean I should form a pact with someone who is revolting. "Unless you know something more, you haven't convinced me of anything."

He steps to the front door and peers at the sky. When he returns, he speaks in a hushed tone. "This world isn't what it seems."

That gets my undivided attention. "Oh? In what way?"

"I can't say."

My hands move to grab him, but since we are basically naked, I settle for letting them form fists between us. "You need to do better than that."

"I've been sworn to secrecy."

"Is that what the leprechaun told you?"

His thin lips curl. "You're stalking me. I'm flattered."

"Don't be. I don't trust you."

"What if I can change something?"

"You think you're a virtual god?" I say with a chuckle.

"No, nothing like that." He rubs his plain chin. "Small changes."

Hating myself, I fall into the trap. "Like?"

"I can nullify the libido inhibitors."

"Sex?"

"Yes, watch."

While I'm ambivalent about sex as Suri's way to overcome the control of the overlords, thoughts of sex combined with Syd are more unappealing than anything I can imagine. "Why don't you try something else?"

"Just watch."

Instead of fleeing to the farthest reaches of Home, I stand like an idiot as he closes his eyes in concentration. When his cheeks puff from the effort, he looks a second from exploding into little body parts.

One can only hope...

A triumphant smile crosses his face as he opens his eyes. "There, it's done."

"What?"

"I've become sexually aroused."

My eyes betray me by glancing at the slight bulge in his sheer underwear. "It's the same."

"No, it's harder. Put your hand there and touch it."

"Seriously?"

"This was a lot of work. Just reach inside my underwear and you'll see."

I retreat a couple of steps, tightening my fists, my nails digging deep into my palms. "Are you insane?"

His voice rises. "You think I've set this up as an elaborate ruse to get you to fondle me?"

That's exactly what I believe. "I am not touching you anywhere or getting into any kind of partnership. My husband was my partner and you're not replacing him."

"He's gone from your life. Like everything else prior to your download!"

My frustrations boil past my common sense. "Before this, I couldn't even hurt a fly. Now, I can't even feel guilty about killing all of those people on that stupid platform. I'm staying loyal to my husband because it's my last bond to humanity."

Even with Syd acting as my confessor, it feels good to finally enunciate my worst fears.

"To survive, you'll do a lot worse," he retorts. "Get over yourself. What you're really afraid of is that you'll grow to enjoy the killing."

My fists shake. "I am not a sadist. You make my skin crawl. If you were the last person on Earth and every last virtual world, I wouldn't form a partnership with you."

As I brush past him to leave, he grabs my wrist.

The training of the threads kicks in and I twist my arm from his hand and snap the flat of my elbow into his jaw.

He rocks to the side but doesn't fall. The features of his plain face flare with anger as his fingers curl to strike.

I wait in a defensive posture while his eyes waver as he fights some internal war.

Instead of doing anything provocative, he faces his palms toward me. "This isn't how I wanted this conversation to go." Although his tone is level, his eyes rage.

"Because you're part of the team, I'll fight with you. Other than that, stay the hell away from me."

"I'm getting out of here and into the actual world. I'll do whatever I need to do, and nobody will stop me. In the end, you'll see I'm right."

His surety cancels out my anger, and my stomach churns. "I'm not abandoning my friends."

"You'll see, Brin. I'll look forward to the day when you come and accept my offer. That's the only way you'll survive what comes next."

Somehow, he knows what tomorrow will bring.

A chill rushes over me as I turn and hustle into the night.

FIFTEEN

My RETURN to the barracks meets with no further incident, but after I crawl into my bunk, my mind whirls in anxiety. I absolutely detest Syd, but a sliver of me knows his words carried some truth.

When the soft glow of dawn creeps over my bed and heralds the arrival of the pivotal day, I haven't slept a wink.

However, small discomforts don't matter to Sergeant Rick, who decides we need sunrise calisthenics.

With bleary eyes and barely functioning limbs, I trudge through the workout, trying to determine who I hate more, Syd the Lewd One or Sergeant Rick the Make Work Jerk.

After nothing happens in the morning, we journey to the cafeteria for brunch. The highlight of my meal is imagining the blue liquid tasting like a million cups of coffee. The cynic inside me applauds when the placebo effect lasts for the whole of seven seconds.

During the entire time, Syd stays cordial, sipping with a blissful stare of stupidity as if nothing happened in the museum.

On Sergeant Rick's direction, we spend midday and the late afternoon performing more calisthenics we don't need and target practice we need even less. Despite my lack of rest and anxieties, I finish first in the sharpshooting contest. An astounded Sergeant Rick rewards me with a "Nobody Likes a Showoff" speech.

I don't want to believe it, but perhaps Syd's words about thread integration carry a little weight.

By the time the sun scrapes against the tops of the mountains, I'm antsy with anticipation.

Fortunately, the wait isn't long, and as the last rays of light disappear, static wraps over my body and we're back sitting in the group room. It might be my imagination, but the glow of the elementary shapes appears muted, even somber.

The air pops, and a beaming Haiku materializes in the center of the semicircle.

"Welcome! Are you eager for your first scenario?"

Subdued stares and tightened lips meet her cheerfulness. The only movements come from Walt tapping his toes and Carol twirling her hair.

I chew on my thumbnail while the moment stretches.

Sergeant Rick announces, "We're ready."

"That is indeed wonderful," Haiku says. "Now, here are the details of the next phase of the Ten Sigma Program."

People shift into attentive postures with sharp intakes of breath.

"You will be placed in a series of scenarios. Every scenario contains its own virtual environment, generally representing something in the real world. It can be jungle, desert, arctic, mountain, ocean, or anything else you can imagine on Earth. Scenarios begin with a specific mission, which can be defending or attacking or a specified task or some mixture of them. Additionally, other parameters will be presented on a case-by-case basis. This can include a command structure and boundaries."

"Will you be coming with us?" Walt asks nervously.

"None of the guides may enter a scenario. Rules are rules and cannot be broken," Haiku replies.

"Can you tell us more about this upcoming scenario?" Rick asks.

"Only that the forces will always be roughly in parity in addition to the strengths and skills of the individuals."

An image of the bald giant crashes into my mind. I take short breaths as tightness constricts my chest. What's she talking about? He wasn't like everyone else. I'm not sure how I survived the hammering at the end of the first battle, and I'm still terrified of meeting him again.

My hand quivers but otherwise doesn't respond when I try to raise it to ask about his existence.

Haiku takes on a serious countenance. The focused eyes, taut cheeks, and tight lips look wrong on her face. "This is important. Your bodies react as they would in the real world. You need air to survive and if you are shot or stabbed or punched, the injuries will be the same. However, no matter how terrible, any and all wounds shall be healed upon completion of the scenario. But..." She pauses, sweeping a glance over the team. "If you perish, you shall be expunged from the system."

"Dead? As in forever?" Suri says.

"Your consciousness can't be duplicated, and once extinguished, cannot be revived," Haiku replies.

Simon pops to his feet. "I don't understand. Everyone has the threads. Why do we need these scenarios!"

Haiku slowly turns him. "The threads are only a starting point. To prove worthy of graduating this program, you must hone your skills and steel your mind and that can only be achieved through trials by fire."

The ex-politician sinks back into his chair. "I mean, it just seems like a waste," he says, looking to the rest of us.

Carol raises her hand. "If we survive, but don't accomplish the mission are we expunged from the system too?"

Haiku admonishes her. "Don't be such a worrywart. If you fail to complete your mission, you restart from the beginning."

There are groans I would join, except I notice Syd staring at me. When I quizzically raise an eyebrow, he asks Haiku, "What are the parameters to complete the program and get back to the actual world?"

Haiku claps, her happy face returning. "That is a wonderful question and my favorite part of the briefing. Everyone receives a score. And soon, you'll be able to sense not only your score but everyone else's too."

Everyone pushes their heads forward, squinting.

"Not now," Haiku says. "Like the rest of the acclimation process, it will manifest according to the talents of each mind."

"We all start at zero?" Rick asks.

"No, everyone's score is 2.5 sigmas," Haiku replies.

I sit up with a start, the mathematician within me shivering.

"What's a sigma?" asks Walt.

"It's also called a standard deviation and is a measure of population," she replies. "We only want special people of great skill to return to the real world, so it is the highest standard of measurement."

"So, 2.5 sigmas were our odds of winning the first battle?" Sergeant Rick says.

"Exactly, one in one hundred and sixty-two," Haiku replies in her happiest voice, dismissing the one hundred and sixty-one people that died for each of us to be here.

Her next words confirm my worst fears. "The risks from each scenario are cumulative, and to graduate this program, you must achieve a level of ten sigmas."

While she gleefully claps, I cover my mouth, hoping I misunderstood.

Grumbles and yips of consternation come from around the semicircle.

"Seven and a half sigmas to go?" says Jock in a heavy voice.

"One out of a hundred and sixty-two to get 2.5 sigmas—what's that make, one in a couple of thousand to get to ten?" adds Walt.

Syd looks at me with laughter dancing in his dark eyes.

I avoid his gaze. Walt thinks the odds are additive with the sigmas but that's not the way it works. I have the math background and wish I didn't. Everything operates on a bell curve. The further you move toward the tail ends, the less there is. It's like trying to gather oxygen at higher and higher altitudes. While easy at sea level, Mount Everest is harder, the stratosphere harder than that, and it's impossible when you get into space. The finish line for this program is like trying to breathe outside the orbit of Pluto.

It's not that 2.5 sigmas are one out of one hundred and sixty-two while four sigmas are roughly one half more.

Four sigmas are one out of thirty thousand.

Five is one in 3.5 million.

Ten would be—

131,248,150,000,000,000,000,000 to 1.

The giant number representing the odds materializes in my head accompanied by Haiku's cheery voice. *"About one in one hundred and thirty-one sextillion but don't tell anyone!"*

As the others wrestle with the basics of statistics, my fingers rub along my bottom teeth.

Syd sends a knowing nod, while Haiku secretly speaks again, *"Remember, keep that between us!"*

The astronomical number has twenty-four digits and is greater than the number of people who have ever lived or will ever live by factors of ten. Even if we had a billion lives instead of just the one, in the face of one hundred and thirty sextillion to one odds, zero people would be expected to survive the gauntlet of scenarios to reach a ten sigma level.

We're all dead men walking.

SIXTEEN

Scenario one begins when I materialize in a new world, wearing a snug skinsuit. My hand grips a silenced .22 caliber assault rifle while sprays of water hit my face. I lie with four others—Suri, Carol, Rick, and Syd—in a speeding rubber craft, bobbing over shallow waves. Three other identical boats travel in a line with us for a total force size of twenty—two teams worth of people.

I want to scream, *"We're all dead! What does it matter!"* but the words die against the knot constricting my throat.

From the horizon, a lengthy triangle of land grows against the nighttime blanket of stars. My body tenses from apprehension as I squint to gather more details. Gnarled rocks dot a landing beach that leads to lurking bluffs formed from twisted crags. Between the fractured veins of moonlight spilling down the slope lie deep gouges of blackness. And offset to the moon side of the island, a single menacing peak completes the foreboding picture.

This is a deathmatch. Kill everyone on the opposing force.

The grim task isn't spoken; it appears in my mind.

Filling my lungs with sea air, I shake my head. While I'm torn between hoping to get used to the brutality and never falling into the trap of guiltless murder, the weight of the ten sigma odds dwarfs everything. No matter what we do here, an endless line of battles awaits, and our long-term survivability is, for all intents and purposes, zero. We are corpses with temporary control of our bodies and besides Syd, I'm the only one who knows it.

I don't want to die.

My fingers twitch as I wipe water from my eye.

A gentle hand touches my shoulder. "Are you okay?" Suri asks.

Skirting around the deadly truth, I reply, "Yeah, just anxious about what's coming."

As the boat vibrates, the moonlight jitters over her pretty eyes. "Think about something good in your life. Something to live for."

She's right. Besides surviving the coming violence, I need to keep reminding myself of who I was in the real world. I search for the most iconic of my remaining memories.

My husband flashes a winning smile. An intimate moment consisting of him, red wine, a silky comforter over a small bed, and homework appears in my head.

As I enter, I relax.

The imaginary room flares into a blinding white. When the brightness fades, only the two of us remain in a black space.

The big dreamer voice says, *"People win lotteries all the time."*

My sarcastic self responds, *"Getting to ten sigmas is exactly like that, except a thousand million million times worse."*

"But, no matter the odds, everyone buying a ticket thinks they are going to win. Why not you?"

"Incredible, your imaginary attitude is on steroids too!"

"The ten sigma lottery ticket in your pocket will be the winner!"

"I'm changing your name to Major Optimism."

"I'm calling you Private Downer."

"Touché."

His tone becomes serious. *"Before, we made a great team because my optimism and your realism were unbeatable together. Now, you're alone, but to survive, you'll need to be the best of both of us."*

I have no snarky answer to this imaginary version of my husband.

"Get out of here and make sure you win!"

"Whoop-Dee-Doo! I love imaginary you," I say and give him a kiss.

The salty air blows past my face as the warm touch of his lips fade. In spite of the situation, I force my lips into a tight smirk.

Although only a small step, I set my goal to survive the coming battle with as many teammates as possible. Bigger things, requiring a crazy optimism I don't have, will need to wait until I completely lose my sanity.

Suri notices my expression and chuckles.

"Stay frosty," says Sergeant Rick.

I return my attention to the island.

Although everyone has the capabilities of the black and red threads, the former ranger captain has real experience. And considering the crap is about to become real, that counts for something.

———

Minutes later, when the boat scrapes ashore, I've identified a myriad of ambush points across the faint gleams and intervening shadows of the long side of the island but strangely, no threats.

Hating the conundrum, I hop over the foam of the surf and land on a flat rock. As I flick the rifle's safety off, Syd shows his amusement with a feral grin.

"Virgin territory," he whispers.

Although I frown at the odd words, I appreciate their meaning. Something about this place is pristine.

Suri brushes past and I follow her to a low embankment and form part of a defensive perimeter while Rick jogs off to discuss strategy with the other team leader.

As the two of them huddle, I study the dark forms of the second team. While it's hard to distinguish any features, they seem familiar, and I wonder about their backgrounds, imagining them to be accountants or parents or grandparents. Maybe they even have a Sergeant Rick type leading them.

I shake my head. These people are part of the Ten Sigma Program and subject to the same odds as us.

More dead people walking.

Vela sidles next to me, and I'm relieved to shift my attention to my friends.

"What are we waiting for?" she asks nervously.

"Just remember to use your training."

"That's easy for you to say."

She still thinks I have some special power.

Instead of answering, I look to the rest of the group. Although expertly holding their weapons, they have varying expressions. Surprisingly, the calmest is Walt, while unsurprisingly, Simon has the widest eyes and jitters with the most fear. Everyone else falls somewhere between those two extremes, except for Syd, who alone looks eager.

While I'm not sure where I belong in that spectrum, I hope I won't let anybody down.

A black thread whispers, *"One can never tell how one will react until the bullets fly."*

Rick returns and kneels in the damp sand. Under his cool gaze and relaxed demeanor, the anxiety lessens. He explains the strategy. "The second team is the reserve. We'll form a skirmish line and flush the enemy out. Pairs only, stay alert. Carol and Syd will hold the far right." He points to Suri and myself. "You two are next. I'll be in the center with Simon, then Walt and Vela. Jock and Ally will take the far left. Let's go."

While I provide cover, Suri scrambles up the meter-high wall and to the gnarled rocks forming the cliffs. The awkward climb is the perfect place to get attacked, especially from the tabletop peak dominating the landmass to the left. After her black form gets to the top, Suri waits, scanning for enemies.

Upset with Rick for volunteering us to lead the assault through this dangerous terrain, I sling my rifle and jump on top of the sandy barrier and then slip into a deep crevasse. Keeping inside the shadows, I use my fingers to find handholds and pull myself up the steep slope. With little noise or trouble, I negotiate my body over the rim of the cliff and crouch next to Suri with my weapon ready.

Ahead of us, bluish moonlight shines on a landscape created from the paths of many lava flows. The twinkles of metallic particles rise into the distance. For no good reason, a black thread informs me the volcanic material resembles Iwo Jima, the home of one of the bloodiest battles of the Second World War.

I suppress a shudder.

Suri motions and we scamper over a ripple of rock. With our expert knowledge, we use the cover of the stones and indents in the harsh terrain to advance swiftly inland.

Despite the cool air, sweat trickles down my spine. While I tug at the nape of my outfit, only the soft padding of our boots and the fading crashes of the surf disturb the stillness.

Something is wrong.

I want to relay my misgivings to Suri but stay quiet, overriding my fears and trusting to Rick's plan.

Another fifty meters pass before we proceed into the long night shadow of the heights. Although I draw anxious breaths expecting gunfire, during the entire heart-pounding advance, I've found no sign of our enemies, not even around the ominous peak that is the premium defensive position on the island.

A strong breeze greets us as we cross the dimpled ridge forming the spine of the landmass. The terrain changes into a smallish plain that spills into the opposite shoreline. The lack of cover forces us to slink into a groove between two colliding lava streams to keep pace with the others.

While my clammy skinsuit enjoys sticking to my sweaty body, a chilling sensation wanders over my skin and the tingly spiders of doom stab at my nape.

My steps slow, and I stop.

Fright from threats tucked into black recesses of this crazy place I understand, but this concern is different. Syd said this place was virginal.

"Why are your thoughts wandering?" my husband says.

I imagine a big smile plastered on his face while he adds, *"Because..."*

Because there is nobody here.

Suri backtracks. "We're falling behind. What's wrong?"

"It's just nerves."

Her features harden as her dark eyes focus on me. "That's not it, what are you thinking?"

"I haven't seen anything."

"They're trained like us and very skilled."

"The best option would have been attacking when we landed. But we're more than halfway to the other side and nothing. Look at the peak."

Her eyes flicker to the ominous mass blocking the moonlight.

"Anyone up there would have already fired," I say.

After drawing a long breath and swallowing, she says, "Okay, you have a point."

Gesturing at the mostly smooth terrain leading to the opposite shore, I say, "This is terrible for defense. There isn't enough cover left, and they can't be waiting to get surrounded." I take a deep breath. "What if they aren't on the island?"

She grabs my shoulder. "Let's go."

"Where?"

"To Rick."

We abandon caution as we rush to the center of the line. Rick scowls when we arrive. "What are you two doing?"

"Rick," I say.

Simon interjects, "Shut up. Both of you idiots get back to your position."

Suri holds up her hand, saying in an urgent voice, "Listen to her."

Rick says, "If we're attacked now—"

My anger rises at his rigidity. "We won't be. There's nobody here."

"What?"

I jab my finger to our front. "Has anyone heard or seen anything? Why would they wait for us to sweep them into a flat, undefendable area?"

Rick wipes sweat from his knitted brows. Too many precious seconds fly past as he processes the information.

"What do you want to do?" I hiss.

His cool demeanor evaporates, and after spewing a long string of creative curses, he says, "We reform the line for an attack from behind us."

"We need to warn the others," I say.

"Defense first, then the reserve team. Go get Carol and Syd. We'll set up the rest."

"What about them?" I point to our landing spot and our allies.

Rick says with an angry undertone, "We will protect our people first. Move, now!"

You're welcome.

However, I'm not upset with him. The deliberate words cover his fear because our first scenario is in danger of becoming our last scenario.

Suri and I hurry in an adrenaline-powered sprint, the rubber soles of our boots thumping on the uneven lava. I should be used to it, but my speed and coordination still amaze me. My old gimpy self would have broken an ankle by this point. When Carol and Syd come into sight, we're breathing heavily.

"Problems," I say as we hit the ground next to them.

Soft clicks from silenced guns and impacts of bullets on stone cascade across the landing beach. The four of us flatten.

Rick was right, anyone running back to warn the other team would be in deep trouble.

A couple of figures, possibly the people I mused were parents or grandparents, clear the beach ridge only to be gunned down a moment later.

Dead.

As experiences from the black threads fill my mind with advice, I fight a growing panic. Suri stays reserved, sucking in slow breaths, while Carol wipes moisture from her pretty face, letting her hand linger on her long hair. Syd's eyes gleam, and he produces a vicious smile, announcing he's ready to defy any set of odds.

"We have to rejoin the others. Rick has a plan," I say.

Syd huffs but otherwise stays quiet.

I lead them back to Rick with a wary eye toward the beach. The sounds of battle soon still.

Suri stops. "The other team's gone."

"We're alone," Carol adds with consternation.

I've been in the virtual world for only a short time, but these people are the closest thing I have to a family.

"Guys," I say, surprising myself. "The fun and games of training are finished, but stay calm. We can do this."

Syd nods and says in a hungry voice, "Our enemies don't know what they're in for."

Neither do our friends.

Unsure of the reasoning behind the last thought, I move at a faster pace, and we swiftly arrive at Rick's position.

He's organized the rest of the team to defend behind the mid-island ridge stretching to the heights. Except for a few rocks near the beach, the exposed ground to our rear ensures there will be no retreat.

Rick points at the peak. "Brin, cover the main part of the line from there and shore up any breaches. You're our last line of defense."

My reward for winning the morning's marksmanship contest. Although I want to stay with Suri, there's no time to argue. With my eyes darting toward the beach, I scamper behind a pitted river of lava and follow its channel to my position.

When a silhouette rises over the lip of the cliffs and ducks into cover, I slow my pace, keeping low.

Over the next minute, I catch enough movement to map out their advance. Each attacker expertly uses the bumpy terrain, presenting little or no opportunity to receive fire. I count thirteen, and given the silence from the shore, assume our ten allies are gone, having killed seven of our twenty enemies.

My boots hit the shallow part of the heights before the next set of shooting starts. While the sharp impacts of bullets register on the rocks, the attackers don't press their slight numerical advantage, unexpectedly staying content to hold their position.

The slope steepens, and I exert more effort to maintain my progress. After a few steps, I find a narrow curving trail, which allows me to negotiate the nearly impassable rockface to reach the top.

When the path ends, I pull myself over a two-meter-high stone lip, flopping onto a large tabletop of dirt. After I scoot to the battle side, I have a commanding view of the action.

Nothing has changed during my climb. Although bullets crackle along the length of line, the enemy hasn't advanced.

A disturbing thought washes over me. Haiku said the forces should have parity. My assumption was twenty enemies overwhelmed the reserve force, taking seven casualties. What if it was fifteen with only two dead? That would leave five coming from an unknown direction and explain the temerity of their approach.

Frantically, I weigh the different options for the opposing commander. Our defense is anchored at the peak and extends with the mid-island ridge. Because our half of the island is smooth, a flanking attack at the far end of the line or from directly behind would destroy us.

Soft footsteps pad up the narrow trail.

I raise my rifle.

Syd's head pops over the rock lip.

With many regrets, I refrain from pulling the trigger. We need everyone.

After he scoots next to me, I ask, "What the hell are you doing here?"

"Just checking to see if you've changed your mind about my offer."

"Now?"

"I didn't feel like following Rick's strategy. They should have made you the leader."

Ugh.

"I don't have time for this."

Twisting my body, I scan the miniature plain toward the long tip of the island. There's nothing.

Could I be wrong?

Tugging at the skinsuit sticking to my chest, I squint at the barely visible triangle of sand. The glitters of the quartz particles wink from dark forms, moving with caution.

"Wow," Syd says. "That's an unfortunate turn of events. They'll roll up the flank starting with poor Carol. Then, Suri and Walt. Glad I'm not down there."

I should have killed him.

"Shut up. We have to help."

"Our weapons don't have the power to cover the flank at this distance."

This I know. At over two hundred meters, and with the enemy's movement and cover skills in addition to the silencer limiting the rounds to subsonic speeds, a hit isn't a realistic expectation from this range. "We have to get closer."

"I'm not moving. If we stay here and pick off the enemy as they advance up the hill, we'll win."

"Everyone else will die."

He shrugs. "Mostly."

It's all I can do not to throttle him. I take deep breaths, letting the battle unfold in my mind. I can impede but not stop the flanking attack from this position. If I call out and we pull back and try to form a defense around the heights, they will still swamp past Carol and Suri before we can slow them down. With the higher ground, we might win, but plenty of my friends aren't going home.

Or I can run and try to take out the second team by myself. If successful, I can save the flank. If I get killed, then everyone in their stretched-out positions dies with me.

I wish I had someone to talk with besides Syd. My chatty, optimistic, and imaginary husband is silent.

"You're running out of time, Brin. Stay here with me. We'll form a great partnership."

My mood turns angry as I ignore him and scrutinize the battlefield.

Screw it.

Taking the crazy option, I abandon my post and dash down the slope, accompanied only by Syd's fading laughter.

SEVENTEEN

I LEAVE THE PATH, and staying inside the shadow of a tapering ridge, slide down the slope. After I hit more forgiving ground, I use my long strides to make good use of the meager time we have left.

A picture of steam erupting from the ears of Sergeant Rick or Simon for yet again disobeying orders crashes into my mind. I stifle a laugh; they can shoot me after we're dead.

Still hidden by darkness, I plow into the surf, stopping when the freezing water reaches my waist. Because of the flatness of this side of the island, pushing through the ocean is the only way I can cross the exposed terrain without alerting anyone to my presence and getting shot to pieces. I rush toward the end of our line, my legs churning against the undertow threatening to pull me out to sea and the rest of my body fighting the waves trying to send me onto the exposed beach.

When I pass behind Rick at the halfway point, I wave frantically to get his attention.

He's too focused on the battle to notice a bobbing form lost against waves of darkness.

When I escape the shadow of the heights, moonlight brightens the surrounding ocean. Now visible, I lower my aching body until my chin scrapes the top of the shifting water. I attempt to match the rhythm of the swells, which works less often than I'd prefer, and after a few steps, my nostrils and eyes sting from crests of saltwater lapping over my head.

Then a powerful breaker knocks me to a knee, and it's all I can do to avoid being dragged ashore.

The returning undertow pulls out my leg.

I flop underwater with a mouthful of the sea spilling down my throat. Unlike the blue cafeteria liquid, this tastes exactly as it should, briny and full of salt. With the nasty taste sputtering from my mouth, I push my head above the surface. Although my muscles burn with fatigue and my rapid breaths can't supply enough oxygen, I force myself to keep moving by focusing on terrible images of my team lying dead from my incompetence.

After what feels like an eternity, but in reality is only a minute or two, I finally arrive near the exposed flank—numb, but just in time.

The dark forms rise, getting ready to wipe out my teammates.

With barely enough strength to heft my rifle, my hands shake as I aim. As the surging water threatens to knock me over, I draw a steadying breath. Hitting anything doesn't matter, I only need to get everyone's attention. I empty the thirty-round magazine in the general direction of the enemy, the bullets peppering nothing except for a few scattered rocks.

The exhausted effort attracts just enough attention. Carol and Suri swivel to meet the fresh attack, and a new firefight breaks out.

However, my plan's too successful. From beyond the beach, a dim figure points a rifle at me.

A bullet zips past my ear as I twist my head.

I tumble underwater while more impacts splash around me. A wave flips me over, then the undercurrent drags me along the sandy bottom. More seawater spills into my mouth, up my nose, and then down the wrong passage of my throat. I expel valuable air coughing out the foul liquid, then even as my lungs beg for oxygen, I clench my jaw and tighten my lips.

Engulfed by blackness, the roiling currents grab my limbs and whirl my body in every direction. Panic explodes through my dimming consciousness. I have a terrible fear of drowning, but if I try to get air, I'll wind up getting shot.

This is only ending with my death.

My chest heaves as fleeting thoughts race through my mind. My team. Fragments of my prior life. I clutch at the one of my husband. His confident face flashes his winning smile.

Imaginary him says, *"It's only a little water and a single shooter. Grab some air and don't lollygag on the surface. Don't give him too much credit either; he's one guy struggling to hit a head bobbing in the middle of the ocean."*

"Kisses, Major Optimism."

"That's General Optimism to you."

More bubbles escape from my burning lungs as I snicker. Instead of heading up, I push downward and when my fingers touch the sandy bottom, I flip and finding my footing, shoot to the surface.

I gulp one greedy breath before more bullets force me back underwater. At least I'm getting them to waste ammunition. I thank the virtual overlords for leaving my sarcasm intact.

When I next breach the surface, Carol and Suri are distracting the enemy with cover fire. Although my insane actions almost got me killed, at least they're momentarily safe and helping me.

As I bob with relative anonymity in the swells, I spy an egg-shaped boulder sitting at the boundary of the beach. It's an opportunity, but my exhausted muscles can barely stop the pulling currents and powerful eddies in the water from drowning me.

It's too far. I can't do it.

My frustration boils. Why is everything ridiculously hard? As one of a hundred and sixty-two people surrounded by a rising sea of red acid, fighting was so simple. I barely had a chance to think.

"Then stop thinking and act!" Major Optimism screams.

A wave hits my back and instead of resisting, I angle toward the protection of the boulder, letting the force of the water propel me ashore. When my hands scrape sand under the foam of the surf, I rise and, using more of a stumbling crawl than run and dragging the rifle, which has miraculously stayed with me during the ordeal, cross the narrow beach and flop behind the big rock.

Amazingly, I haven't been hit. While not based on talent, I'll welcome the dumb luck. I want to do something but have to wait a moment to stop shivering and expel saltwater from my nostrils and mouth. After setting the weapon against the boulder, I wipe mucus from my chin and then rub my arms and legs to rid them of numbness.

Still trembling, I peer past the shaded side of the rock. Four of the enemy, dark against the glittery terrain, duel with Carol and Suri. The fifth points his rifle at me.

I tumble back as a three-round burst spikes into the rock, whizzing splinters past my head. As blood trickles down my cheek, I close my eyes.

They're good.

My anger rises.

So am I.

After shakily reloading the rifle, I twist past the opposite side of the boulder with gritted teeth and snap off a shot. My main opponent isn't at the same location, but it feels good to do something proactive.

Against this caliber of enemy, staying put isn't an option. Even though I'm not reaching the ten sigma level, dying in scenario one would be an embarrassment.

I roll to my right and crawl away from the egg-shaped boulder. Not needing a stray bullet to find my head, I slither into a fissure running behind a lava channel.

As I slip around my enemies, I hug the bottom of the shallow cut, the rough surface painfully scraping through the skinsuit over my knees and elbows.

From the faint clicks of the triggers to the zips and sharp impacts of the bullets, I develop a mental map of the nearby fighting. However, the most important piece, the location of the person hunting me is missing.

Since my team has to stay in the cover of the mid-island ridge, our position is extended and vulnerable with Carol bearing the brunt of the attack and Suri only able to provide sporadic suppressing fire.

The situation is tenuous at best. When the main force coming from the rocky side of the island reaches us, the two prongs will envelop Carol and Suri and then the rest of the line will collapse.

With growing desperation, I move another ten meters and edge into the long shadow of the peak. I peer from the darkness. Everyone is where I expect them to be, except for the last enemy. I roll back into cover and take long breaths to slow down the speed of combat. I have to end my opponent quickly to rescue my friends.

Something clicks in my thoughts. My most important enemy doesn't know I'm the only one making a headlong rush through the ocean. When I mentally review the flattish landscape, only one place is suitable for protecting the beach and covering the flank against Carol and Suri.

The sounds of fighting from beyond the ridge edge closer. Suri turns and engages the new threats, leaving Carol and myself matched against five opponents.

No more time to waste.

I prop myself up on an elbow. With my aim centered on a dark space extending from a large rock slab near the water, I empty the rifle.

Most of the shots fly into the ocean except for a single dull impact. A second later a body crumples into the sand.

Amazed, I pop up, and slapping in a fresh magazine, move forward in a combat crouch, shooting at the nearest enemy.

Fleshy impacts erupt across his body.

The one behind reacts by rolling and firing.

I jump to the side, the rushed shots nicking the ground behind me, and return fire.

More dull thuds. Two left.

The one after lies in a lava channel dueling with Carol and doesn't notice me.

I fire a headshot that ends with a sharp crack of skull. The remaining enemy jumps for better cover, but Carol kills him with a three-round burst.

The flank is secure, and I'm stunned to be alive and unhurt.

"Score one for Major Optimism," declares my cheery husband.

"Score one for General Optimism," I reply.

"Yay, a promotion on my first day!"

I reload, letting my frayed nerves calm.

Carol steps onto a lava pipe, wide eyes wandering over the entire scene. "Wow." She puffs out a relieved breath.

Two moonlit forms appear over the ridge. I dive and hit the rough ground, jamming my shoulder as they fire. Suri twists away, but blood and brains fly as Carol jerks backward from bullet impacts.

While leaping to my feet, I fire in fully automatic mode and in three seconds, shower the entire magazine over a wide arc.

The nearest enemy collapses while the other tumbles and disappears behind the ridge.

Ignoring the dull throbs from my shoulder, I reload and run to my friends.

Suri is hit, and I jump into cover next to her. Located in the stomach and arm, her bloody wounds are awful but not immediately life-threatening.

Ten meters away, Carol lies on the round top of a lava flow, her long hair splayed over the glittering ground with blood from a neat hole in her forehead spilling over her face.

I hold my revulsion inside and curse myself for getting lulled into complacency. Even though we're all dead anyway, dying for a mistake is stupid.

"Victory is no cause for celebration," a black thread chirps.

Despite all the knowledge in the threads, we aren't real soldiers. Killers maybe, but not soldiers.

Heavy breathing from the opposite slope pulls me from my self-loathing. I've wounded the second attacker who killed Carol. A coldness settles inside me.

After taking a quick peek to ensure I'm not being ambushed, I scuttle over the crest and slide into a groove pinched between two veins of jagged rock. At the bottom, my thigh brushes against a fallen weapon. Even with an unarmed opponent, I won't repeat the mistake of being complacent. Carefully scanning every shadow in every nook, I inch closer to my enemy.

My finger tightens on the trigger as I leap past the last of the rock formation. A breath catches in my throat and I freeze.

The moonlight shines on violet eyes. It's the final girl I killed on "Acid Island."

Dead is dead and never to return, so how can she be here?

Despite leaking blood from the chest and abdomen, her stare is lucid. However, as I lower my face into her vision, she displays no signs of recognition.

If she's in front of me, then…

Consumed by fear, I swivel and search for the bald giant. Although things are quiet, I'm not fooled. Tunneling my focus, I sweep my weapon over the dark patches in the landscape, not sure if I'm going to fight or flee when he appears.

Syd's voice drags me from the terror. Hidden by a deep shadow, he repeats, "Well, do you want the honors?"

"What?"

Walt jumps past Syd. "We won!"

While my heart leaps at the sight of the teen, I'm puzzled. "I don't understand."

Walt replies, "The fighting's over. Syd was awesome, he swept through their line from the opposite side."

Syd's thin lips form a bashful smile as he steps closer. It's fake because he would have just as easily let everyone die. As he idly uses the suppressor of his rifle to fondle our last enemy's wounds, she groans.

Rick steps into view. "Don't drag it out."

Syd looks to me. "Well?"

My eyes burn with disgust while I deliberately shake my head. Then without a backward glance, I walk away.

Scenario one ends with the faint click of a trigger pull.

———

The salty breeze changes into citrus and honey scented air, and I sink into the soft leather of my ready room seat.

I roll my previously injured shoulder. True to Haiku's word, it's in perfect condition, as is the rest of my almost naked body.

My adrenaline rush drains until I wrap my arms around myself, only wanting to shiver from the terror of combat and fear of the bald giant. With the violet-eyed girl coming back to haunt me, can he be far behind? And by some mystical power, I somehow can't vocalize my anxieties to anyone.

Across the semicircle, the other survivors express the span of emotions one would expect from surviving a life and death situation. Vela sheds a tear as she touches her cheek. Suri runs her hands over her now-healed wounds in disbelief. A nervous giggle leaves Walt as his toes tap dance on the floor.

On my right, Ally rubs her cheeks hard enough to remove her freckles. At least narcissism still exists in the virtual world. Rick sits at attention, a satisfied expression over his face.

And Syd. He stares hungrily as if needing another battle.

Nine of the seats have an occupant. Given the circumstances, the survival rate is amazing, but my eyes linger on the empty chair. Carol was the burn victim, and I liked her and her idiosyncrasies. She should be sitting with us, twirling her long blonde hair instead of being dead.

I should feel worse. Everyone should feel worse.

Simon stands, letting out a hoot, his fists shaking at the ceiling. "That was better than election night! I love winning!"

Although he's probably happier at being alive than anything else, his bravado pulls everyone from their introspection. Except for Syd and myself, relieved snickers and sheepish looks spread across the group.

The former politician continues in a louder tone. "And I nailed one! Right between the eyes."

"I don't think I hit anything, but I didn't get hit either," Ally cheerfully says. "How many did everyone else get?"

Jock and Suri each hold up a finger. Rick pops up two. Walt shrugs his shoulders while Syd stays surprisingly quiet despite his obviously high score.

"I got one too," Vela says. "Brin, how about you?"

Five people died by my hand. The remainder of the team got six. There were eighteen of the final attackers. That means Syd's tally is seven if I give him credit for the violet-eyed girl I wounded. Regardless, the two of us did the lion's share of the hard work.

Just like he said we would.

I shake my head, staring at Carol's seat. My count isn't right. Carol, whom I didn't warn to stay frosty, got one too.

"Brin?" Vela repeats, pulling me from my remorse.

Before I reply, Rick stands, clapping. "Don't be concerned with the number of kills. This is a team. The first time for combat is always rough, and we came through with flying colors."

For emphasis, he sweeps around the semicircle, extending his hand and giving the appropriate handshake, fist bump, or high-five to each member of the team. My interaction is more of a light touch with his knuckles grazing my extended fingers, but he doesn't notice my dour mood.

When Sergeant Rick returns to his chair, Syd laughs, switching to his gentleman persona. "The outcome was in doubt for several minutes."

Rick points to me. "I want to commend you for your initiative. If you hadn't saved the flank, we would have lost."

I'm surprised. Although Simon scrunches his face in disapproval, Sergeant Rick isn't going to put me in front of the firing squad like I half-expected. And I need to hand his real-world combat experience credit. He made the right call setting up the defense first and unlike myself or Carol, he would not have lowered his guard in the lull of a battle.

I reply, "Can we have a minute's silence for Carol?"

Suri sends a nod. At least I'm not the only one noting the loss.

Rick rubs his chin. "Of course. I'm not sure why I didn't think of that myself."

Because you're not fighting the optimizations of the overlords like me.

Before we give the poor woman her just due, a hum rises and Haiku floats in the middle of the group, her strawberry scent flooding into my nostrils and her silvery eyes twinkling with pride.

"An amazing performance by all," she says with light claps. "That tactical situation would have destroyed most teams, yet you sustained only a single casualty."

Suri interjects sarcasm into the cheery atmosphere. "If we had all perished, would you have been sad?"

Haiku doesn't recognize the rhetorical nature of the question. "Absolutely I would. Until I took over my next team."

I give props for the honesty of our software therapist, but I'm annoyed Carol has been forgotten.

Before I can point this out, Haiku speaks again. "Everyone has increased to a 2.6 sigma score. With those having a kill getting an extra hundredth. Brin, who performed exceptionally well, receives an extra nine-hundredths!"

Vela breaks her reserved character with a loud shout. "Superhero!"

I tighten my lips, not needing or feeling worthy of the accolade.

Haiku continues, "And for having the most kills, Syd gets an extra tenth."

It's left unsaid, but Syd was instrumental to the victory. Although he doesn't believe in teamwork and I still don't trust him, I raise my estimation of the plain-faced man. On a battlefield, he has value, and without him, there would be more empty seats gracing the semicircle.

However, when I look across the delighted group, his face has reverted to a mask of indifference.

Some people are born for combat.

Haiku turns serious. "This was the first of many scenarios and it's imperative for you to do well in each of the coming ones.

"This has been a long day. Now is time for rest and relaxation. If anyone has any trouble, call my name."

Although she's speaking to the team, I sense her words are directed at me. Why? I have no idea and she doesn't meet my inquisitive glance.

Instead, she raises her hand and the soft glows of the room disappear.

After the static fades, I'm lying in the spongy mattress of my bunk. Only faint rectangles of starlight leaking from the cuts along the top of the wall disturb the darkness, and except for soft rustles and faint snoring, the place is still.

Across the aisle, Carol's bed is vacant. Although disappointed to discover I'm past her death, a sadness rises inside me when I glance at the other occupied bunks. Many, if not all will be empty in the near future.

With nothing else to do, I close my eyes.

Mixed images of violence, the bald giant, and the violet-eyed girl swirl in my mind. After a few minutes of frustration, I pull myself from the bleak thoughts and stare at the blank underside of the upper bunk.

My conscience won't let me sleep, but I can't force myself to suffer a shred of guilt over the dead. I'm losing the battle against the optimization the virtual overlords require in their servants.

What have I gotten myself into?

Mentally exhausted and bursting with exasperation, I think of my family.

Nick, Darla, and Emily.

As long as I can remember them and draw strength from their love, all will be okay.

I repeat the names as I search through my memories, trying to hold on to my past.

Later, as the gray of dawn crawls into the room, I fall asleep watching the last recollections of my wedding collapse into dust.

EIGHTEEN

Surrounded on the battlement by four attackers, my threads coordinate perfectly as I lunge with my arm fully extended. My sword catches enough of the battle ax to deflect its arc past a terrified Walt's helmet.

The reverberations of the block numb my forearm while the curved end of the ax carves a chunk of stone from the castle wall. As Walt scuttles to safety, the ax-head whirls around the soldier's heavyset middle and comes at my face.

I twist, arching my body to let the sharp edge fly past, and then completing the turn, guide a spear thrust from my midsection with my free hand.

After a pirouette along the wooden shaft, I swipe my sword at my second opponent's neck.

The tip meets his carotid artery. Blood splashes over my cheek and cascades down my leather shoulder protection.

A quick sidestep brings me past a downward cut from the ax, which cleaves the walkway with a resounding clang.

With a twitch of my wrist, I reverse my sword and launch it through the armpit gap under the man's bulky armor. The blade sinks into his body and gets yanked from my hand when he crumples.

Before my dead enemy tumbles over the outer embrasure, I pull the long ax from his hands and whirl it against the slashes of my last two foes. The hefty weapon is difficult to use, and I give ground to a dizzying array of sword strokes.

A wild cut glances off my breastplate even as a more determined attack slices the thinner armor protecting my pelvis.

I leap past the fallen spearman and retreat over a slick puddle of blood. When my enemies follow and slip on the unsure footing, I spin, twirling the long pole of the ax behind my back, and take a giant swing that neatly sends their heads flying from the high wall.

After their bodies collapse, the battlement is full of blood but clear of threats.

Walt rises to stand on shaky legs. Amazingly, his lack of combat skills haven't gotten him killed during the last four scenarios. Adjusting his helmet, he says, "Thanks."

I run through a litany of things he needs to improve in order to survive, but given the dire situation, only say, "Be careful."

My medieval armor and clothing are sodden with blood, the thick fluid slippery over my skin and the heavy metallic odor overpowering my sense of smell. Although silly, I take a moment to wipe my cheeks and shift my shoulders from discomfort before I scan the battlefield.

We are screwed.

Few defenders remain to guard the ramparts. Carol's replacement's replacement, a woman calling herself Joan, lies mangled near an angle in the walkway. Sadly, I feel no guilt over her death.

A battering ram crashes against the main gate while squares of enemies in glittering helmets and chain mail await their chance to charge into the castle. There are at least one hundred and fifty of them. To maybe thirty of us.

We are totally screwed.

A bloody gauntlet grasps the top of the embrasure past the southwest turret of the battlement. Walt follows behind me as I dash down the walkway.

When we arrive, Syd's head rises over the revetment.

Although I still harbor a huge distrust of the man, I'm glad he's returned because we need his skillset now more than ever.

Grabbing his arm and shoulder armor, we pull him into the castle. While he labors for breath and finds his footing, I peer over the thick stone to find empty ground. "You're the only one left?"

He takes a moment, wiping the spittle from his chin with his wrist. Although the sole survivor of a fifty-person attack and covered in ash and blood, his plain face is remarkably composed. However, when he points to the burning siege engines at the far end of the battlefield, his eyes blaze with fury. "This was a stupid plan."

"Why? It worked."

"They have plenty of troops. The catapults and scorpions weren't big enough to breach the wall. Just a damn decoy."

"This scenario was three against one," says Walt. "Haiku said the forces would always be equal."

"The castle counts as the difference," I reply.

Syd ignores our comments. "I told Rick this was a terrible idea. You knew it too. Why didn't you speak up?"

"What for? He has the combat experience," I say defensively. I'm upset too. While I need to voice my opinion more, I don't need Syd lecturing me on my shortcomings. On the surface, the strategy was sound. A raiding force destroys the siege machines in a surprise attack. But now, the lack of defenders negates the advantages of being behind solid walls. And all wasted to eliminate a nonexistent threat.

"Rick is going to get us killed," Syd says.

I glare because this is the third time we are having this debate. When he says "Us," he means himself and myself. Not Walt, not Suri, not Vela or anyone else. Syd never raises his voice, relying on repetition to make his point, but in the midst of a battle and expanding his audience to include teenage Walt, he's being insubordinate.

More than usual.

Walt's eyes wander, pretending to study the battlefield.

Not wanting to escalate the heated conversation, I remember my own inexperience when Carol died and try appealing to reason. "Rick's real-world battle experience counts for something. He wants to save the rest of the team. You keep telling me we're special and we're getting more sigmas than everyone else."

His unblinking eyes bore into me. "The more risk, the more dumb luck comes into play. How many times will we survive facing five or ten-to-one? A random patrol. One lucky shot. Some slob taking a piss at the wrong time—"

"Then I guess it's a good thing nobody ever needs to pee."

"You know what I mean, and you know I'm right."

Despite his mood swings and anger from this battle, Syd speaks in a level tone because he doesn't need theatrics. Everything is true and although he refrains from saying it, I hear the words from his last argument. *"If you get killed, what's your altruism worth? They're all going to die."*

I set my jaw. Although I'm bearing greater risks, I don't begrudge saving the members of my team. I'd rather not have to witness another friend like Carol having a hole blown in her head.

"Um, guys," says Walt.

The gates groan and the locking bar splinters. Shouts rise from the courtyard as the few defenders rally, trying to save the castle.

Our differences won't be settled in a day or week. I might hit Syd if he utters another syllable, but he only shakes his head in disgust.

"What are we going to do?" Walt asks.

Before Syd can suggest a brute force plan like "Kill everyone," which will wind up getting us killed too, I say, "I have an idea."

It's something I've considered since the scenario started but didn't mention because no one asked me and I'm not in charge.

I motion to the highest part of the tall keep. "We get the royal family in there. There are narrow passages, and the flying bridge needs to be crossed to reach that point. This force is undisciplined and will pursue. I'll take Walt and get Rick to move the family. Syd, you collect the surviving defenders and when they follow, hit them from behind. We'll trap them between the two of us in a long confined space. The narrowness will negate their numbers and we'll destroy them."

There isn't any disagreement regarding the risky plan because Syd and I will somehow make it work, and besides, what other options do we have? "The castle's ready to fall. Let's move," I say.

Syd sends a final look of admonishment before dashing away.

After trading my ax for a sword, I lead Walt in the other direction.

The remains of the gate splinter, and clashes of metal ring across the courtyard as we reach the edge of the revetment. When Walt pauses, watching the action, I smack his helmet to keep him moving.

In his haste, he runs too high, his head bobbing above the teeth of the battlement. When he breaks cover without stopping, I leap, and grabbing his shoulder, yank him behind a waist-high parapet. Arrows whiz over our heads.

I explain to his gaping mouth and wide eyes, "They've had archers waiting since the battle began."

He sighs. "I'll never be able to do what you can. Thanks for watching out for me."

I puff up, deciding to take my given talents less for granted. Despite all the imparted knowledge of the threads, the teen isn't combat ready, but I can't spend the entire scenario being a mother hen. However, I make a note that if we survive, I will spend more time teaching him the common-sense nuances of battle in a more sedate setting. "Keep moving, and be careful."

By staying low, and with my hand guiding Walt from danger, we reach the stone building without further incident. The royal residence sits at the top of four flights of a winding staircase, and although weighed down by our armor, we sprint up every step. When we arrive at the thick wooden door protecting the royal chambers, Walt is winded but doesn't complain.

I give a tired smile. Despite his many combat flaws, the teen has his good points too.

When we enter, Suri glances at our bloody armor and wrinkles her nose.

"That bad?" she asks.

Between gasps, I nod. "Dire. We're breached and they're coming through the last defenders. We have a few minutes while they search the lower areas."

Although the chambers and medieval castle are classical designs of hewn stones and pointed arches, the mission for this scenario, a royal family, is an afterthought. The king, queen, and princely child sit on elegant thrones with blank expressions stamped on their faces. Unlike the combatants, these caricatures resemble carved statues. Or the super cheap sexbots that proliferated society before I entered the virtual universe.

Suri tries to lighten the situation. "You should try talking to them."

Walt says, "It's hard to believe they're that important."

I nod, understanding his meaning. As the mission objective, if the enemy touches them, we lose the scenario and have our sigma score reset to zero, possibly a fate worse than death.

No more time to waste.

I call Rick over and explain my plan. As always, he wastes precious seconds evaluating its subtleties, but luckily, he agrees before I scream at him. Although he generally makes rational decisions, his deliberate nature in the heat of battle is infuriating.

With Suri and Walt protecting them, Vela, Ally, and Simon grab the royals and run toward the flying bridge and the sanctuary of the keep while I yell to them to make sure they're spotted.

Rick asks, "Brin, can you delay the attack?"

I would have volunteered to do this impossible assignment, but coming from Rick, it causes Syd's words to echo in my head, *"Rick is going to get us killed."*

Turning, I utter a curt "Yes," and then march to meet our foes as the throne room empties.

After clumping down two flights of the narrow staircase, I choose a defensive position at a square corner landing and wait, growing more pensive as the rush of enemy boots echoes from the passageways below.

"This could be worse," says General Optimism, who has been strangely quiet until now.

"How's that?"

"I don't actually know."

Not helping…

Walt steps next to me.

"You shouldn't be here. This is going to get dangerous," I say.

Although fright pools in his eyes, he bravely replies, "It's the royal family. They creep me out. I'm more comfortable with you."

I don't believe him, but there isn't time to argue. His never-complain attitude apparently comes in second to his loyalty. I try not to grin. "Okay, stand behind me. When I get tired, or we get pushed into a wide front, help out."

He nods.

A few seconds later, another person settles next to us. "Hi," Suri says cheerfully. "I got lonely."

My confidence should brighten because I'm with friends and I might yet live through this scenario, but my insides only contain a gnawing fear. While I'm not scared of combat, I'm scared that Syd might be right. When I die, my altruism will mean nothing if nobody else survives.

And on the path to ten sigmas, there are too many ways to get killed.

More footfalls echo in the stone confines.

Jock says, "This party's getting crowded."

"Hey Brin, save some for me," Vela adds.

A new person pats my sodden armor. Ally slyly grins, which makes her freckled face too cute for the upcoming medieval bloodbath.

While I stare straight ahead, a genuine optimism rises inside me.

As the stairs below fill with enemies, another pair of boots arrives. "Move aside people, let me show you how a real soldier does it," Rick says.

Tightening my lips into a smirk, I hold back a snarky remark as people part to allow Sergeant Rick to stand next to me.

I glance at him. His blue eyes radiate anticipation.

He says with a dry voice, "I'm thrilled with how everyone obeys orders."

While he might get us killed, at least he has true intentions. That has to count for something.

"Well, what are you waiting for," I shout to the crowd congregating on the landing below.

Covered in chainmail and wearing a tapered helmet, a woman who my threads tell me is a 2.9 sigma, charges up the stairs.

I rush to meet her and as we cross swords, my trepidations vanish.

———

The glowing shapes of the ready room appear while sighs of relief and nervous giggles erupt across the semicircle. Against all odds, everyone including Walt has returned and nobody harbors any guilt for those we killed.

Personally, being mostly bare-skinned and clean has never felt better. I rub my hands down my body and check my underwear, making sure that none of the dozens of cuts along my arms and legs nor buckets of blood and entrails that spilled over me remain.

Suri makes a face, pointing to the tip of my nose. When I wipe with my finger, she laughs.

I send her my best snort and eyeroll combination. Of course, we're free of stains. Even though the ghostly tingle of my sodden medieval outfit still registers on my skin, I force my hands to my sides to prevent further embarrassment.

Syd doesn't join the gaiety, instead focusing a glare on the opposite wall. While he's angry because I won't agree to his partnership plans, the cynical part of me believes he's upset that everyone except for the two of us didn't get killed.

Unfortunately, his dour attitude matches my worst fears. We were lucky the enemy did exactly as I expected. What happens when the luck leaves, or worse, when ill fortune arrives? Or we meet someone using better tactics? Those things and worse are guaranteed to happen in the innumerable scenarios required to pass the ten sigma gauntlet.

Haiku appears with a pop. "It is amazing," she says. "During that whole day of battle, this team has sustained only a single loss."

In my joy of returning with all my friends, I had forgotten about the replacement. Slinking into my chair, I glance at the empty seat, trying to muster a sense of guilt or at least a sliver of sympathy. There is nothing.

"And you protected the royal family. This is the greatest team performance I have ever witnessed. You are all wonderful!" Haiku finishes with a clap.

She fails to mention the other teams lying strewn in the virtual castle and surrounding virtual valley. Since Haiku bound me to secrecy over the true ten sigma odds, the only way I can impress the perils of the Ten Sigma Program upon my friends is a roundabout question. "How long do teams usually last?"

Haiku mulls for a moment, and just as I assume she is going to ignore me, her silver eyes focus. "The average lifespan of a team is 1.56 scenarios."

Suri uncomfortably shifts. "That's until the team is ineffective?"

"No, that is the one hundred percent killed in action median. But, you have now won six scenarios only having lost three people. I have great hopes for all of you," Haiku says as she sweeps her gaze over the semicircle. "Everyone has added one-tenth of a sigma point, except for Syd and Brin who are now both at the 3.8 sigma level."

Claps of optimism permeate the air.

But it will only take one mistake to get everyone killed, rendering any score increase moot. We are too far from the end to consider anything but survival.

While Rick spends too much time analyzing unimportant details, he cares about people. Syd is an excellent fighter but will sacrifice anyone to succeed. We need them both.

I need to support Rick, and despite my misgivings, keep Syd in line. Also, I promised to help Walt. "Rick, if we are going to survive, we should alter our team building to improve our individual recognition skills."

Rick happily says, "Great idea."

I turn to Syd. "Syd, I hope you'll be on board with this?"

While flashing an ambiguous smile, the rest of his plain face stays expressionless.

NINETEEN

My hands slam on the mattress.

The soft surface produces a disappointingly muffled sound.

Sitting cross-legged on the opposite end of the bunk, Suri repeats my actions with the same dull results. "Just like that?"

Laughing, I say, "No. The effect was more impressive. Remember, we were in this dingy room in the basement that had concrete walls. The echo was really loud. Definitely an attention grabber."

"So, then what happened?"

I tell the rest of the story about the first time I met my husband in the computer class so long ago, leaving out several unflattering details because if Suri is going to recite the whole thing back to me, my preference is having the event told the way I wished things would have happened. No dinner salad on my lap. My body not covered with old sweat. No runny nose from a winter cold. It's cheating, but a series of white lies won't be the worst thing I've done since entering the Ten Sigma Program.

When I finish, she tips her legs over the side of the mattress and leans against the corner of the metal frame. "So, the true love of your life was born out of the hatred of computer programming?"

It isn't romantic when she puts it that way, but I respond with a slow nod.

"At least that one's better than losing your virginity to that nerd from high school," she says in a heartless criticism.

With two fingers, I tap my temple and wink. "Some of your better moments are in here. Be nice or maybe I'll start mixing your stories."

In mock indignation, she crosses her hands over her breasts, one of her many endearing gestures.

"Tell me another," she says.

"It's your turn. Quid pro quo."

She huffs. "Your life is more compelling. I grew up in a strict household, and my life was planned. Take dominating but loving parents, strict adherence to Hinduism, a long happy marriage, and make up a story. The truth wouldn't be too far off."

"That's just an excuse. Everyone thinks their life is boring. Haven't you ever done anything absolutely crazy?"

Her eyes expand a fraction while her lips make the slightest of curls.

Without my senses enhanced by combat, I wouldn't have noticed. I point at her, but before an accusation can leave my lips, Walt butts into our conversation.

"I don't know why you want to save your memories. The more I forget, the better I feel." Rubbing the pimple on his chin, he nervously smiles and watches his feet twitch below his bunk.

Walt tried suicide on his eighteenth birthday as a precursor to entering this world. Since I've known him, he's alluded to a horrible family life but never shared any details. I can only imagine what he went through even to contemplate such a drastic solution.

However, he receives my angry stare for listening to the private conversation. Telling my important tales to Suri, so she can recite them back when my memories have eroded, is one thing. Despite wanting to protect Walt in the battles, having him know the intimacies of my life is entirely another matter.

Suri picks up on my reticence. Like me, the fighting, and the acclimation process have hardened her. "Did we ask for your opinion? Or anyone else's?" She throws a mean glance to Syd, sitting three bunks away with his head cocked in our direction.

Walt rubs his longish hair, and his agitated feet grind harder. "No, I assumed that since we were part of the same team—"

"Which means fighting together, not sharing histories," Suri says politely. "Now, leave us alone. Both of you." She looks to the many empty areas around the formerly full barracks. "The two of you have plenty of places to hang around without eavesdropping on us."

I mollify them. "Walt, I think you need to practice a few things to increase your battle reactions. Syd, can you help him?"

A glare crosses Syd's face before he composes himself. It's the simmering part of his nature, always ready to explode, and he's again angry with me for trying to protect my friends. "*A fool's folly*," he keeps repeating. But I've committed to helping Rick do the best we can.

When he doesn't move, I add, "Unless you want to share something about yourself?"

Instead of retorting, he walks to Walt and gives him a fist bump. "Let's leave the ladies to their gossip." As they turn, I get an eyeful of male crotch, the shape overly enhanced by the sheer, tight material of the scanty underwear.

Despite my lack of libido, I avert my gaze as they walk away.

A snicker erupts from Suri's mouth. "You're such a prude."

"Me? What about you with your strict upbringing?"

"When I joined this program, I was ninety-two, and there are no ninety-two-year-old prudes."

"Well, I'm not prudish either."

She taps her temple. "Remember, you told me about your love life."

"Not all the nitty-gritty details."

"Enough of them."

"I'm not even sure of why you're talking like this. Nothing is exciting here."

Her eyes widen again and her lips tremble. It's like in her stories where she tries to hide something mischievous from her parents.

I arch an eyebrow.

"What?" she protests.

Wagging my finger, I say, "You can't keep anything from me. You told me every one of your tells."

She blows out a sigh and scoots across the bed, only stopping when our bare hips touch. Then tucking her chin onto her collarbone, she softly says, "Have you wondered what it would be like?"

A moment passes before I realize her meaning. "Sex? Here?"

"Yes."

"But why? Any desires disappeared a long time ago."

"Because I can't let the virtual overlords take everything from me. Being human means having a light and a dark side. Life and death. Sex and violence. Love and hate. If we don't have sex or love, we're not living, it's only violence, hate, and death. What's the point of that?"

I snort in deference to her logic. Despite the lack of desire, on certain nights after particularly violent scenarios, my hands have wandered below my waist when I've tired of watching my memories crumble. I've explored enough to know all the right parts are in all the right places, but no amount of stimulation causes any excitement. "Nobody's horny. Or anywhere near it."

After her eyes travel over our immediate area to ensure our privacy, she leans close.

Warm air tingles my earlobe when she whispers, "I know. But I haven't gotten any in twenty years. Now with this hot body and all these yummy, naked men, I figured that once the fooling around started, you know, something could happen, or even the attempt might be fun." After a pause, she continues with heavier breaths, "I would kill for an orgasm. So, that crazy thing I was about to admit to doing…"

Her eyes cautiously make another circuit, then fingers caressing my bicep and bringing her mouth close enough to kiss my ear, she says, "I tried doing it—here."

"What! With who?"

While the warmth from her body increases, she tightens her grip on my arm. "Be quiet. With a guy who had a 2.7 sigma score three rows to our left. He's gone now."

Gone is the nice euphemism for killed. But I'm so calloused, it's unimportant.

"How was it?"

She shakes her head. "Not very enjoyable. He was completely soft, and I was completely dry. The experience was more like a weird kind of grinding than sex. And the whole time he kept apologizing. Which was so distracting." She straightens, sucking in an exasperated breath. "We tried every trick you can imagine, but nothing worked."

"Everything?" I say, hiding my disappointment.

"Yes, everything. The Kama Sutra would be proud. It was a ton of effort for no results. Not even a tiny spark." She pinches her fingers to emphasize the futility. "And the problem's not physical. Our anatomies are correct."

We join sighs. This I know although I don't offer any information. She has enough of my secrets from the real world.

My husband is a widower. While a loyalty to his fading memory lingers inside me, I want to do something different outside of the life and mostly death scenarios we face. If I had any sexual drive, or if there was any golden pot at the end of the rainbow, I'm pretty certain I would try it too. Now, it's not worth the effort. "Well, let me know if things change for you."

After rubbing her chin and frowning, she states the obvious. "I don't think it will." Then the corners of her mouth rise into a mischievous grin and her eyes sparkle. "But, you can be sure I'll be trying again. And again."

I laugh, and although our uncomfortably close bodies rub together, the contact is more sisterly than anything else.

"At least the trying broke the boredom," she says.

I wouldn't mind trying something new to fill the monotony between the extreme violence either. "Having real food—even horrible army rations—would be great."

A dreamy stare glosses over her eyes. "Anything would be better than the liquid diet. My imagination is running thin, and I miss eating. If this keeps going, I might look forward to the scenarios."

"Don't be a killjoy. Every time can be the last time." While I can't mention the meaning of ten sigma or my fears of the bald giant, I take every opportunity to impress upon Suri to be careful.

She shifts to create space between us and chuckles. "That's why I want a last orgasm. Or five. Or ten. I wasn't kidding too much when I mentioned I'd kill for one."

I snort. "Hopefully, you won't have to do anything that drastic. But whenever it happens, you have to promise to tell me the secret."

"Deal," she says, leaning and putting a friendly arm around my shoulder. "There are a lot of empty bunks now. A restocking is coming soon."

I turn to her, tilting my head in puzzlement. When the surviving population of the sanctuary gets too low, we're combined with other sanctuaries in what's called a restocking. "What does that mean?"

She smirks. "That means there'll be a lot of new yummy hunks running around."

With a faint chuckle, I shake my head. "You're incorrigible."

"Let's keep going. Tell me another story about your husband. I love those quirky romantic tales."

"Quirky?"

"You're right, we'll skip the mundane parts. Tell me about the first time you had sex with him. What's his name?"

"Who?"

"Your spouse."

My mouth opens but nothing follows. Then my heart skips a beat. While I can visualize his face and our first time, his name draws a blank. After further searching my memories, I'm horrified.

The people I still remember have no names.

TWENTY

WALT PURSES his full lips and squints his grayish eyes from the midday sun. Aside from the teen, I stand in the bright sunlight with Suri and Syd on the path outside the barracks' entrance. We're practicing determining someone's sigma score, the skill Haiku said would manifest as we moved into the scenarios.

"2.8?" Walt says, guessing the level of the bearded man walking into the museum.

The guesstimate's close enough, and I give him a pass, while Suri shows an encouraging smile. Syd, however, stands with arms folded, tapping his foot.

Not helping…

I reply, "That was a simple one." Almost everyone is between 2.5 and three. "What about that skinny guy sitting by the pool?"

After a few seconds, the frustrated teen says, "How is this important? I mean, don't we all have the same skills because of the threads?"

Exasperated, Syd rolls his eyes and blows out a long breath.

These are the times I think Syd helps solely to show me the folly of helping others. Despite the outward pleasantness, his pestering about pairing up is only growing worse.

Trying to save the teen's waning confidence, I compose a constructive response.

"This isn't about having the knowledge or experience. It's about how correctly it's used. And how quickly."

"I'm not even sure how this works," Walt says.

"Reading a sigma score is a virtual skill. Call it a gift of the threads. Everyone has a score associated with them, and it's only a matter of allowing yourself to see it. Stop thinking so hard."

Walt nods, understanding the gist of my words without being able to make use of them.

"And you're right—anyone you meet in combat is dangerous. But a person who's won a lot of scenarios is more so because they've proven themselves repeatedly. This is an indicator of true talent, not theoretical skill."

"What about that woman with the bob cut?" Syd says. "Or that guy with the hooked nose? Or the two exiting the museum? You have to know instantly."

I try to give Syd the benefit of the doubt, hoping the barrage of questions is a form of tough love.

Walt's eyes trail after Syd's leaping finger. Instead of trusting his instincts, he tightens his lips and squints in concentration, struggling to go through each thread on a case-by-case basis to come up with the answer. It's the worst manifestation of the thread inefficiency I've seen and a painstakingly long process.

"Syd," I say. "We'll take it one step at a time, so he'll learn something."

"The first woman is a 3.3?" Walt guesses.

"Walt," I reply as gently as possible. "She's a four, very near Syd and myself and extremely dangerous." The meaning hits me only after my brain processes the words; even for this company, I am a very dangerous individual.

Syd throws up his hands. "This is something he should know. He has to size up his opponents in an instant, or he's dead. Or worse, he'll get one of us killed."

Walt's posture hunches as each statement hammers his fragile ego.

Syd referring to Walt in the third person makes the tone creepy rather than angry and reinforces my belief he's only being helpful as a means to partner with me.

"That's why we're out practicing," I reply to the group.

Suri touches Syd's arm. "The lad's getting better."

While Syd doesn't pull away, he blurts, "How did you ever beat the hundred and sixty-one other people in your version of Acid Island?"

It's a fair question and one I've been asking myself. The more I know of the passive teen, the more I rationalize he must have some hidden talent, some battle rage coming out like a superpower when he's threatened, even though it's impossible in this universe.

While Walt refuses to divulge stories from the real world, he is freer with his virtual experiences. In a shaky voice, he says, "I started near the edge. When the first person jumped at me, I ducked and she went into the ocean. Her screams were terrible. Then I shied away from the fights. When the bodies piled up, I laid between them for camouflage until the acid rose high enough to burn me." His eyes flicker as he pauses, remembering something from his past. "I have a high pain threshold. Whenever the fighting increased, I rolled higher up the platform. Nobody noticed me as they butchered each other. Eventually, only a single guy was left, doing a victory dance. So, I grabbed a torn off arm and using the sharp edge of the bone, I stabbed him in the back of the neck."

Using the remains of the dead is unconventional to say the least. While Suri's dark eyes reserve judgment, I waver between being fearful and being impressed. I want to ask if he had a bald giant come and beat the snot out of him, but my mouth refuses to open.

Switching my thoughts from my internal demon, I say, "No matter how you did it, coming out as the winner is impressive."

Walt releases a tense giggle as if he was secretly terrified of uttering the wrong thing to me.

Embarrassed by the pedestal he's put me on, I return a tight smile. His history is a mountain to overcome, but I'm praying he'll survive because of the compassion Suri, Rick, myself, and even Syd are showing.

Syd sends Walt a salute of unabashed approval. "That's brilliant."

As the teen gains confidence, Suri adds, "Walt, it's a clever solution."

I suspect Walt needed to be very careful in his home life. The slightest infraction, perceived or otherwise, would lead to some kind of abuse. And possibly worse. "Thinking on your feet and reacting quickly are important, and that's why we're working with you to improve your perception. You haven't mentioned your past and you don't need to. But it will save your life to focus further than worrying about what's just in front of you."

"Everyone on the team is like the family I wished I'd had," Walt says. After a moment to consider what he's willing to share, he finishes, "I'll try to do what you ask."

Before I can give him a "Don't Try—Do," lecture, Rick exits the barracks, his ramrod-straight posture straighter than usual. When he has everyone's attention, he turns his blue eyes to Suri. "Vela, Jock, and Simon are doing snap fire drills. Can you take Walt and get him up to speed?"

Taking the hint, Suri grabs Walt's arm for the exercise. Anything to distance Walt from his other life and concentrate on not getting killed will be a huge benefit.

After they walk out of sight, Rick says, "He's a great kid. Let's make sure he won't cause any of our deaths."

Syd huffs.

"We'll get him to be competent," I say. I can't promise more until he gets over his past.

Rick clears his throat. "That's not why I need to talk with the two of you. This is painful to admit, but the team's healthy fortune is primarily because of your skills and a dose of good luck."

When neither of us responds to the true statement, he continues, "Besides the training, I'm making alterations in the command structure. Simon is entrenched as my number two."

Although he doesn't sigh after the last sentence, Rick's tone makes it obvious that Simon is less than desirable as a second.

"Brin, I need you to be my chief of staff. We'll always discuss strategy when we enter any scenario. And Syd, I'd like you to be the main scout."

The changes make logical sense, but Syd will always be in the riskiest position. It's his worst-case nightmare come true.

"Syd and I can alternate doing the scouting," I offer.

Rick replies, "With all due respect, Syd's better at close combat. You both understand how perilous the scenarios are. As a team, we're doing well, better than anyone has any right to expect and if we're to keep it up, we have to maximize everyone's abilities by putting them in the right place." He turns to Syd with a fatherly stare. "You've come a long way, and we really need you in this position."

I wait for the explosion, but Syd simply replies, "No problem, Rick."

Rick expels a breath I didn't realize he was holding. "Outstanding. This is a tough world, and I'm glad you're both with me." He extends his hand and Syd shakes it, saying, "I better go and make sure everyone else can back me up."

Surprisingly, Rick stays as Syd wanders from sight.

While waiting for him to break the silence, I shift my shoulders and pull at the band over my breasts. Although I'm more comfortable with my appearance, my body at times still feels like a tent draped over my persona.

Finally Rick says, "I'm a little surprised that you of all people suggested more drills. I thought you hated them."

"They're okay," I tentatively say.

The corners of his lips rise into a smirk. "I'll admit it. They're boring."

That brings a chuckle from me. "Yeah, they're repetitive, dull, and also stuff we already understand."

"I know."

"Then why?"

"Fighting is more than just the threads and how they interact with our bodies. Winning a scenario is also about teamwork but more importantly it's about being decisive and having the confidence to beat any odds. That's not in any thread. Part of being a leader is inspiring people to be better than they think they are. And that not only comes from the battlefield, it comes from practice too."

"Since we're being honest, I only suggested the extra drills as a way to get Syd closer to the rest of us."

Rick snorts. "That's as good a reason as any. You must be doing something right. I wasn't expecting him to agree so easily to my proposal."

"Me too."

"You think I'm crazy for trusting Syd, especially after the fight where he tried to kill me and Jock."

I shrug.

"We need him."

But, does he need us?

Rick reads my hard stare then rubs his sunken eyes. The expenditure required for being a tireless leader is taking its toll.

"Being in charge isn't about doing what you'd like or something simplistic like handling all the details. Leadership is about doing what's best for everyone regardless of your feelings. Dispensing with smaller things for the bigger picture. And sacrifice.

"Not to get you down, but at some point, we'll meet an organized team or a better fighter. So far, we've been lucky. Without everyone, including Syd, working together, we won't win."

Although I stoically nod, I'm rattled on the inside. Why is he singling me out for the lecture? I'm no leader.

Rick's next statement startles me. "Syd's not like us."

I think of following Syd to the strange place under the building and the witch. Given the more imminent and dire threat of the scenarios, I've suppressed my suspicions.

"He's different, that's for sure."

"There's more than that, Brin. Look, when I said he was better than you at close fighting, I didn't mean that from a skill standpoint. You're both the best I've seen."

"But," I add.

Rick tightens his lips. "But, Syd was born for this."

"The scenarios?"

"No, the killing. He loves it." Rick faces me. "And that's the difference between you two. Syd wants to be here, doing this. You do this because you have to.

"And we can only succeed with both of you. So just talk to him. Keep him in line, for the good of all of us."

"Just never trust him," I say.

Sergeant Rick smiles. "I'm practical, not stupid. I can't remember the details, but he's meaner and more vindictive than the worst people I've dealt with. I wish we didn't need him, but we do."

This I've known since the beginning, but regardless, a chill forms in my bones.

TWENTY-ONE

BLACK FLECKS of ash settle over my helmet and thick woolen uniform while cordite-tainted air stings my nostrils.

As I watch for danger, I chew on my thumbnail.

To my front, sunlight pierces through a quilt of ugly clouds and cuts into the gloomy atmosphere of a smoldering alpine village. The shifting beams brighten an array of smashed V-shaped rooftops, and in particular, one tall steeple. In the murkiness beneath, dying fires consume broken red and white buildings while pouring greasy smoke over the cobblestone streets.

Although it's a virtual construct, a sadness from the destruction of the old-style architecture touches me. I wonder if the emotion stems from my forgotten past, then shake my head. Extraneous thoughts will get me killed.

Even with my plan working, the enemy on the road to defeat, and our mission objective sitting in the town square, the tingly spiders of doom cling to my nape.

"You are such a worrywart," says the disembodied voice of my husband.

"Just trying to stay alive, General Optimistic."

"That's General Optimism to you."

Brushing aside the ash lying under my tired eyes, I ignore my imaginary spouse and focus, looking for any oddity in the swirls of smoke, listening for any sound besides the crackling pops of the embers, desperate to sense anything straying from the ordinary.

Something is bad, but I can't figure out what.

Boots crunch on the frozen ground behind me.

I tug at my collar and check my remaining weapons. The assault rifle has two reloads and a leather sheath strapped around my right thigh holds a double-edged combat knife. Given the few left alive from the morning's battle, it should be enough to finish the scenario.

Suri and Walt kneel in the snow next to me. Lines of soot are streaked over their exhausted expressions.

"Any word from Syd?" Suri says between misty breaths.

I shake my head. My bloodthirsty teammate is once again by his merry self. "Nothing. But I bet he's in the village somewhere."

Walt pushes forward, and I grab the collar of his uniform. Although his skills have improved from the training and the practical experience of the last scenarios, he still has a lot to learn. Starting with patience. "We stick with the plan."

"That place looks like a deathtrap," Suri says.

Happy not to be the only one with misgivings, I let go of Walt and rub the imaginary arachnids dancing on my neck. "We need to be really careful," I say for the impatient teen's benefit.

Suri points. "Rick's ready. He's got the leftovers from the other teams with him."

His force sits at the edge of a pine forest two hundred meters to my left. It's composed of the other five members of my team, in addition to six stragglers from the other three teams. Everyone else is gone.

"You should see the other guy," my optimistic husband chimes.

Not helping...

Rick charges from cover, leading his group in a loose line toward the town.

Despite my apprehensions, we're committed. "Let's go," I say, hopping from the bluff and landing on a crust of snow. Scanning for danger, we head over the brittle ground toward the nearest structure, the blackened remains of a smashed cottage.

Rick's team drops out of sight as they plow into a cloud of smoke. What could go wrong?

Everything.

I leap past the remnants of the quaint abode, and jamming myself into the rough stones of the front staircase, peek into the street.

A few meters away, heaps of reddish rubble lie around a single bent streetlight. Beyond that, only orange embers glow through the haze swallowing up the shattered buildings.

Rooting out our last enemies in this muck will be costly.

Gunfire erupts from the direction of Rick's group.

Everything can go wrong.

I rise into a crouch and indicate for Suri and Walt to follow as I sprint across the narrow street.

Enough remaining structures, piles of broken rocks, and craters lie along the periphery of the village to allow a slow but safe passage. As we proceed, the tangled sounds of gunshots and sharp cracks of impacts grow in frequency, adding urgency to our movements. I keep a wary gaze toward the spire of the church and the treacherous black spaces lodged under the jagged rooftops poking above the haze. There are far too many places for a talented enemy to wreak havoc on us.

After what seems a lifetime of sliding or crawling, we finally arrive at a dire situation. Sporadic gunfire pins the rest of our team inside the horseshoe-shaped remains of a row of townhouses. Vela and Jock defend the flanks. Rick pops up from the middle and fires a shot, then disappears before return fire chips the shallow brick wall in front of him.

Walt leaps up and empties his rifle at the church.

I tackle him, pulling his body past the curb, and push him flat on the pebbles layering the cobblestone street.

Bullets fly at us, their impacts pulverizing the surrounding walls and rocks.

As wave after wave of debris cascade over our prone forms, I hunch and close my eyes.

Something yanks at the thick sleeve of my uniform.

"Are you trying to get yourself killed?" I scream at the struggling teen.

"That's our team. Our family. We have to help them," Walt says in anguish as he wriggles to free himself.

"We will but not by doing anything stupid. I don't want to lose you too."

I twist his wrist into his back and keep him pinned. A crease of pain runs over my bicep and my damp uniform sleeve clings to my upper arm.

Great, I'm shot.

As I wiggle my fingers and determine the wound is only superficial, Suri slides down the rubble pile, contorting herself to fit into the remaining cover. "Three of them, and one's really formidable. At least a six and a half sigma."

From my quick glimpse of the woman, my guess is a seven, which is downright terrifying. "Stay here," I say in an angry whisper to Walt. I look at Suri. "Sit on top of him until he calms down, then follow me."

After shoving Walt into the cobblestones a final time to emphasize safety, I roll away, staying behind a low brick wall and below the line of sight from the dark openings in the looming structures. While my heart thumps wildly and rising blood pressure in my ears mutes the surrounding battle, I keep my thoughts cold. One mistake will end my life.

When I reach the edge of my cover, I lean up, and remembering the best sniper positions, snap fire a round into each opening. As I duck, return fire sprays through the oily haze and pelts the protecting bricks, showering me in a hail of dust and sandy debris.

The remaining enemies are really good.

Another firefight breaks out on street level and adds to the chaos. It could be Syd or one of the other stragglers. From my sheltered position, I have no idea.

"Rick. Rick," I yell. Keeping my head low, I frantically wave, but he's fully focused on the battle.

He motions for a gung-ho charge into the enemy.

I scream. The man doesn't realize we are dealing with a superior foe and normal tactics won't work. We have to change the axis of our attack and use our greater numbers.

My efforts attract unwanted attention, and a fusillade thuds around me.

I hunker deeper into the frost-covered street.

Before I can recover, Rick jumps up and Jock follows. The gunfire shifts to them.

Twisting past the shallow wall, I pop up, finding a sniper in a cutout window of the church steeple. An instant after I shoot a three-round burst, the man staggers from a hit and falls into the haze. I dive back to cover, expecting return fire, but the area goes quiet.

The fighting is done for now.

Blinking my eyes, I open my jaw, attempting to restore some hearing as I reload. Then holding my rifle in a combat posture, I scoot across the exposed street and scramble the remaining distance to the team.

When I arrive, Jock coughs blood. From above his sternum, bubbles leak from a gaping wound. He won't last long, but I can't worry about him.

There is a far bigger problem. Lying sprawled on a slope of broken bricks is my worst nightmare, Rick with one of his blue eyes staring at the sky and a gory hole where the other should be.

TWENTY-TWO

CURSING, I dive behind a low wall pitted from gunfire because there's still a risk of getting sniped. After I crawl the rest of the way to Vela, I ask, "Why did Rick charge?"

"Ally was hit. We had to do something."

While I understand the need for action, Rick never had a chance against the seven sigma.

"I counted three of them," she says.

"Two. I got one."

"One." A huge man with streaks of blood and dust covering his rough face steps over the low stone wall with five others in tow.

"Who are you?" I ask.

"Blue," he responds with the tainted air reverberating from his deep voice.

Despite the dire situation, his stare lingers on me.

Ugh.

I break the awkward moment, glancing to Walt and Suri as they arrive in wary crouches.

When the teen sees Rick, tears moisten his eyes.

Pebbles spill as Simon stumbles into the rubble-strewn enclosure.

His wild gaze roams over Rick and then to the nearest buildings. "The last one's a six," he breathlessly says.

"The last one's a seven," I announce.

Everyone looks around in panic.

"What do we do now?" Vela says as she moves to help Jock.

Walt answers, "We go on and win."

Blue draws his huge hand across his chest. "A rah-rah attitude isn't going to cut it."

While Suri slides over to take care of Ally, I ask, "What do you suggest?"

"We do a building-by-building search for this last one and kill her," Blue replies.

With a finger bloodied from staunching Ally's wound, Suri indicates the wounded. "In this visibility? Ally and Jock need us to win and win quickly."

Blue shrugs his massive shoulders. "That's not my problem. I need to do what's best for my people."

My anger flashes, but he's only saying what I'm guilty of doing in every single scenario. I can't allow Jock and Ally to die from a methodical solution. "We'll get destroyed in a town-wide search."

With that dissension, everyone offers their opinions to the point where the seven sigma won't need to do anything, we are on the verge of slaughtering each other.

My gaze strays to Rick, who tried to coach me to be his next in command. Although I can't remember why, I'm frightened of the responsibility. And in this crap-fest, no matter what we decide, quite a few of us won't return. However, with the wrong choices, everyone dies.

Jock coughs blood. Without immediate action, he and Ally are finished.

I slam my hands onto the rubble to cut through the chaos. Controlling my own nervous feelings and the throbbing pain shooting up my wounded arm, I say in a level tone, "I'm in charge."

"Says whom?" Blue asks with disdain.

A coldness pools inside me. Rick is gone. Ally and Jock are dying.

And while everyone is sinking into raw emotion, the scenario still needs to be won.

And bring as many people back to Home as possible.

"Says me. I was the chief of staff to Rick and now I'm in charge."

"I'm the next in command," says Simon. "And I say we hunt this last one down."

Although thinking ill of the deceased isn't polite, part of me is furious with Rick for leaving Simon as the second. A little bit of heartbreak would have avoided this issue.

Suri says, "Rick listened to Brin and we should too."

"Look where that got Rick!" Simon screeches, the politician in him working overtime.

Before anyone answers, Syd jumps next to me, appearing as if by magic, and says in a confident tone, "If you're smart, you'll listen to her. She's got more battle sense than any of us or any seven sigma."

Even though he was missing, I'm not surprised Syd is alive. I blow a misty breath into my hand and wait for Blue and Simon to weigh their options.

Finally, the large man responds, "I'm going to watch out for my own."

As he gathers his remaining people, I reply in a loud voice, "We're going to die if we don't handle this situation correctly. Panic won't help and being on different pages won't either."

Blue stops.

Despite my distaste for being the center of attention, I force myself to straighten against his withering gaze. "We can win this scenario by killing this last opponent or capturing the fountain in the middle of the town square. If we let this get personal, and try to kill a seven sigma in this mess, we'll lose. So we probe in force to the town center and push to the fountain."

"Then that seven will know where we're heading and pick us off," Simon argues.

Not helping.

"We dictate the action. If we threaten the mission objective, the seven will have to stay in front of us."

"You think you can force a seven sigma to do anything?" Blue says.

"Yes," I reply with more conviction than I feel.

Blue shakes his head. "Good luck."

I watch helplessly as he leaves with his people.

Simon rises. "That's the plan. We take our time and hunt with the safety of numbers. Who's coming?"

The rest of the group looks to me with expectant stares.

"Great," the ex-politician says. "You'll get yourselves killed." Pebbles fall down the slope when he crosses the remaining shreds of the broken wall.

"Simon," I say.

"I'm second in command, and that means I'm in charge now. You're the one disobeying my orders," he says before sprinting after Blue's bigger group.

Syd steps over a rubble pile. "Well, that didn't go so well."

"Are you coming with us?"

"No. I work alone. See ya."

After he disappears, my muscles tense with frustration, and I blast out a curse. We have three different groups running three different plans.

So be it.

As I speak, I look to the people placing themselves in my care, Vela, Suri, and Walt. "Fine. We'll work on their left and use them to protect our flank. First one to reach the fountain, just touch it."

"What about Jock and Ally?" asks Vela.

"We've done everything we can. If we don't succeed, they'll die anyway."

Although not a democracy, everyone nods in approval.

"Okay, stay alert and we'll win this thing," I say, almost grimacing at the over-confident white lie.

I lead my friends onto the street, careful to avoid looking at Rick's face as the others disappear into the haze.

Like a group of medieval hunters, we head off to defeat the mythical seven sigma dragon. I've never envisioned anyone getting that far. Nothing comes as I try to conceive of what it would take to reach that level. And now we're looking to end that person's life. It's a pity.

"You know what would be a bigger pity?" asks General Optimism with what I imagine is a broad smile.

"What?"

"Getting yourself killed!"

Not helping…

The tension in my group rises with each step toward certain doom. We've never fought anyone of this caliber before, and I'm pretty sure none of them have a "General Optimism" rooting them onward.

TWENTY-THREE

As the four of us turn onto a curving lane bordered by broken store-fronts, I refrain from thinking of Jock and Ally bleeding out. Worrying about matters out of my control will only cloud my judgment.

We cautiously push forward, paralleling Blue's team on the adjacent street and letting them inadvertently protect our flank. Considering the quality of our opponent, I don't give them much of a chance.

Also, Syd and Simon are roaming around, but I can't waste precious time thinking about them either. They made their decisions.

Four blocks away, through the oily swirls of smoke, a glimpse of the town square comes into view.

Icicles hanging from a second-floor balcony drip water onto my shoulder as I signal a halt near a smoldering townhouse. While the distance to our objective seems short, a quick stroll on a lazy summer day, moving through the low visibility with our enemy possibly located behind every fractured facade or mound of broken stone is daunting at best.

Aware of the heightened danger, the others stay alert, searching for any clue in the haze-filled environment.

Unsurprisingly, nobody sees anything out of the ordinary, and even if anyone did notice something, part of me thinks that something would be a trap.

I frown at the ridiculous conundrum.

Time's running out for the wounded.

As we renew the advance, my boots splash through slushy puddles, and the first block passes without incident. That is a cause for concern. Three blocks left. Why is the enemy waiting? While we edge past a narrow cross street, I catch one of Blue's group moving into a tailor shop on my right.

We are going to get hit where we least expect it.

But where could that be?

A crawling sensation covers my neck as I scan the surroundings. I motion to Walt. "Cover the rear."

"What?"

"Behind us. Move slow, I think the attack is coming from there."

He doesn't believe me but does as I ask.

Searching to my right for a gap in the wall of alpine structures, I try to signal someone from the other group. Waiting for the next cross street will be too late for them.

A single shot echoes. Panicked return fire peppers the neighboring buildings. Because Blue and his people aren't prepared to be the hunted, it's a terrifyingly logical tactic.

When Walt steps to help, I grab his shoulder, resisting my own urge to run to the fighting. "Suri, Vela, stop," I say loud enough to get their attention. "Move to the square."

The words are cold, but realistically, getting mired in a firefight only helps our enemy. Forcing the seven sigma to react is the best way to save Blue's team as well as Simon and Syd. My guess is anyone winning enough battles to reach that level won't allow herself to lose and restart the program as a zero.

Suri leads at a faster pace, adjusting her movements to avoid piles of debris while twisting her head and searching for likely points of ambush. Vela follows, her eyes wide, pushing ahead despite her fears.

And she's right to be worried—the seven sigma is taking full advantage of the disorganized attack. I motion for Walt to stay close for protection, then take quicker steps to catch Suri.

The gunshot staccato rises to a climax then stops. No time to tell if the lull is because Blue's group and Simon are dead, or the seven sigma had to disengage to stop us.

We hit the adjoining intersection at a decent clip. Two blocks left. The gunfire opera starts again. I wince, expecting the next burst to be at my head. It's the major problem with everyone having the threads— given a clean, unobstructed shot, we never miss.

My fingers tighten on the trigger because I want to fire randomly at the surrounding structures on the slim chance of flushing out our opponent. I force myself to relax with a deep breath. Besides being impatient, the shooting will only alert the enemy to my location, and with only one reload left, I can't waste any bullets.

Walt's broken shuffle on the cobblestones stops and he fires.

Not sure if he's sighted the seven sigma or a shadow, I duck behind a concrete staircase.

Shots come from the second floor to our right.

Not wanting to die in a narrow, exposed passageway, I signal the others to enter the husks of the busted buildings across the cobblestones.

Although I don't have a clear handle on the situation, we have to keep advancing because we can't allow the seven sigma to dictate the action.

And we have to save Ally and Jock.

As soon as we plow into a store with empty glass counters, I slide forward on a heap of bricks and gesture for Suri to continue in the lead with Vela and Walt guarding the rear. We proceed with halting progress between oddly shaped gaps in the adjoining walls and pass beyond the main line of smoldering fires.

While the air clears, an eerie quiet again falls over everything— something that sets the tingly spiders trampling over my neck. The seven sigma is getting ahead of us and into a superior position.

Bullets splinter molding in front of Suri. She dives behind a cornerstone. Walt and Vela rush to the open windows to provide support. Suspicious, I watch for tripwires and other traps. There is nothing, but it's obvious we are being funneled into this location.

I rush next to Walt and peer past the jagged edges of a shell hole.

Opposite, through windows and gaps in the wounded facades, I catch movement, but the seven sigma isn't waiting or trying to find a firing position. I tap Walt, and we pull back, maintaining pace with our adversary by moving through a hallway and toward the center of town. Although constantly watching, nothing happens, and at the next intersection, we stop, anticipating an attack if we try to cross the open space of the street.

A shadow darts past a second-story window of the building opposite our position.

We fire, splintering wood and murdering bricks.

The seven sigma reappears on the first floor. She aims high and away from any meaningful target.

Before anyone can react, a bullet flies into a ledge above us and a grenade tumbles into our midst.

"Trap, get out!" I yell.

Walt and Vela look up in surprise. Suri dives to the side.

I crash through the front window with my injured arm flaring in pain as I shoulder roll down a heap of broken bricks and into the freezing wetness of a slush puddle.

The explosion flattens an unstable wall and the building collapses with a deafening crunch.

Rising as a cloud of dust rolls past me, I fire blindly at the last location of the opponent and nearby storefront, emptying the rifle. Then, loading my final magazine, I run for the next bit of protection: the remains of the corner house.

Beyond the shell of the buildings, Simon stumbles into the intersection, eyes wide in shock. Before I can wave him into cover, blood spurts from his neck then as he twirls, a second bullet zips into his face. And with that, the ex-politician I detested is gone.

However, he was one of my team. I let out a futile curse and move. Although nothing can be done for him, I can help everyone else by ending the scenario.

Suri is thankfully uninjured and has reached the same conclusion. She dashes to the intersection.

I scan the sniper points for movement and signal her to get across the street to the last block before the town square. We need to keep the pressure up by attacking the goal and forcing our opponent into a space with limited mobility.

Another fusillade rises in the distance.

Not understanding how the seven sigma could change locations so quickly, I rise from hiding and run. Suri covers me until I slam into the wall next to her.

"Simon's gone," I say.

"Walt? Vela?"

"Not sure. They got caught in the grenade trap. The seven sigma has the entire area mapped out. Speed is important but be careful."

Suri sets her jaw. We have to finish the battle—and soon—to have any chance of saving the wounded. But we need to avoid the foolishness that comes with desperation.

Rather than running through the thinning haze to the fountain, an obvious trap, we head to the nearest building, a blown-out cafe with dust covering a hatched tile pattern.

After we clear the first floor, the square remains quiet, and once again, we've lost track of our enemy.

General Optimism announces with a gratingly cheery voice, *"But she's lost track of you too."*

"If I survive this, you are getting demoted."

"Only if you survive!"

Really, really, not helping…

I motion Suri to get past a rustic table and upstairs to the surprisingly intact second floor. The staircase is skinny and decorated with flowery wallpaper. Suri climbs the stairs lightly, carefully advancing in a combat crouch. At a cone of light coming from a bullet hole, she stops. When nothing happens, she takes a step. The wooden floorboard squeaks.

Just as the stairs shred, I shove her forward. Wood splinters and bullets rocket past my face.

Suri screams from sharp debris slicing through her legs.

I fall and tumble down the narrow steps. When I hit the floor, I fire into the bottom of the staircase. The impacts produce loud sounds and make impressive holes but strike nothing of substance. Footsteps pound into the square and I rise and smash through the front door, alone and matched against a tougher, shrewder, and meaner opponent.

TWENTY-FOUR

THE MISSION OBJECTIVE; a frost-covered fountain consisting of a dry concrete basin circling a sculpture of three leaping dolphins, sits in the middle of the town square. Barriers formed from rows of alpine buildings with red and white facades, paneled windows, and peaked roofs surround the wide space. Gashes ripping through several of the storefronts leak shallow veins of debris over the stone tiles layering the ground. The rest of the place is quiet, and except for trailing wisps of smoke, desolate.

The dolphins beckon with playful grins and mischievous eyes. All I need to do is run forward and touch any part of their bodies. But it's an obvious setup for an ambush. The seven sigma won't miss an open shot. As a matter of fact, the seven sigma is better than me in every facet of warfare and has been one step ahead for the entire battle. Given the lack of gunfire, I can only assume all my allies have been neutralized.

My panicked breaths fog in the icy air as the prospect of single combat with the monster seven sigma causes shivers to run up my spine.

"Remember, you're just as good. The only difference is that this person has had more opportunities to earn a higher score," General Optimism chirps.

"That easy for you to say, you aren't the one getting killed."

"If she kills you, then imaginary me dies too. So that means we're partners."

Imaginary husband receives an imaginary eye roll.

"Did you want to live forever?" he says quoting a line from something I've forgotten.

"If you don't shut up, I'm demoting you from General Optimism straight to Captain Cliché."

"No fair!" he whines.

Although I don't respond, imaginary husband is right and I take his words to heart. While the seven sigma and I have the same threads, the difference, as always, is in the application of their skills and experiences, and of course, the confidence in one's self.

Paying attention to every detail, I make a slow sweep and clear every nook, cranny, and opening in the neighboring area. After nothing presents itself as an obvious target, which is in no way surprising, I cautiously take a path to the nearest group of buildings and cross under the looming church steeple.

Rocks slide behind me.

I twist, rolling over a fat pile of pebbles, as a knife flashes past my face. Snapping myself to a knee, I fire but my target turns and the bullets smack into the church door.

A tossed stone ruins the aim of my next attempt and the rifle clicks empty.

Knife glinting in a shifting ray of sunlight, the seven sigma flies over the pebble mound.

I toss the useless rifle at her and dive to the side, which allows enough time to yank out my knife. Holding the weapon in a defensive position, I rise and slowly shift my feet, trying to arc around her.

Up close, the seven sigma is, surprisingly, an appealing young woman with only an average height and build. Long black hair outlines her oval face and cascades past her shoulders. Not dangerous at all except that she's probably killed a few thousand people to reach her level. The empty ammo pouches around her waist explain why I'm not already dead.

While her brown eyes gather every detail of my being, she matches each of my actions, ready to fall on my back if I break to the fountain.

To my surprise, she speaks. "I love your red hair and you have expressive eyes. You're quite the looker."

Although my expressive eyes make stupid blinks, I mercifully refrain from doing any of the "I'm Uncomfortable With My Body" gestures.

"A bit insecure?" she asks demurely.

Silent and not at all sure about conversing with the enemy, I sidle away from the slippery footing of a frost patch.

She mimics my movement with lighter steps, taking a casual, even cute posture, although her fingers remain tense around the hilt of her knife and her eyes linger on my bloodied sleeve.

The wound isn't bad, but I keep the arm's motions stilted to make it seem worse.

She smirks. "We are allowed to talk."

"What for?"

"Haven't you wondered what it takes to reach my level, Ms. 4.2 Sigma?" she says, purring my rank. The score I have fought so hard to achieve is metaphorical light-years behind hers.

"I just worry about getting past the next battle."

While the tension remains in her knife hand, she chuckles. "That used to be me."

Against my better judgment, I ask, "What changed?"

"Fighting what's in front of you just isn't good enough. To survive, you have to consider everything. Even things beyond the scenarios. Your team. Your avatar. Your mindset. Use everything at your disposal to your advantage."

Although spoken convincingly and with a sincere expression, everything is an act. She only wants me to lower my guard. However, I stupidly process her words and find they contain a level of truth.

If only her victory condition wasn't my death.

"The final attack was—how should I say this?" She gives a polite shrug. "Haphazard. Your allies were fools for not following your plan. Which is really too bad, because with a more coordinated effort, you might have won."

"We haven't lost," I retort even as her perfect composure wilts my confidence and the back of my neck reacts with a familiar tingle.

Her boots scrape to a stop while a disarming smile plays on her face. There is a slight shift of her weight and the knife flashes at my throat.

I react with a block while angling my body and stepping backward to evade the lightning thrust.

The combination is barely enough as the sharp edge grazes my cheek.

My return strike meets air.

Her lips tighten into a thin line, letting me see the lethal aspect of her nature for the first time. Instead of being afraid, the spiders stop dancing on my neck. At least I know what I'm fighting.

"That's the spirit," says my imaginary companion.

"Cheerleading doesn't help."

"You're as good as advertised, girl with the red mane. That knife thrust should have killed you. And the grenade attack and when I fired my last bullets on the staircase too."

Is there anything she doesn't notice?

Idle banter won't help, and I keep my mouth shut.

"Don't you want to know how I know who you are?"

I do, but all of my attention needs to be focused if I'm going to survive.

Her lips change into a pouty expression. "Done talking?"

Forcing myself to remain calm, I edge closer to the fountain.

She lunges to block my path while making a quick pivot and slashing at my waist.

Even though I'm prepared for the attack, the speed and force make it almost impossible to stop and I can barely coordinate a step back with a shift of my body to dodge. The hand on my wounded arm arrives just in time to prevent a reverse slash, and then I have to retreat further when she kicks at my knee.

After a quick half-shuffle, she fires the knife at my heart.

I parry and riposte.

Her balance is amazing. Faster than possible, she dodges and hits again. In the next five seconds, we hack at each other's hands and arms in close quarters combat.

When we separate, like all knife fights, there is no winning, just varying degrees of losing. The big problem is I'm the clear loser. Although we're both bleeding, I'm in a far worse shape with a serious stab wound in the ribs along with a dozen other cuts.

There's no time to rest. She renews the assault with a dazzling array of thrusts, the blade moving faster than my eyes can follow.

Relying on my experiences and instincts, I defeat most of the attacks and manage to launch my knife at her arm in a defensive swipe.

As she pulls back, blood flows from a gash in her sleeve.

But again, I'm in worse shape, a cut on my forehead drips blood around my eyes and my left arm dangles from a deep wound in my shoulder and a slash along my collarbone.

Blood trickles onto her knife hand, but the damage isn't enough to degrade her abilities. And she's between me and the fountain. A knowing smile crosses her face and she winks; I'm going down in defeat.

Dizzying from the loss of blood, I think of Walt and Suri and everyone else who will die if I lose. With that in mind, I grit my teeth and move forward, leading with the knife, ready to let her impale me if I can only land a death blow for a double kill.

"That's right. Think of your friends and make this personal," she says, staying one step ahead of my plans.

I don't care and launch an attack, but she side-steps and slashes at my hand, scoring a deep cut on my wrist. Wincing from the pain, I squeeze my fingers to hold onto the knife.

"Do you think there is anything I haven't seen? Anything you can hide from me? Like faking a wound on your arm," she taunts.

I'm really starting to hate this person, but resist the urge to scream by grinding my teeth.

To add insult to my crappy position, she does a quick shuffle like a prima ballerina while weaving the knife in front of her. Every bit of her fighting skill is intact.

My stomach sinks, but I won't accept the inevitable.

"If you want to kill me, just kill me," I hiss.

After the last syllable leaves my mouth, I want to smack myself because I can't believe my final words are going to be the most cliché retort in history.

"If you weren't dying in the next ten seconds, if you could just get past your insecurities, you might have enough talent to get out of here." Her eyes make the tiniest of flickers over my shoulder.

It's her first mistake. She's worried one of my wounded friends might help. Someone is still functional.

"Bingo!" says my husband.

She thrusts at my hobbled knife hand and cuts a tendon.

The blade falls to the tiles with a clatter.

I'm defenseless. As she speeds in for the kill, I tumble to my side, grimacing from my injured ribs and winding up on my back. A red thread forces my heavy combat boots in the air, ready to kick out and defeat any attack. The ground fighting style, so deeply embedded into my psyche that I don't remember its name, is from a remote place with treacherous footing.

As she comes at me, slashing and stabbing, I rotate and use my boots to meet her strikes. The knife isn't sharp enough to hurt the thick rubber soles or tough leather of the footwear. I concentrate solely on defense, content to allow her to waste energy while I pray one of my missing companions comes to my aid.

She gets agitated as her attacks fail, taking wilder swings and leaning her body forward to land a damaging blow. In her zeal, she loses her footing on an ice patch and stumbles.

Kicking out, I catch the ankle holding her full weight. Bone crunches. As she falls, stabbing at me, I roll to the side, catching her reverse swipe on my back, which cuts a painful groove through my skin but somehow misses my spine.

I rise to my feet, grunting in pain.

When she tries to stand, because her ankle won't hold her weight, she collapses to a knee.

"Bitch!" she screams when I take my first step. "I have children."

That's not fair. "As a seven sigma, you've been around long enough to have forgotten everything."

"I used my fingernails to cut their names into my arm every time my body was restored."

The woman's tenacity terrifies me, and not yet believing, I limp around her, willing myself not to meet her eyes.

"Melody and Melissa, those are my children," she yells.

That's worse than not fair. It's a hardcore mind game and although the words tug at my insides, I keep my focus on saving my friends, and not trusting her, I back away.

"Those are their names, and I will return to them."

She pushes onto her hands and knees, struggling to rise. Even after she stands, her first footstep is so hobbled, she has no chance of catching me.

But with each of my steps, the names of her children ring louder in my ears, until I can't stand it any longer and turn to the fountain.

When she's out of my sight, instead of relief, there is only remorse. I wipe a drop of blood trickling past my eye. This woman almost gutted me, and I'm filled with sorrow. From beating the mythical dragon? Because of her children?

"Don't you touch that fountain. Come back and fight!"

There is a wet thud and a stab of agony. My leg crumples with her thrown knife sticking from the hollow of my knee. I groan, more from anger at not realizing the woman would never run out of tricks than actual pain.

Uneven steps approach from behind.

Clawing at the icy tiles with the palm of my hacked-up hand, I drag myself forward, trying to slither the final distance to salvation. When I turn my head, I see her staggering after me, ready to kill with her teeth bared in anger.

She's going to bite me to death.

"It's actually a pretty terrifying look," says Lieutenant Optimism. *"Lieutenant? You can't demote me again."*

"I hate you."

In agonizing fashion, I drag myself another couple of arm-lengths. The grinning dolphins are only five meters away, but her wounded strides are faster than my tortured scrapes.

"I'm not going back to that island. You hear me?"

As I roll onto my back, I flinch from the snarl on her face.

"That's right. Let's fight to your death," she shrieks.

Half of me forgets my training and wallows in terror. The other half tries to delay the inevitable by using my good arm to toss my helmet at her.

She laughs and tilts her head to dodge the wobbly projectile. Then baring her teeth in a wide victory smile, she straightens and steps close.

With one of my legs out of commission, I can't block her attacks with the same ground defense. I will the fingers of my working arm to pull the knife from my knee. Although I can wiggle the handle enough to cause agony, the cut tendons in my wrist can't supply enough power to free the blade.

My life is finished.

The moment stretches and when my optimistic self remains silent, I realize the thought is true. I can't defeat my implacable opponent.

As she looms high over my shaking body, a stray beam of sunlight outlines her dark form.

I raise my arm in a futile attempt to stop the final assault.

Her chest explodes, and a shot echoes as she falls next to my boot.

Syd stands near the church steps, uniform drenched in blood, using one hand to hold in his stomach and the other to cradle a smoking gun.

Gurgling, the seven sigma grabs my leg. As her life fades, her eyes dart wildly, still seeking some way to win.

When she doesn't find one and her grip weakens, I'm stunned.

She dies with a hateful stare trying to cleave my body into gory chunks.

Although the scenario is over and I'm thrilled to be alive, the tingly sensations from the spiders of doom return to my neck.

Something is very wrong.

TWENTY-FIVE

THE SCENTS of citrus and honey assault my nose as I materialize into the ready room.

I should be happy, or at the very least, relieved at the narrow escape. But my freshly healed body does nothing to alleviate my mental fatigue or the stinking suspicion eating at my core.

I'm missing something.

Seven seats are occupied around the semicircle. By some miracle, all the wounded have survived, their bodies shivering as their minds adjust to a sudden healthy state. The three vacant places belong to Carol's replacement, Rick, and Simon.

I have trouble generating any sympathy for the old politician. While he meant well, that and a cup of coffee would be the same as a cup of coffee. Simon in charge would have gotten everyone killed, and I'm not sad to see him gone.

Ally recovers first, her hands grabbing her knees and pulling herself upright. "I thought I was dead," she says, relief filling her voice. "What happened?"

Mired in my own thoughts, I keep silent.

Vela speaks, "We went after that seven sigma, but I only remember a building coming down on me and choking from dust."

"Wow. A seven?" Ally says in disbelief.

"I should have helped more," Jock says.

Their faces turn to me, waiting for the answer.

Suri sits up, folding her arms. "Brin?"

I don't want to relive the battle with the seven sigma.

Her children are named Melody and Melissa.

My response is barely audible. "Syd killed her."

"Mostly, the credit belongs with Brin," Syd says, letting his hungry eyes shift around the circle. "However, between the two of us, we got the job done. We make a great team."

Before I can deliver a retort to Syd's insinuations of the two of us making a team, Jock hangs his head in shame, saying, "Sorry, Brin. I promise I'll do better next time. It's not up to you to shoulder the whole load."

I nod, hoping his promise doesn't turn into some stupidly gallant action.

Ally gasps. "Oh, no. Rick and Simon?"

Staring at the empty chairs, Jock slumps his huge shoulders.

To my left, Walt sniffles with watery eyes, staring at the back of Rick's seat.

While wanting to lean over and hug the teen, I stay fixed to my chair. It's not the awkwardness of our minimal outfits. My face flushes when I silently admit I'm more afraid of loss than being close to someone who could be killed in the next instant.

Given the abilities of our last opponent, we were lucky to have lost only Rick and Simon. However, besides her devotion to her children, something else about the seven sigma haunts me. It could be an item from the weird conversation or her final hateful stare, but I'm still unnerved by the whole experience.

Suri sends a contemplative smile. I wonder if she's grateful to be alive, sympathetic to my feelings of detachment, or happy Simon is gone.

Probably all three.

Syd rises and walks over to hug Walt, which is a little surprising. Then he looks at me.

Remembering Syd asking me to touch his privates in the museum foyer, I shiver because I'm not touching, let alone, hugging him.

Before he takes any action that would lead to a confrontation, the room mercifully brightens and Haiku appears with a gentle pop. While Syd sits back down, everyone's attention shifts to the avatar.

"Welcome back," she says in her cheery voice. "That was a difficult scenario, but you came through nicely."

"Not all of us," I reply.

If Haiku notices my anger, she hides it well. "That scenario usually culminates with one hundred percent losses. Especially against such a formidable opponent. Returning with so many of your team is a victory." Her hands rise high above her head to emphasize the point.

While Syd mildly applauds through the somberness blanketing the semicircle, I slouch into my seat. I'm sick of Haiku's cheeriness and tired of the fighting. I just want to plop into my stupid bed and sleep through the next five scenarios.

"Without Rick, we need a new commander," Jock says.

"Oh, that is an excellent point," Haiku replies. "Picking a new leader is my second favorite activity."

A faint groan escapes my lips.

Good luck to whoever gets selected.

The room stays quiet. Everyone is stunned by the loss of Rick, and of course, without Simon, nobody volunteers.

Walt holds up his hand. "I think Brin should be in charge."

Murmurs of general agreement follow.

After studying their hopeful faces, I decide against making the decisions that will get them slaughtered. "Suri would be better."

Suri shakes her head. "With all due respect, Brin, you think better on your feet than any of us."

"I'm good at planning things, not being in charge," I say, tired and wishing to be anywhere else.

Vela says, "That sounds like Simon talking."

I blow out a listless breath. "It isn't Simon, it's me. I know myself and my limitations. Being in charge and making decisions that get people killed is something I'm not ready to do."

Jock says in a confident voice, "Brin, you need to lead us."

Before I respond, Haiku says, "Brin cannot be coerced to be the team leader. Is there anyone else?"

Syd sends me a mysterious smirk then lifts his hand. "I would volunteer myself."

"That is an excellent suggestion," Haiku says. "Syd has the highest score and did kill the seven sigma from the last scenario."

Suddenly, being in charge isn't a horrific idea. Syd's planning would most likely be limited to *"Kill everyone you can!"* And we would only last one or two scenarios.

Suri stands and looks to everyone. "Brin, I'm not sure anyone is ever ready for this kind of responsibility. However, I'm sure this is something you will grow into."

Jock rises too. "You're the most qualified and I promise we'll make it work."

I can't remember the stories from the real world that make me unfit to be the leader, and the alternative is Syd. I accept with a woeful nod.

Syd laughs. "I withdraw my candidacy."

Haiku says, "This is wonderful. Now that the leadership position is settled, we can go on to the debrief."

While she spends the next few minutes in her usual gleeful post-scenario chatter, my eyes wander over the semicircle as I ponder how I can possibly save all my friends, and even Syd, from a certain death.

Except for me, everyone straightens in expectation when Haiku begins announcing the sigma score increases for the team.

With each new number, I slump further into my seat, the enormity of my task weighing on my shoulders.

They are all light-years from reaching the magical ten sigma goal.

But now, it will be my decisions that get them killed.

TWENTY-SIX

THOUGHTS OF FAILURE disturb my nights. An uninformed choice leads to Suri's death. Ally, Jock, and Vela get butchered from a tactical mistake. I'm indecisive and Walt dies. These aren't nightmares; a week has passed since I've slept for more than ten minutes, a period encompassing four scenarios and twelve training sessions.

Although we're on the third set of replacements, everyone from the original team has survived.

I hate myself for being happy about that.

Command isn't easy, and worse than being worn out, I'm second guessing myself. Given the lethal nature of the program that's a state that can't endure. Just one mistake or less than optimal decision and one of my friends will be dead.

Rick was right: I have to be bigger than my misgivings.

I really need Syd's help.

However, he's more detached than usual. We've won the last two scenarios because I've accounted for his random rampages across the battlefield. That's not a recipe for continued success.

As I cross under the portcullis to the museum, I chew on the corner of a thumbnail.

The serenity of the artwork amid the rustic red brick and oiled wood interior used to bring me pleasure. But then Syd decided he enjoyed spending his spare time in my favorite place.

This is a stupid idea.

But the only option I can choose to save my friends.

As I enter the main courtyard, a tall woman and a round-faced man brush past me. Resisting the urge to lash out at them, I raise my head and search for my reticent teammate.

He isn't hiding. Directly in the middle of the central viewing area, he sits on a bench built from polished rails of wood, facing a massive landscape painting. A skylight shines a broken halo over his spiky hair.

I stop chewing my thumbnail and wipe my bleary eyes. With conspicuous movements, I walk and stand behind him.

Ugh.

Even though he knows I'm waiting and why I've come, his attention stays riveted on the artwork.

Placing my hand over my mouth, I clear my throat.

His head slowly twists to look over his shoulder. "Hi Brin, I didn't notice you there."

I edge around the bench and interpose myself between him and the painting. As I stand in a loose posture, his eyes linger on my body while a bland smile creases his face. Although a flush rises on my cheeks, I resist an urge to fold my arms.

"That's my favorite thing here," he says, pointing through me. "For some reason, the dark clouds of the onrushing storm and the flashes of lightning feel like home."

Not wanting to discuss the finer points of culture, I say, "Let's talk."

He pats the polished wood next to his thigh.

I shake my head. "Someplace private." Looking past the main hall, I locate a secluded nook obscured by hanging vines and gesture for him to follow.

When I enter the confined location, although low stone chairs with inviting leather cushions sit against opposite red-bricked walls, I stand near one of the small sunlit windows, preferring to keep the conversation in a serious tone.

On the other hand, Syd marches straight in and plops into a seat. "So, how's the integration going with John, Brine, and Catty?"

"Jack, Brie, and Kate," I reply with irritation. It figures Syd wouldn't care enough to know everyone's name.

Giving a dismissive wave, he leans into the back cushion. "Whatever. They won't be around that long anyway."

I resist the urge to smack him. "They might survive if you were on board with the teamwork."

A vapid grin appears on his face. "I thought Walt and Suri were integrating them nicely with your standards."

His dragging out the conversation hints at a past life involving some aspect of sadism. Or maybe being a professional torturer. "If you worked with us, everything would be better and smoother."

"No."

"No?"

"What about this situation has changed that would cause me to alter any of my behavior?"

The question is rhetorical, and although my eyes narrow, I stay silent.

"The game is whoever reaches ten sigmas. It's not how many and it's not how you do it. Whatever happens, the overlords will keep putting us into battles and keep restocking the team with replacements. The lesser talents will die while the greater ones will advance. This is simple evolution."

"If we work together, we'll do much better. Haiku keeps saying we are the best team ever. And that's because of our teamwork."

"No. That's because of me and you. Without us, they'd die like every other team. An average lifespan of 1.56 scenarios. And no matter what you do, they won't get to ten sigmas."

"Winning isn't only about how vicious you can be. Everyone has something to contribute."

"Mostly, they contribute as extra targets for our enemies to kill."

"You like Walt, don't you? And I see the way you glance at Ally and Suri. They're our friends and deserve to make it out of here just as much as you or I."

He snickers. "*Deserve* has nothing to do with anything."

I grind my teeth, hating the truth of the statement.

"Don't get angry. You came to me because I'm better at killing than you."

"I'm not sure why that makes any difference."

"Just say it."

My lips tighten.

Leaning forward, he says, "I'll consider your offer if you say I'm better at combat than you are and that's why you need me."

"Fine," I say, rolling my eyes. "You're better at combat than I am and that's why it's important for you to be part of the team."

"I don't care about your accolades. I merely wish for you to see reality. And reality doesn't give a damn how hard you try or how much you care."

"If we all get killed because of you, then one day, you'll be alone against a horde. What will you do then?"

"I'd win. But fine, if you want me to assist with your strategy, I want something too."

"What?"

As he pauses and licks his lips, a feeling of dread rises in me.

"I want us to be partners—in every sense of the word."

"You mean sex?"

He nods.

"Nobody can have sex in this place."

As a response, he squeezes his eyes closed. Deep lines crease his forehead and his cheeks puff as he concentrates, reminding me of the first time when he made his offer in the foyer of this building. After an uncomfortable minute, he stands. "Look at it."

Once again, my eyes betray me and trail down his body. Instead of being flaccid, it's poking from the top of his underwear. "How did you do that?"

"Touch it."

"I am not touching it."

He grabs my hand. Not resisting enough, I let him move it to his privates. Although not fully erect, it's enough for intercourse.

"How?"

"I have my secrets. But if we were partners, I'd share everything with you." He completes the statement with a lecherous stare.

"No!" I spin and brush past the vines.

His fingers leech onto my shoulder and as I twist away, his hand slips to my breast.

Cringing from the clammy touch, I leap backward.

"That's too bad for you and your friends. Poor Suri and Walt. Ally and Vela. And what about Jock?"

I snap a right cross into his smug face.

He staggers and falls against a stone armrest. As he glares, I step into the entranceway, taking a defensive posture. But instead of attacking, he laughs.

"Why are you fighting the inevitable?"

Slowly shaking my head, I reply, "I should call Haiku and break up the team."

He rises and wipes a sliver of blood from his lip. "But you won't. Like it or not, you're stuck with me."

I frown because he's right. Given the life and death scenarios, Syd dashing off and killing anyone he finds has a significant value for winning. And if I disband everyone, the others won't have either myself or Syd to protect them.

Pointing my finger, I say, "Get the whole idea out of your thick skull. We will never be together."

A haughty smile crosses his plain face. "You came to me. The next time you ask for my help, make sure you come begging."

I turn and stomp away from the nook, hoping he comes to his senses before someone I really care about gets killed.

The callous statement should stop me, and as I exit the museum, I add that to the list of how I should feel.

TWENTY-SEVEN

"Then, you slam your palms on the desk," Suri says. She raises her hands high above her head. After a dramatic pause, she fires them into the mattress. The huge slap produces a disappointingly muffled sound from the soft surface.

Exhausted, I give a bland smile.

Suri continues recounting a story that should help restore my memories because if nothing else, the stress of leadership has accelerated their destruction.

However, her words wander past without triggering any reaction, partially because of my lack of sleep but more due to the distant nature of the topic.

I barely even remember what I used to look like.

Struggling to prop my eyes open and keep from yawning, I say, "This is exactly how I told it?"

"Yes. This is the first time you and your husband meet."

I shrug. The words evoke none of the images or feelings that should accompany an actual experience. The whole effort is more akin to a crappy attempt of inserting myself within a trashy romance novel. Or at least the way my fading memories recollect trashy romance novels.

Suri taps her chin. "I can see this isn't ringing any bells. What if I recount your first time with your husband?"

Ugh, so not excited about sex.

Although I'm forgetting my life in the physical world, the incident of touching a semi-erect Syd is seared into my brain. I rub my fingers, cleansing them from imaginary grime.

Her eyes widen. "I promise, this one's exciting."

Hoping the excitement is contagious, I blow out a long breath. "Okay."

"Amazing dinner, plush sheets, romantic candlelight."

None of the phrases stimulate any recollection, but I politely return her stare and nod as if I'm interested in hearing the rest.

"This was your third date on a warm summer evening. He took you to an Italian cafe where you drank sangria and had the porcini mushroom ravioli while you talked about the future. Afterward, you invited him back to your room, where at the door, you gave him a sultry kiss."

As the story progresses, Suri's eyes burn brighter as if she, not I, was reliving the tale.

I cover my mouth, stifling another yawn.

"Then each kiss becomes more passionate as you push yourselves toward the bed."

As she relates the lurid details of our first time, the words revive nothing. However, my cynicism increases with each perfect happening within the story. I want to accuse Suri of embellishing things, but from her earnest expression I know she's being honest.

How many white lies did I tell?

Not only do the details mean nothing, the story is so clean and idealized because I've added or subtracted things to make myself better, more desirable, more passionate, and more exciting, that I don't have the foggiest idea of what I exaggerated and what's the truth. But the overall effect makes everything worse since the parts that aren't true undermine those that are.

By the time she gets to the climax and moves on to the pillow talk, my legs are fidgeting and I'm impatient for the ending.

When she finally finishes, I sigh quietly in relief.

"Do you want me to tell another one?" Suri asks with more excitement.

The truth smacks me. The strangeness underlying her demeanor is arousal, which leads to a single awful conclusion. Suri's had sex recently and her most likely partner is Syd.

"No," I reply sharply. If she recites another tale from my sex life, I'm going to superimpose her as myself and Syd as my husband. The thought of my best friend writhing with Syd is too much for my weary brain to handle.

She raises an eyebrow.

I tighten my lips. The stories aren't making me want to remember and even as we engage in a stare-down, her words fade from my mind. I'd have trouble repeating the most basic parts of what she just said. And that was before polluting the entire tale with images of an excited Syd. At the last thought, I once again rub my fingers clean of imaginary grime.

The mattress in the bunk across from us shifts. Walt sits up, saying, "I wish I had a story like that in my past."

"We've had this conversation on not eavesdropping before," Suri replies.

For some reason, now I don't mind him listening to the intimate details of my prior life.

Because the stories mean nothing.

"It's okay," I say.

Walt explains, "I mean, it amazes me you put so much trouble into trying to save the memories of your family."

"Because I loved them, Walt. More than my own life," I reply, a little surprised to have lasting feelings of people I barely remember.

In a quiet voice, he says, "I killed my neighbor's dog."

Both Suri and I turn to him as much from the unexpected sharing as the horrible content.

Walt continues in a monotone, "I liked him too. Big shaggy dog with a wet nose. Always stupidly friendly. That family was so perfect, and I hated them for it.

"One day, I couldn't take it anymore. It was the middle of summer, a really hot afternoon, and I had on a long sleeve shirt to hide marks on my arms. I got some rat poison and wrapped it in a hunk of meat and fed it to that dog. They took it to the vet, and a day later, it died. I'd think I would have felt bad, but I don't remember anything of the sort."

Despite the shocking nature of the words, his voice remains level, even calm.

"That's awful," Suri says.

"I know this makes me sound like a horrible person, but I had my reasons."

"Then why did you do it?"

"That's it. I don't remember. That or anything else from the real world. Except for this one thing. One big shaggy dog. I hope I forget soon."

"Walt, for better or worse, our memories define us," I whisper.

Suri picks up from where I stop. "Even the rotten things. It's how we handle them and go forward that makes us who we are."

"You both grew up with a loving, supportive family. I don't remember mine, but I know that wasn't my upbringing. You can't understand what I went through."

In that respect, although I don't want to admit it, he's right. He's experienced horrors I can't imagine. "If we don't remember what we did wrong, how can we learn to do what's right?"

"This is my last memory. Without any past, don't I become my true self? Aren't we all decent at heart? That's why even though I wanted you to understand my decisions, I've never shared a shred of my past with you. I don't want any of it—the anger, the humiliation, anything —to come back and haunt me.

"I've done terrible things, but I'll change who I am. I know it. With both of your help, I can create new memories from here on out. It won't be hard to be a better person than I was. I'll be like both of you."

Suri nods with watery eyes. "I'm sure you can be virtuous."

I wonder about my own lost memories and if I'm better without them. Somehow, my skill set is improving. It might be from the confidence I've gained from winning so many scenarios, or because of the sheer amount of practice from the fighting. Even now, I don't want to admit that, maybe, the things I've forgotten were holding me back.

"Brin?" Suri says, returning me to Walt's issue.

For his sake, I hope he can shed his past and become a better person, just as for my sake, I'm counting on staying a decent person without my past. Now, unless he was a good person, harmed by unbearable surroundings, Walt needs to change who he was. But it's hard to justify causing pain by killing an innocent animal as a means to feel better about yourself. No matter what the justification.

This is a conundrum I don't need. Walt's a member of my new family, and besides being loyal to him, my job is to get him out of here alive. Regardless of any prior incidents.

Time to act the part of a team leader.

Folding my hands on my lap, I reply, "Sure. Everyone deserves a second chance."

Walt nods, biting his lip, his eyes happy with my approval.

"Brin, do you want to hear about your first date with high school nerd boy?" Suri says, anxious to switch subjects.

I scrunch my lips. The memories Suri wants to recite are as good as gone.

And the remaining ones are crumbling into ash. How long they last or if my morality still remains after they've disintegrated, I have no idea.

What will I become without them?

I draw an angry breath.

What's better for Walt isn't better for me. I've lost good things too, like how I learned to stay loyal and love my family and friends. While the virtual overlords want me to forget who I am, it's not in my or the team's best interests.

I have to save a piece of myself.

"That's enough for today's stories. Practice would be better. Walt, you need a refresher course for moving in cover, right?"

The teen smiles. "I need a lot of things."

"Then, we'll be practicing a lot of things," I reply, forcing a grin.

"That sounds like a great idea," Suri says.

As we stand and head out of the barracks, I focus on the man in the hospital room, determined to preserve the image against the might of the virtual overlords.

However, inevitability weighs on my soul with each passing step because deep down, I know only a matter of time will pass before my prior life is lost, just like I know practice will only delay the loss of my friends.

But, no matter what happens, I'll never surrender.

TWENTY-EIGHT

THE FIRST ORANGE wisps of dawn creep into the sky, and the chaos of the night ends. I'm not sorry to see the darkness leave.

In the faint light, an accusing expression graces the pretty heart-shaped face. I don't understand why; quite a few scenarios have passed since I've slain the girl with the violet eyes. With an unsteady hand, I wrench my knife from her chest and gently let her body sink into the murky water, feeling relief when her sightless stare disappears below the floating patches of algae.

Rules are rules and dead is dead, and yet...

Without a ready answer, I return my focus to the battle because I have bigger problems than a strange sense of guilt over killing her again.

The miasma of the swampland smells like rotten eggs infused with equal measures of blood and death, but I take a deep breath to steady my fears.

As the leader, I've been separated from my splintered team and that's turned the scenario into a crap sandwich. The chaotic night skirmish has destroyed the other six teams from my side, and the few stragglers are being hunted. It's taken every bit of my intuition and training to keep things from completely unraveling.

I'm terrified of losing any of my friends.

Heavy discharges from AK-47s chatter among the tangles between the drooping cottonwood and tall cypress trees a hundred meters in front of me. The fusillade dies as quickly as it started. Without insects in this virtual environment, an unnatural stillness falls over everything.

My wool uniform clings to my skin with an uncomfortable dampness.

I push my wet hand past the collar and rub along my sweaty nape. Then, poking my head above the stalks of the surrounding vegetation, I assess the situation.

"*Take a gander at the bright side, you can at least save some of your team,*" says my sidekick.

"*Shut up, Corporal Sunshine,*" I reply.

"*Hey, when did you demote me again?*"

"*Just now.*"

"*Well, like you said, it's a real crap sandwich, but you can do it! Not like you have any choice.*"

Not helping…

In spite of being exasperating, my optimistic inner voice is correct. It's my responsibility to save the situation.

As I slide the knife into my belt sheath, I motion to Jock, who has fought well and doggedly remained with me throughout the worst of the fighting.

When his boots sink into the mud at my side, the brackish water sloshes past my legs and into the stalks of grass surrounding the violet-eyed girl.

Before I can fret too much about her corpse resurfacing, Jock says between broken breaths, "I would never have expected them to attack that way."

"Neither did I." But it's not his or anyone else's job to anticipate these things, it's mine and I've failed miserably. The opposition only needed to defend a set of boulders. Instead, they attacked leaving my forces shattered from a hammer and anvil assault.

Expect the unexpected.

I nibble on a wet and dirty nail, ignoring the awful taste.

Jock gently takes my finger and pulls it from my mouth. It's the first time he's ever deliberately touched me. His large hands are surprisingly soft. "Relax, Brin," he says. "Under the worst circumstances, you made the best decisions possible. We're still in this fight because of you. And now, you're the only one who can get us out of this mess. Don't worry, it'll be the same as a nice walk through the sanctuary."

"Exactly. Except for the noxious air and the flying bullets," I reply, neglecting to mention our elite enemy.

He nods. "I've been through a lot worse. I just wish I could remember what it was." A reassuring smile follows the last word.

Somehow, the expression reminds me of my husband. At least from what's left of my real-world memories.

When I respond with a tense grin, he points beyond the boundary of the tree line to three boulders carved in the shape of obelisks. They are about a kilometer away in a wide clearing illuminated by eerie patches of phosphorescence. "Their base should be undefended."

That's the obvious choice. By attacking us, their defenses should be empty. Should be. Against these enemies, I can't make the mistake of conventional thinking again.

Expect the unexpected.

"Either the place is booby trapped or they have an ambush ready," I reply. The enemy could be regrouping for a final attack too. In the murkiness of dawn, it's impossible to tell.

More waves spill beyond my boots as Jock shifts his stance. The pale outline of the girl ripples under the water.

Keeping my focus away from my guilt, I sweep my arm in a wide arc. "Our team is spread over the flat swamp past that patch of trees."

"What about Syd?"

He's still alive, I'm sure, doing his own thing, which is killing me in my position as a leader. With his talents, we could have already won this scenario. "I have no idea," I answer while forcing the bitterness from my voice.

Jock refrains from giving another pep talk. Brows knitted, he searches through his threads and experiences trying to help.

I'm not surprised when no suggestion is forthcoming.

A burst of gunfire signals the renewal of hostilities.

"Let's move. We'll swing around the clearing toward the fighting. It's getting light enough to look for signs of a sniper or ambush defending the boulders. We might get lucky." I hate myself for the compromise, but until I know more, avoiding a firm decision is the best course of action.

Jock nods as if he believes I know what I'm doing.

I unsling my AK-47, the perfect weapon for this filthy map, and snap check it. After I'm satisfied, I rise. Crouching, I push into the tall grass while avoiding the girl's body.

Jock follows a moment later.

As we push ahead, the morning sun pokes over the low-lying flora and casts soft beams of light between tree trunks and their interwoven branches. The effect creates lengthy and confusing shadows across the surrounding grass and water, while under our boots, the muck of the swamp grabs at each of our plodding steps.

Sporadic cracks of gunfire spill past our cautious advance. We hunch low to the murky surface. "There," Jock whispers, pointing at several flashes to our left.

Before he can move, I grab his shoulder. "That's one of us. Sweep around the side."

As we hustle to navigate a quieter path to the rear of our enemies, I scan for signs of ambush.

Jock disappears, splashing off into tall masses of brownish reeds.

"Hey," I hiss. After he doesn't respond, I noisily trail after him.

More chaotic gunfire erupts.

I head toward a patchwork of sedges interspersed between thick cypress trees. As several bullets whiz past me, skipping off the water and scything through nearby stalks of grass, I freeze.

Heavy footsteps splash from my right.

I swivel and raise my rifle.

Ally bursts through a thick curtain of reeds. Spatters of mud add to the freckles on her face, and her blue eyes are wide, but she's otherwise uninjured.

Sighing in relief, I lower my weapon and point to the obvious trail. "Jock's ahead."

She tightens her lips and nods, understanding the need for a heightened fire discipline.

I lead her down the path of broken vegetation.

Before we get far, we hear the wet thud of a knife spearing into soft tissue. A gurgle and splash follow.

Abandoning our caution, Ally and I run under the hanging branches of a cottonwood tree and onto a thick mat of grass.

Jock returns, putting away his knife. "That was the ambush team," he proudly announces.

He's trying to fix each of my mistakes by himself. "Don't take unnecessary chances."

"That's nothing," he says in a cavalier tone.

"We handle this together. As a team." No more time for admonishment. "How many did you kill?"

He holds up three fingers.

"That's not anywhere near all of them," I say.

Although the harsh statement is unwarranted, his nonchalant attitude bothers me. Taking on three opponents in the current crap-storm qualifies as an unnecessary risk.

He doesn't answer.

"You okay?" I indicate a rip in his left sleeve.

"Nothing that winning this scenario won't cure." He flashes another wide smile.

For some reason, I don't find the confidence reassuring and even with Ally, my trepidations remain.

I shake my head and edge past a fat tree trunk to a thicket growing along an embankment. Using the extra light from the full ball of the sun, I peer over the brambles to survey the battle.

Cursing, I kneel back into the muck.

"What's wrong?" Ally says, rushing to me.

Without responding, I bite the corner of my thumbnail.

Two hundred meters away, in the golden hue pouring over the depressing brown and gray of the swampland, an ambush is waiting.

And Suri is leading the surviving members of the team right into it.

TWENTY-NINE

THE INEVITABLE COURSE of events unfolds in my mind. Fourteen of the enemy lie in wait. Heading into the L-shaped deathtrap, Suri leads a group of six strong. The outcome is simple math. A few moments after the shooting starts, Suri and her people will be dead.

There is no way to save everyone without Syd. I search my virtual memories trying to figure out where he is.

He's been having relations with Suri, which has to count for something. I think. Then again, knowing Syd, he probably doesn't care.

I grind my teeth in frustration.

"The rocks are unprotected," Ally says.

This I know, but almost a thousand meters of boggy swamp lies between us and the goal. "We'll never get there in time."

"But we'll win."

I swivel to face her. "That's Suri, Walt, and Vela."

While Ally scrunches her lips into a tight circle, Jock says, "Brin, think clearly on this."

My mind races around the simple problem. Take the easy path to the trio of obelisks and let Suri and the others fend for themselves. Or rescue our friends against superior numbers, come what may.

"I have to try to save them," I whisper.

"Brin," Ally says.

I raise my hand to stop further discussion. "If anyone wants to go to the objective by themselves, there won't be any hard feelings. I can't guarantee anyone's safety, but I need to help my friends."

Jock laughs. "We're soldiers. This is what we do for a living."

A moment passes before Ally pushes out a grim smile. Despite the mud dusting her freckles, the expression makes her too cute to be a soldier. "I have an awful feeling about this, but they would do the same for us."

I release a breath I had no idea was lodged in my throat. "Okay, it's settled."

Except for the killing and dying.

"No worries. We got this," Jock says with his newfound and annoying overconfidence.

I grab his arm. "Don't get too cocky. With all the racket you made taking down the sniper team, they'll be sending someone to investigate."

His touch is warm as he peels away my grip. Instead of letting go, his fingers circle my palm. "Don't worry. We've got this."

Although I want to believe him, and for the moment to last longer, it's time for action. I pull my hand from his grasp. "Let's move. Stay low and be careful."

With light splashes coming from my movements, I quickly enter the wide patch of flat-topped cottonwoods and tall cypress trees.

Jock trots next to me. "Suri will hold things together long enough for us to rescue them."

Although he has a point, I'm worried about the hundred things besides Suri that could go wrong.

I blow out my exasperation. Despite my adrenaline rush from the impending contact, I'm even more tired and stressed than ever.

Damn it all.

Tall reeds ripple to our front.

Spying a two-person scout team, I kneel and signal a halt. Both have higher scores than four.

Not having the time for a drawn-out battle against such formidable enemies, I get Jock and Ally's attention, then sling my rifle and yank out my knife. After they draw their own knives, I motion for them to protect the flanks.

Crouching almost to my knees, I creep past thick clumps of grass and into a shallow channel covered with spots of green algae. As I avoid gnarled roots from the cypress trees, the water deepens to the top of my boots.

While the threads enable me to navigate the swamp in silence, my understanding and intuition of the current situation determine the direction and pacing of my actions. For everything I hate about Syd, he's right about one thing—I'm better than anyone at processing and choosing from the competing information.

Trusting to Suri's skills, I roll slowly into the chilly water, only stopping when the algae laps around my face. Then I take a deep breath before sinking into the muddy bottom.

The ripples distorting the overhanging branches and patches of green die as the water stills.

I wait, listening to my heart thump, until the surroundings tremble from dull vibrations. Grabbing a root, I back into the wide base of the cypress tree and twist my head to watch the channel.

My fingers tense around the knife handle when a boot splashes two meters from my face.

Too far away for a quick kill.

While my lungs beg for air, I stay motionless, watching the outline of my enemy shimmer through the water's surface.

When he takes a tentative step, I angle and thrust my legs at him. My boots catch either side of his knee, and I twist.

He crashes into the channel.

I pop to my knees and suck in a blessed lungful of air.

Sloshing his boots into the muck, the man struggles to escape.

Before he succeeds, I land on him with my shoulder plowing into his back and pinning his AK underwater. My free hand drives the knife into his side. As he flails, I jam and wrench the blade further into his body, damaging as many internal organs as possible.

Torrents of blood spill over my forearm and foul the surrounding water as his thrashing weakens.

Rustles come from behind me.

I flop to the side, sinking into the muck and propping up my victim as a shield just before his partner emerges from behind a tree.

Ally springs from the undergrowth and stabs into the back of her neck. The woman spasms as Ally guides her dying body onto a patch of mud.

Even though my victim lies motionless, I hold his head underwater for a few seconds before yanking out the knife.

"Jock?" Ally mouths, sheathing her blade.

Reddish water rolls off me as I rise and survey the area.

Splashes come from my left.

"Crap! Move," I say.

Loud, heavy cracks from AK-47s echo through the trees as we stumble through the channel, avoiding roots and stray rocks.

"That's the ambush," Ally says.

Angrily, I nod. That's where Jock is heading, foolishly trying to save everyone by himself. Clenching my teeth, I force back a scream. "Come on."

Abandoning good sense for speed, we add urgency to our steps, creating loud splashes as we zigzag under hanging branches and around twisted tree trunks.

At the edge of the trees, Jock fires, distracting the ambushers from Suri's team.

I crash into the thick base of a cottonwood, and wiping wet strands of hair from my face, peer across the open ground. Heated gunfire from two directions pins Suri's group behind a rise of grass. Thanks to Jock's intervention, they're still alive. At least for the moment.

The heavy stock of the rifle thumps against my shoulder as I empty the magazine, the bullets landing in a loose arc around the ambushers.

Ally arrives as I reload and fires in a more controlled fashion, actually trying to hit something.

Large 7.62mm rounds pop into the nearby trees, showering us in wood splinters. I hunker closer to the ground and cover my eyes. Although our weapons aren't the most accurate at distance, the enemy are experts at maximizing their value.

Twisting my head, I get Ally's attention and have her move to a flanking position to widen our field of fire. Then I turn to Jock.

"Jock," I yell, waving my hand at him.

Caught in a battle rage, he stays myopically focused on the firefight.

The enemy leader turns his scrutiny to us and advances, slicing from cover to cover while minimizing his profile.

I curse; he's a six sigma.

Jock empties his thirty-round magazine, forcing the man to dive behind a low bramble-topped embankment. The stray bullets take down one of the ambushers near him, her body exploding from multiple hits. Jock moves to the next tree, reloading and shooting in amazing time.

Behind the scant cover provided by the tree line, I trail after him, desperately trying to get his attention. The pace of the battle is accelerating, and now isn't the time to be impulsive. Especially against an elite enemy.

One of Suri's group, a replacement, goes down screaming. Their position is getting overrun.

Jock jumps past the protecting trees and sloshes into the exposed terrain.

I chase after him, but my feet can't move quickly enough through the muck.

With his AK chattering, Jock peppers the ground around the six sigma, who coolly hunkers behind his protection.

After a few steps, taking an eternity to cover, I'm close enough to tackle him.

Just as I leap, Jock reloads, and the six sigma rises to a knee firing a trio of shots. My over-hyped imagination thinks it can follow the tracks of the projectiles. Of course, that's impossible.

The frozen instant passes and the bullets arrive. The first heavy slug spears into the center of Jock's chest. His body jerks backward. The second whistles past my ear as I knock him aside. The third splinters my leg, and I shriek as we tumble into the shallow water.

Despite the pain, I force my hands to keep Jock's face above the waterline. His eyes are unresponsive and gaze skyward.

More firing erupts.

I peek over a patch of brown weeds.

Syd has appeared. With impossibly swift movements, he's among the ambushers in a flash. The six sigma falls in a gory trail of splashes. With their leader gone, the enemy resistance breaks, the survivors scampering in full retreat over the low tufts of vegetation.

The water ripples as someone approaches. A moment later, Ally kneels next to me, her face masked with concern.

"Help Jock," I say.

Ally glances at him then shakes her head. "Let's stop the bleeding from your leg first."

Looking down, I gasp. Blood pours from the wound, pooling around the green algae. The bullet has shattered my femur and the leg kinks at an odd angle. My head feels woozy looking at the massive pools of red tainting the water.

After pulling out her med kit, she grabs a rubber tube and wraps it around my thigh near the pelvis. She knots the ends over the handle of her knife and twists, the tube tightening enough for me to wince. It's fortunate that I only need to survive. In real life, the mangled leg would be amputated.

I don't care.

"Jock's dying. Kill them, quickly," I say, fighting dizziness.

Ally returns my stare with sadness in her pale blue eyes. Then a resigned smile appears on her face. She quickly nods and rushes toward the finale of the scenario.

Water sputters from Jock's mouth as his nose sinks below the murky surface.

I adjust my position to prop his head high and lean myself next to his ear.

His blood-laden cough spews over my cheeks. "I'm not going to make it," he says in a weak voice. "I can't feel anything. Everything's so dark and cold."

"No. You need to concentrate."

His body trembles as he goes into shock.

"Jock. Listen to me. Concentrate on staying awake."

The warmth of the morning sun spills over us as his eyes, still staring at the blue dome, lose focus.

My leg throbs in agony and I feel lightheaded from the loss of blood. I'm so tired, but I force myself to speak.

"Jock, the blue dome's right above you. It's beautiful, and you said it's the way out of this place. That's what you said. Never lose sight of what's beyond the blue dome.

"Remember the walks we took when we got to this world? The clean air and wonderful views that reminded you of the mountains of West Virginia? That's your true home and what waits for you on the other side. You want to go there don't you?"

Although I remember more about his life than he does, the edges of his lips rise into a faint smile.

"I can't lose another friend. I can't lose you too. You have the optimism and confidence I don't have."

His body shudders and stills.

"Jock?"

My eyes moisten when there is no response.

Besides the heavy chatter of guns battling in the distance, the swamp is quiet—almost peaceful.

Although Jock's gone, I hold him tightly, unable to let him slip under the water. His unseeing eyes deserve a few moments of looking at his way home.

My decision got him killed. I'm not sure what I could have done differently, but it's my fault. Lips trembling from fighting back a cascade of tears, I release a tiny sniffle.

Minutes pass before the final gunshots fade into silence.

As the golden flecks of static crawl over my form, I press my lips against his cheek and give him a kiss before the world disappears.

———

Shaking with self-loathing, I arrive in the ready room.

Five of us fill the chairs, Suri, Walt, Vela, and Syd. We weren't fast enough for Jock.

Ally's seat is empty. It's not possible. She was healthy and chasing down the last enemies.

As my eyes stare in disbelief, I know the oversight will be

corrected. I concentrate on the oval back of her chair, willing the pale girl to materialize. Just one more time I want to see her freckled face and too cute smile.

Nothing happens because the virtual overlords do not make errors of that magnitude.

Surrendering to the inevitable, I slump. Ally is a casualty from my orders to pursue with abandon in a futile effort to save Jock.

Although I gave them a choice and they volunteered, their deaths are my responsibility. I could have ordered them to get to the rocks and saved their lives. But I look at Suri, Walt, and Vela.

Could I have withstood seeing those three chairs empty?

The newbies are dead too, but the virtual overlords will replace them. I despise myself for not caring that they died under my leadership.

"That was touch and go," Syd says in his gentleman's voice.

My anger erupts, and I charge at the plain-faced man, stopping just short of his feet because the thought of touching his bare skin revolts me. "Where were you? We needed your help!"

He stares, unperturbed. "I do what I always do. I killed ten of the enemy including their leader, who was a 6.2 sigma."

"If we had coordinated, maybe we wouldn't have lost Jock or Ally," I say, hating myself for not mentioning the other three teammates.

"I didn't make the plans, and you wouldn't have won without me."

My palms smash into his chest.

His chair tips backward and when he crashes on the floor, I dive on top of him.

Instead of fighting, he only lifts his hands to block my punches.

Suri and Vela grab my arms and pull me away before I can do any damage.

"Brin! Stop," Walt says.

Suri adds in a pleading voice, "We need him. He's right, we needed him to win. They had another six sigma. That's the one who got Ally."

A pained expression crosses Suri's face as I stare into her brown eyes. She's right of course. These are the highest-ranking people we've faced since the disaster with the seven sigma who killed Rick and Simon.

I shake myself from Vela and Suri and stalk back to my seat.

Syd stands and speaks in a rational tone, "Another four of them were better than fives."

After Suri sits, she says, "This was a miserable draw. Having losses was inevitable."

Walt adds with sad eyes, "We were lucky we didn't all die."

Ignoring their words, I glower at Syd.

The air pops and Haiku floats in the middle of us. "Is there a problem?"

While Walt and Vela return to their places, Suri shakes her head. "No."

Syd pulls his chair upright and sits with a smile. "Let's proceed with the debrief. Right, Brin?"

I clench my jaw and respond with a curt nod.

Happy and oblivious to the underlying tension, Haiku launches into her post-battle report.

In it, she confirms the quality of the opposing team, and we receive corresponding bumps in our scores. Although I've surpassed five sigmas and the midpoint of my journey, the milestone doesn't matter. While disgust brews in my mind, my thoughts wander from Haiku's words and into the maelstrom of my guilt.

Still caught in the foul mood when Haiku finishes her mandatory speech, I'm returned to my bed.

As I lie still, scarcely breathing and staring at the dark bottom of the upper bunk, my anger ebbs.

I can't allow emotions to cloud my judgment. My remaining friends need me to act like a leader. As slow as Rick was with in-fight strategies, he looked and acted the part, keeping the team together beyond anything that should have been possible.

Now, it's my turn, and I can't worry about the dead. Only the living matter.

With a long sigh, I roll onto my side, burying my face into the pillow.

Suri's right. I shouldn't be battling with Syd. The team needs him and is better with him than without him.

I take a calming breath, which helps me focus on solving the problem.

Syd's been proposing a partnership with me. I'll accept his offer, but only under the condition that my remaining friends must be protected as well.

I set my jaw and close my eyes.

The whole idea revolts me.

THIRTY

It's well past lights out as I walk between the giant buildings of the deserted sanctuary. Although the air is warm and pleasant, shivers run through my exhausted body.

The faces of my dead friends have haunted my past two sleepless nights.

Jock and Ally were my responsibility.

Only five of the originals remain, and while I don't care about Syd, I'm completely stressed over losing Suri, Walt, or Vela.

To make matters worse, the irrational idea that making a deal with Syd would be like making a deal with Satan, or at least with the plain-faced devil of this universe, keeps rattling in my mind.

Like Eve in this screwed up Garden of Eden.

As I reach the museum, I suck in a long breath. What once was my favorite spot in Home is now polluted by his presence.

Nibbling on a thumbnail, I try finding a different solution.

No alternatives present themselves.

After the metal entrance grate opens with an exaggerated groan, I step over the threshold and under the caged foyer light.

Beyond the entryway, lonely cones of illumination fall from glowing circles scattered in the high ceiling. Between them, many shadows lurk within the empty brick halls and exhibition spaces. Not that I fear anything or anyone I might encounter, but the effect only adds to the overall dreariness of the undertaking.

"Syd?" I say quietly.

No response.

"Syd!"

A shifting sound comes from the side wing dedicated to neoclassical sculpture.

Folding my arms, I take timid steps into an arched hallway populated by bleak and looming statues. Except for my breathing and pounding heart, all remains quiet in the foreboding confines.

As I pass a sequestered space between a tall, naked king extending his hands to a domed skylight and an armless Greek goddess under a ceiling dimple, I wonder if Syd and Suri have been having trysts in this place.

A disgusted sigh leaves my lips.

Of course, they have.

But that's not important. My concentration needs to remain on my current task.

Moments later, suffering only an accidental cut on my hand from the wingtip of an angelic statue, I reach a stained-glass window at the end of the corridor. The dim orange and red patterns shift across my body as I turn and face Syd, who is sitting on a low chair in a darkened corner.

Although feeling conspicuous in my thin coverings, I straighten. "We need to talk."

Hidden in the shadows, Syd shifts, and then the voice from his charming persona floats past. "About what?"

"About your behavior and doing what's best for the team."

"I believe I've made my position clear on that subject," he states with maddening calmness.

"There are only five of us left. Don't you have any feelings for them?"

"Certainly, I do. However, that isn't the object of this game. The end goal is getting out of here alive. I would think you had that part figured out. While you've always disapproved of me, my behavior is perfectly rational in light of this situation."

Despite the lack of details in the blackness, I know he's smiling. While my arms tighten because I want nothing more than to rearrange his plain face, I force my hands open because surrendering to the temptation would only jeopardize the harmony Haiku demands within the sanctuary.

"This is only three more than just pairing up with me. How can that make any difference?"

"That's three more than just adding you to the list of bodies to protect. And three lesser talents susceptible to making mistakes. That's too much risk."

"Did you ever consider a bigger team could help you survive?"

"No, that's idiotic. Extra points aren't given for teamwork." He leans from the shadows, letting his smiling expression turn serious in the mottled orange and red light. "If you want my help, I must have something too."

Full of dread, I draw in a deep breath. "What?"

"Only what I've been asking for since the beginning. The two of us share command and mutually protect each other during scenarios. In addition to our partnership extending in every other way."

"Sex?"

He nods. "I want the relationship to be like a marriage where you surrender to my every wish."

Besides having a medieval concept of marriage, Syd has never been close to being one of my fantasies. However, while I can handle the physical aspects, the emotional bonds he's seeking are an entirely different, unappealing animal. I wait for him to say the whole thing's a joke, but his unblinking, dark eyes never waver.

"That's not going to happen."

"The terms are not negotiable."

Walking away is an option. But that keeps the status quo, and I can't stay awake forever from stress until the choices I'm forced to make whittle me into nothing.

Then everyone dies.

But the man in front of me turns my stomach. And that's before adding in the idea of becoming everything he desires. I swivel to leave.

"It's this or your friends," he says.

Images of the gory, broken bodies of Suri, Walt, and Vela, pop into my head. Given the odds, the gruesome outcome is destined to happen, but can I forgive myself when I could have chosen a different path?

As I face him, my words fall small and distant. "You need to promise to do everything possible to save the others."

Sure of my affirmative answer, he lets out a genuine smile. "I will do everything practical under the circumstances." Before I can protest the peculiar language, he hastily adds, "This is a combat environment, and I can't guarantee everyone will get out alive."

He's right about that. Without another reason to delay, I expel a wary breath. "Okay."

"Great!"

"Let's see how this works for one or two scenarios before we consummate this deal."

The plain-faced man rises. "If this is going to work, we'll perform our wedding night duties now." When I hesitate because of the creepy term "Wedding Night," Syd adds, "Think of how wonderful it'll be to save our friends."

Under normal circumstances, I have no libido. Now, I'm revolted by thoughts of sex. "I'm not in the mood."

"What do you mean? This is something you want. You've been trying at night."

"How could you possibly think that?"

"After lights out, I've watched you in the starlight coming from the windows, when you're restless and your hands move between your thighs."

A flush spreads over my face. Privacy issues notwithstanding, there were only three scattered instances after particularly violent scenarios with each ending in total failure.

And apparently performed with an unwanted audience.

I was sure I couldn't feel any worse...

Rather than groaning, I say, "What about Suri?"

"Suri?"

"You've been having sex with her."

Nonplussed, Syd purses his lips in indecision.

"If we're going to be fully invested partners, you need to always tell the truth. Or I'm done."

Syd blurts, "The women I've bedded mean nothing. You are the lover of my dreams, the most beautiful goddess in this or any universe. I've wanted you ever since the first time we met. As long as I'm with you, I'll never touch another woman. I promise always to be truthful." When he finishes, his eyes radiate sincerity.

I have no retort. "Fine."

He grabs my hand. "This is great, Brin. You won't regret it."

The statues cast disapproving stares as Syd leads me down the hallway.

"How have you managed to produce any sexual energy?"

He doesn't reply until we reach an alcove where cushions stolen from chairs and couches form a crude mattress under a solitary light. "That's my secret. Maybe after we make love a few times, I'll tell you."

When he tries to guide me onto the makeshift wedding bed, I resist. "There are no secrets."

He pauses, eyes shifting and eyebrows knitted, his mind raging in debate.

"No secrets," I repeat in a louder voice. "Only the truth. Or no deal."

A tense moment passes before he nods.

The pads emit a long sigh as my bottom sinks onto their chilly surfaces.

After Syd settles next to me, he pulls off his underwear. As I try not to watch, his eyes close, his face wrinkling in concentration. Seconds later, the weird expression fades and he turns, his erect penis rubbing against my thigh.

My shoulders press into the clammy brick wall as I shrink away. "How did you do that?"

"Relax, you won't be able to feel anything tonight, so just enjoy what's coming." He shoves his mouth onto mine.

Scrunching my lips, I twist from the sloppy kiss. "Secret."

A heavy sigh rolls over my shoulder. "You use the blue liquid in the cafeteria to expand your mind."

Despite my skin crawling as his fingers trace a line on my cleavage, I snort.

"You expect me to believe that glop gets you horny?"

He grabs my cut hand then pinches it to draw a drop of blood.

"Ouch!"

I'm more shocked when he licks it off.

"What the hell are you doing?"

Through a red-tainted smile, he says, "This is how you use it. By imagining the taste of sex."

"Really? You've got to be kidding."

"That's the truth. Its power is greater than reproducing eating sensations. The blue liquid enhances the desires in your brain, especially for sex and violence."

Although super creepy, the ideas are way outside of the box, and I grudgingly credit Syd for his creativity. "How did you discover that?"

"Oh, I'm a multi-talented individual." He scoots backward and pulls my lower body from the wall. With excitement brimming in his eyes, he pushes me flat on the cushions.

"Blood makes you think of sex?"

After he swivels on me, his body heat seeping uncomfortably into my skin, he replies, "Sex and violence intertwine. One triggers the other. The scenarios get easier too. You'll see. A lot of avenues will open for you."

"Like what?"

Desire laces his answer. "I enjoy sex. I love killing. Just wait until you try it. With your natural talents, fighting will become trivial. You'll see how entertaining the scenarios become." A devilish grin creases his face.

I've fought and killed, but somehow his statements scare me more than anything about combat.

"But—"

His finger presses against my lips. "I'll explain more after we do this."

I clench my teeth, trying not to cringe as his hands wander down my body, sliding the band covering my breasts to my panties and then yanking both strips of material past my legs.

After tossing them aside, Syd stares at my nakedness, saying in a husky voice, "Everything is more perfect than I imagined."

Not into the act or compliments, I shy from the attention, trying to control my apprehension.

He rises over me, wedging between my legs and prying them apart.

"Stop, I'm not ready. Stop!"

The gentleman voice emerges, saying, "I know you're not into this right now."

"This isn't how I thought things would turn out." Embarrassed by my next words, I sigh. "But I guess you were right; this is for the best."

He offers a sly grin. "Don't be sad. We were destined to be together."

The confidence underlying the statement sends the dancing spiders stinging into my nape and running down my spine.

I'm missing something.

"That's wonderful," I reply, searching for a distraction to hide my fears. Although the idea is nauseating, I put my hand on his spiky hair and push downward. "Spend a little time there."

Warm to the innuendo, he slithers down my body.

My legs tremble, but after he begins, I relax. Surprisingly, it feels like nothing. Except for my revulsion of Syd and the sounds coming from his actions, the whole awkward situation is as exciting as watching paint dry.

Grasping for clues, I say, "So, I guess this wouldn't be happening if Rick didn't die."

The mound of spiky hair bobbing between my thighs doesn't answer.

"Simon died too, but I don't feel bad about that. He would have gotten everyone killed."

Syd pokes his head up. A blissful countenance covers his face, his eyes yearning with lust.

It reminds me of the stupid expression he wears when sipping the blue liquid. No, not stupid. The peculiar look is powered by the impulses of violence and sex in his fantasies.

My jaw clenches. The lewd thoughts were about me...

And I didn't think I could feel any worse.

"What?" Syd asks.

Relieved to change my focus, I say, "About Rick and Simon dying."

"I'm glad they're both gone."

Both Rick and Simon dead by the hand of the seven sigma.

The notion is odd, but she's the only enemy ever to talk to me, and she knew things she shouldn't have. During the following whirlwind and under the stress of leadership, I haven't pondered any misgivings. Could she have spoken with Syd? And what would they have talked about?

I push his head back down.

This time, he uses his fingers, which along with his rough breaths and sloppy licks give tickling sensations more than anything sensual.

As the cringe-worthy moments pass, a plan develops in my mind. Syd is holding something back. But trying to match his deviousness would be a losing proposition.

Although scary, my sole advantage stems from his lust-filled obsession for me, and the path to his secrets lies in dragging his thoughts down into the cesspool of his most depraved desires.

Syd raises his head. "We're ready."

I check and amazingly, my body has responded to his actions. "How did you do that?"

After he plants a last kiss, he says with a grin, "I told you, I'm a man of many talents."

My lips wrinkle and not just at the implications of his statement.

He pulls himself up. While he settles on me, I regain the initiative by twisting and reaching between his legs.

A moan leaves his mouth as I wrap my fingers around him.

"Should we be feeling guilty?" I ask.

"Why?"

As my hand gently rubs up and down, I say, "Because this wouldn't be happening if Rick and Simon hadn't died."

"Those two were lesser talents who didn't survive."

"But you don't feel guilty?"

His eyes focus—a bad sign.

Guiding his hand to my breast, I say, "It's sad to think this way, but things might be better because Rick is dead. Does that make me an evil person?"

When Syd ponders, I quickly add, "I mean, I'd like to thank that seven sigma."

"Really?"

As he roughly squeezes and runs his hand over my chest and down to my navel, I let out a long moan, which I hope sounds sexy.

"I'm surprised you're aroused," he says.

My battle sense kicks in because I'm pushing too far too fast. "Not that much," I say with contrition. "But, this would be better if I was more excited."

"Sex will be simple after you use the blue liquid, but for now, concentrate on violence," he says and moves his mouth to my breasts.

As he slurps, I force away disgust. "Imagine how amazing this will be when my sex drive comes back. The things I'll do for you. With my hands. With my mouth. Is that what you fantasize about?"

"That and more," he says with lust creeping back into his voice.

I tighten my fingers, tugging harder. "Tell me."

His eyes glisten as he replies, "I want to pound myself inside you. To hammer you until you scream with ecstasy and plead for mercy. To teach you things you've never dreamed about. To—"

"That's wonderful," I say, partially to retain control but mostly from not wanting to hear any more of the lurid details running through his head. "Stay with those thoughts. Imagine everything you've ever wanted to do to me."

He grunts with a malicious smirk.

After forcing a smile, I say, "Now, let yourself go."

I gasp through clenched teeth when he slaps my breast, squeezing the areola between his fingers and twisting. Before I can overcome the shock, he bites into my shoulder.

A whimper leaves my lips.

When he rises, his fantasy expression from drinking the blue liquid reappears.

Fearful of what I'm unleashing, I brace myself and say with a rougher tone, "Do it again, harder."

Instantly, Syd dips his head and stabs his teeth into the softness below my collarbone while his hand clutches my breast, his thumb and forefinger crushing and rolling the nipple.

I grimace, stifling a groan from the excruciating pain.

After he finishes abusing my flesh, blood drips down his chin while hunger fills his gaze.

Good.

Trying to mimic the heaviness of his breathing and layer sensuality onto my voice, I say, "You can take me any way you want. Use this perfect body in any way you can imagine."

He tenses, his organ hardening into steel. As his breath rolls out in deep gasps, he angrily slams his pelvis against my lower body. "I need to be inside you."

To fight off his impatience, I squeeze my fingers, digging the thumbnail into the head of his erection.

A sigh of pleasure oozes from his lips as his eyes roll from the ecstasy of the pain.

Now!

"You like that. You want me to be like you? To love what you love about sex and violence?"

"Yes."

"Then tell me everything. No secrets, I want to be just like that," I reply, shifting to allow his erection to settle onto my vulva. "You want this, right?"

Although his lips scrunch and his brows furrow, he bobs his head.

"What did you and the seven sigma talk about?"

When he doesn't immediately respond, I add, "You hated Rick and Simon, didn't you?"

He quickly nods.

"I think you were right to hate them. That seven sigma did us a favor." To drive him over the edge, I tighten my grip and guide him short of entering me. "Be honest. I need to know what you did so I can do it too."

His glazed eyes wander to my face.

Against all I hold dear, I meet his stare. "Remember, no secrets. Then everything you've dreamed of and more is yours."

Intoxicated by my blood and wallowing in blue liquid fueled desires, he doesn't notice the suspicion seeping into my voice. He huskily replies, "It was me. I made a tiny mention of where Rick would attack and who to shoot."

"That's so sexy," I say, rubbing the tip over the entrance. "Tell me the rest and I'm yours."

The words arrive between heavy pants. "In the swamp, I could have acted faster. I should have saved you from getting shot."

I nibble at his neck and chin, ignoring the taste of my blood. "The wound's healed, but I don't understand your meaning."

When he hesitates, I bring him to the point of penetration. "Just explain, and this will happen."

His pelvis rears as he says, "The ambush, I had it mapped out. When you fired on them, I could have coordinated, but I waited."

On the last word, he thrusts, but I twist and shove my hand over my privates, shaking with rage.

He let Ally and Jock die.

"What?" he says through a lust-filled haze.

Putting my free hand under his chin, I push him aside and then still trembling, roll to my feet.

Ugh! I almost let him inside me.

While I use my shivering hands to wipe every place he soiled on my body, my thoughts whirl. I can scarcely believe it, but his obsession with me combined with the urges of the blue liquid clouded his judgment enough to share the awful truth. How could I have been so stupid? Regardless of what happens, Syd will sacrifice everyone until only the two of us remain in some unimaginably twisted partnership. I'm not saving anyone; I'm only guaranteeing the inevitable.

As the arousal infecting his demeanor fades into bewilderment, Syd props himself on a knee. "Why should these people mean anything to you? If I hadn't taken action, Rick would have gotten us butchered. Protecting everyone else will get us killed too. I'd do everything over again. I'm glad they're gone."

"They trusted you as a teammate."

After Syd wipes the red drips from his lower lip and chin, the gentleman persona returns. "Brin, let's be sensible about this. The women I've bedded, the others on the team, none of them matter, especially fools like Rick. Only you're special to me."

While he believes his decisions are perfectly rational, I drill him with a right cross when he rises to follow me.

He falls with surprise plastered on his face. As he pushes himself upright, his eyes narrow with anger.

I back from the alcove, unsure if he's going to attack and more unsure if I can defeat him in single empty-handed combat.

Instead of pursuing, he hesitates, embroiled in another internal argument. Then his expression hardens as he rises. "These other idiots would be dead if it weren't for us. Us!" he says, thumping his chest. "I know the odds are tough, but together, we'll make it to the actual world."

I reach down and pick up the thin bands of my clothing. As I frantically tug them back over my body, I decide what painfully needs to be done.

"Haiku. Haiku!" I scream.

A pop, loud in the secluded space, signals her arrival. "What is the meaning of this altercation?"

"Nothing," Syd says, still naked.

After adjusting the sheer material to cover as much skin as possible, I turn to the avatar. "That's not true."

While she waits with a placid stare, I take a deep breath. The solution isn't teaming up with Syd; the solution is getting everyone as far from him as possible.

"Syd and I have irreconcilable differences."

Her eyes blink in surprise, and then she faces Syd. "Is this true?"

"No." Palms outward, he raises his hands. "This is something we can handle. We don't require your help."

I shout in an angrier and crazier tone than I intend, "Split up everyone. Syd and I can never go on another mission together."

Syd reverts to the gentleman persona. "Haiku, bring the rest of our original team here."

Before I can object to the unfair tactic, Haiku waves and Suri, Walt, and Vela, appear with confused looks. They probably assumed they would materialize into the ready room.

"Brin wishes to break up the team," Haiku announces. "In order to keep the peace, all will be sent to different teams in different sanctuaries."

"Why?" Walt asks with trepidation.

Suri looks first at me and then to naked Syd, guessing what happened. "Don't do this Brin, we can work through these issues."

If only we could. She doesn't know Syd as well as I do. Nobody does. I lock eyes with Walt's fearful stare. There is nothing I can do to comfort him.

Syd speaks in his most charming voice, "This is a tiny misunderstanding. Suri's right, Brin. There's no reason for this."

Vela says, "Brin? Let's stay together. It's our only chance to reach ten sigmas."

"Quite true," Syd adds, ignoring every last thing he just said about these people. Stunned by how sincere he sounds, I'm tempted to believe him too.

"We can't do this without you," Walt adds in a helpless voice.

I harden my resolve because, with Syd as a teammate, they're dead anyway. At least on their own, they have a fighting chance. It hurts me to think like that, but a hidden enemy like Syd is far worse than anything anyone could face in a scenario.

"A thousand enemies outside the house are better than one within," a black thread chirps, unnecessarily quoting an old Arab proverb.

Sorrowfully shaking my head, I turn to Haiku. "This issue can't be fixed. End the team."

"So be it."

As my remaining friends, whom I dearly love, scream protests, sparks flow over their bodies and they dissipate into the ether.

I hope they understand.

THIRTY-ONE

AFTER THE OTHERS VANISH, Haiku is my only companion in the deserted museum. While the little avatar looks satisfied, I'm haunted by the final expressions of my only friends in this universe.

I ask, "Did you go with them too?"

"No, there's only one of me, and I preferred to remain with you."

"That's so touching."

Not noticing the sarcasm laced in my reply, she says, "You took the wise course of action by breaking up the team."

"Oh?"

"Yes, the others were holding you back. It was a prudent decision to get rid of them."

"What's that supposed to mean?"

My hands curl into fists as she responds. "The emotional bonds you created with your teammates are stifling the progress of your acclimation. This program isn't designed to produce great teams, the success of your group notwithstanding. The goal of this program is to identify exceptional people. Your friends are irrelevant to your individual accomplishment."

"Then why have the team?"

"To make you immune to losing people you are close to," she says with complete innocence.

My fist rises, and I punch her square in the nose.

Her silver outfit shimmers as she passes under a light and flies into the far wall. Like a balloon, she rebounds unharmed.

Furious with the results, I surrender to my rage and leap after her, sending blows into her body while screaming, "They were my friends. Not a set of statistics. And I wanted to save them."

After each attack, she remains unscathed, impervious to any force I can deliver.

As my frustrations mount, I channel more fury into ever wilder swings and kicks. One hand breaks when I miss the bounding avatar and shatter the armless Greek goddess. The toes on my left foot plow under her and snap, fracturing a wall. Knocking the supplicating king to the tiles with a mistimed punch, I destroy three fingers from my other hand. My ankle twists after I kick a pedestal, toppling a huge marble warrior. His shield shatters into jagged pieces over the floor. Ignoring the injuries to my annoyingly perfect body, I hobble after the waif, a one-woman machine, demolishing artwork and furniture from my formerly favorite place with reckless abandon.

Haiku absorbs the punishment with a patient gaze.

After the pain from the broken bones in my swollen hands and feet becomes too great to endure, I stop, pressing my elbows into my thighs to hold myself upright.

From the middle of the marble and red-bricked destruction, the disembodied head of the statue king stares with stoic disapproval.

Still raging, I glare at Haiku.

The silence lengthens, interrupted by only my labored breaths and angry sniffles.

When it's clear my tirade is finished, Haiku snaps her fingers and my wounds heal. The surrounding corridor and statues return to their prior state, erasing the entirety of my tantrum.

I straighten and step toward her, never wavering in my hatred of the little avatar and the virtual overlords.

Haiku calmly says, "If it helps you to get over your anger, you may continue to assault me."

Realizing the whole effort has been a futile disaster, I shriek and sink to the brick floor. "Teamwork, friends, family, all of it should be cherished. People are stronger together, not by themselves."

"Under normal circumstances, that is true, but it isn't always possible to place five or ten or a hundred people where you need them. In every situation, one extraordinary person can change defeat into victory. The harshness of the Ten Sigma Program finds those individuals."

"Don't you care about producing someone like Syd? Do you understand what he's become?"

Her expression darkens.

"You know?"

There's a pause as her eyes lose focus. In the dimness, they seem to fade from pale silver into a cobalt blue. "Yes."

"Then why can't you do something?"

A hint of frustration accompanies her next statement. "Because he has powerful allies."

Apparently, there are divisions within the ranks of the virtual overlords. "Can't you do anything?"

"The rules are embedded into the deepest layers of code. They are set in stone. Everyone, including the overseers, must conform to the design of the system. Syd can only be stopped in a scenario."

I bury my face in my hands. Polluted by the enhanced emotions of the blue liquid, Syd is going to achieve a ten sigma score and leave this place.

Haiku politely asks, "Do you require anything else?"

"Go away," I whisper between my fingers.

She doesn't, instead floating closer. "This program is in disarray and worse things are coming. Far worse. Regardless of your sentiments, this is something you won't be able to hide from."

While Haiku patiently waits for my response to the warning, images of the hateful avatars cross my mind. I wonder how they fit into everything and how anything in my current situation could possibly get worse.

My friends are gone, scattered to the ends of the virtual universe.

Courtesy of my decision, everyone is now alone, fighting for their lives.

I had to save them from Syd.

Because a sliver of relief is part of my angry thoughts, I shake my head. My biggest anxiety is ordering one of my friends to their death or not ordering them to their death. Altering a battlefield decision trying to protect Suri or Walt or Vela could get many people killed. While I hate myself for not being strong enough, disbanding the team was the painfully right choice.

And nothing will be worse than letting them go.

Slapping my palms on the floor, I force the thoughts aside and rise. Staring into the avatar's eyes, I say, "I don't care about the problems of the overlords. Their fights aren't my fights. Go away."

She whispers, "What will you do?"

The barely audible question echoes in my mind, triggering another wave of anger.

"What will I do?" I say. "I've done everything possible. I've charged into every situation when it mattered, and I've been on the winning side in every scenario."

With sad eyes, she shakes her head and makes the leave motion. "If only it were that simple."

A little more than baffled, I try to fathom the meaning of her words as a halo of golden sparks wraps around her silver form. Somehow, they are the key to the whole Ten Sigma Program.

After she disappears, I'm no closer to a solution.

My eyes water from frustration.

Although I have no idea of what anything means, it doesn't matter. Looking to the judgmental faces of the newly fixed statues, I make my resolution for the virtual universe. I will escape this place, but outside of surviving, I won't succumb to the overlords' vision of being a perfect soldier.

No matter how alone I am or how much I forget, I'll fight with all my being to keep my essence intact.

Regardless of how much worse it gets.

THIRTY-TWO

MY NEXT TEAM is freshly recruited and eager. Despite my best efforts, they die storming a sandy stretch of beach under a dreary sky. A brutal First World War trench battle whittles the group after that into nothing. Infiltrating a stronghold inside a snow-capped mountain gets the next enthusiastic bunch slaughtered. Three more sets of nine follow and the meat grinder of the scenarios eliminate them in different ways, some creative, some not.

Without having Syd and Suri in addition to Rick's training, it's impossible to save any of them for much longer than statistical expectations of 1.56 scenarios.

Worse, with the destruction of each successive team, my guilt over their deaths dwindles even as the shell surrounding my fading emotions thickens. I'm not sure if it's my morality crumbling or the futility of being close to people who will soon be gone, but whatever the reason, I stop trying to befriend my new teammates and force the names and faces of the dead ones from my mind.

Each night, I lie in my bunk, attempting to save my dying past. However, nothing stops the brittle images from collapsing into dust. I'm terrified of what I'll become when the final memory disintegrates.

Besides those dire thoughts, I reserve any remaining slivers of emotions or pangs of guilt for Suri, Walt, and Vela. I wonder how they are doing and if they're still alive. Haiku isn't helpful with any of my queries.

On the other hand, I don't concern myself with Syd, who I'm positive is doing well. A part of me hopes we'll wind up on opposite sides in a scenario. The remaining larger, more rational part wants to avoid that tough contest.

And above everything else, as my emptiness increases, the killing becomes easier.

I'm losing the battle for my humanity.

A bowstring twangs. I raise my small shield and flick away an arrow. At a full gallop, the last Mongol horseman flees from the battlefield. He has talent, being a four sigma, but without the combined firepower of his dead group of a hundred, he lacks the ability to harm me.

As my stallion pursues through tall stalks of browning steppe grass, I enjoy the rush of clean air over my face and the hooves thundering under my body. With no ambush or other nasty trick in sight, I loose an arrow at his horse, aiming to hobble it.

Alertly, he whips to the left, and the long shaft flies into an open patch of dirt.

I use the pressure of my knees to guide my mount inside his turn and gain ground.

A husky woman, bulging into the joints of her leather armor and streaming a flying ponytail of blonde hair, slashes into my vision and forces him to reverse direction.

As he loses speed, I narrow the distance.

He draws back the bowstring, and I brace for an attack. The arrow speeds at my ally. She tumbles from her horse with the feathered end of the shaft sticking from her eye socket.

I'm close enough to put away my bow and draw my sickle-shaped sword, brandishing it high over my head.

Realizing he can't escape, the man slows, grabbing the handle of his scimitar. It's too late.

I fly past, leaning over and swiping at his horse's hindquarters. The upper curve of the metal slices through hide and muscle. Amid bellows of pain, the beast crumples.

Before I can swing around, a mustached man and darkly tanned woman gallop past me. There is a guttural sound as they ride in and slice at the fallen enemy across his leather protection. The thin material isn't good for close-in defense, and after they pass, he's bleeding from a couple cuts.

Uninterested in the final coup de grâce, I halt and watch from a distance.

The tenacious man rolls and slices at the front leg of the horse of the lead attacker. The terrified animal rears and tosses the mustached man. Before my ally can recover, the Mongol rushes up and stabs him in the neck.

I swivel and gallop toward the combat. As I near, he cuts under and slices the belly of the second charging horse. The huge animal tumbles, its rider getting crushed in a tumbling mass of hooves and limbs.

The Mongol dives as I thunder by, sliding beneath my sword and tossing his blade into my horse's flank.

I leap at an angle and tuck into a rolling ball, only stopping after flattening a long swath of waist-high grass. With a massive thud of flesh slamming against earth, my horse lands a meter from my prone body, shrieking in pain.

My enemy runs and grabs a sickle sword from one of my fallen allies.

Waiting for reinforcements is one strategy, but my curiosity gets the better of me. I rise and sprint at him with my weapon held in a strike position.

As I near, brutal, unblinking eyes greet me from a blood-painted face.

There are worse things coming.

As Haiku's forgotten warning reverberates in my mind, I slow.

He senses my trepidation and charges with a snarl. Two steps from me, he swings his curved sword in a flashing arc.

I quickly react with a high block. The blades meet with a terrific clang, and unnerved from the force, I step backward.

While he follows with sharper attacks, the swirling hatred in his eyes evoke an odd familiarity.

Whirling my sword for defense, I give ground to my meaner opponent. After my fifth step in retreat, his thread inefficiencies become apparent—his choice of strikes are predictable and repetitive. Inner rage notwithstanding, he's not even close to the seven sigma and I'm far better than when I fought her. With rising confidence, I avoid a sharp thrust and step forward, launching a riposte at his neck.

He delivers a heavy parry, and we slash back and forth. As he struggles to match my attacks, I take advantage of his prior wounds to hobble his leg, then after a high feint, deliver a vicious slice across his belly.

Steam rises as his guts pour over the trampled grass, and after collapsing, he uses his last breaths to scream curses not only at me but at my family and ancestors, none of whom I remember.

As he crosses into death, a peculiar happiness infects my mood and I shiver. The weird emotion scares me more than anything that happened in the battle.

I wonder if I've moved one step closer to being the sociopath the virtual overlords desire or if he's the harbinger of worse things to come. After a moment's reflection, I sigh. It may be a little of both.

A totally irrational thought strikes as the golden sparkles ending the scenario appear.

The man is familiar because he reminds me of Syd.

THIRTY-THREE

FIVE OF THE seats are unoccupied when we reassemble in the ready room. I spend a moment trying to remember the missing but give up when Haiku appears.

As she delivers her happy speech, my thoughts return to my final opponent. He performed much better than he should have, and I search for why he reminded me of Syd. They share none of the same physical characteristics.

A minute later, I'm no closer to solving the riddle but find my hand rubbing my nape. It's a strange sensation because in the ready room, there should be no danger. I glance at my surviving teammates, who are enthralled by Haiku's words.

It's only when my attention shifts to the little avatar that I notice something funny. Between every sentence, her silver eyes wander in my direction. In contrast to the rest of her happy countenance, they are angry.

Her normal expression reappears when I flash her a quizzical look. I don't have the vaguest notion of why she would be upset with me and chalk it up to a software quirk.

I hate computer programming.

Bewildered by the strange thought, I adopt a posture of mild interest until Haiku finishes.

When we're finally plopped into the late afternoon sun of the sanctuary, I'm still perplexed at the behavior. Although I'm glad to be out of her company, another more annoying issue presents itself. While crawling into my bunk and pretending my reality doesn't exist is my only concern, the others want to celebrate our victory in the cafeteria.

I'm not hungry, have no food fantasies, and have been avoiding the place because Syd's sexual rediscovery from the blue liquid has fouled my appetite.

Unfortunately, the survivors insist on a celebration, planning on making the blue liquid morph into the finest champagne.

While not wanting to get attached to anyone, I trudge along because I haven't hit the point of catatonic depression and really have nothing better to do.

After receiving our squishy meal packs, a hairy man calling himself Lou or Larry, takes charge. "I'll be describing my tasting of the finest champagne, which is the greatest beverage in the history of mankind, so follow along and be liberal with your imagination."

Katie, a four sigma, calls out, "How do we know it's not cheap soda water?"

Although mocking everyone's memory loss, she has a point. Lou or Larry points a thick finger at her, saying, "As long as you enjoy the experience, who cares?"

A tanned girl with big blue eyes and raven-colored hair says, "I love champagne. Let's get started."

Everyone else nods while I take an impatient breath.

He starts by saying, "Imagine holding a flute of the most beautiful crystal, the elegant stem between your thumb and forefinger gracefully curving into a reservoir for the divine. There's a pop followed by a soft sigh as the cork is withdrawn. As the exquisitely sculpted bottle tilts, a wonderful peach-tinted champagne pours into your glass. Listen closely to the delicate hiss of its tiny bubbles crawling to freedom. Wave your hand over the nectar. The amazing aromas of citrus and strawberry with hints of vanilla flow into your nose."

As he proceeds, he weaves the different nuances of sight, smell, and touch into the description. His speech is grander and more detailed than anything I could have imagined.

My mind tells me the most expensive champagne is sitting in my hand.

"Now, take the barest sip," he says.

I do.

"Allow the lovely juice to caress your palate. Notice the complexity of the fruit flavors, the bold citrus, the hidden orange, the touch of vanilla, the lightness of the bubbles tingling your tongue."

To my surprise, not only is the taste wonderful, in all aspects, the blue liquid physically matches his amazing description. Even when I swallow, the alcohol warms my throat before settling into my stomach. Stunned the gloppy fluid has an influence on not only my mind but my body, I take another sip, becoming a bit tipsy.

Was I a lightweight in real life?

When everyone nods in appreciation of our host's efforts, he begins the toasts. Squeezing his bag in his pudgy fingers, he thrusts it in my direction. "First, to Brin, for conquering the six sigma level. Someone we can all aspire to be."

Katie sighs. "That seems so far away."

I return an embarrassed smile but stop short of making a "You Can Make It Too!" speech.

Everyone sips and our host moves onward to the next toasts, giving generous platitudes to each survivor. Soon, they carry on carefree and inebriated, embedded in the throes of the blue liquid with the dead forgotten. Whether a real or placebo effect, I'm not sure, since I've wandered away from the fantasy.

Bored with the antics of my team and wishing to be anywhere else, I watch as other survivors enter triumphantly through the plain doors. They are uninteresting too.

As my attention wanders across the busy space, I catch the stare of the leprechaun avatar. Although his comically green outfit combined with his ruddy cheeks and scraggly red beard create a jovial appearance, his eyes are narrowed into slits. A moment passes before I realize he's glowering at me with a simmering anger akin to disdain.

What the hell is wrong with the software today?

Instead of joining the pissing contest, I focus on the package in my fingers. A curious idea hits me. If Suri was telling me about my past when I was drinking the blue liquid, perhaps, I could regain my memories.

I sigh, missing her. Even if she's still alive, she's somewhere lost in the vastness of the virtual universe.

As I sip, thinking of nothing, the liquid tasting like thickened tap water, I spy a familiar brunette, her hair tied in a loose bun, exiting the room with her team.

Vela!

Amazed to find my friend and former teammate, I toss my pouch on the table and push past my drunken companions. I rush to the doors, eager for any news of Suri and Walt.

By the time I get out of the cafeteria, Vela's disappeared. A miniature unicorn avatar glares before popping away and leaving me alone in the long hallway.

THIRTY-FOUR

THE REMAINDER of the afternoon and evening can't end soon enough.

Night arrives and when the lights darken, the sleeping spaces fill with exhausted men and women.

An hour after the shuffling ends, I get up, searching the barracks for my former teammate. As I wander through the dim aisles of metal-framed bunks, only the light sounds of snoring and tiny rustles of sheets disturb the stillness.

Roughly half the beds are empty, casualties since the last restocking, which makes my job easier. A few of her sleeping teammates are in the fourth aisle I check. As I near the wall, I'm surprised to find Vela on a lower bunk, sitting knees tucked into chest against a support post.

Staring at her toes, she says in a quiet voice, "Hello, Brin. I've been waiting for you."

"Vela, how have you been?"

Her fingers brush over her cheek, a residual habit of the animal attack that disfigured her face.

When she does nothing else, I sit in the middle of her bed, resting my feet on the floor. Although I'm close enough to touch her, the gulf between us is unmistakable. "It's great to see you. I've missed you guys so much. You're all I ever think about."

"I think about you a lot too. So gorgeous and so perfect. I watched you in the cafeteria. You were having such a grand meal with your new team. Are they your new best friends?" She enunciates each word with increasing venom.

"There's no one I care for more than my original team."

Slowly tilting her head up, she fixes me with a lifeless gaze. "Is that right?"

And I thought I was unsurpassed at sarcasm. "Yes, that's right. I had to end the team."

"I'm sure it has nothing to do with you not wanting to be the team leader."

Scrunching my lips, I use a moment to compose an answer. "That's true. Making life and death decisions for my friends is one of my biggest fears. But that's not why I separated everyone." I stop, realizing how crazy I would sound speaking of Syd and not wanting to reveal his secret of the blue liquid.

"Then, why did you do it?"

"I had my reasons."

A sarcastic chuckle leaves her lips. "Well, I guess that makes everything okay."

"Have you seen Walt or Suri?"

"Except for my new teams, I haven't seen anyone. But who cares about them? They're all dead." In a quiet tone, she adds, "Just like me."

"That's not true. There's always a chance. You need to keep trying."

Her watery eyes gleam in the faint starlight. She folds both arms around her shins, pulling herself into an upright ball. "I understand what ten sigma means. Not that I have your math background, but I know it's impossible to get to that level. Especially without your help."

"You don't need me. You're an excellent fighter, and you've made it this far."

Her voice flares with anger. "Keep your praise to yourself. You and Syd are the two best." After a gentle sigh, she continues in a softer tone, "Suri's good too. For a moment, I let myself believe we were getting out of this nightmare. Wouldn't that have been great?"

The system's not designed for that...

When I stay silent, she huffs. "So much for that. Just let me die in peace."

"No," I say, considering how much I want to share. After weighing the options, I decide. "There's a trick. Something to get better at fighting. Syd told me about it."

While she evaluates my words, her lips purse. Vela has always been the most suspicious of our group, and a moment passes before she unwraps her arms and leans forward, grasping at the single shred of hope I've offered.

"I'm sorry, Brin. It's not you. I just have trouble trusting anyone."

"It's okay. I understand about the animal attack."

"That's not the problem." She pauses to wipe a tear. "I loved all the animals in the zoo. Now, I can't even remember which one attacked me. But it wasn't personal."

"You don't need to say anything if you don't want to."

"I wanted to be a vet."

Tilting my head, I send her a questioning look.

"Sorry, I don't know why I said that. My memories are mostly gone, and I don't understand why I'm this way. I assumed I would become normal and start trusting people as I forgot, but nothing has changed." She wipes her nose. "I shouldn't have doubted you. I'm sorry. Of everyone here, you've tried to help me the most."

"That's okay, Vela."

"I can't even remember why I dropped out of vet school. Pathetic isn't it?"

I reach out and touch her leg, forcing her to return my stare. "It isn't. You're like everyone else, losing memories and just trying to survive. I promise I'll do whatever I can to help. We'll even practice in the off hours just like with Rick."

Nodding, she blows out a long breath. "I know you're a good person Brin, and I can trust you. What's this trick?"

Before I can reveal the secret of the blue liquid, a static tingle wraps around my body.

There's so much more I need to say, but "Don't give up…," is all I can express before I'm in the ready room, prepping to enter another scenario.

THIRTY-FIVE

My worries for Vela evaporate when I materialize in a new environment, a powder-covered ten-street-by-ten-street maze comprised by rows of broken two and three-story brownstones that apparently were dropped from a small mountaintop.

Besides myself, clad in a skin-tight black outfit, my weapons are a wire garrote looped in my hair, three throwing knives in a holder wrapped around my forearm, a long blade—more sword than knife—resting in a sheath running along my thigh, and a cold stiletto against my back. Basically, I'm a ninja.

Dressed in black, four teams make up my side. Our opposition is also four teams but dressed in gray. Forty against forty dueling in artful hand-to-hand combat until one side eliminates the other.

In other words, a total crap sandwich of a deathmatch with the sole promise of absolute brutality.

"Better to worry about yourself than an ex-teammate," Private Optimism says.

He's right but I hate myself for agreeing with him.

"I can hear your thoughts—"

"You are so getting busted down another rank."

"Seriously? You can't demote me any further."

"The dog-catcher post is vacant."

"You're kicking me out of the army? That's plain mean."

This is so not helping...

I promise to tell Vela the secret of the blue liquid when I return.

If I return...

"Brin, how do you want to handle this?" asks the 3.57 sigma named Lou or Larry, who is better at describing champagne than fighting.

Not wanting to have more blood on my hands from making decisions, I say, "Just roam around and kill everyone from the other team." Somehow, the statement comes out like a comment from Syd, and I cringe.

"Shouldn't we have a strategy?"

Because being a six sigma gives me a ridiculous level of seniority, the faces of the people, all ranked between 2.5 and up to Katie's four sigmas, watch me with expectation.

My resolve to shy from being the center of attention fades.

"Give me a minute," I say while studying the surroundings. Through the thin haze, the falling sun glints on broken glass and casts a reddish pall over the shattered walls of the buildings.

"We'll set up a defense in something sturdy with height to hold the wounded. Afterward, we'll send out two-person scout teams. Be careful and don't engage unless you have a definite advantage."

After a brief search, I select the remains of a roofless three-story construction in the western corner of the map as a home base. It fulfills all of my requirements along with having the sun at its back.

Inside the busted structure, piles of dust take the place of furniture. Aside from that odd feature, the other basic aesthetics are a simple molding, and, curiously, when I wipe the white powder aside near an oblong hole over the staircase, a lavish herringbone tiled floor.

After studying the thin interior walls, narrow staircases, and broken ceilings, I assign people to guard the entrances and place spotters on the open third story. When the dispositions are set, I instruct two pairs of scouts to locate the enemy without being discovered or running unnecessary chances.

As they vanish down the dusty street, the tension embracing the remainder of the black team rises.

I turn my focus to plotting the tactics of the battle. Absent long-range weapons, we'll be fighting hand-to-hand and building-to-building, which will be as much fun as Stalingrad.

Depending on the enemy's strategy, we have alternatives. If they are in small groups, we can swing through in larger groups. We just need to watch for people with street smarts. Ambushes will be abundant, and given the talent level of the participants, deadly.

Or we can move in kill teams, only engaging the enemy when tactically possible. With our skill, the throwing knives are lethal. And I need to have people gathering expended weapons in case the fighting becomes protracted.

I roam through other possibilities, hating the complexity of my thoughts. However, without further details of the enemy's movements, we have to make do.

This environment would be perfect for a bunch of Syds to operate.

A returning scout hustles over the street, a long cloud of dust trailing in his wake.

It's too soon.

Myriads of possible catastrophes trample through my mind. "What's wrong?" I ask.

Although breathing hard, he's not winded. "There's a broad main street four blocks from here. All of them are there."

"All forty of them?"

"Yes, we each counted twice. I left the others to keep watch, but they weren't doing anything but waiting."

It must be a trap, but how? No explosives are present and they're all accounted for. With wariness filling my thoughts, I gather the team leaders and instruct each of them to take their team to a different side in order to envelop the enemy. Then everyone hits them at the same time and hopefully, we all return home happy.

"A real Cannae maneuver," chirps one of my black threads.

I ignore it. This type of fortunate circumstance is reserved for people who are not me, or anyone else in this forsaken program. But I can't figure out what's wrong.

After the other three teams leave, I motion for my nine charges to follow. Still not trusting the good fortune, I make my way in stealth, taking advantage of the ample cover to move over the dust-covered asphalt of the street. Instead of using a direct path, I wend through different structures, adding to my knowledge of the area and planning escape routes if things go awry.

The other teams are in position when we finally arrive. I signal to my people to complete the encirclement. Then I enter the rear of a large building and tread lightly to the second floor. Besides a thick dust layer, the inside is empty and similar to our home base, except a brown pinstriped wallpaper decorates the hallway instead of molding. I shake my head; the predilections of the virtual overlords are not worth thinking about.

Lou or Larry and two others, the raven-haired girl with the big blue eyes who loved champagne, and a teen reminding me of Walt, follow me into a wide room overlooking the street.

I signal for them to move to the front windows.

"They're all there?" I whisper.

Lou or Larry answers, "Yes."

"What's your name again?"

Tilting his head, he narrows his eyes. "Leo."

Ugh.

I really need to take the distance from teammates thing less seriously. "No one hiding in the buildings on the sides?"

A few seconds pass as he rechecks his tally. "Forty. See for yourself."

Already knowing the answer, I count anyway. There are forty of them. Forty athletic bodies in form-fitting gray outfits doing nothing except waiting for a bloodbath.

Although they are out of throwing knife range, we have them surrounded and at every other disadvantage. While we only need to fight what's in front of us, they have to watch what's happening everywhere around them.

The raven-haired girl turns from the window. "They look oblivious."

"They know we're here," I counter. "They just don't care."

Leo shrugs. "I don't have your experience, but that's all of them and the rules are the rules."

Every word is true. The sides are equal, but I hesitate.

The others give me anticipatory looks.

"So, why are you worried?" says my internal voice.

"I'm not. Not really," I reply, biting my lip.

"Confidence, I love it!"

"You are the least helpful person I've ever met."

"That you remember—don't forget that!"

So, not helping…

"Why are we waiting?" Leo asks. "If they decide to attack, they can blow through our lines with ease."

He's right. We won't get a better opportunity.

Against my instincts, I raise my hand and give the go sign. Then I lead the charge, leaping through the window and landing with a dust-raising thump on the street.

From the surrounding rows of buildings, the others do the same, most drawing their smallish swords while the remaining toss their throwing weapons.

Although one or two of the other side falls, they react quickly and without surprise.

Both sides advance and metal clashes as the oversized brawl begins.

At the edge of the mayhem, I need to tilt my head higher to see the face of the ox-like woman opposing me. Her giant shoulders ripple as she brandishes her blade. Then emitting a deep growl, she charges.

Using a lightning draw, I meet her attack with a stinging block, but her ferocity drives me backward.

She's mostly strength and size without any finesse, and after weathering the brunt of the assault, I riposte, slicing her hand and landing a swipe across her ribs.

Relishing in the pain, she redoubles her effort, somehow getting stronger and faster.

Shocked and forced to react quickly, I parry a thrust then block a lethal two-handed swing. My counter forces her to back away, and I pull out one of the throwing knives. Instead of tossing it, I use it as teeth for my non-sword hand.

She delivers an overhand swing.

While stepping backward, I parry and then stab her free hand with my throwing knife.

Furious, she counters with a ferocious thrust. It's sloppy and her first mistake.

I take advantage of her open position with a glancing block and pirouette past her extended arm, nicking her carotid artery with the small knife.

Blood spews from her neck, and she collapses onto the asphalt with an angry gurgle.

A thrill shivers through my body.

Forcing aside the strange reaction to her death, I peer down the block, trying to make sense of the chaotic flesh and steel clashes swirling throughout the clouds of dust. My limited viewpoint is mostly glimpsing a bobbing head or swinging arm, popping out of the curls of white. Further away, swords glint in the low sunlight. I can't tell who's winning or losing.

A scream of death rises over the vicious clangs of metal. The raven-haired girl with the big blue eyes falls at my feet, her mouth leaking blood, a long slash running from her shoulder to her pelvis.

Her killer leaps at me with a feral challenge. In spite of the dust, he doesn't blink, instead staring with an unnatural focus.

I shuffle back with a quick step, stretching the line but not allowing him to break past.

He flicks a throwing knife.

I jerk to my left and it flies by my temple, clattering against the building behind me.

In a single swift motion, he draws his sword and fires a thrust.

As I twist my upper body to avoid the attack, I snap my sword at his leg.

The edge of his weapon grazes my shoulder while the tip of my weapon hits above his knee, cutting tendons.

He grunts and swipes at my midsection.

Sucking in my stomach, I jump back, his attack missing by a millimeter. Then I toss my throwing knife at his head.

He twists, but it slices over his right eye. Blood pours down his face, blinding him.

I sweep his sword aside with a loud clang and deliver a vicious sidekick.

His ribcage collapses as he goes flying into the melee and lands somewhere amid the roiling dust.

Champagne-loving Leo staggers toward me, covered in dusty whiteness, blood cascading from bite marks on his throat. His eyes roll into his head, and he dies, falling onto the heap that was once the raven-haired girl.

More people drop. The fighting subsides and with fewer struggles, the obscuring clouds thin. Down the avenue, many contorted bodies with horrible wounds lie between thickened pools of blood.

Something is very wrong. Many of the enemy have fallen, but the vast majority of my side is dead. The gray team is far more talented than they should be. Impossibly, my team is going down to defeat despite holding every advantage.

Who are these guys?

The loud clangs ebb as the fighting ends.

Katie, the four sigma and next highest ranking from my side, collapses with bright red blood fountaining from a slice across her throat.

The fine powder settles enough to reveal the entire battleground. Nine people stand among the dead.

I'm one.

The other eight are dressed in gray, their dark eyes sending me hungry stares.

I run.

THIRTY-SIX

THINGS ARE ONLY GOING to get worse. A lot worse.

Haiku's words rush through my mind as I execute a full-blown retreat, my hurried steps leaving an obvious trail over the dust-filled streets. Remembering the details I noticed on the meandering path to the battle and using all of my experience threads, I dash between the reddish constructs to limit my exposure.

Although facing impending death and having my options cut to a single desperate idea, I'm perplexed. None of the gray team scores are noteworthy, not even as good as poor Katie's four sigmas. Yet, they fight like demons. Although one or two of them could have the skill to rise to a significant level, eight is a statistically impossible number.

However, they exist and are close behind, hunting me in four teams of two. If I fight with one pair, the other six will be on me in a flash. Worse, my limited area to hide shrinks with every step. It's a total crap-fest.

Jagged pebbles fall in a mini-avalanche as I pick my way over a rubble pile and clamber through a small street-level window.

Instantly, my enemies converge toward the sound.

As I rush down a narrow hallway, I admonish myself for not using Leo's time with the champagne to increase my power via thoughts of sex and violence, because I really need Syd's close-quarter viciousness to prevent my opponents from hacking me into chunks of gore.

After slipping through a ruined doorway, I stumble into the kitchen. As my hunters converge, I slither out a small window frame and using a low profile, cut down a cramped passage between high brick walls.

The narrow path is perfect for an ambush, and the pursuit slows, affording me precious seconds to execute my crappy idea.

By design, I'm letting them funnel me in this direction. The original three-story structure I picked as the home base is nearby, and I have the advantage of knowing its layout.

When I pass the end of the alley, the front of the building is steps away. I sprint up the stairs, and not caring about the noise, smash through the double doors.

Nobody crashes into the foyer after me, which is a relief because I have a spare moment, but dire because they're trying a simultaneous assault, and I can't defend against eight opponents at the same time.

I dash up the cramped staircase to the second story. As I turn the corner, I sheath my undersized sword and pull the garrote from my hair. Heart thumping, and hating the wretched plan, I kneel just past the staircase and wait.

As the front door swings open, I take a steadying breath and slip the thin wire through the gap in the herringbone tiles.

When the top of a man pops into sight, I tap the floor.

He glances up.

I lower the garrote and yank backward with both hands.

The loop catches his neck, and he gurgles, kicking out.

Muscles straining, I pull him up and struggle to the balustrade. With a final tug, I knot the garrote handles below the corner ball and then sprint to the top of the staircase.

As I skid to a stop, a woman with short black hair shoves past her twitching partner.

My eyes widen. Her face is painted with an elegant pattern of blood stripes eerily similar to the Mongol warrior who reminded me of Syd.

She whips a throwing knife at my head.

I duck.

It punches through the stairway window, leaving thick slices of glass embedded in the frame.

Unwilling to waste one of my two remaining throwing knives, I step back and breaking off sharp pieces of the jagged glass, fling them at her.

The first sails high and hits her partner in the throat. Amid the spurts of blood, he stops moving. As she side-steps the next, her feet slip on a dusty stair. I fire another shard that stabs her thigh, and then one more that leaves a slice on her arm.

She screams, and in a rage, lurches up the steps.

I meet the charge with a stomp kick into her face.

Her neck breaks with a disgusting crunch as her head snaps backward. She tumbles past her dead teammate and limply slides into the dusty foyer.

One pair gone, three pairs left.

Glass shatters in the adjacent room while a thump comes from the ceiling. Two more sets of feet appear near the double entrance door.

"Time for Plan B."

I ignore my optimistic voice.

"There is a Plan B, right?"

So not helpful…

Retreating through the hallway, I slide on the dust-covered tiles and spin into a modest room. With no other option, I plow my way out the single front window.

Before I touch the street, I tumble to lessen the impact, wiping a long smear through the layer of dust. As a powdery haze settles around me, I wipe my eyes and catch an overzealous enemy stupidly leaping from the same window. I reflexively roll under his arcing form and yank out my blade. As he flies over, I thrust upward. The tip spears into soft tissue, gouging away a chunk of his inner thigh.

His leg buckles as he lands and face-plants onto the layer of fine powder. He feebly attempts to rise, then collapses into the slushy red puddle growing from his spewing artery.

My five remaining opponents sprint and bar both sides of the street, taking their time to circle me as I stand.

The three women and two men each have a different pattern of blood drawn over their faces. Their vicious eyes beam with a sinister hardness, examining me like an animal to be slaughtered in an ancient ritual. Although none have anywhere near my six sigma score, the hatred rolling off their bodies makes up for any differential in skill level.

My confidence ebbs. They aren't natural.

"You've got them right where you want them!"

"What the hell do you mean?"

"Stop thinking and react."

"That's easy for you to say."

"Syd would eat these people for breakfast."

"You're an idiot!"

In front of me, a rough woman with a circle of blood on her forehead arches an eyebrow.

Irritated at the universe, I puff out a breath but refrain from smacking myself.

However, Mr. Optimism is right. Syd would demolish my opponents. If I survive this predicament, I promise myself I'm joining Vela in sampling the extremes of the blue liquid.

Someone heavy shifts in the dust behind me.

I whirl to face a large man with three blood stripes running down each cheek. He grins.

My control snaps. "Are we going to finish this sometime today? I have to meet a friend after I kill you all."

A smallish woman with a dot of blood decorating her nose yanks out her sword and lunges at me.

With a sharp clang, I stop the thrust then sidestep an attack from the striped-cheeks man.

A swipe draws blood from my back, but the second man who is decorated with smears of blood under his eyes leaps back before I can strike.

I'm totally outmatched.

After setting my feet, the next attack comes from the final woman whose face is painted like a hawk. I deflect an arcing sword then parry a thrust from the circle-forehead woman. I twist but the tip of a sword nicks the back of my leg.

Powder spills from me as I blow out a frustrated huff. They are hacking me into shreds one gory piece at a time. I grit my teeth, suppressing any sound of pain, and tighten the muscles in my face. Although defeat appears inevitable, I'm not giving them the satisfaction of seeing fear.

The eye-smears man charges from behind and I pivot to block his thrust. The circle-forehead woman swings an overhead strike, and I dodge, but a kick knocks me to the ground.

Squinting from the cloud of dust, I roll from a flying foot, which still manages to glance off my ribs. After slamming my hand on the ground in frustration, I wobble to my feet, bruised and bleeding.

"Focus!"

Two pairs of uneasy boots shift to my rear. The dotted-nose woman steps to my front and takes a deep breath. From behind, the striped-cheeks man shifts his posture for an overhand strike. The eye-smears man adjusts his sword position on my right while opposite, the hawk-face woman fondles her throwing knives.

I'm not sure how but my perception has widened to encompass their every movement. Each intended attack is clear to me. I haven't felt this ready since being tossed into the battle on "Acid Island."

Before I can think myself out of the perfect fighting state, the dotted-nose woman shuffles closer and fires her sword at my chest.

Trusting to my intuitions, I sidestep, hearing the movements of the person behind me and sweep my sword to block his attack while dodging a flying knife coming from the other side.

The circle-forehead woman swipes her sword.

Stepping inside her guard, I block the swing and jam my blade at her throat.

She stops it with her free hand and when I pull it back, the sharp edge slices two of her fingers off.

While keeping her sword hand in my grip, I swing my sword to ward off attacks from two others.

The circle-forehead woman tries to bite me, but expecting it, I twist to throw her into the striped-cheeks man.

I jump through the gap to break the encirclement and turn, backpedaling to create space.

The eye-smears man whips a knife at my face.

Jerking my body in a half-swivel, I deflect it with my sword then block a slash from the striped-cheeks man. As my head twists to evade another knife, I spy a powder covered wall a few steps to my right. I dash to it and whirl, raising my sword for a high stroke.

On my heels, the striped-cheeks man moves to block my attack.

Instead of assaulting him directly, I swipe the flat of the blade through a pile of dust on the wall and fling it at him.

The powder hits smack in the center of his unblinking eyes. He raises his hands, blinded.

I snap the second knife from my holster into his throat.

Blood erupts from his neck and wheezing for air, the striped-cheeks man crumples in a heap.

Four left, including the one missing her fingers.

Another knife speeds at me and my body automatically shifts to let it fly past.

The circle-forehead woman charges and I deflect her blade, twisting my shoulders and letting her momentum carry her into the wall. With a fleshy thump, she tumbles over it, raising a powdery cloud.

There's no time to finish her. The eye-smears man pounces at me.

I swipe aside his overly aggressive sword strokes, and when the circle-forehead woman pops above the wall, I snap throw my last knife.

In her disoriented and missing finger state, she offers no defense, and the blade hits her in the eye with a squishy sound. Dead, she vanishes behind the low barrier.

The eye-smears man snarls under his blood paint and redoubles his attack, launching an overextended swing with too wide a stance.

I dodge and cut his arm as I shuffle past to avoid being encircled.

This is the best I've ever fought. I even sense the thread inefficiencies in my opponents. There aren't many, but every single millisecond delay or suboptimal movement gives me a subtle edge.

With measured fury, I jump at the remaining three, who don't have a chance. Using deft sword strikes, I advance and feint, taking advantage of everything the environment has to offer.

When the dotted-nose woman slips on the slush leaking from my face-planted enemy, I rush in and slice her throat.

Seconds afterward, my stiletto finds the chin of the eye-smears man and plows through his brain.

As the hawk-face woman, my last opponent, charges with a bellow, I fling my sword into her chest. Terribly wounded but refusing to die, she stumbles at me.

With each staggering step, my fear rises and although winded, I raise my fists to meet her.

As she nears, her arms droop and her sword clatters on the street. Two steps from me, her mouth opens to flash a wide set of bright teeth.

I blast my right fist into the center of the bloody beak painted on her face.

Bone shatters and with blood and bits of teeth pouring from her smashed lips, she crumples at my feet.

As she draws her last breath, a happy shriek leaves my mouth even as my strength falters and I sink to the dusty street.

Who were these people?

———

The static fades and despite sitting alone in the semicircle, I've never been happier to be in a healthy body.

Because I'm lucky to be alive.

It was the best and most natural I've fought since the beginning. But I can't celebrate because I'm not sure how to recapture that ability.

Who were those people?

I hunch and bury my face in my palms, letting my pent-up fears flow through my head.

When a soft pop announces Haiku's arrival, I peek from between my fingers.

She applauds. "Finally, I was wondering if you ever would."

Pulling my hands down to prop up my chin, I ask, "If I ever would what?"

"By yourself and outnumbered, you harnessed all of your talents and fought to your true potential."

Although I hate to admit it, part of my success was not having worries about any teammates. "Why do you care?"

"It's important for you to do well."

Straightening, I slap my palms on my thighs. "I mean, of everyone who has died from your teams, why am I so special?"

As Haiku floats close, shades of blue float throughout her normally silver eyes, giving her a strange depth.

"Brin," she says with enough emotion to get my attention. "Your performance in this scenario was very important. More than you know."

It's an odd admission.

"What do you mean?"

"You need to use your situational awareness more. Against every opponent, not only the toughest, you always need to perform at your best level. For every single battle."

"I survived. Let's not make a big deal out of it."

"You should understand your importance in the world."

The tone seems familiar, but I can't place it.

"Who were those opponents?"

Her newly expressive eyes blink. "Each team varies in the quality according to a normal distribution."

"No, they were different. You said worse things were coming. Were they part of that?"

She purses her lips, deep in thought. "Today, you won a great victory. And you need to continue to grow and perform at a higher level in the scenarios."

"But what about them? The stares, the bloody face paint. What's inside them!"

I shiver at the last words. The hatred and malice rolling from their bodies was unnatural.

"They are participants in the Ten Sigma Program, nothing more."

"Weren't you watching?"

"Of course, and you performed magnificently. By yourself and outnumbered, you harnessed all of your talents and fought to your true potential."

I scrunch my lips, fuming at the repeated sentence. While I want more information about the strange opponents and why worse things are coming, Haiku won't be forthcoming with any more details into the inner workings of the virtual world for today. I need to speak with Vela and making convoluted arguments to the little avatar falls around a million places below that. "Being that I'm the sole survivor, can we skip the debrief?"

"There is no substitute for procedures. Rules must be obeyed."

I groan. Her insistence on performing a debrief promises to be excruciating. Letting my frustration take over, I say, "You send me to battles. I come back. You increase my score. I ask you questions. You skirt around them, not giving me any answers with any value. And I'm not interested in hearing a psychoanalysis."

She glares.

I respond with a shrug because ultimately, I don't care about an unhappy software construct.

After a moment, her cheery face returns along with her shallow personality. Then she politely chatters away while I stare and will her to finish.

Finally, as I reach the end of my patience, she floats back to the center of the room. Her happy voice gets happier. "And your sigma score has increased to 6.2!"

I might have imagined the whole emotional depth thing.

"Are we finished?"

She waves her hands, and I materialize on my mattress.

Under the faint starlight crawling through the high slats, everything is still. There's no need to wait.

Determined to save Vela with the secret of the blue liquid, I pop out of my bunk and rush down the aisle.

When I get to her bed, it's empty. With a nervous breath, I collapse beside it, waiting.

Hours later, when dawn peeks into the barracks, I have to accept my worst fears.

Vela is gone.

THIRTY-SEVEN

SIX SCENARIOS PASS after Vela's non-return to the barracks. Besides killing and surviving, my seminal moment occurs when I come back alone from an impossible mission into the heart of a fiery city and cross the seven sigma barrier.

And mercifully, during this time, I haven't seen any more face-painting opponents and have no reason to treat the blue liquid as anything other than a culinary-based entertainment source. At least for the moment, things haven't gotten worse from that standpoint.

Kneeling behind the apex of a shallow hill, I shield my eyes from the midday sun hanging in the clear sky. In front of me, stout hedgerows growing on shallow embankments divide the green land into square fields. While a soft breeze laden with the smells of flora and trampled grass brushes past my face, I watch the last of the other side flee to the map's edge, their panicked forms plowing through shrubs and stumbling over scruffy tracts of grass. Seeking easy kills to raise their scores, overzealous sigma chasers from my team pursue. Despite the gospel preaching parity between the competing forces, sometimes lopsided battles happen.

However, I don't care about the impending victory. The alien sensation of happiness has replaced the dullness smothering my emotions.

I'm almost shaking with nerves like a schoolgirl which, of course, I have no recollection of being.

Suri is on my side, but I've kept my distance. The disaster with Vela weighs over any desire to speak with another member of my original team. I wonder if she despises me too.

"You're not a despicable person," my annoying internal voice says.

Not needing the conversation, I pressure my temples with my fingers while shaking my head.

"Hey, are you trying to fling me out of your mind?"

"Maybe…"

"Well, it won't work."

"Ugh, you make me want to walk in front of the next bullet."

"That's not happening either."

I hate my optimistic internal voice.

"I can still hear you."

So not helping…

Despite the possible adverse reaction, the idea of speaking with Suri consumes my thoughts. If I don't take the chance before she joins the chasers, she'll be gone. I yell, "Suri!"

She stops and turns her head, her brows knit in puzzlement.

I stand, sending a tense wave.

For a moment, she waffles in indecision before the corners of her lips rise into a smile. She jogs up to my position, eyeing me as if I might be a mirage. Her cheerfulness is genuine, and when she arrives, I wrap her in a hug.

After we separate, she says, "I'm surprised to see you."

"Pretty coincidental."

Her eyes flick to the stragglers fleeing in the distance.

"Can we chat?" I say. When she hesitates, I add, "It'll be good to not kill for a bit."

"Sure." She sits and pats the ground by her side. "This is as nice a location as anywhere else."

As I settle next to her, my anxiety dissipates. Despite the macabre situation of watching people being hunted down and killed in the background, almost giddy feelings wash over me. It's been so long and there are so many things I need to say.

"Congratulations on making seven sigmas," Suri says.

I scrunch my lips. Strangely, being the primary cause of the death of the seven sigma who etched her children's names into her arm still bothers me.

Melody and Melissa.

"And to you too," I reply.

"I'm only a six."

"Don't worry, you'll get there."

Suri's expression flattens as she turns to watch the chase of the stragglers.

Nervously, I change the topic. "This is just like when we swapped stories to keep our memories." I tug at my shirt. "Except for the clothing."

In spite of the gulf between us, she grins at the lame joke. "Sometimes I miss those days."

Me too.

"Do you want to hear one of your stories?" I ask.

"No, I don't think so."

"That's surprising."

"Repeating the stories doesn't work. I thought you knew this."

Although part of me wants her to tell a story from my past, she's right. I stupidly nod. "Aren't you afraid of what will happen when the last of your past fades away?"

"It already has. I stopped fighting a while back."

"Why?"

"I have my reasons. Perhaps you should ask yourself why you're so afraid of losing yours."

The many answers to the question are obvious, and her casual response scares me. Being adrift without the moral anchor of the last links to my loved ones and the real world is terrifying, especially in this universe of violence and death. "I'm not giving up that easily."

"Eventually, you're going to lose."

Resignation fills my answer. "I know but I still can't let it happen."

She sighs. "When I was still trying, I used a different technique to reflate my memories."

"What?"

"Ever try painting?"

"This I would remember how?"

A chuckle floats from her lips, one of her many endearing qualities. "You understand how it works right? Having a paintbrush and paint, then dipping—"

"Yes, I know that."

"You need to imagine painting over the image."

"Does that work?"

"For a while."

Another silence follows.

"Vela's gone." It's a rough segue, but I have to get the guilt off my chest.

Her lips edge into a frown before she replies in a neutral tone, "That's too bad."

"Have you seen anyone else?"

"Just Syd, and he has a new team that's completely loyal to him."

"There was a secret Syd told me that could help you in the scenarios."

"Anything Syd considers good, I have no interest in. Especially any secrets. He's not trustworthy."

"Oh? I was under the impression you had something going on with him."

Her face tenses, and she spends a moment watching several teammates stab an enemy to death. "I did some outlandish things getting caught up in this body and fighting the will of the virtual overlords. But having sex as a petty form of rebellion isn't victory or anything even close to it. At best, it was a diversion. I realize now those actions were mistakes."

Although there is more to add, she falls silent again.

"I've made a few of them too."

"I miss Haiku."

"That's a little shocking. What's your new avatar like?"

"He's a bland gremlin named Grel. At least Haiku had some depth."

I snort. "Depth? She's annoying."

Suri tilts her head and looks at me from the corners of her eyes.

"Every time I come back, she badgers me about doing better. And when we're alone, she gets really agitated. We've had some major arguments."

"Why?"

"Haiku has a vision for me as a perfect warrior. She wants me to lose my humanity and become a pure killer so I can advance faster. I won't stand for that."

"At least she cares."

The stilted conversation lapses into another silence because we're stepping around the central issue. Since I might never see her again, I gather my courage for the great confession.

"I feel awful about breaking up the team."

"Why? That's the best decision you made."

"I thought you'd be angry because I separated everyone."

"A little at first." She turns away from the chase to gaze at me. "But, I understand why you did it."

Although I'm relieved she doesn't hate me and doesn't think I'm a coward for not wanting to lead, I still need the truth. "Why aren't you upset?"

"That was the best for everyone. We had to go our separate ways. Wasn't that your reason?"

"No, it was Syd. He was going to get everyone killed."

"Eventually, we'd all have to make tough choices about surviving. At least now, I don't have to worry about sacrificing someone who's a friend."

"That doesn't sound like you."

She shrugs. "I've changed in many ways."

"That's the lack of memories talking."

"No, that's not it. I've changed for practical reasons. Here, the overlords control all the rules. This is a rigged game. The only true way to win is to reach ten sigmas and leave this miserable place. Nothing else matters.

"Brin, take Haiku's advice. Worry about getting yourself out of here. Become a ten sigma."

"Remember what we discussed? Life and death, sex and violence, love and hate. Everything about a human being is balanced. The overlords only care about death, violence, and hate. Winning isn't worth it if you don't retain any of your essence."

"If you die here, it won't be worth anything."

I have no answer for that.

Deep in the corner shadow of a distant hedgerow, two of our teammates hack apart the last of our enemies.

After the bloody form falls, Suri says with finality, "Don't worry about saving your humanity. Let go of the past."

Coming from my best friend in this place, the statement is shocking. I return a somber glance.

Unlike Suri, I need my memories and loved ones, and I'm afraid of existing without them. I silently repeat my promise to do everything in my power to remain myself.

As the golden sparkles signifying the end of scenario cover us, she adds one final sentence.

"Brin, it's time to end our friendship."

———

In the full semicircle of the debrief, everybody is ecstatic, except for me and Haiku.

Suri's words weigh on my psyche. I can't believe she's become so callous.

What the little avatar's issue is, I have no idea. However, now and then between her speaking and hand waving to the team, her eyes flick angrily in my direction. The color and depth of the silver orbs vary wildly depending on whether she is being shallow to everyone else, or she's directing dark emotions at me. My head spins from trying to follow her mood.

Finally, after announcing everyone's new sigma scores, she concludes with the usual happy clap and wide smile.

A quiet hum echoes in the room as the others disappear under a glittery sheen of sparks.

Although never happening before, I'm not surprised to find myself sitting in the same chair with Haiku floating in front of me. I clench my jaw, waiting for the opening salvo.

The little avatar doesn't disappoint. A deeper, angrier expression infects her face before she screams, "Your performance in the last scenario was abominable."

Suri misses this?

"Given that we won with nobody dead, I'm sure I don't know what you're talking about." The tone is snarky and oddly feels right. How obnoxious was I in the real world?

"Staying in your past isn't in your best interests nor is it the end goal of this program."

"Suri was there, and I wanted to catch up with her."

Her hands rise. "Suri!"

I return a defiant stare but speak in a level voice. "Yes, my friend, Suri."

Strangely, I can sense the wheels grinding in her mind.

"You should have been killing the final enemies."

"Why? To add a millionth of a point to my sigma score?"

"You are falling behind. You can't kill only when you feel like it. Every little bit matters."

"Behind who?" Not waiting for an answer, I fire out the other questions bothering me. "Why are worse things coming? What's with the people who paint their faces?"

Her voice rises. "Given your abysmal performance you should be happy not to be facing them."

"So they are different. Who are they?"

"You have enemies that exist and want you to fail."

"Finally! What enemies?"

Haiku pushes out a heavy sigh as if she's already said too much. Her voice lowers when she continues.

"Please don't concern yourself with things that are out of your control.

"While your skills are superior, amongst other things, the longer you're in these scenarios the more vulnerable you are to the perils. Given enough opportunities, even the chances of an insignificant event increase. And given the millions of misfortunes that can befall you in the scenarios, dawdling will cause your demise to become a certainty."

In the simplest terms, her wordy speech parrots Syd's warnings.

"The more risk, the more dumb luck comes into play. How many times will we survive facing five or ten-to-one? A random patrol. One lucky shot. Some slob taking a piss at the wrong time…"

However, the sympathies of a software construct don't interest me. "Aren't the others from my team deserving of higher scores too?"

She pauses, pursing her lips and breaking eye contact.

Happy with the rattled reaction, I decide snarky works as a good counter to my fading emotions. Part of me hopes I was a complete bitch in my prior life.

"Well?"

"Here, only individual achievement is rewarded. The others will or won't advance. They will or won't die. You must keep your focus on your own situation and reach ten sigmas."

I stand and peer directly into her face. "What's it all for?"

She takes an indignant breath to calm herself. "You want to survive and return to the real world, don't you?"

Of course, she's right. I made a promise to never give up. However, I don't want to hear it from her. I'm not sure why, but something about the little avatar rubs me the wrong way. "From your perspective, why does my life matter so much? I don't see you giving this kind of treatment to anyone else."

Haiku doesn't answer.

Faces of my dead friends, Vela, Carol, Jock, Ally, Rick, and even Simon appear in my mind. My voice rises in exasperation. "Given all the death, why should I matter more than anybody else?"

Her eyes flatten as a smile returns to her face. She cheerily says, "We'll talk later when you're in a better mood."

The static wraps around me, signaling the end of the meeting.

I'll never be in a better mood.

THIRTY-EIGHT

THE UNRELENTING STREAM of battles speeds past, blending together into a drawn-out smear of death as my sigma score marches higher. I slaughter Spartans, Romans, Carthaginians, Nazis, people from long-lost civilizations, and others from places that never existed. Soldiers dressed in everything spanning from modern battle armor to loincloths fall to me in every type of combat the meat grinder of the scenarios can supply.

I lose count of the number of lost teammates while my mind muddles their here-one-moment-and-gone-the-next faces into a hazy set of bloody features.

From time to time, I'm reminded of my original team, but there isn't a whiff of them in any part of my virtual universe.

Upon every return, an increasingly agitated Haiku admonishes me with growing severity to perform better while not providing any additional information. Although I haven't recaptured my performance against the unnatural opponents in the dusty brownstones, I angrily retort to each criticism with the fact that at least I'm still alive.

When I reach eight sigmas, the congratulations from my team and Haiku ring hollow.

I have bigger worries.

My real world remembrances have withered into black specks of dust. In place of my childhood, teenage years, and young adult life sits a deep, virtually empty cavern. Between the huge gaps in the space reside fading brushstrokes that carry no meaning. And even they are crumbling into ash. Was I smart enough to attend college? Was I married? Other than my parents, did I have a family? Friends?

Although I still revere the blue dome, I'm not even sure if blue was my favorite color.

My constant state is wondering 'what was I just trying to remember?' The feeling is like having something bubbling under the surface of my consciousness echoing what I've lost.

Was I even a decent human being?

That's why, even as I've watched the vibrancy of my past turn brittle and flake away, I pour my energy into retaining the last slivers of a tired man sitting in a hospital room who told me never to give up. In some unknown fashion, he's important in my prior life, and his reassuring smile gives me strength.

It's a losing battle, but I need to save this tiny part of myself because when this last shred is gone, only a bunch of red and black threads forming the backbone of a sociopathic killer may remain.

The floor jostles and a man bumps into me. He nods and shifts to give me room.

The stuffy atmosphere is saturated with the sweaty scents of soldiers packed into every nook and cranny of the aerial transport. The unwelcoming faces in the dim light are typical of the combatants before each battle.

I lean against a support strut and fiddle with the straps of my parachute. Then, I perform a final check of my kit, a tactical electromagnetic (EM) rifle, old-fashioned pistol, med-pack, and extra ammunition. It will be a long fight.

A small bulb glows red from the ceiling. The engines whine and the floor pushes against my boots as we rise for the attack drop.

I slap my aerial visor over my face and through the reddish gleams on the thin material, return a stony stare to the nervous glances from my teammates.

Look to someone else for reassurance.

The light switches to green and an alarm sounds. A second later, the floor splits.

Thin air whistles past my helmet as I plunge through darkness. While I orient myself into a stable falling position, the black silhouettes of my team scatter against the backdrop of the predawn sky. Below, the starburst pattern of lights from a sleepy city winks through wispy clouds.

It's beautiful.

As the approaching skyscrapers and streets grow in detail, my heart pounds, and I beam at the thought of the impending scenario.

———

After I land, a six-hour battle ensues between two sides of twelve teams.

Now, except for the bodies, the black avenues of the modern cityscape mostly lie deserted. Tall rectangular buildings sheathed in massive glass panels, and impervious to hypervelocity pellets or entry, curve high above me while the late morning sun casts my surroundings in shadow.

My reflection follows on glass storefronts as I wend my way along a concrete sidewalk. Taking cautious steps, I scan for any signs of my remaining enemies.

In the lonely street ahead lay my contorted victims from a prior pass, two gory bodies with blown-out torsos. Beyond them, a broken sanitation truck carelessly tossed on its side fills an intersection.

I jerk the tapered EM rifle higher, swinging the muzzle to cover a recessed second-floor balcony.

A loose newspaper flaps against a metal railing protecting plastic outdoor furniture. The rest of the reflections on the nearby glass stay still. A moment later, a harsh breeze bearing a burnt stench sweeps past me, softly whistling to the next intersection.

Blowing out a breath, I return my gaze to ground level, forcing myself to stay alert. Few combatants remain, but I've only survived by being too careful.

"They're probably just as scared of you," a strange internal voice says.

"Your pie-in-the-sky happy thoughts aren't helping anyone," I reply in as testy a tone as an imaginary voice can carry.

"You could use a dose of optimism for your thoughts."

"Didn't I fire you or kick you out of my life?"

"I'm not sure. Did you?"

"Who the hell are you?"

"If you don't know, how would I?"

This is so not helping...

Even the stick figures from the empty halls of my memories are piles of ash. Except for one image, nothing remaining is more than a shadow or innuendo of something I used to know.

I'm so lonely.

Yet, all my semantics for fighting are intact. Everything I need to function but nothing that makes up for my dying individuality.

"This is for the better," the strange voice says.

"What do you mean?"

"Well, without extra baggage, you're probably a better fighter and you'll survive a little longer."

I stay quiet.

"So there is that—"

"Who the hell are you again? Why should I listen to anything you have to say?" The final sentence is thought so loudly, I'm surprised my head doesn't explode.

My unknown passenger falls silent.

Great.

I'm angry at it and more angry at its words. Once the last vestige of my past fades, all that's left might be a mindless automaton doing the sole bidding of the virtual overlords. I'm not better off without my memories.

Not one bit.

Detouring from the mission, I park myself into a cubic entranceway walled by thick glass panels.

From across the space, the reflection of my perfect form stares at me. I can't remember why this body made me so uncomfortable or what I used to look like.

What was I in the real world? A saint? A sinner? Rich? Poor? There was a poem covering all the possibilities. Of course, I remember none of it.

Who am I without knowing?

I run my fingers down my face.

Even though I have materialized after every scenario in the exact same body, I'm different. While I have the same beautiful mane of red hair and classical features under an ivory complexion, the difference rests in my eyes. Although still a deep shade of blue, they are flat and lacking any sparkle of life, the weight of the scenarios and loss of my prior life catching up to me.

I can't let myself fade into oblivion.

After double checking my surroundings, I concentrate on the trick Suri taught me to reflate my sole remaining memory.

I recall the remnants of the image. The few details resemble a hastily sketched set of lines and curves more than a person or place. I imagine a paintbrush and dip it into a multicolored can of paint.

The memory pulsates as I focus and swipe the brush over the brittle lines. Increasing my concentration, I repeat the process. Color drips into the frame. After a few more strokes, a huge reassuring smile with glistening white teeth blossoms on a handsome face, and my anxieties fade. He's someone who loved me.

My mood brightens as I draw strength from his confidence. I had to be a decent person. Maybe not a saint but definitely not a sinner.

When I open my eyes, a gleam of life sparkles from my reflection.

That's enough.

The wide avenue remains empty, and I breathe a sigh of relief. Although worrying about my past in the midst of combat was a foolish endeavor, and Haiku will have an admonishment waiting for me when I return, I don't care. Keeping a part of my individuality is worth the risk. For however long this works, I have no idea, but I'll resist the will of the virtual overlords for as long as possible.

After resetting the EM rifle on my shoulder, I edge along the glass of the entranceway. When I scan to the left and right, it's all clear. Still cautious, I step onto the sidewalk.

My nape crawls with imaginary spiders.

I freeze.

A hypervelocity pellet tears across my midsection, expanding upon impact to maximize bodily harm. An instant later, the distinctive crack of the EM weapon reverberates off the hard surfaces of the buildings.

Another second passes before my mind realizes my body has received a mortal wound. My legs wobble, and then I collapse, my intestines spilling from my abdomen and onto my thighs.

THIRTY-NINE

SHRIEKS ROLL past my ears and agonizing seconds pass before I realize the hideous sounds are spewing from my lips. While my throat constricts with panic, my eyes widen. Curled tracts of bloody intestines lie everywhere. My intestines.

I bite my tongue to stay quiet and suck in sharp breaths of air tainted by my gory insides. Because I was trying to recapture a memory that doesn't even matter, I'm going to die.

Another pellet ricochets off the sidewalk next to my exposed boot. A third plinks into the opposite wall, cracking a spiderweb into the corner of the tough glass.

Eyes darting and falling into a full-blown panic, I quickly search my surroundings. Although I can't see anything from my prone position, lying in the open will be my death.

With gritted teeth, I fight the delirium from the overwhelming pain and pull the squishy mass of digestive tract into my abdomen. At least as much of it as I can gather. While I drag myself into the cover of the entranceway, using a quivering hand to prevent my innards from falling back out, moans of agony undercut my rushed breaths.

If I survive, I'll be whole again when the next scenario starts.

If I survive…

Each movement becomes more excruciating than the last and fighting off the urge to scream, I arrive at the far wall and slump against the glass. My mind swims in dizziness, and I shiver from cold. Around the gore, my skin is turning blue as my body succumbs to shock.

But I can't surrender to the wounds, someone is still coming to kill me.

When I grab at my pistol, the holster flap is difficult and the weapon won't come out. I struggle to steady my fingers. If I'm found, I'm dead.

After more groggy efforts, I finally succeed, my shaking hand grasping my salvation, although in the interim, I've lost enough blood that my head wobbles and my intestines have leaked past my other hand and onto the concrete.

I made a promise to never give up.

Sucking in calming breaths, I force myself to stay upright, even as my attention wanes and my heavy eyelids flutter.

Nothing matters. Not the horrible injuries and not the awful pain. Using every last bit of stamina, I push my gun through the curls of my insides for a clean shot at the street. Then ignoring the agony, I close my eyes and play dead.

After several delirious moments pass, the patter of rubber-soled boots arrives through a whistling breeze. The enemy is near.

I count to five then open my eyes.

The bald giant from Acid Island fills the square entranceway.

Terrified, I empty the magazine with the gun jerking wildly in my hand.

Bullets walk over his body, peppering him in red bursts. His mouth opens in shock as he collapses to the pavement, his weapon clattering on the street. As he stills, the breeze blows through thin wisps of hair on his head. His body isn't large or muscular.

My fear gives way to disappointment, and I frown through my suffering. Thinking I had slain my virtual demon was stupid. The real bald giant wouldn't need a bullet when he could march up and just beat the snot out of me.

More shots echo off the glass of the tall buildings. From nearby, another body thumps onto the asphalt. Footsteps approach on the sidewalk.

Someone's coming.

I panic. My EM rifle lies past the entranceway while the pistol is empty. My free hand twitches as I try to eject the finished magazine. It's a futile gesture; my fingers are shaking too much.

Sighing, I resign myself to fate as a dark figure approaches. A moment lapses before I pierce the haze shrouding my mind and recognize the girl with the violet eyes. Her rifle points directly at me.

When I attempt to shoot, my hand is empty. The useless pistol rests on the ground next to my thigh. I don't remember dropping it.

Instead of killing me, she kneels at my side and pulls out her med-pack.

I loll my head back to her, stunned. The girl with the violet eyes isn't an enemy. I don't know what to make of this crazy universe. Besides the worse things coming, dissension between the overlords, and my loss of memory, I can't explain why she resurrects in different scenarios and why of everyone I've killed, she's the one I remember.

Death is final here, and I'm one hundred percent certain of it.

Yet, now she's back and helping me.

This is worse than being wounded. While I don't want to rely on anyone else, I've killed her so many times, the shame I feel from receiving her help crushes my soul.

After a quick check, she sprays an analgesic over the injury.

As the pain lessens, my guilt swells. I have to allow her the chance to seek revenge. "I've killed you. Leave me."

A puzzled look covers her pretty face while she touches my lips to keep me quiet. Similar to every other time I've encountered her, she never speaks.

Faint shots echo, and she spends a moment scanning the neighborhood. When satisfied everything is clear, she pulls out a roll of bandages and, wrinkling her nose from the smell, gets to work patching me up.

I hate being helpless.

If I am to survive, I have to eliminate the weakness of holding onto my past. However, if only an endless supply of battles would remain until I reach ten sigmas, what's the point? I wouldn't be me. My choices are to die as myself or live as a shadow of my former self.

Wishing to be anywhere else, I release a helpless breath.

When the girl with the violet eyes finishes closing the wound and applying bandages to the best of her ability, my body is somewhat functional.

With a clearer head, I decide.

Never give up.

To keep my promise, I need to survive, and the last vestige of my prior life needs to crumble into dust, come what may. I hope I'm a good person at heart and can withstand whatever moral drift comes without the anchor of a past.

That will have to be enough.

Still leaking blood from my abdomen, I grab my pistol and, twisting my face into a pain-fueled snarl, rise to help the girl with the violet eyes finish our enemies.

———

Before my materialization into the ready room completes, I notice a livid Haiku waiting for me. Her presence is a gigantic breach of etiquette; she should only enter after the team finishes acclimating from the scenario.

When the cushion sinks under my weight, she screams in a rage that's wholly at odds with her dainty appearance. "What was that about?"

Because my teeth are chattering and I'm still in shock from having most of my insides spilled over a nice sidewalk and then stuffed back into my body, I can't answer.

While I struggle to regain control of my faculties, the little avatar fumes, floating over me with her small arms folded and her face scrunched in fury.

When the shivering stops, a moment passes before my mind adjusts to the lack of pain stabbing throughout my insides. Hands involuntarily rubbing over my pristine abdomen, I overcome my disbelief that my internal organs are where they should be.

Instead of answering, I let my eyes roam over the empty semi-circle of chairs. Once again, I am the sole survivor from my group of ten.

Letting her anger simmer, Haiku descends to my eye level. "Are you listening? This type of behavior cannot happen again." The concern radiating from her is more disconcerting than her apoplectic rage.

While I need a lecture, I don't need one from a childish therapist. "I don't care."

"You should care!" Back to raging, she clenches her tiny hands in front of her chest. "You are too close to the end. To success. Doesn't that mean anything?"

"I'm just another person in this program. Why am I so valuable?"

"Why throw all your hard work away?"

My exasperation spikes at the question answering my question. The virtual overlords have won. There is nothing I will do to resurrect the disintegrating outline of my last memory. I'll become someone without a past, their ideal servant. But I won't mention it and give her the satisfaction of cooperation.

"Okay, I screwed up. But, it's my life."

"Greater things are involved than just yourself."

"Aside from saying something worse is coming, what greater things? And you still won't answer my questions about why I'm so special."

"Your score is over eight sigmas. That's why you're so special."

The words spill in a pleading tone. The emotional depth underlying the shallow personality of the computer program is off-putting, and although truthful, yet again, her statements tell me nothing.

"You needn't concern yourself with my well-being."

"Your well-being is of paramount importance."

Slowly drawing in a breath, I lean forward. "I have some specific questions."

She sighs. "Very well, I will answer from what I am able to answer."

Finally.

An image of the violet-eyed girl and the bald giant form in my mind. But my mouth won't ask what's on my lips. Imagining the leprechaun and other weird avatars brings the same result, nothing.

My hands slam on the sides of the seat.

"You're unhappy again. Perhaps I should schedule a therapy session. Or if you physically desire to assault me?" Haiku asks hopefully.

I glare. If I could hurt her or any of the virtual characters, I would gladly accept the offer.

Strangely, the emotion leaves the little avatar, and she matches my rage with a blank expression.

Perplexed more than usual at her erratic behavior, I take a deep breath. While lacking any memories as evidence, I know prior me would be appalled at the ease with which I slip into violence as a means of expression. "No, none of that will be necessary."

"It is exceedingly important—more important than you realize—for you to be successful."

"I'm just a person trying to survive. Without the threads, I'm nothing."

"That's not true. You need to take the best of your experiences and personality and sync them to your situational awareness. Only then will you rise to your potential."

The déjà vu of the statements isn't lost on me.

"Haiku, can you tell me anything else?"

"What knowledge do you require?"

There is an opening, but nothing of what I want to ask will come out.

Again.

Disgustedly, I shake my head. While I'm curious about the behind the scenes interactions of the virtual universe, they ultimately aren't essential to my survival.

In the heat of agony, I promised to let my past die without further resistance and only work on moving forward and surviving. Now, in a relaxed atmosphere, I know it was the right decision.

Although I'm not sure what I will become, I made a promise in a long-forgotten context to never quit. That's the best course for me to follow.

"This is exhausting. Can we just get to the debrief?"

Her eyes narrow as she descends to glare at me. "We'll dispense with the debrief for today, but to ensure there are no more lapses, I'll be watching you closely."

Great.

She waves her hand and static envelops my body.

FORTY

"Do you think we're going to win?" a frightened voice asks.

I don't respond, my mood matching the dark, still atmosphere. With the collapse of the outline forming my last real-world image, I've finished my acclimation to the Ten Sigma Program. I'm officially the person with no past, someone who has completed the journey to becoming the sociopath desired by the virtual overlords.

Gripping my ax tighter, I listen for signs of our enemies but only hear the tree branches scraping against the roof.

The log cabin providing our shelter from the frost-covered forest is a modest space built over a frozen dirt floor. A lone keg-shaped stove occupies a corner, while a stout plank bars the crude wooden door. The sole reminder there is an outside arrives in the shape of distorted rectangles of starlight leaking through the broken glass of a six-paned window.

A wet cough leaves my shivering companion, who lays on his side, huddled under a thick cloak. As he patiently waits for an answer, his pain-filled breaths fog in the icy air and drift through the dim orange slats radiating from the stove's grill. I can barely make out his young face in the intervening shadows.

He's the last person on my team.

"How old are you?"

"Sixteen."

Younger than Walt.

"Keep your hands on that wound or you'll bleed out."

With a grimace, he nods. "I'm sorry, it's just that I can't stop shaking."

My detached self informs me I should be in the forest where I can be hunting and finding an advantageous situation to defeat my three remaining enemies. Instead, I'm trapped in an obvious position next to the only heat source on the map with a person I only met in the ready room right before this scenario started.

Why can't I just leave him?

I stand, sighing. The frosty air finds every opening in my flannel garments as I pull off my heavy wool cloak and toss it over him.

"Don't you need this?"

"No, it'll only restrict my movements when I fight."

"Thank you," he says, accepting the flimsy explanation. "They're going to be coming to rescue us soon. Right?"

The other eight from our side in this brutal single team versus single team affair are already dead.

"Right?" he repeats.

Because the kid's only a 2.6 sigma and newbies don't know any better, I resist the urge to admonish him for the useless conversation.

"Let me concentrate."

"Sorry, I'm just a little scared. I was always close to my parents, I hadn't even finished high school and now this."

The words die in the empty shell of my emotions.

"Well, with that attitude, we'll be at ten sigmas in no time," my internal voice announces.

"Shut up, I hate you. Whoever you are."

"There's the passion you've been missing! Aren't you glad I'm around?"

"No!"

The winter wind rises, funneling through the shards of glass embedded in the window frame and rattling the loose planks of the door. The swirling air finishes rushing through the confines by brightening the dying coals nestled in the stove.

I switch my attention back to my companion. "Hey kid, don't fall asleep."

His head lolls as he opens his eyes.

"Tell me what you remember about your parents."

As he searches for coherent thoughts, his stare wanders. A few labored breaths pass before he says, "Sorry, you know with the memory loss, it's hard to focus."

I send him an encouraging nod.

"We lived in one of the projects, assisted housing, one of the red-bricked buildings. Nothing special. You know."

Although I don't, I don't interrupt.

"My father did some job for the government, I forget which, while my mother was a great cook. We used to have all the relatives over for big dinners every weekend. It's funny, the blue pouch goo mimics her meals perfectly. I love the cafeteria."

"So how did you wind up here?" I say, shifting the subject away from Syd and his secrets.

He stops, looking for the right memories. "There were riots. A lot of buildings in the neighborhood burned down."

"Is the world that bad?"

"There are lots of politics. I don't understand all the specifics, not even why, but a few border states left the country. And in the middle, the stuff got really bad."

These tidings I should know or at least have some sentiment for, but without memories, I have no reference for what the real world should or even might be like.

I sigh. I can deal with that issue if I survive.

The kid continues, "The protesters rioted in our city. They started a fire in our building. My father managed to get us through the flames, but when we got to the street, the mob attacked because he worked for the government."

As more of his words pour out in fogged breaths, the terrible tale wanders through the barren cavern of my memories like a dusting of snow, finding nothing to resuscitate, not even a speck of emotion. When he speaks of his father's murder, I futilely search for something to trigger meaning, some fact to rhyme and bring alive any part of my past. When the story arrives at the point where the kid gets fatally wounded defending his mother, no remembrance has resurrected itself, not the faint lines of an image, not even a shadow of something I should feel.

Everything is gone. Except for disappointment that I haven't any empathy for his plight or his circumstances for joining the Ten Sigma Program.

"I'm sorry about that," my mouth says in an empty tone. "I guess it's good you'll be losing your memories too."

He blinks away a tear and changes the conversation from my pathetic answer. "Can I ask you a question?"

"Sure."

"It's hard to tell, but I think you're at least a six sigma and you've seen a lot more than me."

I shrug. "What are you getting at?"

"Just that the other side is tough. I'm not very experienced, but if you include the acid platform battle, I've been in three scenarios and these guys are like nothing I've seen."

In a loose sense, he's right. Our enemies are face-painters, the likes of which I haven't fought since the ninja scenario in the dusty brown-stones. And despite the distance between us, I'm impressed. He noticed and came to the correct conclusion with little information. If he could survive a few more scenarios, he might have a chance.

"Everything about this program is dangerous and you should always be prepared for anything. These people are tough, but they can be killed like anyone else. Never forget, as long as you're alive you have a chance."

Even against ten sigma odds.

Faint footsteps crunch on the brittle ground outside.

The worse things are coming. I keep my voice level. "They're almost here. Do me a favor, when they attack, stay hidden and I'll take care of the fighting."

Taking quiet steps to the side of the doorway, I ready my ax and slide my long Bowie knife from its sheath.

Two pairs of feet stop short of entering. Nervous moments pass, the silence interrupted only by their heavy breathing.

An earth-shattering kick slams the door inward, splintering the holding bar over the floor.

I leap, swinging the ax at the fur-clad forms jumping into the cabin.

The first enemy anticipates a side attack and blocks the ax handle with his forearm.

Striking with my other hand, I embed my knife into his ribs.

He bull-rushes into me with a grunt.

Expecting the move because I understand the brutality of the face-painters, I twist before my back hits the wall and using his momentum, plow his face into a fat log.

His twisted laughter intermixes with the crunch of his bones.

I kick the back of his knee, driving him to the dirt floor. Before I can finish the job, he rolls away. As I ready to take on his female partner, a fur cloak rises, blocking the orange glow from the stove.

That stupid kid.

Instead of staying safe as I asked, he charges into her back. She turns and stabs him. He squeals, sinking to the ground. As she raises her ax to kill him, I throw mine. The heavy ax-head sinks deep into her neck, and she tumbles, knocking over the stove in a crash of metal, flesh, and flying embers. As her body stills, ash from the broken stovepipe spills over her cloak.

A gust rattles the open door, swirling the dust throughout the room.

Raising my hand and squinting through the stinging cloud, I spy the first man rising, his face a dirty mess of flesh and teeth. With hatred in his unnatural, unblinking stare, he rushes and thrusts his knife at me. I deflect the strike with my empty hand, then sidestep and like a matador, drive my knife into the base of his neck as he flies past. His momentum carries him into the wall where he splats with a heavy thud.

The cabin settles into stillness as his limp form sinks onto the frozen floor.

I walk to the kid and kneel next to his unmoving body. There is no response when I shake him. Putting my ear by his mouth, I listen for any breathing.

Nothing.

After standing, I stare at his face, wondering what emotion I should be expressing. Perhaps sadness at this death would be appropriate. Maybe happiness at remaining alive could be suitable. I have no idea, only vaguely understanding the dispassion flowing through my being is wrong.

However, there's nothing to take its place.

Another frigid wind cuts through the open door and brings a last bit of life to the sparks scattered over the floor. They brighten for a moment then fade, disappearing into the surrounding shadows.

Besides me, everything in the cabin is cold, dark, and dead.

Shivering, I grab my wool cloak. After brushing away some loose ash, I wrap it over myself and step to the door frame.

Dappled light spills on the frost-covered ground in front of me. High above, a myriad of stars covering the clear night sky shines through the barren forest canopy.

I suck icy air through my teeth, scorching my throat and filling my lungs with the breath of winter.

When I glance back, the lump of the kid's form is indistinguishable from the rest of the blackness hiding the floor.

Only death is inside.

Perturbed, I pause at the last thought. I'm not sure if I'm thinking of the cabin or myself.

The lifelessness consuming me isn't right. Although I can't imagine any other way of living, I know this isn't how I'm supposed to be. Determined but uncertain of how to change it, I close the door and march off to kill my final opponent.

FORTY-ONE

A RAUCOUS TONE from my newest collection of teammates rolls through the cafeteria. No casualties during a victorious scenario will do that for morale. Especially for a lowly bunch of sub-three-something sigmas.

I've witnessed this same victory celebration on more occasions than I care to remember.

From the empty husk of my emotions, I watch Jay, a former comedian, tell a brave tale about battling two samurai warriors with glee plastered on his pudgy face. As he speaks with exaggerated bravado, his nostrils flare and his hands make wild gestures, betraying his relief for still residing amongst the living. A middle-aged woman stuffed into a young rosy-cheeked body interrupts to add further details of her own Japanese inspired ordeals.

Except for me, everyone contributes to the glorious conversation while trying to conceal their innermost fears.

Because they don't realize they're statistically dead.

Even sitting in the center of the group, the gulf between myself and their camaraderie spans an infinite distance, their happiness stirring nothing inside me. Haiku, no matter how much I despise her, is correct. The Ten Sigma Program rewards individual achievement.

Teamwork is incidental to the final goal, and because of the nature of combat, the people surrounding me are only temporary.

But it seems wrong...

Everyone's focus shifts when I blow out a long breath. As an 8.63 sigma, the highest ranked participant they've seen and most likely ever will see, my every action is steeped in gravitas.

Rather than give another sign of melancholy, I pull my cheeks higher, forcing a smile into my expression.

Satisfied with my apparent approval, they return to their grand tales.

Without real-world memories or friends from my original group, I'm a shadow, a person only finding solace during the life and death fighting of the scenarios. While saving my closest friends from Syd was the best decision for everyone, I despise where that choice has led.

Vela's gone and who knows what happened to Walt or Suri.

Laughter spills from the team as a lanky woman, who is called either Jill or Jan, arrives at the table with ten blue pouches cradled in her arms. She tosses one to each of us.

Under the expectant gazes of the others, I punch my straw through the plastic. Again satisfied with the approval of the war-weary veteran, my temporary companions copy me and plunge their straws into the gloppy substance.

More smiles appear as everyone enjoys the psychosomatic food, their finest meals remembered amid their desperation to retain a fading past.

Bereft of real memories, I recall my best blue liquid inspired moment and take a sip. The aroma of bacon runs into my nostrils while the flavor of buttery waffles coats my tongue. The fake experience does nothing for my listless spirit.

Moans of pleasure cross the table. Judging from their placid expressions, everyone on the team is having a marvelous time.

For me, being a mindless drone and conforming with what is expected of every other ten sigma participant holds no appeal. Letting my food fantasy vanish, I swirl the tasteless gloop around my mouth, contemplating Syd's secret as I have for the past three meals.

I wonder...

The notion is dumb, but I need to do something to defy the overlords. Besides the possibility of death taking me at any moment, what would be the point of not sampling everything available?

I scrutinize the pouch resting between my fingers. If Syd was being honest, the blue liquid would be my path to get out of this lifeless existence. Although I have no reason to doubt his words or his erect penis, Suri despised him, wanting to know nothing of his secrets. And both Jock and Rick warned me long ago never to trust the plain-faced man.

I wish I could speak to them now.

An image of an admonishing Haiku pops into my head. If anything, her constant badgering has only inflamed my appetite for change.

Screw the little stalking avatar.

Taking a sip, I picture a man and woman copulating and focus.

The gelatinous liquid stays the same.

I haven't surpassed eight sigmas by giving up so easily. Letting the gloppy fluid slosh over my tongue, I reduce my focus to just the triangle around the male's private parts and suck a larger portion through the straw. I imagine a gorgeous man in the midst of ardent lust.

Although the unappealing texture in my mouth disappears, there are no fireworks.

Scrunching my face, I mount another attempt by picking out smaller, more sensual details.

More bland frustration.

Because the blue liquid worked for Syd, I know there must be something else, but everything I recall from the scenarios leads nowhere.

I huff. The others have half-empty bags. It's time to quit.

Or...

Although not in the scenarios, there were victory toasts. The man who performed them was killed in the dusty brownstones against the face-painting opponents. His name was Luke or Lou. I can't remember; it was too long ago.

But his description of the champagne was so perfect, I could taste the alcohol and feel the inebriation.

Leo!

I congratulate myself for remembering his name.

Leo nailed the five senses at the same time. All of touch, taste, smell, sight, and sound needed to be correct in order to get the most from the blue liquid.

I have to do the same.

What are the prevalent features of all five of the senses during sex?

Dim candlelight surrounds a handsome lover. Sensual scents from rose petals caress my nose. Silk sheets rustle under my back. The gentle, warm touch of his fingertips. Husky sounds of breathing. The flavor of a passionate kiss.

A salty taste runs over my tongue. Musky odors bleed into my nostrils. Faint grunts from exultations nuzzle my ears. The cozy feel of strong hands tingles my skin.

My body quivers as heat seeps into the junction of my thighs.

After so long, the sliver of emotion threatens to overwhelm me.

Pulling my knees together, I wince and shift uncomfortably on the plastic chair. In the crowded cafeteria in front of my newest teammates, I should stop. However, everyone else is lost in their liquid-fueled eating fantasies and I'm bordering on the throes of passion.

I need more.

What does sex taste like?

My tongue runs over his body. I imagine sweat and salt. My other senses add to the fantasy as I slip further into the moment. The wetness of a French kiss. The heat produced by writhing bodies. Heavier scents and deeper, more sensual flavors. My heart pumps faster while my breaths grow husky.

The warm buds of an orgasm form in my lower abdomen.

Gasping, I allow my knees to part but tighten my hands and tense my arms to stop my fingers from moving there. Staying in the fantasy and forgetting the bustle of the cafeteria, I stifle my amazement and suck another pool of the wonderful fluid into my mouth.

A man rolls on top of me and places himself between my legs. The nascent feelings of delight spread from my loins and build into a steepening wave of pleasure that threatens to engulf my being.

I shiver as he pushes into me.

Lost in ecstasy, I painfully bite my lip to stop from crying out.

A second passes before I realize blood has tainted the liquid with malevolence. Murder has its own distinct flavor. I've killed many in the scenarios, but before now, I never understood the wonders of ending a life.

My hands wrap around the throat of my fantasy lover. As my fingers tighten, raw emotions flood into my being. Murder gives more pleasure than sex. Hatred is better than love. Tighter, tighter, I squeeze, enjoying his wheezy breaths and bulging eyes. It's mesmerizing. When his breathing stops and his eyes glaze, my body shudders with joy.

No!

I slam my hands on the tabletop. The bag explodes between my fingers, sending a shower of thick blue droplets everywhere.

Wiping the liquid from their faces, my confused companions stare at me in silence. Then they raise their pouches to smash them too.

I face my palms toward them and thrust out my hands. "Don't."

"What's wrong?" Jay says in bewilderment.

"It's nothing." Standing and knocking my chair to the floor, I angrily wave for everyone to stay seated. Then ignoring their surprised expressions and the curious stares of the other teams, I pivot and leave the cafeteria.

When I get into the hallway, I stop and wipe strands of red hair and glops of blue liquid from my face, which ignites an odd sense of déjà vu.

Fighting the malevolence infecting my mouth, I force my fingers into my throat and retch, but nothing comes out.

The foul desires of the blue liquid won't go away.

I want more.

With renewed determination, I shove my fingers down my throat again, achieving the same results.

Rather than force my hand into my stomach, I settle for "Plan B" and take a few minutes to spit out the vileness.

Afterward, I press my forearms into my thighs, holding myself in a hunched position and using deep breaths to shake off my embarrassment. Attempting to have an orgasm while sitting in a bustling cafeteria was an awful idea.

And that was the best part of the experience.

While I've obliterated the wall separating me from my emotions, murder has infected my desires. I need to feel someone's life being extinguished in my hands. To watch the sparkles in my victim's eyes fade. Taking a life is better than sex.

If I give into it, I'll plow through the scenarios.

I rattle my head, struggling to force the craziness from my mind. The substance has more power than I imagined, corrupting even an act as beautiful as making love.

Although trying to do something like Syd was a stupid idea with predictably terrible results, I now understand his motivations. However, while he controlled the blue liquid, my single experience skirted the edge of insanity.

Sadly, I feel a bit of redemption for not telling Vela his secret.

Better to be dead than a monster.

I can't surrender to that fate. My mind protests but I concentrate on Suri and Walt and the good things from the virtual universe.

As the remembrances calm me, I straighten and gather in my surroundings.

Near the end of the hallway, the witch I met under the bowels of Home floats on her broom. Even though it's not a private place, I'm angry she's intruding on my private moment.

I march to confront her.

She speaks in a neutral voice as I approach. "While you can lose your life in the scenarios, here is where you can lose your soul."

Although I'm tempted to grab her as she performs the hand gesture and disappears, I watch in stony silence, troubled by her words.

Because you probably feel like Eve after she ate the apple.

FORTY-TWO

In the cavern of the opera-styled theater, the black and white motion picture flickers on the giant screen. The light-hearted romp seems familiar with the two lead actors performing a classic comedic routine, but I don't recall any of the details nor does it matter. I'm just glad the humorous movie lacks any sinister undertones.

My violent desires don't need any triggers.

Resisting the urge to wipe my tongue and spit, I clench my jaw and squeeze my lips closed with my fingers. Although my foray into Syd's universe of sex and violence crushed my lifeless state, six days have passed and the cloying thoughts of the blue liquid won't leave. Unlike normal emotions, they hang like a cloud, ever-present, malevolent, and constantly prodding me toward evil. In each scenario, with each kill, the joy of violence surges, threatening to overwhelm me. Only with a huge effort have I avoided slipping into the clutches of insanity.

While the audience erupts in hysterics at a punchline, I focus on one particular deep, rumbling laugh.

Sex on the other hand...

With a gentle twist, I clandestinely look three rows behind me. The exquisite man arrived with the last restocking of Home, and I'm disgusted with myself because, with the return of my libido, I've been stalking him for two days.

When he returns my covert glance, I sink into my seat, pushing my attention back to the entertainment.

The deep laugh rumbles at another sight gag.

Without the grounding from my memories, my moral compass remains adrift. While I think I'm a good person, I remember nothing to validate that claim. Besides being hard to kill and victorious in the scenarios, I'm not sure of what separates me from a sociopath. And now with the blue liquid pushing in the wrong direction...

Life can't be this bleak.

I gnaw on a fingernail, and closing my eyes, switch my thoughts to the first movie night with Suri and the rest of the team before our initial battle, which seems like ages ago.

Despite resolving to avoid making new friends, I miss my old ones. I hate the loneliness consuming my being.

Great warriors are lonely.

It's the first time I've viewed myself in that context, but the statement is accurate. Fighting alone is what I do and do well.

I release a soft sigh. Although my past is gone, somehow, I know I'm exactly where I never wanted to be.

When a hairy leg brushes against my knees, I open my eyes. The end credits scroll up the screen while the crowd streams into the aisles and exits up the inclined ramp.

After reorienting myself, I stand, feeling antsy to jump into a new scenario. Combat has sadly become my sole comfort activity.

Masculine fingers brush across my bicep as I step into the aisle. It's my stalking target, the gorgeous man with the deep laugh.

Afraid of igniting any dark desires, I avoid staring at his V-shaped body and take faster steps, elbowing into the middle of the slow-moving crowd. Irritated people, whom I consider mere fodder to be fed into the meat grinder of the scenarios, grumble as I rush under the ornate doorway and through the opulent lobby.

When the clean air of the sanctuary hits my face, I dash down the staircase. At the bottom, I stop, and clearing my head with quick breaths, fight to control the urges of the blue liquid.

The handsome man pauses next to me, his gorgeous eyes innocently meeting my gaze. Up close, he's more chiseled and sexier than I imagined. His perfect lips widen into a reassuring smile, reminding me of someone I've forgotten.

Before he can leave, I reach through my jumbled emotions and touch his arm.

Words are unnecessary and we remain motionless as the crowd files past, just two metaphorical ships passing in the night.

That's appealing.

More appealing is the prospect of any physical contact to get rid of the feelings of isolation. Although the rational part of my being warns of the danger, my yearnings are only one part blue liquid against ten parts loneliness and a hundred parts wanting a release that's unrelated to killing.

While the fantasy in the mess hall turned disastrous, I know that with a little willpower, I can make sex absolutely pleasurable and without a trace of violence.

After we're alone, I ask, "Do you find me attractive?"

Although he tilts his head like I've asked a trick question, his eyes wander from my face to my breasts as if studying a work of art.

A distant part of me wonders if I should be bashful.

I dismiss the thought. Nothing matters from my prior life; there is only the here and now. I stand taller, basking in the undivided attention.

After a small bow, he says in a rich voice, "You're the girl with the red mane of hair. Nobody is more divine."

Although spoken without vulgarity, the compliment is plenty for my mood. I grab his hand and drag him toward the museum. As we pass a tall iron lamp, I pull him off the path and march at a faster pace, the longing and anticipation in addition to my resentment at the virtual overlords driving my impatience.

Screw the witch and her warnings.

When we reach the museum, I force him into a dim rectangle sequestered between two parallel exhibit wings where the shadows from tall fern trees afford plenty of privacy.

After forcing him into a secluded corner under a resting overhang of ivy, I yank off my skimpy clothing and shove his wonderful body next to a barred window. Before he resists, I run my palms up his chest and jamming his back against the side of the metal bars, grab his head and force a passionate kiss on his lips.

With heavy pants, he responds as best as he can.

As my naked body writhes against him in the shadows, I push out my tongue and thrust it deep into his mouth. Struggling to breathe, he battles back as we desperately try to share an intimate moment.

At the height of the ferocious efforts, I feel only disappointment. On the inside, I'm wooden, even frigid. Although our bodies squirm and our lips twist with our tongues darting back and forth, the labored movements resemble those of cheap sex robots more than impassioned lovers.

Powered by my almost nine sigma level tenacity and my hatred at the entire virtual universe, I send my hands down his wonderfully sculpted body, taking care to caress his muscular pecs and six-pack abs. However, despite the motions being correct, our actions are performed analytically. Neither of us shows any involuntary throes of passion or uncontrolled fits of ecstasy. Nothing registers, not even the tiniest spark of desire.

When I arrive at his privates, he's flaccid.

I won't give up.

There has to be something more. I grab his arms and yank him from the wall. He yields to my brutality as I shove him to the manicured grass. After pulling his underwear to his thighs, I straddle his pelvis and push him flat, using my hand to stimulate him.

Nothing.

Frustrated, I drive myself onto his shriveled penis. When that fails, I grind back and forth in a frantic attempt to generate excitement.

Watching paint dry would be more fun.

My growing anger fuels the need for something more than the violence and death of the scenarios. With rough movements, I shift higher, rubbing my sex over his chest and proceeding until it's poised under his chin.

He shows his willingness with a grin.

Not requiring another hint, I move myself over his lips until only the top of his nose and forehead are visible and then press down, closing my eyes and searching for something arousing from my empty memories.

His tongue springs out.

I squirm to enhance the pleasures the act should generate. Seconds pass without kindling any passion. With exasperation, I command, "Push it in as far as it will go."

As he complies, I grind harder.

More nothing.

My anger bristles at the futility of the exercise, and I ram my pelvis into his face, plowing his head into the ground.

I want to punish him.

A muffled cry comes from between my legs, but he continues, his teeth cutting into my privates from my crude motions, making my inner thighs and his lips slippery with blood.

I gasp. The pain is amazing.

The buds of the orgasm that spread during my blue liquid fantasy reappear in my loins. There's no need to stop in this secluded setting. I embrace the ever-present cloud of dark emotions forcing its way into my thoughts. The pleasures that have been missing from my virtual life are coming.

Arching my back, I buck with as much force as I can muster.

In spite of the obvious discomfort, the man's tongue moves faster and deeper to match my excitement.

The joyful radiance expands from my sex and spreads into my pelvis and up to my pounding chest while the wonderfulness of murder rises from my throat.

A moan of delight leaves my mouth as I let go of my self-restraint. I peer downward, enjoying the sight of my undulations over his blood-stained face, never imagining the act could be so beautiful.

Between my rough thrusts, he struggles to suck in air while still pleasuring me.

That helplessness adds to the intoxication and drives me to wilder heights. My hands glide from my knees and hover over him. I gleefully slam them into his head and tussle his thick hair.

A muffled squeal escapes from his mouth as he squirms for breath.

The desperate gasps between my tightening thighs send me further into fantasy. Fingers squeezing his temples, I move my thumbs over his closed eyes and lick my lips in anticipation of pushing them through his eyeballs and into his brain. After he's dead, I can pull out his heart and drink his blood.

Murder is wonderful.

Muscles tensing across my body, my lungs holding in a giant breath, I let insanity fill my mind.

"What are you doing?"

The strange internal voice from the scenarios yanks me from the abyss. Jerking my hands away from killing my lover, I scream and then slam my palms on the soft ground.

The impact produces a disappointingly muffled sound.

Shivering, I force the foulness from my thoughts. This place is worse than a dysfunctional Garden of Eden. Death, hate, and violence taint everything. Even the simple act of making love is intertwined with the desire for murder, exactly the opposite of what it should be.

When my emotions calm, I lift myself off his face.

He gasps, sucking in a lungful of air.

I swing my leg over his body and stand.

Propping himself up with his elbows, he faces me. His rich voice sounds funny with a split lip. "Do you wish to continue?" he naively asks. "It seemed to be working for you."

Murder lingers in my mind. He's at 2.72 sigmas, and killing him would be so easy. I gnash my teeth, disgusted. Somehow, violence defines everything.

I've become precisely what I didn't want to be.

I spit onto the grass. "No," I say with vehemence.

He sits up, a confident smile spread over his face. "If you wish to attempt this again, I'll be willing. Or perhaps you can tell me the secret for enjoying sex?"

I wipe my mouth clean of spittle. "Have your avatar take care of that lip."

Without waiting for a response, I grab my clothing and march through the long shadows of the ferns, exiting the sequestered space.

As I near the path, a dismayed Haiku hovers in the yellow light of the wrought iron lamp.

Naked, and realizing that besides the nudity, my adventure must be plain from my grass-stained knees, flushed face, and blood smeared between my legs, I embrace my slut-walk and brush past her, readying myself for the inevitable tirade.

Silently, she floats alongside me with her eyes downcast.

After a few annoyed steps, I turn and say in a louder voice than I intend, "What?"

She speaks from disappointment. "Certain activities aren't suitable for you."

While I'm surprised she doesn't yell in anger or indignation, I understand exactly what the cryptic statement means. "I'm shocked you care so much for my virtue."

For a fleeting instant, a deepness lurks in her computer-generated eyes, and I think she's going to sigh.

She opts for her usual happy smile. "To be a successful member of this program, please focus on performing well in the scenarios."

Spoken like a scout leader. I wonder if I was in one of those organizations then shake my head. Those memories are gone. "Whatever I do in my own time is none of your business."

Her smile flattens as her silver eyes blink.

My hands ball into fists. "Or do you want to make it your business?"

We both know the implied threat is pointless, and the little avatar holds her ground.

"I merely stress that there are certain emotional boundaries from where there is no return."

The frustration seeping into her voice causes an odd satisfaction within me. I frown at my pettiness. "Unless you have something specific to say, leave."

Her eyes lose focus as she makes pouty lips. Then waving her hand, the air pops and I'm alone.

Being the victor by retaining possession of the battlefield does nothing to lift my mood. After putting the skimpy garments back on, I trudge toward the barracks, my thoughts swirling in a dark cloud, upset with the loss of my past, angry with being so susceptible to the liquid, and frustrated from my unfulfilled desires.

I hate the virtual overlords.

By the time I get in sight of the domed building, I'm no closer to dispelling my anger.

It's tempting to drift into the darkness of the blue liquid and enjoy the killing. It'll make the time pass much faster and I'll be better at the scenarios.

But what will remain if I fall to such base desires? A murderer addicted to dispensing death? A person like Syd, worshiping at the altar of evil?

I won't live that way.

Sex, violence, Haiku, and the virtual overlords, none of them have any importance. Even the worse things Haiku keeps mentioning. I only need to survive a bit longer. A little more combat. A few more scenarios. My sole focus will be on the important task of getting out of the virtual universe.

I grimace. It was the advice Suri gave me. Don't care about anyone else, concentrate on reaching ten sigmas. Just like I was when I listened to the boy in the icy cabin whose parents died in the real-world riots.

That's not acceptable either.

At the entrance of the barracks, the leprechaun floats, his eyes full of resentment as they track me.

His demeanor strikes the exact wrong chord in my malice-laden mind. "What do you want?" I yell.

He stays silent but narrows his eyes and scrunches his face into a hate-filled expression.

As his hand rises to perform the leave gesture, my anger explodes through my frustrations and self-loathing. I dive and grab him as he pops away.

The world vanishes.

FORTY-THREE

Biting cold stings my skin, but consumed by hatred, I rush down an endless tunnel in a myopic pursuit of the leprechaun, who represents the embodiment of everything I find wrong about the virtual universe. Besides the violent character of the Ten Sigma Program, I'm sick of Haiku and the other weird little avatars with their clandestine glares and overtly hostile expressions. And that's not even mentioning all the riddles.

I want answers.

Faint vibrations emanate from my tissues as I move faster. However, despite my hurried pace, he increases his lead. His flying form shrinks in the distance, and his grass scent lessens with each of my plodding steps.

It's like being mired in quicksand.

Worse, my body is betraying me. A growing nausea clutches at my insides, and as the debilitating feeling spreads throughout my being, my flesh and skin soften while my bones become rubbery.

The passageway abruptly spills into a vast space, and my wobbly self tumbles into a strange buoyant medium.

There is no trace of the leprechaun.

When I nibble on a fingernail, my teeth only find mush.

What have I gotten myself into?

Terrified, I search the surroundings for anything recognizable. Although boundaries define the expanse, no solid walls exist. Projected as shades throughout the area are frightening, evil caricatures of people. Their malice washes over me, stomping my anger into insignificance.

As I fight the urge to curl into a mass of puddling flesh, a familiarity tickles my distorted senses. I can't fathom how but things feel similar to when I followed Syd under the bowels of Home.

Even though there's no hint of his presence, I know that somehow this incomprehensible mess is connected to the mystery of Syd.

Something I was warned against pursuing.

Sobered by the rational thought, I hunt for an escape from the crazy place.

Ripples in the medium brush through me.

I dive away, doing a motion that's not quite running or swimming, and speeding as fast as my disintegrating body can move.

After slicing between a couple of projections that quake with sadistic humor at my predicament, I plow through an invisible barrier, falling into a bright, infinite space that dwarfs anything I thought could be imagined.

What in all hell have I gotten myself into?

I struggle to draw calming breaths to combat my growing fear. After a few attempts, I realize I don't have any lungs. What's worse is that I don't appear to have a heart either.

Outside of the nebulous substance pretending to be my body, no colors exist, nor is anything black and white. The medium shakes from titanic indeterminate forms treading on nearby billowing clouds.

While everything near is out of focus, further away—above, below, front, back, and to each side—are dots like an array of stars, each representing one of an infinite number of maps for the different scenarios and sanctuaries floating at an infinite distance.

That's too many infinities to contemplate.

The surroundings quiver as I rattle my head, searching for a logical explanation.

All virtual environments are created from software and have laws subject solely to the whims of their designers. I'm in a place far beyond Home—someplace exceeding the bounds of my reality and a place I shouldn't be.

My vision isn't blurry; my entire body is blurry. While not ethereal, my substance resembles nothing of gas, liquid, or solid. In this universe, my abilities and training have no value.

This is the home of virtual overlords. The idea makes sense and I wonder why it's taken so long to arrive at this obvious answer. Perhaps it's because my mind is made from the same indescribable mush as the rest of my body and my reasoning is impaired.

Something huge bumps against me. While I quiver, the being wanders past, oblivious to my puny presence. As it recedes, I notice others approaching.

Besides my fear, a sickly concern rises in me. If this is the virtual version of heaven, given the dysfunctional nature of everything else, I'm in big trouble. I'm unsure of how to escape from this mess or where I should even begin looking.

However, anywhere seems better than my current position. I spin, focusing my smeared eyesight through the thin swaths of white drifting nearby, and head in the quietest direction along the path providing the least resistance. If I can avoid meeting anyone, I'll consider myself fortunate.

As I travel, none of the infinitely far away dots move closer, but other sensations pass through me. In shadows between the streaky clouds, there are people. Why are they here?

I try to blink, but my current form comes without eyelids.

More objects of varying size and intensity wander nearby.

A wrinkle in the surroundings rumbles through my form. The other beings are close.

Afraid to be discovered, I retreat as dizziness overcomes my thoughts. Despite my nonexistent lungs, my body still needs oxygen. With the gigantic forms of the virtual overlords looming close, I can only wobble helplessly.

From next to the spot where my ear should be, an unmistakably feminine voice whispers. "How did you get here?"

"I touched that leprechaun when he disappeared."

"You've made a dreadful mistake. I told you to follow the rules."

It's the witch avatar.

"No kidding. I'm sick," I say, slurring each word into the next.

"Yes, you don't belong here. Your body can't survive in this environment. We need to get you back to where you belong before anyone notices."

An invisible force grabs my form, whipping me through countless mists. As I streak through the strange universe, tiny against the backdrop of infinity, the true nature of my insignificance isn't lost on me.

In the Ten Sigma Program, the virtual overlords can't be defeated. It was ridiculous to even try to be rebellious. Sex, trying to keep my memories, all were futile attempts to stop their limitless and unrelenting power. Suri was right. The only way to rebel is to win and get out of their grasp. If I'm lucky, with a modicum of my soul intact.

That can be my only revenge.

"You are a player in something far larger than yourself," she chides.

Given the nature of my thoughts, I laugh.

"What is this place?"

"Be quiet. You have enemies here."

Full of nausea, my mind whirls at the implications. They're part of the worse things, the face-painters. But the turbulence buffeting my body interrupts the train of logic. Not sure what would happen if I vomit, I force my energy to maintain control of myself as the mists speed past and we travel at greater and greater speeds.

A single dot grows in the distance. Although it radiates a familiarity, like everything else, the details become more unfocused as we near.

The witch says, "I believe you're safe."

"How do you know?"

"I don't with any certainty. But you better hope nobody noticed you."

"Why?"

"Because then there will be consequences. Remember, I told you, if you bend the rules, they can be bent against you too."

"Who are you?"

There is no answer.

Solid again, I lie flat on my mattress staring at the top bunk. The world is in focus. Air fills my lungs and my heart pounds in my chest.

I move my hands and run them over my healthy body, happy to be back in my perfect form.

The whole experience was so alien it must have been a dream.

"If not, there will be consequences."

Before I can ponder the meaning of the faint words, the entire thought evaporates.

"The whole thing was a dream," I whisper to myself.

I hope.

FORTY-FOUR

My CELEBRATORY BATTLE after breaking the nine sigma level starts under brilliant sunshine with an arid breeze brushing fine particles past my face.

I shade my eyes.

The map is a parched, hilly terrain sprinkled with patches of dull green flora and crossed by tall berms of earth packed in wooden frames. On each hilltop stands a defense structure resembling a log tower constructed from cut timber. Here and there, a lonely pool of blue water under a wide-topped acacia tree interrupts the glittering sand carpeting the low-lying areas.

Another tranquil place to boost my sigma score.

A baggy robe with a loose hood rests over my body. It's mostly white and woven from a coarse material. A pair of plastic goggles strapped over my eyes and a bandanna covering my mouth protect against the dust. Around my waist, a cinched gray sash holds a wide scimitar along with a sheathed dagger. Soft-soled slippers nestled over my feet complete the outfit.

It is desert garb designed for the modern day pirate.

Our mission is to defend a flag planted at the junction of two ramparts in a shallow valley below my position.

Although nothing threatens, the familiar spiders tap dance over my nape.

There are ramifications. This will be a disaster.

Troubled by the strange premonition, I survey the features of the landscape, but besides the usual map idiosyncrasies and scenario details, everything is normal.

My teammates shuffle their feet in the sand, awaiting my instructions.

Deciding not to be indecisive, I signal to meet with the four other team leaders.

As the teams trickle toward me, my blue-liquid-freed emotions spew out a stream of happiness. Instead of fighting it, I rejoice in the long-lost feeling as a familiar figure runs to me. While part of me is stunned he's still breathing, all of me is ecstatic. I wrap my arms around him and whirl in a circle. "Walt," I scream.

"Stop squeezing so hard, I can't breathe." He giggles, a truly strange sound to hear before a battle.

The rest of my team sends us dubious glances.

What? Can't I be happy?

Apparently not. I surrender to their dour mood and put the teen down. Then pulling my bandanna under my chin, I force aside the excitement and assume a stately pose. "How have you been?"

His wide eyes stare as if I might be a mirage. After he catches his breath, a smile lights up his face. "Not bad. I'm surprised to see you. I didn't think I'd get this far."

That makes two of us.

"You took Rick's training to heart," I say before the moment becomes awkward.

"I'm only a 4.6. I've got a long way to go."

While his low score indicates a lack of risk-taking, to survive as long as he has, he's certainly had to have more than his share of luck. But he'll need more than good fortune to reach ten sigmas. For an instant, I consider mentioning the secret of the blue liquid. However, when I weigh that against the near-disastrous consequences of my foray into its clutches, and its still hovering presence, I say with a straight face, "You'll get there."

"Well, it looks like we're having a reunion," says the familiar voice of a man owning a staggering 9.82 sigma score.

My warm feelings for Walt evaporate, reinforcing the temporary nature of anything scenario-related.

"Hello, Syd."

The plain-faced man joins us, holding his fist out to Walt. The teen removes his eyes from me and sheepishly completes the fist bump.

After Syd pulls back his hand, he faces me. "Brin. It's wonderful to be in your company again. You seem to be doing well."

The politeness is chilling. I expected a harsh greeting after our last parting. "I've been doing fine, Syd," I reply, omitting the suspicions from my voice.

A woman, pale but attractive with dark eyes and sporting streaks of red in her long, Goth-like hair, sexily wraps her arms around him. "Is this her?" she asks with a hungry stare.

"Brin, meet Belle, my second," Syd says in his gentleman persona. When another pretty girl with a narrow face attaches herself to the couple, he adds, "And Syrin, my other partner."

"And so much more," Syrin purrs as she gathers me in with leering eyes. "I love her hair, and she's quite fetching."

Belle chimes in, "Although not as beautiful as you said she was."

I ignore the catty remark, maintaining a cool gaze as the other four men and three women of his team approach in silence. While none of them look exceptional, they are not in the least intimidated by my sigma score and project an indescribable confidence into their arrogant postures. And underneath each of them lurks the blue liquid's dark insanity.

What I would have become if I had stayed with Syd.

In their presence, the ever-present cloud of evil pushing at the edge of my thoughts calls for me to join them.

Clenching my jaw, I shove the malevolence away. The horrible temptations won't be a part of my existence.

Syd breaks the tension with a chivalrous grin then makes quick introductions. Unlike my teammates, I remember each of their names. And unlike everyone else, they throw appraising stares at my body.

Not giving a damn one way or the other about their attention, I hold my ground with an indifferent expression.

However, Walt and the others shy away from our passive-aggressive standoff.

Syd says, "Come, Brin, let's meet with the team leaders and formulate a plan."

I do a double take. While Syd caring is out of character, Syd strategizing is really out of character.

He smiles. "I've evolved since we were last together."

Belle shoots him a glare.

From the glint in his eyes, I know he's imagining the failed sex act between the two of us succeeding, and I want to scrape the skin from my body.

"Fine," I say. "Let's do this as fast as possible." Even if it would be great to catch up with Walt, I'm not spending an extra minute here.

Despite Syd's charming words, I most certainly do not trust him. He caused the death of my friends, and I broke up the team because of him.

However, his presence is comforting because it explains my unease. As long as I don't let him screw me or anyone else over, everything should be okay.

Hopefully…

———

Under the broken shade of a watchtower, Syd and I gather with the other three leaders.

The last one to join us, a dark complexioned 4.23 sigma, pulls off her bandanna, revealing a mouth gaping in shock. As her eyes dart between Syd and myself, she says, "Never thought I'd see one let alone two nines!"

"This should be an easy scenario," adds a lanky man with a 3.1 score.

Don't be so sure.

Maintaining the gentleman persona, Syd says, "The pleasure is all ours, isn't it, Brin?"

I stupidly nod, struggling not to roll my eyes. While I understand everything about Syd and his possible treachery, I have no way of explaining this to the others in the few minutes before the battle starts.

"You can if you want to sound paranoid," my annoying internal voice chimes.

To prevent my hand from smacking my head, I tighten my lips and let my eyes roll.

The 4.23 sigma sends a puzzled glance.

Syd speaks, saving me from having to make an embarrassing explanation. "The best approach is for me to lead my team on a killing mission outside the perimeter while everyone else remains on guard."

It takes a moment for the others to override their respect for Syd's sigma score.

"The victory condition is the flag. Wasting resources hunting for them doesn't make any sense," the 4.23 sigma protests. "They have to come to us, and without projectile weapons, we can mass to meet them."

The other two leaders nod vigorously in support.

"Nonsense," Syd says to more groans of disapproval.

While their tactical assessment is correct, my opinion differs. I'm encouraged because the lack of sophistication means Syd hasn't really changed, and if he and his people are outside the perimeter defense, he can't betray anyone else.

Before the argument gets heated, I raise my hand and say, "It's an unorthodox plan, but Syd has more knowledge than we do, so this is for the best."

I maintain a straight face to their incredulous stares because technically, the different parts of the statement are truthful.

Unconvinced by the tenuous logic, the 4.23 shakes her head. "But—"

"We'll make this work," I say with as much confidence as I can muster.

An awkward moment passes before she replies, "I guess if you made it past nine sigmas, you must know what you're doing."

With tight frowns, the other two leaders begrudgingly follow with their agreement.

If they only knew Syd like I know Syd.

Yanking out his sword, Syd smiles, his dark eyes gleaming with anticipation. The bladed weapons ensure the killing will be face-to-face, perhaps the type of combat he loves most. My heart races at the remembrance of fighting him during the training session.

"Well, that settles that," Syd says. His gentleman persona vanishes as he offers a twisted smile. "Good luck to everyone."

I remain in contemplation as the others respond with good lucks of their own.

As Syd rejoins his waiting team, Syrin casts a final appraising leer while Belle uses one corner of her mouth to send me a half smirk.

While my skin crawls, I return a confident smile.

They're all just creepy extensions of Syd.

Syd marches his team away with Belle and Syrin somehow inflecting sexy strides through the puffiness of their desert garb.

Everybody relaxes when the strange people disappear behind a curving berm.

I'm not the only one with uneasy thoughts.

Since the highest remaining sigma score belongs to me, I direct the other three teams to guard thirds while holding my team in reserve. It should be a flexible enough plan to handle any contingency from the opposition during the battle.

As the desert-clad figures disperse behind the berms and scattered dark green flora around our flag, I rub my neck. Something is still bothering me.

Then the enemy attacks and everything is put on the back-burner as I shift my concentration solely to defense.

———

As the scenario progresses, my hands get metaphorically full. Like in the swamp where Jock and Ally died, the opposing leaders are formidable, combining incisive attacks, clever feints, and diabolical ambushes to create a gigantic crap sandwich.

The problem is the stupid map and weapons. Because the enemy only needs to touch our flag and we can't shoot them, we have to defend in depth. This faulty strategy allows them to gather in strength and destroy us in pieces, and I've had to use every bit of my skill to stay one step ahead of disaster. My concentration on staying alive and not losing has been so complete, it's even drowned out the cries from the ever-present cloud of the blue liquid.

While I'm intact, only losing my goggles and having huge swathes of blood staining my white outfit from several desperate fights, the scenario has savaged the rest of my side. The other three leaders are long gone, and only a few exhausted stragglers remain.

Mercifully, although he's solely alive because of my best efforts, Walt crouches near me, his clothing bloodied and torn, but none the worse for wear. While I can't drag him to ten sigmas, and still don't believe he's survived this long, the least I can do is get him through the remainder of this battle.

On the other hand, similar to most scenarios, the opposing side has taken a beating during the ferocious fighting too. Especially from me.

I pull down my bandanna. "Where in the hell is Syd? Having a picnic?"

Walt responds to the rhetorical question with a nervous shrug. Of course, he doesn't know, and of course, he wants to give Syd the benefit of the doubt because he naively believes the best in everyone.

However, as an adult with firsthand experience, I'm free to think the worst of my blue liquid tainted former teammate. Without his team, the enemy outnumbers us five to four. I haven't seen anything from them since the fighting started, but I'm sure they aren't dead, and, worse, they've contributed nothing. We're being completely screwed by their inaction.

I roll my eyes to the blue dome. Escape is so close.

Wishes don't win scenarios.

Grinding my teeth in frustration, I listen to distant clangs of heavy scimitars, my over nine sigma experience warning that the fighting is reaching a climax. From opposite our flag, a swirling battle rages near a wooden defense tower. Other sharp noises come from my right, drawing attention to a huge cloud of dust rising over a sharply crested hill.

Both are decoys.

After a day facing these opponents, I finally understand their strategy. Both signs of obvious strength lack decisive action. No danger is coming from either threat.

Their plan is to sneak a single person to the flag from the tranquil part of the map.

For the hundredth time, I curse at Syd. This scenario should already be won.

I point at a wide earthwork slightly taller than myself, which curves along the rear of our position, and most importantly, rests in a quiet area opposite the fighting. "Let's go this way."

Walt glances behind us. "Isn't the fight over there?"

"That's a diversion. The breach point will be near that berm."

"I don't understand."

"There isn't time to explain, just trust me," I say with urgency.

After he nods, I lead him away from the sounds of clashing swords. Crouched and with careful steps, we wend our way down a shallow slope and around the twisted trunk of a huge acacia tree. After we leave the broad shadow of its flat crown, I increase the pace, hustling over the damp sand skirting a pool of water.

With our soft shoes silent, we sprint past some bodies and to a collapsed portion of the earthwork. I scramble up the crumbling dirt with my hands grabbing at the exposed wooden frame.

When Walt follows, his feet slip while his arms flail and I have to reach past my ankles to drag him the final way to the top.

After we flatten ourselves on the three-meter wide surface, we peer over the wooden lip and wait.

Our timing is none too soon. A moment later, a female form clad in a dark gray version of my pirate outfit approaches.

I'm right!

As she disappears from view under the rim of the embankment, I slither forward and raise my head.

Situated at the edge of my vision, the lithe figure hesitates against the wall of dirt. Her movements are strangely familiar, but her face is buried under the bandanna and shrouded by the loose hood.

After taking a quick survey, she sneaks away to reach our flag.

A chill runs up my spine.

"Brin," Walt says, his goggles magnifying the terror in his eyes.

I finish the sentence for him. "It's Suri."

FORTY-FIVE

THERE WILL BE REPERCUSSIONS.

I don't understand why the words won't stay away.

"What do we do?" Walt says.

Panicked thoughts flood into my mind as I push him back and down the crumbling slope. While I desperately search for a solution, my heart leaps into my throat and my breaths shorten. In our last meeting, Suri ended our friendship for the good of both of us, but she's still the person closest to me in this crazy place. If I kill her, the scenario will end, but can I live with myself? Unlike my real world memories, there are no guarantees I'll ever forget anything I've done in the virtual universe. Certainly to this point, it hasn't happened.

"Brin?"

Through taut lips, I reply, "We're not killing her."

"You're going to let Syd do it?"

"No, that's not what I mean."

"Then how do we end this scenario?"

I look to the blue dome. The vast distance to the real world seems further away than ever. "We let her win."

The idea sounds worse leaving my mouth than it did in my head.

"Brin," Walt pleads. "Think about what you're saying. You're almost out of here. I love Suri, but you'll be sending everyone to level zero."

"But with more experience, coming back will be easier. We'll have a chance that Suri doesn't, not against Syd's super-team and not against me. She'll die unless we let her win."

He frowns, knowing my reply is truthful. "I'm not that good."

It kills me but he's right. I wrestle in my mind before blowing out a sigh.

"Syd taught me a secret you can use to get out of here. When you drink the blue liquid in the cafeteria, imagine the taste of murder and you'll become a better fighter like him."

While I hope I haven't made anything worse, I can't condemn Walt to death either.

"What about the others on our side?"

"Everyone else is dead or less than a three. This is a small step backward. Except for Syd's team. You saw them. They'll need to take their chances like everyone else."

The teen bites his lip, his posture shrinking.

"To win this scenario, we need to kill the other team. That means Suri has to die. Is this what you want?"

He shakes his head. "What do you need me to do?"

"Make Syd and his teammates stay away from the area. I'll get her around the guards and to the flag." I put my hand on his shoulder. "Be brave and do this."

"Okay, Brin, I trust you believe you know what you're doing."

The response is a bit strange, but we need to act now. "Go, there isn't much time."

After quickly nodding, he leaps down the incline and rushes away.

The hasty plan is full of terrible logic, but I don't know what else to do. Suri's death at my hands would rob me of any humanity I have left.

I dash after her, hoping I don't change my mind and everything turns out for the best.

———

Implementing the other half of my impulsive plan will be harder than convincing Walt. I have to grab Suri without harm to either of us and get her safely to the flag.

Improvisation isn't my strength and anxiety fills my thoughts. Things are happening too quickly, but I can't let her die.

"This is a terrible idea, and I'm having nothing to do with it," says the strange voice inside my head.

"Shut up."

I already feel queasy enough without internal me eroding my resolve.

The berm curves outward and away from the flag, affording me a precious minute to find another alternative as I catch up. While I run, my mind speeds into overdrive, searching through nonexistent alternatives. When Suri reaches the end of the wall and prepares to race for the flag, I'm not surprised when nothing offers itself.

My trepidations mount as I sprint over the remaining distance to the stealthy form, the brittle earth crunching under my heavy steps. The thudding approach is far too conspicuous and when I leap, she turns.

Her sword flashes in the sunlight and in midair, I yank out my own to block her swing.

The two blades meet with a clang, then I roll to the side, dodging a riposte. Loud crescendos of swordplay aren't part of my hastily-conceived plan.

Before she can launch another attack, I jump to my feet and yank back my hood. "Suri, it's me."

A moment passes before the surprise in her eyes fades into recognition. "Brin? Oh, no," she laments, sinking to her knees.

Suspiciously, I say, "You ended our friendship."

She pulls off her bandanna. "I said that so you would move past breaking up the team and concentrate on surviving the program."

"Get up," I say, lowering my sword.

She tosses aside her weapons. "Please hurry and finish it."

"Stop acting like an ass, Suri."

"I won't fight you."

"That makes two of us. But Syd's here too, and he and his team won't have any problems hacking you into little shreds. You're going to lose."

She releases a heavy sigh. "What do you want to do?"

"I'll get you around the guards and to the flag."

"I can't allow you to do that. Not for me."

"That's where you're wrong. I have to do this for myself. Not for anyone else." When she doesn't reply, I add, "This isn't bragging, but I'm better equipped to reach ten sigmas than you. We both know it's true."

Despite the situation, I see she wants to make a joke, but thankfully, she holds off. "Even with more skill, you might not return to this level."

I force a grin. Going to zero and returning will be virtually impossible. "Don't worry, I'll make it."

The sounds of fighting dim.

"Do you hear that?" I say. "That's the last of your team dying. We have to move, now."

"I'll owe you big time."

"Yes, you will. When we're sitting in the real world, you'll be buying the first and second round of drinks."

"Okay, but I hate doing this."

"We'll send Syd and his people to level zero, which at least is a good thing."

A genuine smile crosses her face. "Let's go before I change my mind."

Me too.

I lead and guide her past an acacia tree and a shimmering pond instead of following the direct route. Although time-consuming, the serpentine path allows us to get behind the guards.

With nothing further to say, we move in silence. But with each step I take in Suri's company, my conviction for the crazy plan strengthens.

Finally, I understand. The length of time Rick and then I held the original team together against all odds allowed friendships to form that should have been impossible given the nature of this program. And the overlords couldn't erase those feelings because they're a part of the fighters we've become. As long as I keep true to my friends, nothing can harm my humanity.

Although I'll be heading back to level zero, for the first time since the loss of my memories, my moral compass is pointing in the right direction. After so much emptiness followed by the misguided emotions of the blue liquid, the sparks of life flooding into my being feel wonderful.

My footsteps lighten.

It's good to care again.

As we leave the wet dirt surrounding the pond, Suri's strides force me to move at a faster pace than I'd like. She's serious about getting it done quickly. I want to slow her down, but I'm more afraid she'll change her mind.

I grit my teeth. There are risks with whatever we do.

When the flag comes into view, I hesitate, rubbing my neck.

Instead of waiting, Suri runs to the goal.

We need caution, not speed. I sprint after her, struggling to close the distance and trying not to holler.

Sand sprays as a huge form erupts from the ground and grabs at her legs. It's Mick, the largest of Syd's team.

I fling my dagger at him, the blade catching perfectly in his neck. An irrational happiness passes over me as he falls.

Another dagger hisses through the air and hits Suri's leg, and she tumbles to the ground.

Footsteps rush from behind me.

As I roll away from the ambush, two people rise from the sand and grab at my legs. I lash out with kicks and twist myself free from an arm lock.

Before I can regain my balance, a leaping form drives a stomp kick into my side, bruising several ribs. I groan in pain. But I have to reach Suri who is buried under a pile of attackers.

Another fist flies at my face.

I duck but a painful elbow jams into my kidney. I slam my head back and cartilage breaks.

As I crawl forward, someone else, heavier, kicks me in the stomach. I roll onto my side, pain radiating from my bruised ribs.

More people grab me, pinning my arms behind my back.

"Well, what do we have here?" Belle whispers in my ear.

Rough hands push my face into the hot sand.

Blowing out a dust-laden breath, I twist my head while futilely struggling against the many bodies restraining me.

Two people step forward and grab a battered Suri and drag her from the flag.

"I told you I hated this plan. It's everything you're not good at," says internal me.

"Shut up."

Belle and her companions haul me upright, careful to keep my arms immobilized.

I shiver. Their faces are painted in various blood designs.

They're part of the worse things.

Belle leans into my vision, circles of red surrounding her eyes. "Syd will want you for himself, but we can have fun with your friend."

I scream as the people pound Suri with their fists and rip her clothing to shreds. When she's naked, they use the strips of her outfit to bind her arms and legs. Then trussed up like an animal for slaughter, they toss her at my feet.

The crowd parts for Syd.

When I see Walt walking next to him, my heart breaks.

As the teen approaches with tentative strides, I understand where happiness clouded my judgment. The lengthy stares, the unblinking eyes. Walt has been using the blue liquid, which is why he's survived for so long. Syd must have taken the training part with him seriously enough to reveal the secret.

Syd stops in front of me and removes his goggles and pulls down his bandanna.

"You killed Mick, one of your own side," he says with a smile. "That requires a consequence."

"Go to hell."

He delivers a backhand across my cheek and before I can straighten, follows with a punch into my body.

My injured ribs scream in agony.

With a mysterious smirk, he steps backward.

Although terrified of what's coming, I'm more ashamed of my plan failing and losing to Syd.

"Just finish it," I say to end Suri's suffering.

"No, we won't be killing her for at least a little while. First, we're going to teach you a little lesson," Syd says as he draws his dagger and slices my clothing.

FORTY-SIX

COVERED by the shade of the rampart, I struggle from my knees against the unbreakable grips of Syd's people. Ragged breaths spew through my clenched teeth while my bruised ribs cry with dull waves of pain. Except for my bra and panties, my clothing lies in tatters over the surrounding sand.

Suri writhes, the blood from many cuts flowing down her body.

I jerk my shoulders against the grasping hands and receive an agonizing kick to my ribs. Although I force back whimpers, my grimace draws a smile from Syd.

He turns his attention to Suri and runs his fingers down the blood covering her back, slowly tracing a pattern to her thighs.

Both Belle and Syrin chuckle at her cries of disgust.

After painting a rendition of some ancient god on his face, Syd gazes with a strange reverence to the blue dome, listening to something no one can see.

When the odd communion finishes, he stands and points at me. "No switching sides, Brin."

Without any snarky retorts available, I only return a glare to the truthful accusation.

He raises his hands to his people. "This woman is a traitor to our cause, and we shall do everything to her that we desire."

The statement garners many nods of approval. Belle kneels, stroking my hair. "So thick, so luxurious."

Syd walks to us. "I've been studying anatomy with my prisoners," he says with calm detachment. "It's amazing what you can learn by taking time to enjoy the fruits of the scenarios. I'd like to teach you a few of the finer points of torture."

I unclench my jaw long enough to say, "That's okay."

His dagger glints as he yanks it out. Then he steps into the shadow and uses it to tap his cheek. "I insist."

"Syd, just end this," Suri mumbles from the ground.

The plain-faced man rolls his eyes. "Gag the bitch."

Syrin grabs Suri and places a dagger over her throat. "I can do better than that."

Syd twists his head, saying with exasperation, "She's the last one. The scenario's over if you kill her."

Flushing from embarrassment, Syrin shoves a ball of cloth between Suri's lips then unwraps her sash and binds it over her mouth.

Syd fixes his attention on me. "I was very fond of you. We should have been partners in everything, but you broke your word."

For unnecessary emphasis, Belle glares from behind him.

I spit. "You were trying to get everyone except us killed."

He shrugs. "They were going to die, anyway."

"You said you would save them—who's lying?"

"Within reason, I would have done my best. However, no matter what was going to happen, they were going to die."

Ugh.

While I hate the idiotic circular arguments with Haiku, this is worse. "Just get on with it."

With a steady gaze coming from behind the crazy war paint, Syd says, "I've discovered a way to cut the nerves of your limbs without damaging the arteries. I'll have you flopping around in no time."

From the scenarios and our time in the sanctuary, I know Syd perhaps better than anyone in this universe, and he means every word. Despite my training and experiences, the loss of body control terrifies me. I twist and pull, struggling with everything I have, but only succeed in amusing the sadistic faces crowding behind Syd.

The tip of his dagger trails down my shoulder to the inside of my right arm.

I flinch.

"Careful, if you squirm too much, I might cut something I shouldn't. That would be harmful to my pleasure."

My scowl only excites the glow in his eyes.

There is a sharp pinch, and a splash of blood drips on the blade. The arm goes numb. Terrified, I thrash my body, but none of the muscles below my right shoulder will respond to my desperate commands.

A sting touches the inner part of my left arm, which fails too.

Despite trying to remain stoic, a shriek of terror leaves my throat.

When Syd leans over to slice inside my thighs, I thrust out with a knee.

"Cut her spine," says Syrin with a hungry grin spread on her narrow face.

"No, that's too much, I want her to enjoy certain things," Syd replies, scraping the tip of his dagger down the triangle of my panties.

"Let me do it, I've been practicing," Belle says.

Syd nods to her and steps away.

Rough hands yank me backward as my feet and legs are pulled apart. Belle sinks between my knees.

When she dips her head and kisses the material covering my privates, I snarl. Her dagger runs along the inside of my thigh, then my left leg goes numb.

I cry out more from the idea than any actual suffering. A moment later, the feeling leaves my other leg. Helpless, I gasp. Only my torso can move.

Belle stands and gives Syd a steamy kiss.

"That's perfect," he says with appreciation.

The sky rises above my head as I'm shoved flat to the ground. My wriggling only adds to the terror. Although there is minimal pain, the limitations are worse than any wound, surpassing even when my intestines were spilled over the street and the violet-eyed girl saved me.

Syd's people leer, making lewd comments, as they remove their clothing. Some even have blood symbols painted down their chests and over their genitals.

Thinking of the bizarre things they must have been performing on Suri's team, I tense my lips into a line to prevent my panic from exploding.

Syd kneels and brings his blood-decorated face close to mine. His breath rolls past as he speaks. "We perform a ritual to bind ourselves to the thoughts of the blue liquid. Don't you wish you had married me when you had the chance?"

"You're insane," I sputter.

A hunched Walt stands behind the crowd, trembling.

Syd follows my stare. "Walt, you want to be the first?"

The teen edges backward.

"Oh, don't worry. Once you've combined sex with violence, you won't be so scared. Or impotent."

Everyone laughs at the crude joke.

Syd returns his attention to me and slices away my remaining garments with deft flicks.

A whimper comes from Walt while more snickers fill the air.

I twist my head when Syd plants a sloppy kiss on my lips.

The part of my body that can still move trembles as his dagger scrapes past my navel and stops between my legs.

One of Syd's men stomps forward, removing his underwear. I'm not surprised to see him erect. "This will be fun."

Syrin yanks out her dagger. "Leave something for my turn."

The tallest one, peeking above the tops of the others, yells in a deep voice, "Wow. I've never seen anything that sweet. I can't wait to get into her."

Instantly, Syd leaps to his feet and wades into the crowd. Bodies tumble amid loud smacks and yelps of pain while those lucky enough to escape cower from his wrath. Syd is far more powerful than the last time we met.

His voice rises over the terror. "This one is mine. We'll use her body for the ritual, and everyone will have a taste. But, any sex is for my pleasure alone. Understood?"

Belle pushes to a knee and rubs her cheek, saying, "She betrayed us and wanted to send us back to zero."

"And she'll suffer," Syd replies. Then jabbing his finger at my privates, he says loudly, "Everyone remember, this is mine."

There are fearful nods and murmurs of acquiescence.

Erect from the violence and thoughts of sex, a gleeful Syd returns and lies on top of me, rubbing his body over my squirming torso. Past his heavy breaths and adding to my shame and humiliation are blood-painted faces gawking in anticipation of the act.

Desperately, I twist, grimacing from the pain radiating out of my ribs, but without the use of arms or legs, my struggles are useless.

Syd jams his head down and sinks his teeth into my shoulder.

A throttled scream leaves my throat.

As he rises, his blood-coated lips widen into satisfied smile.

I can only tremble and fight away tears while he adjusts himself to complete what was started in the museum so long ago.

"Hey, Syd," Suri says.

Heads swivel toward her voice.

One of her hands is free and holds a dagger. Helplessly, I watch as she draws it across her neck, splattering a torrent of red over the beige sand. Her eyes dim as she collapses.

My last friend is gone.

Syd screams, grabbing my throat and raising his dagger.

My mouth opens in horror as the blade comes impossibly fast toward my face.

A millimeter from my eye, it freezes.

Static wraps around me, and Syd's demonic countenance vanishes.

FORTY-SEVEN

As the static tingle dissipates, I shiver. Squeezing my eyes shut and tensing my now healthy limbs, I push a scream through my anger and grief. When it finishes, I grit my teeth and examine my surroundings.

It's not the citrus and honey scented ready room. A dank and oppressive atmosphere drapes over me. Stacked rows of flattish gray stones with sharp edges climb to create high, looming walls. At the top of the square space, narrow slats of light stab through elongated openings and form a misty halo under a reinforced stone ceiling. A singular door made from thick iron bars wrapped over stout planks of wood provides the only means of entry.

I'm in a dungeon and naked.

Feeling small and wishing for even the tiny covering of the usual sanctuary outfit, I draw my legs into my chest and wrap my arms around them, struggling to control the residual shivers running over my body.

The attempt to save Suri was a hasty decision, although it was the only one I could have chosen under the extreme circumstances. Given another chance, I would do it again. It's the first time I've been truly alive since the destruction of my past.

But now she's gone, betrayed by Walt, whom we both have saved many times. I should have known he couldn't stomach going back to level zero.

Syd will reach ten sigmas while I...

I don't know what my fate will be, but the price I'm going to pay for saving my humanity will be on the worse side of bad. I don't care. Suri, my best friend in this horrible universe, is gone. Walt is dead to me. Everyone from my prior life is long forgotten. I'm completely alone.

All while evil such as Syd marches forward.

What can they do to make anything worse?

A pop reverberates across the cell. An agitated Haiku floats above me with her tiny hands waving in front of her chest and her dirty feet shaking. "You cannot physically assist the other team under any circumstances."

"You never said we couldn't."

"It's common sense, and you purposefully killed one of your team-mates. There's no way I can help you." The impassioned words sound strangely human.

"Screw it. I made my decision. I don't need your help."

"Please understand. If it was my judgment, you would receive no punishment. But the others are furious. Uncontrollably so."

I return a defiant shrug.

Her lips part in terror, then wide-eyed, she glances at the door and shrieks, "Oh, why did you have to go where you shouldn't have?"

Despite my exterior bravado, I chew on the tip of my thumbnail.

Although I'm not in a scenario, my neck tingles in warning. While I'm used to the weird mood swings of the little avatar, the raw fear emanating from her is infectious.

There is a rumble, and dust falls from heavy thuds shaking the walls. The hinges of the door rattle.

I suck in a fearful breath.

Haiku trembles. "No. No!" she screams and disappears.

The sharp edges of the freezing stones dig into my back as I press against the wall, struggling to escape what's coming.

Metal groans as the door blasts outward. The bald giant, constantly in my thoughts but absent since "Acid Island," fills the open frame.

Bare feet scraping against the dirt floor, I try to push myself through the unyielding stones while my eyes wildly search for a place to hide in the confined space.

The naked man enters and closes the door with an ominous thud. When he steps forward, I fire my heel at his knee. Leaning over, he slaps it aside. With a massive hand grabbing a fistful of hair, he lifts me to my toes.

I punch his chest and head with no effects.

A fist blasts into my diaphragm.

The air pours from my lungs as I raise my arms to protect myself.

An uppercut smashes my nose and jerks my head upright, my eyes rolling into their sockets. Blood dribbles down my chin as he lets go of my hair and slams me into the wall. The razor edges cut my shoulder blades while a pain-filled whimper leaves my mouth.

I counter by launching a weak hook into his jaw, which does more harm to my knuckles than his face.

Another blow from a meaty fist cracks a few of my ribs.

The ground rises as I crumble to my knees.

He kicks me in the head and the world goes black.

FORTY-EIGHT

WHITE MISTS SWIRL IN VASTNESS.

My mind journeys through an infinite space as my substance ripples from the movements of giant beings. I feel funny because my hazy body has no heart and my lungs can't gather any air. There is only numbness. Blessed numbness.

You shouldn't be here. There will be repercussions.

My swollen eyelids crack open, and through the crusted slits, I find everything in my reality is the same. The same layered walls with razor edges, the same dull halo of sunlight, and the same discolored, bloodied body sending screams of misery into my brain. My life has morphed into a continuous existence of torture.

There have been five beatings during this never-ending time. I think. With no healthy restoration of my being after each visitation from the bald giant, the wounds have accumulated into a mass of throbbing agony interspersed by spikes of intense pain.

Strangely, it's been a mechanical brutality. Excruciating to be sure but lacking any artistry or personal touch. My tormentor is no Syd in terms of sadistic imagination.

And like everything else outside of the blue liquid portion of the virtual universe, nothing concerns sex. Although my brutal antagonist has grabbed and punched and kicked my private areas, there has never been a threat of rape amid the violence.

I wonder if that would be better, then I dismiss the awful notion. Not worrying about being violated is a good thing.

When I shift, fiery waves of suffering from my fractured right forearm and left leg cause a sob to slip through my cracked lips. After the torment subsides, I search across the gigantic bruises and broken bones of my damaged body for something still working. To my chagrin, only my terror remains intact. It's irrational: I should be used to the poundings, yet every time I think of the bald giant, my panicky feelings swamp any rational thought.

I open my broken jaw with an unsettling crack. Whimpering through the pain, I push the fingers of my good arm across my teeth and yank out a loose molar.

As I wince, blood leaks onto my tongue. Horrible thoughts of murder inject a sliver of happiness into the agony filling my mind. A rush of energy consumes me.

Amazingly, my single foray into the blue liquid's dark side persists. Like the dozen other times blood has seeped onto my taste buds during the beatings, I force the euphoria away. The virtual overlords can't make me enjoy the madness of killing. No matter what, I'm keeping a shred of my humanity.

I squeeze my fingers and crush the bloody tooth.

I'm going to die.

Rather than the resignation comforting me, I search for a way out of the predicament. I'm trapped and wounded, my body working at a shadow of my normal abilities. That's a far cry from the giant, who is always stronger, faster, perfectly healthy, and meaner. A lot meaner. While I would never beat a helpless prisoner, my fear only seems to stoke his sadism.

Ominous footsteps shake the room. Dust falls onto my shoulders.

Against every bit of my pride and training, my heart thumps wildly as my terror rises. It's starting again.

The iron and wood barrier swings open, and the bulging muscles of the bald giant fill the opening. Instead of striding into the cell and pummeling me, he pauses with a grin, admiring his handiwork.

Rage overcomes fear. I won't be bullied. Ignoring the pain in my fractured leg, other broken bones, and bruised tissues, I push myself off the floor.

I'm barely upright when he steps into the dungeon, the door slamming behind him. I flail at his head as he grabs my hair and crashes his fist into my damaged ribs. There is a nauseating crunch as bone splinters shred my internal organs.

Doubling over, I gasp from the fresh agony.

Instead of proceeding with blows to my battered body, he jams me against the sharp rock, which gouges more cuts over the exposed meat in my shoulders.

A cry leaves my lips.

His meaty fingers wrap around my throat and squeeze.

As my breaths shorten, my eyes expand. This time, he's going to kill me.

I don't want to die.

Whiny thoughts won't prevent anything. Forcing my broken right arm into action, I bring up my hands to break his grip.

The helpless effort brings a smile to his face.

Blackness creeps from the edges of my vision. I thrash in panic, trying to loosen my throat from his grasp. His beady eyes fill my tunneling sight while his grunting exaltations flow into my nostrils. My lungs scream for oxygen with each tightening of his death grip as my mind threatens to slip into unconsciousness.

The cell rumbles from his booming laughter.

It's finished. My eyes flutter while my muscles weaken.

I clench my broken jaw in a final effort to cling to life, wincing from the pain.

More blood leaks from the hole in my gums. I try to spit the foulness away, but only a wheezing breath sputters from my mouth. Then my lungs spasm and a cough leaves my throat, spilling a wash of blood over my tongue.

Images of murder and torture appear. Without any energy to restrain them, they march into my mind and release the lingering emotions of the blue liquid. While malevolence fills my thoughts, my pain shockingly lessens even as a newfound strength floods through my body.

A fresh goal consumes me. Although I'm dying, the bald giant is going to be my companion on the journey to hell. If it's the last thing I do, and the only worthwhile thing I accomplish in this crappy virtual existence, this thing's life will end. While my real world memories have vanished, I intuitively know I've never desired anything more than killing this one horrible creature in front of me.

I wouldn't trade this opportunity for anything.

My eyes pop open, and I offer my mortal nemesis a bloody smile.

The giant hesitates.

With my good hand, I launch a left hook into his jaw.

It bounces off, and he chuckles as his hands return to squeezing the life out of me.

After another worthless punch, I hunt through my dizziness for a different solution. Since my nemesis is impervious to blunt force, I need a weapon. Something pointy or sharp. My eyes wildly roam the confines of the cell. Only the edges of the stones are available, but I lack the strength to impale him on the wall. Besides that, there is nothing.

When I try to bite his wrists, he's waiting for it.

His fist plows into my mouth, shredding my lips and knocking out my front teeth. More wonderful blood washes over my tongue.

A single lucid thought enters my mind.

Walt.

The teen is the worst fighter I've known, but he won "Acid Island," by using the protruding bone from a torn off limb.

No body parts lie around the cell, but in my deranged state, that's not a problem. My right arm has plenty of bones, including one that's already broken.

I slam it against the wall. Pain, greater than anything I've ever imagined, resonates from the self-inflicted wound. Embracing the torment, I hit the sharp stones harder with my fist. The broken bone shatters and bulges from under my skin.

Although my hand dangles at an odd angle, I strike again and again, until the craziness works. Through the agony, I gurgle with delight when a splintered edge pops into sight.

The giant freezes from my sudden insanity.

I swipe the pointy protrusion at his neck and when it draws blood, a throttled scream of joy infused with exquisite layers of derangement leaves my shredded lips.

His mouth falls open from shock.

Before he reacts further, I jab under his jaw and into the carotid artery.

Beautiful, glorious red blood spurts over my shattered arm.

Through my wheezing breaths, I chuckle.

Fear seeps into his eyes, and as he trembles, his fingers weaken their death grip.

My lungs struggle to fill themselves. Despite the lessening pressure, only whistles of precious oxygen scorch through my battered wind-pipe. But it gives me enough energy to fire a couple more jabs into his neck.

Stunned, the bald giant grabs his fresh wounds in a hopeless effort to staunch the torrents of blood. His massive legs wobble as his strength ebbs. A second later, he crashes to the floor with a monstrous thump.

Without his hands propping up my body, I fall too, slamming onto my knees and good arm as I give a hollow cry of relief.

While the red of his life fluid leaks through his fingers and spills over his hands, the bald giant bellows in fear.

Although experiencing more pain than I've ever endured in any scenario, I cackle. His discomfort is hilarious. For a moment, my remaining splinter of humanity wonders if I'm going insane. Then it evaporates, and I bellow with laughter, embracing my psychotic state. Shattering an arm to use the sharp end of a compound fracture as a weapon is the grandest thing I've ever done. I bring the gory tip to my lips and lick it. The combined taste of our blood is amazing.

An expression of horror explodes over his brutish face.

A guffaw leaves my mouth as heat rushes into my private areas.

While my thighs twitch to increase the pleasurable sensation, I ignore the lewd distraction.

Murder is so much better than sex.

The delicious notion widens my shredded lips into a malicious grin.

Pale and frightened, my victim scuttles backward, pinning himself into a corner.

My shattered arm dangles as I pursue with a three-legged crawl, thrilled to be a participant in the Ten Sigma Program.

How could anyone not want to be a part of this?

Pausing, I laugh. The fleeting thought is the whole answer to "What will you do?"

His whimpers draw me back to my happy task, and when I reach him, he's fading from the loss of blood, but his eyes are wide in terror.

Good.

I rise above him, drawing back my non-fractured arm.

"Don't," he says.

Besides my bloodthirsty rage, the dizziness from my wounds is causing me to process things at a glacial pace. A moment lapses before I comprehend he has spoken a plea for mercy. I hesitate. Then I reply with the only response making sense to my demented mind.

"Fuck you!"

I blast my fist into his face.

The jolt sends a shiver of pleasure up my arm and into my being.

He whimpers, and I drive another punch into his nose.

The crunch of cartilage fills my thoughts with the joy of murder.

His cowering fuels my hate, and as I launch my fist again and again, my focus narrows, tunneling around the sparks of glee erupting in my mind. More laughter pours from my insanity as my muscles quake with hysteria.

When his two front teeth come loose, a rush of desire strikes between my legs. I squirm, adjusting my knees to maximize the spreading waves of euphoria.

My breaths grow ragged and my body writhes as each delivered blow adds a layer of heat to the warmth engulfing me, my mind helplessly spiraling into the abyss of pleasure.

Suddenly, an orgasm flashes from my sex, popping like fireworks and sending pure ecstasy through my damaged tissues. When the wonderfulness erupts past my throat, I shriek with delight.

Blissful moments pass, and then I slowly wander back from the depths of the amazing experience, basking in the after-climax glow, my muscles quivering in elation.

The bald giant twitches, his face a reddish pulp of broken bones, mashed tissue, and torn skin. Most of his blood lies pooled around my knees.

When his jerky movements stop, I lean forward and lick the gore dripping over his body. The wonderful flavor infuses me with a craving for more. Baring my teeth, I dip my face to his chest, but before I can do anything, the electric tingles wrap over me.

As the dungeon disappears, my wrath-filled howls echo to the faint halo of sunlight obscuring the ceiling.

―――――

Swamped by the metallic taste of blood lingering on my tongue and the desire for murder and mayhem raging in my mind, I materialize into a cube-shaped room covered by large glowing white squares. Although I'm still nude, I don't care.

More people need to die by my hands.

Flexing the fingers of my now healthy body and barely containing my boiling rage, I drag my hand over the slick surfaces, searching for a door.

After I complete a circuit around the confined space, it's apparent there's no exit.

My wanton desires explode.

Uttering an incomprehensible shriek, I launch a lethal punch at the nearest square.

It yields and absorbs the blow, air leaking from the squishy padding. When it restores its original shape, I bellow and fire more punches.

For every impact, the pliant material reacts the same way, soaking up all the energy my fists can dish out, and then slowly re-expanding into a flat surface.

After the last punch lands, the squares sit intact, laughing at my struggles.

My rage spikes, and hollering a war cry, I stomp kick the nearest pad, and when that gains nothing, I swivel and run, launching my head into the opposite wall. As I drive with my legs, trying to push myself outside of the room, the square gently rises, forcing my body backward.

Not ready to admit defeat, I push my hands in front of me, struggling to dig into the padding. My fingers find no purchase on the silky surface as the square flattens.

Consumed with rage, I blindly send savage strikes at the immovable objects until I accidentally hit a crease between two of them. Clawing my fingertips around an edge, I find a grip and yank with all my strength.

The covering rips from the wall with a horrible sucking sound.

A howl of happiness escapes from my lips as I toss the hated object. It crumbles against the opposite side of the cube, and the dust evaporates before hitting the floor.

When I turn, an identical glowing white pad has restored the wall.

The moment of glee evaporates, and a primal scream erupts from my belly. I clench my fists and tuck my head under my arms. As my fury overwhelms me, I send useless punches at the soft barriers.

Everything remains impervious to my best efforts.

I must have more blood.

In desperation, I turn, and after taking a running start, launch myself at one of the walls.

I bounce back and land, the thick floor pad preventing me from injury. With heavy breaths and flagging strength, I rise and deliver a climactic, gigantic kick at the hated squares.

A shock reverberates up my leg, but the effort once again yields nothing.

My prison remains white, spotless, and uncaring for my desires.

After releasing a bellow, I step into the middle of the space and whirl, frantically hunting for an escape. As the room spins, I process different options, allowing cold slivers of rational thought into my mind.

Suri.

Her admonishing countenance says, *"I killed myself for this?"*

I stop the wild turning and push out a dizzy sigh. Then focusing on my friendship as the bond to my humanity, I take a deep breath.

The black emotions of the blue liquid crest, and moments later, they fade, leaving only hollowness in my being.

Spent from the physical effort, as well as the emotional toll, I surrender to the situation and sag against a wall, sliding down the slippery surface to the cushioned floor.

After another deep breath, I spit, cleaning my mouth of imaginary blood and washing my thoughts of the horrors I committed while murdering the bald giant.

A few more minutes pass before my mind clears enough for sanity to return. Then I draw my knees into my chest and wait for what comes next.

FORTY-NINE

By the time a soft pop heralds Haiku's arrival, I've reconciled my churning feelings of rage, shame, and glee into a knot of apathy.

As the little avatar floats over me, pleasant strawberry and earthy scents fill the padded space, doing nothing to improve my disposition.

"Get me out of here," I say.

"First, allow me to congratulate you," she replies in a contrite tone.

A flush spreads over my cheeks as I remember the insanity. "I survived, let's not make a big deal out of it."

"Your victory was unexpected."

An odd, masculine timbre underlies her childlike voice.

I squint at her dirty feet. But the black streaks aren't dirt, they're rubber. I pop off the floor and stare into her face.

A blueness deepens her silver eyes.

"What are you?"

Instead of answering, she runs her gaze over her body and her hands over her face.

"Something's weird with your voice and your feet. And there's a blue tint in your eyes."

Before she can protest, broken recollections of a vast space, huge beings, and a tiny witch enter my mind.

"You're one of the virtual overlords."

A dainty huff leaves her lips as she folds her arms.

Furious with all the secrets, I jam my finger into her chest. "Don't deny it. I know what I know."

An awkward moment passes before she raises her hand and snaps her fingers. Her simple tunic shimmers while her small form elongates. A broad-brimmed, black hat sprouts on top of her head and heavy black boots press into the padded floor. The odor of mothballs washes over me.

Ugh.

After the transformation finishes, I squeeze my face, pulling on my cheeks. This revelation shouldn't be a surprise; it's a half-truth that's been egging at the back of my mind since I arrived in the virtual universe.

Cloaked in black, the figure to my front is a younger version of the man in the broad-brimmed hat who extended me the Ten Sigma Program offer. Although his face lacks wrinkles, he has the same electric blue eyes and detestable mustache.

How can I forget everyone I hold dear, yet remember him?

And he's been disguised as Haiku.

I'm naked.

"Clothing, and not that skimpy outfit. Now."

"Really, I'm a scientist—"

"Real clothing. Now!"

Again, he snaps his fingers, and a white smock drapes over my body.

Taking a second to enjoy my modesty, I suppress the remaining vestiges of the blue liquid. I need clear, rational thought now more than ever.

"You promised I would never see your face again." Oddly, saying the snarky statement feels better than any of the potential questions floating in my mind.

He responds with indignity. "I promised you would never see me again in the context of the real world. Given those conditions, I was being forthright."

One nagging thought charges in front of all my questions. "What...

the… hell…"

The remaining words stick in my throat as I hunch in a coughing fit. Looking up, I glare at the virtual overlord.

His hand waves in a complicated motion.

Something in my mind snaps, and words fly from my mouth. "What the hell is up with that bald guy?"

He purses his lips as if there were many better things I could waste my breath asking. "The enforcer has a different form for every person. He represents fear and death."

"Well, that didn't turn out too well for him, did it?"

His mustache widens as an amused smile crosses his face. "No, it didn't."

"And?"

"The enforcer is a method to control you, in case you get back to the real world. With the training you've received, we need to constrain your actions only to your orders and nothing else."

Instead of bedtime stories, they created a virtual bogeyman to perform the same task. But now he's dead and that's removed at least part of their subliminal authority over me. Which explains how I finally recognized the man in the broad-brimmed hat under the Haiku disguise.

"And the girl with the violet eyes. What weird facet of control does she represent?"

"None of them."

I raise an eyebrow.

"She's a coincidence," he offers with a shrug.

"What's that supposed to mean?"

"It's a long story."

Crossing my arms, I glance around the cell. "I have nothing better to do."

He sighs. "Very well, I won't keep any secrets. Your girl with the violet eyes is an AI construct. Considering the nature of battle, you shouldn't remember her. However, you have a niece with the same rare trait and that predisposes you to notice violet eyes."

I search the empty cavern of my prior-life memories. Except for my guilt from killing her, the violet color of her eyes means nothing.

"Since dead means dead, why does she keep showing up in my scenarios?"

"As you know, this program is a means to produce super-warriors. In order to account for the high casualty rate, we originally only used AI combatants. We are continually creating instances from over six thousand baseline models to feed into the Ten Sigma Program."

"And one of these models has violet eyes?"

He nods.

"So she never remembers me because every time I've seen her it's a different copy?"

"They're not exact copies, but in essence you're correct. As I said, she's a coincidence, nothing more."

I spend a moment digesting the new facts. Considering the ten sigma odds, none of his words should be surprising. "You said originally?"

"Yes. Despite the numbers of AIs that we produced, the final yield of ten sigma graduates was too low. A few of us conjectured the issue was computer personas lacked the survival instincts inherent to real people.

"I developed a system to identify human beings as candidates and ensured the ones with no alternatives could join the program. It wasn't so simple of course, creating the download technology, determining the correct parameters, recruiting volunteers, but I'll spare you the details.

"Of all the recruits, you were one of the two most promising."

"Who was the other?"

"You caused her death."

I grimace. The seven sigma trying to return to her children.

Their names are Melody and Melissa.

"The vast majority of your opponents have been AIs. Does that make you feel any better?"

"Have I killed real people?"

He sheepishly says the obvious answer. "Some."

"Then, no it doesn't."

"They were all going to die anyway and volunteered."

Because the last statement improves my mood, I change the subject.

"And where does Syd fit into this?"

"What do you mean?"

"He's at least as skilled as I am, but you didn't list him as one of your top two."

"As I've said before, your perception level is quite high."

I think of the creepy man and the wild variances of his personality. Clues from my rebellious investigations go through my mind—the strange places I've been, following Syd under the bowels of Home, the infinite space with the witch, the feeling of vastness, my body turning into mush, and most importantly, the sensations of fragmented people.

"Syd's not human, is he? He's somehow part of the 'Worse Things' you've said were coming, the face-painters."

"A very astute observation. Yes, besides using real human beings, a second line of research is devoted to creating a human persona to excel at combat.

"Syd is a composite construct. An amalgamation of desirable traits from different people."

"What exactly does that mean?"

"The other faction of scientists raided prisons to find suitable subjects," he says with reticence.

"Suitable?"

"Death row inmates. The worst of the worst criminals. Then they ripped apart the vileness of their beings and created new personas."

Copies of him were under that building. No, not copies, facets of Syd being combined into a complete being like the other terrors floating in the strange place where I followed the leprechaun. Somehow, they were one and the same as Syd. It's evil genius; instead of relying on dumb chance to get a ten sigma, create a person, someone only devoted to the mission, a perfect predator working through everything without conscience or remorse and taking pleasure in the gory details.

But not everything is dark. There are other parts of Syd, incongruous with death row inmates—namely his gentleman persona.

"Syd's always at war with himself, and he seems schizophrenic at points. Those weren't the only traits you gave him."

He bashfully nods. "We added other human aspects for control."

"Let me guess, the gentleman part was taken from you."

"From a few of us."

When I think of Syd and his perversions, with everything enhanced by the secret of the blue liquid, I almost spit at the man's feet. "How are those fear and death controls working?"

A shadow crosses his face. "Certain issues have arisen."

"And you're okay with that?"

"Perhaps, you should be more concerned with your own future."

He's right. "What now?"

"You tried to send your team back to level zero. That is your punishment."

"I'm not going back to zero."

"You killed a teammate, and you have many powerful enemies who want nothing less than your death."

"Then why did you come here?"

"I have a closeness to you, especially after this length of time. I assumed you would be the first one of my subjects to defy the odds and return to the real world."

My promise.

Without any prior memories, and given the destruction of my original team, this man is literally the only friend I have left. And the only opportunity I have to not repeat the entire Ten Sigma Program.

However, I have leverage because I'm the pinnacle of his project while Syd is my opposite amongst his rivals. "Syd will rise to a ten sigma level and go to the real world."

His mouth tightens.

My hunch is correct; he needs Syd to fail. "If Syd reaches ten sigmas before I do, what happens?"

"If he passes the ten sigma level, the achievement validates their hypothesis. The composites will go into mass production with all available resources."

"But that's not the worst part, is it? You craft a means of control, but Syd won't be stopped. You create rules, but he bends them in ways you never considered. No matter how many restraints you create, he's clever enough to avoid them all."

Although he says nothing, his face tightens with worry.

"And that's what you fear—what will happen when Syd and others like him arrive in the real world."

"All that matters is the ability to reach ten sigmas. That is our definition of success."

"I can stop Syd."

"The composites are superior. You are no match for them."

I recall every strange opponent I've encountered, everyone who aroused happiness when I killed them. The ones who reminded me of Syd. The face-painters. "In the dusty brownstones, I beat eight of them at the same time."

"That you did. However, Syd is the crown jewel of the composite program. The one given the most resources and by far their most powerful."

"I beat your bald giant."

"And what did that cost you? Even if I were inclined to listen to this foolish notion, you would need to succumb to the dark emotions from the blue liquid. And this time, you might not be able to escape the insanity. Then we would be in a worse position because that's something you can control even less than him."

It's a fair point, but I've got enough anger from my last meeting with Syd and his team to make up for any blue liquid insanity.

I raise my hand. "I swear I will beat him without resorting to anything from the blue liquid. I would rather be dead than risk losing my sanity again."

"Good intentions don't go very far. They certainly won't stop a creature like Syd."

"We have to try."

He shakes his head. "This is all moot. Syd is at 9.99 and in his last battle."

I shudder thinking of Syd and his tastes on the other side of the blue dome. Not to mention the flood of evil to come after him. "He's not there yet."

"He's better than you and everyone on his team is a composite. You can't defeat them."

Although wondering from where in my lost past I've attained the big dream optimism, I'm sure my confidence in myself has never run higher. Nothing can stop me.

"In this last scenario, I was on the same side as Syd. If the others wanted to validate their hypothesis, they could have pitted me directly against him. But they didn't. They're afraid I'll kill him."

Instead of voicing opposition, he pinches his chin in thought.

"After I broke up the team, you said there are those situations where one person can turn defeat into victory. This program is designed to produce those individuals through the harshest methods possible."

"That is true."

"What better place and time is there to show that? You need Syd defeated before he gets to the real world. You need one person to make a difference." I tap my chest. "Me."

He meets my stare, eyes glimmering with hope.

"What have you got to lose?"

"I'll need to expend a lot of capital…"

"But this is a risk worth taking."

A moment passes before he nods. "Yes, it's time to make a stand."

I smile with tight lips as he performs the leave motion and disappears.

Alone, and with nothing further to accomplish, I lower myself to the cushioned floor and await my fate.

FIFTY

I'M NOT sure how much time passes before the man in the broad-brimmed hat returns, accompanied by a thin, pale woman with long straight hair. Her formal black robe reeks of sage.

"Hello," she says.

The familiar voice belongs to the witch avatar. "Why are you here?"

"I'm part of the group that created Syd and the rest of the composites."

The hateful glances from the leprechaun and several of the other avatars spring into my mind. "Great."

As if reading my thoughts, the man in the broad-brimmed hat says, "The reasonable one and the person in charge."

She adds, "Although I'm a scientist, I'm not like the others because as the lead administrator, I need to do what's optimal for the program.

"Humans or composites, the direction we should follow is not a certainty, as some of my colleagues and rivals feel. While it's difficult to get human subjects, creating and maintaining composites has its own unique challenges.

"When we first met under the sanctuary, we were fine-tuning Syd's traits. The composites require a substantial amount of maintenance, but they're also quite effective."

"And who's going to maintain him when he gets back to the real world?"

"The goal of this program is to produce individuals capable of great deeds. Those who can do whatever it takes to win. And our proof is whoever reaches ten sigmas."

While not a complete answer, she's being honest as always, and I find myself reluctantly liking her. "Okay, what next?"

"We are in agreement to not reset your sigma score and allow you to try your fortunes against Syd," she says.

The man in broad-brimmed hat adds, "That's the good news, the bad news is that while we attempt to ensure parity, Syd is in the middle of his last scenario with a commanding lead. You'll be metaphorically swimming upstream."

"Is that all?"

"Isn't that enough?"

I have more bad news for him.

"This will be my last scenario too."

"That's preposterous," he says. "You are slightly more than a nine sigma. The ten sigma rule cannot be altered."

My big dreamer optimism powers into overdrive. "I don't need the rules bent but live or die this will be the end of my time here. Adjust the odds so that when I win, I'll be at the ten sigma level."

"Why that's," he sputters. "That's the most ridiculous thing I've ever heard."

He's right. The odds are so gigantic, I don't want to know the answer. "You want Syd stopped, and your enemies want me stopped. I'm not spending another extra moment waiting for an angry leprechaun or psychotic teddy bear to set up another scenario to drive me insane or get me killed." I leave out the part of being totally sick of my virtual existence.

"You won't stop Syd with those odds. You'll be dead."

"This is the purpose of the Ten Sigma Program."

"Foolhardiness isn't the purpose of this program."

"I have a proposal."

"Proposal? There is nothing that can justify this," he says, shaking his hands.

"Let her speak," the witch interrupts.

"No," he says, raising his voice. "I won't hear of this. You'd just love her to get killed to prove the superiority of your composites."

The witch turns to him, anger flashing in her eyes. "I've already stated my neutrality. We both want the best for the program, don't we?"

Before their argument boils into a screaming match, a question pops into my mind.

"What will you do?" I say.

They pause, eyeing me with curiosity.

"What will you do?" I repeat, louder. "That's what you asked when I entered the virtual universe. The choice between heading into an unwinnable situation or staying safe. I'm going to the impossible battle."

The man in the broad-brimmed hat flicks his fingers dismissively. "The more important question is, 'How will you win?' This is more than talking your way to victory. You actually need a plan."

I laugh. "No plan survives contact with the enemy. But that's not the point.

"It's not about making the right decision in an impossible situation. That's not what you're looking for in the Ten Sigma Program.

"You're not trying to find someone who can be shoved into a tricky situation and win. That defeats the whole purpose of the program.

"You need someone who relishes being in the thick of things, the person who thrives when things are at their worst. Someone with enough confidence to rush into impossible situations and win. Over and over again. Someone who will always find a path to victory, regardless of the odds."

I pause, stifling a blush because the epiphany only came when I was in the shameful throes of the blue liquid, beating the life from the bald giant.

In a lower voice, I finish. "The question isn't 'What will you do?' The question is 'Do you want to do this?'"

The man in the broad-brimmed hat stays silent, clenching his jaw, while the witch faces me and asks, "What is your proposal?"

"Take all the composites and everyone who knows the secret of the blue liquid and put them on the other team. Every last bad egg in one basket. Then if I win, you end the composite program. No more Syds."

An uncomfortable moment passes as the two overlords weigh their options.

The witch breaks the stalemate. "I accept your challenge. If you are victorious against such odds, the composite program isn't worth continuing."

"No. No! I absolutely won't allow this," the man in the broad-brimmed hat says.

Instead of matching his undercurrent of raw emotion, I appeal to his logic. "You gave me this ideal body, hoping I would grow into it. Now, after everything that's happened, I'm who I'm supposed to be." I step to him and clasp his hand. "Now let me go where I'm supposed to be."

His angry eyes meet my gaze.

"This is for the best," I say softly.

Another moment passes before his anger melts, and he agrees by dipping his head.

I release his hand and step back. "And regardless of anything, this is my last scenario. If I win, I leave this universe and if I lose, I'm dead."

"Agreed," the witch says. "Very well, there is much to prepare. I wish you the best." With those final words, she waves her hand and disappears.

"There is one last thing," I say to the man in the broad-brimmed hat.

"What?"

"I want my memories back."

"That can't be done, they're gone."

"But you can give me the information about my life."

"You've come so far not knowing."

I narrow my eyes. "You've never been close to your family, have you?"

He shrugs. "I'm not, and you've asked me that before, but now that memory is gone forever, along with everything else. What you're proposing is futile."

"I remembered you."

"Yes, you may have echoes of those involved with the Ten Sigma Program."

Shadowy things enter my mind. Mr. Leader, Mr. Scientist, Ms. Lawyer with her irrational devotion to secrecy, and a glassy sphere topped by a golden ring.

"That means?"

"It means nothing because nothing is left from your specific past. Everything was erased to prevent any interference with your optimization process."

"No, I won't accept that." Wildly, I look for something in the cavern of my memories. Zero. Even the ghostly touches of the ten sigma officials have no context. I can't picture any of their details or where I met them.

"The Ten Sigma Program is your present and your future. Accept it," he says with finality.

Letting my rebellious nature loose, I reply, "I react to violet eyes. That means some traces of my family are still inside me."

He draws in a deep breath. "But consider: included in your past is everything that made you weak."

"Those things helped me become what I am now. Better than a nine sigma. The best human you've ever recruited. I don't care what format but give me every detail you have. Somehow, I'll get my memories back."

He blankly returns my stare before performing a strange motion with his hand. "Very well, I hope you find what you're looking for."

Green threads appear in my mind. When I examine them, facts from my prior life pour out like paper sheets spilling from a filing cabinet. While the effect is similar to Suri pointlessly retelling my stories, they are better than nothing.

"Thank you."

"If that is all, it's time for you to have your final battle."

When he raises his hand, I grab his palm.

"The chances of Syd and myself being on the same team were astronomical."

"Perhaps. Good always finds evil," he responds with a smirk.

"Instead of taking responsibility, you're giving me a philosophical answer?"

He laughs. "Believe whatever you wish."

Despite being seconds from entering my final scenario against the most lopsided odds I will ever encounter, I share his good humor with a smile.

Pulling his hand from my grip, he ends the levity. "I wish we could spend more time together, but the other powers aren't particularly patient."

Then he surprises me by leaning over and kissing my forehead. After he straightens, I touch where his lips lingered, confused by the action. I've been living in a universe consumed by violence and hate and death for so long that a few seconds pass before I recognize the emotion. It's love.

His hand begins the weaving pattern as he steps backward. "This time, I truly promise you will never see me again. You will either die or return to the real world."

Still unsettled, I lamely respond. "I wish I could say it's been a pleasure."

As the static wraps around me, his fading voice says, "Best of luck. Please be successful."

The man in the broad-brimmed hat has changed my existence more than anyone I remember, and he never gave me his name.

FIFTY-ONE

HEART THUMPING IN ANTICIPATION, I materialize in my final scenario surrounded by the uncertainty of night. While I want to peek at my personal files, survival ranks as my top priority. I dive onto crusty sand, taking cover behind a curved ripple of land.

Never having entered during the middle of a battle, I expect everything.

When a minute passes without a threat, I assess the situation. Resting on my head is a comfortable helmet, my quick breaths making a light fog on its visor, while a thin ceramic armor encases my body. For weapons, I carry two grenades, a combat knife, one silenced pistol with an extra magazine, and a full ammo belt for my suppressed assault rifle.

Moonlight breaks through a stack of clouds stretching from the horizon and sends a ghostly curtain knifing across the terrain. In the visible portion of the night sky, stars twinkle.

I lift my visor and blink from a smoke-tainted breeze. Wood fires burning in scooped out holes litter the landscape. Not knowing the duration of the scenario, I presume they are everlasting.

After my eyes adjust to the dimness, I move my gaze beyond

several small crests to a lattice of shimmering reflections. It's a network of rivers carving the land into a series of islands with varied, flattish terrains lit by clusters of the orange bonfires.

Besides those oddities, this map has one other notable feature. Starting from just past my boots and spreading as far as my vision allows are shrubs resembling spiky aloe vera plants, with glimmers from the fires dancing on their tapered leaves.

My anticipation wanes. The details don't matter. Syd is here, and my only goal is to kill him and every last one of his companions before my end.

A giggle floats past me.

I twist, my leg breaking a long leaf with a sound of a popping Christmas ornament.

When I check my armor, a deep scratch runs along its surface. The leaf is created from a thin, mottled material resembling a mishmash of metal and glass.

I shake my head at the craziness. These knife-like growths are everywhere.

Leading with my assault rifle, I rise into a combat posture and step over the crest of the land ripple. As my revulsion rises, I cautiously tread down the slope, looking for any sign of movement or ambush.

When my feet touch level ground, I pause, forcing my gaze directly forward, while bodies stripped of armor and staked out in grotesque positions populate my peripheral vision. They've been tortured with presumably their major nerves cut or spines severed. I don't linger over the details because they're too close to my own experience, and besides promising the man in the broad-brimmed hat not to succumb to the evil of the blue liquid, rage will only cloud my judgment.

With measured strides, I walk toward the back of a helmetless figure sitting in a meditative pose and facing a body with a hideously burned torso and mangled limbs.

As I approach, he remains motionless, his flaxen hair and ceramic armor bathed by the flickering orange light from the blazing wood fires to either side of him.

I stop at three paces away, ready to fire.

Without turning, he says, "There aren't any threats. But you should be mindful of the plants, they're dangerous."

Although still suspicious, I ease my weapon to my hip, keeping it pointed at the center of his body mass.

While he slowly swivels to face me, only the steady crackle of the nearby bonfires and my shallow breathing interfere with the silence.

His delicate features form an unreadable mask when he meets my gaze. "Hello, Brin. It's wonderful to see you again."

"Hello, Walt."

Motionless, we let the moment stretch.

Of course Walt is here. Anyone and everyone with knowledge of the blue liquid is on the other team. And none of them can leave this scenario alive.

A rising breeze fans the fires and blows strands of hair over his face.

My fingers tighten on the trigger.

He turns his palms over to show they're empty, then he speaks in a voice radiating serenity. "Do you want me dead, Brin?"

"You killed Suri. You betrayed us."

Yellow dots flash in the distance. A moment later the faint pops of suppressed gunfire arrive.

My eyes scan for threats.

"Weren't you listening? I told you we're alone," he chides. "I didn't kill Suri, she did that to herself. And I didn't betray anyone. You did that."

I pull my attention from the distant battle. In the most literal sense, he's right. "Did you kill these people?"

"Me?" He smiles. "I couldn't kill all these people. I'm not that good." He snickers at some secret joke. An infusion of insanity, courtesy of the blue liquid.

"Why did you do this? Why not just kill them?"

The snickering stops. He politely says, "I told you, I didn't kill them. As far as torture, maybe it was fun. Maybe it's something I enjoyed."

I pull the trigger.

Walt doesn't flinch as my bullet flies under his jaw, leaving an angry red streak on his neck. His eyes express his disappointment. "Suri was on the other team. She had to die." His voice cracks. "Now, I'm on the other team."

The gun barrel wavers as my unsteady hands twitch. Thoughts of our past race through my mind. Of the good times in the barracks. Of the many times I saved his life and our more innocent existence before the first scenario.

Even as I gnash my teeth, my resolve falters. Walt has to die, but someone else has to do it.

When I lower my weapon, his lips contort, trying to suppress his inner workings. The effort fails, and loud cackles erupt from his mouth. "After everyone you've murdered, you're having trouble now?"

Before I can step forward and punch him in the face, the low sound of a motorboat engine rolls by us.

"Last chance, Brin. That's my team coming."

It's a lie. "Go poison another dog, Walt."

Except for biting his lip, he shows no recognition of the only story he's ever told me from his past.

Although there is more to say, I pivot and take deliberate strides away from him, marching over the low rise and another forty meters to the nearest river.

When my feet reach the damp gravel near the water and I haven't been shot in the back, I'm mildly surprised, but angrier with myself for allowing emotions to cloud my judgment. I need to be at my best, not only against Syd, but Walt and anyone else I could encounter.

"Since you're where you're supposed to be, perhaps you should do what you're supposed to be doing?" advises internal me.

Rolling my eyes, I reply, *"Yes, that wasn't my best."*

"I hope not. It might be good to win this scenario."

Unsure of why my optimistic internal voice has developed a snarky streak, I slowly shake my head, watching a five-person assault craft approach. It matches the boat from my very first scenario. Only now, three of the five places are unoccupied.

When the rubber bow scrapes ashore, the man in front lifts his cracked visor. Underneath the sweat and dust streaking his face, he's handsome. With a southern twang and a dubious stare, he says, "You're the reinforcements?"

After I nod, he jerks his head. "Get in."

FIFTY-TWO

I LIE in the middle of the craft as we glide through a forty-meter wide channel of slow-moving water.

From behind me, a woman with long black hair steers a quiet outboard engine and navigates us through the labyrinth of waterways. A patchwork of scars runs over her armor, and fear laces each of her breaths. She's a newbie unlucky enough to have this shit-show as her first scenario. The man with the southern accent, a five, lies next to me, doing a better job of concealing his anxieties. He is in charge.

Their names are Cleo and Bob. Since I'm leading them to their deaths, I figure it's only right to know what to call them.

As we round a bend, Bob points at the central apex of a flattish island. "Our defense is based around that flag."

Syd's objective is a square of glowing material draped from a sturdy two-meter high pole. Concentric ripples in the land emanate from its base and propagate into the surrounding water. Besides the rock dropped in a pond terrain features, the island holds more than a few sprinkled bonfires, casting metallic gleams off the dreaded plants, which appear to be everywhere.

Turning to Cleo, Bob says, "Watch out for the plants, stick to the center of the channel until we get to the landing beach."

"I can handle it," she replies in a frazzled tone.

Bob explains, "We lost a team when their boat impaled on one of the razor leaves." He pats the thick rubber of the hull. "This got shredded, and the whole thing went straight to the bottom. Everyone drowned because of their armor."

I nod. The many sturdy segments can take the small wounds of gunfire but not the long, jagged tear inflicted by a sharp sword pretending to be a leaf.

"After everything we've been through, dying because of some stinking shrubs is a ridiculous way to go," Cleo says.

It's true. But nothing I can add will make it better. "How did you know where to find me?"

Bob says, "Damnedest thing. Got a message for reinforcements. Never happened before." He pulls off a protecting glove and wipes his brow. "We need as much help as we can get. We're getting our asses whooped."

Although I want to offer some reassurance, there is none. What we are up against is beyond anything in his previous experience, prickly flora or not.

His stare lingers on my face, demanding an answer.

"Hopefully, I can help."

The weak reply seems to satisfy him, and pulling his glove back on, he resumes his forward watch as the boat curves around the circular island. The lethal plants dot the high vertical walls, continuing as dark shadows below the water, and render any ingress a death trap.

After another minute, the land tapers into a vegetation-less ribbon of landing beach.

The boat scrapes ashore next to a line of similar craft. Beyond, twenty-one people wearing battle-scarred armor wait with various postures of exhaustion.

Relieved faces cluster around us after we set foot on the sand, and a chorus arises. "A nine sigma!" "Wow." "We're in luck." "We're going to win!"

They're more of a mob than an organized force. Probably the singles and duos remaining from what was once a large number of teams and just thrilled to still reside amongst the living.

Cleo flips up her visor, studying me with wonder. "Nine! I didn't notice. My apologies."

They think they have a chance.

Not wanting to piss on the happy parade, but with no other choice, I ask, "Is this everyone who's left?"

"Two on the bluff," Bob says, pointing across the river. "Ten are scouting in three boats. Everyone else is here."

I frown. It's too few, and I force away a rising sense of guilt from their impending deaths. Regardless of my deal with the overlords, Syd was going to win this scenario and kill them in horrible ways. At least now, their lives can count for something.

Bob motions past the group. "Over there, the scenario's easier to explain."

After I follow him to the edge of the shore, the remaining crowd fills the space behind us.

Indicating the varying shapes and sizes scratched onto a fine patch of sand, he says, "This is the map. Our win condition is to defend our flag to the last. As far as terrain, there are thirty-eight islands, the smallest being about three hundred meters long, the largest is a little over a kilometer. Seventeen are flat with only the spiky shrubs as cover. Dicey to hold at best. We're in the northeast corner, guarding our flag. They keep whittling away at our defenses. Now, all of our outposts are gone. Our scouts should be able to tell us where they're coming from, but..." He looks directly at me. "We can't stop them. They're really talented, better than they should be. Especially in this." He waves at the darkness.

"When is daybreak?"

"Never. It's always night."

As the glints from the fires dance on her eyes, Cleo says, "It seems like we've been here forever."

The low whine of an engine wanders from the gloom. Before anyone can panic, a single boat lands and the lone occupant leaps onto the beach.

"The scouts," Bob says.

Nervousness ripples through the crowd.

The returning scout, a short woman with almost a four sigma score, strides to us. As she brushes past the stunned group, she raises her visor. Although her face is youthful, her eyes carry a great weight. She must have volunteered at a very old age.

Cleo asks, "Odet, where is everyone?"

"Ambushed," Odet replies, scowling. "They took the others alive."

Fearful glances bounce around the crowd. Bob removes his helmet and rubs his matted hair. "I knew a few of them," he mumbles.

Odet gives us more good news. "They've gotten reinforcements too."

"How many?" Bob asks.

"Another fifty. Maybe sixty."

There are grumbles and moans of disbelief.

Facing me, Bob says, "That means they're more than a hundred strong."

"What about us?" Odet asks.

Bob points at me.

"That's it?" she says, considering my sigma score. "I'm sure you're worth a lot and I mean no disrespect, but this isn't fair."

Life's not fair.

Bob curses as despair settles over the group. "With these crazy enemies, I'm not sure about our chances."

A helpless expression covers Cleo's face. "They're not satisfied with winning. They've been doing things."

Everyone understands what that means. Slumped postures and frightened whispers infect the others.

Although my skin crawls and rage rises in my chest, I tighten my lips. I was only in Syd's and his teammates clutches for a few minutes and can only imagine what it would have been like for them to have completed their torture.

This is an opportunity.

I hate myself for the thought, but with fresh prisoners, our enemy will be occupied for some time.

"Stop," I say.

The subdued conversation continues.

These people have been fighting Syd and his followers for the larger part of an endless night. Although it's a wonder they're still alive, they're braver than they believe. I hold up my hand. "Everyone be quiet. You've all fought well, but nobody gets to quit," I scream over them.

The mumbling grinds to a halt, and as their undivided attention shifts to me, my self-assurance soars. Somehow, everything about the situation feels comfortable and right.

I jump into the silence. "I understand what's been happening. But the things they've been doing aren't important. There's no time to feel sorry for ourselves. Now is the time to act."

Not having the slightest idea of how to tell these people what we need to do, I consider my next words carefully.

Opting for the truth, I say, "These opponents, they aren't like everyone else."

Nods of approval.

"They're better, stronger, faster than they should be. And more vicious." I wait for further agreement before adding in a low voice, "Everyone here will probably die."

Instead of despair, unwavering stares of determination meet my gaze. That's good.

In for a penny, in for a pound.

"It's not probably, it's definitely. But we need to stop as many of them as possible. It's a lot to demand, but we're soldiers. And as soldiers, the most we can expect is not losing our lives for nothing." Unlike Simon or Sergeant Rick, I'm not used to or good at making long speeches so I take a deep breath. "These aren't people we're fighting."

While their expressions turn to curiosity, I'm surprised my speech isn't being censored. "This is a good cause. All of you are forgetting your pasts. But no matter how much you've lost, you still remember what evil is.

"These enemies, they are composites of the worst individuals mankind could produce. Sadists and sociopaths. The vilest parts of the murderers, the rapists, the child molesters, all combined into one. And every last one of them is here fighting against us.

"If they win, more will come. You might not remember your loved ones, but you love the real world. If they get through us, that's their next stop.

"There will be no more reinforcements. There are no other scenarios. That means it's up to us. Right here. Right now."

They weigh my words in silence. Many have taut expressions. Others glance to their neighbors, evaluating their options. Cleo stares blankly in front of her, lost in thought and seeing nothing.

Odet stops grinding her teeth long enough to say, "I guess it was stupid to think anyone could become a ten sigma."

Bob asks, "What are we going to do?"

That's a good question.

A fierce wind gusts through us, whipping the nearby flames.

"There's a storm coming," Odet says.

Most of the thin clouds have blown past, and overhead the full moon sits high in the star-dusted dome of the night sky. A wall of foreboding thunderheads towers on the horizon. Muted flashes of lightning form twisted shapes in their angry swirls and crawl along their dark underbellies. I imagine the howling winds, blinding rain, and deafening thunder they will bring. It will be one against one in that chaos—a huge advantage for Syd.

"Do the unexpected," my internal voice whispers.

"We aren't waiting for them to come and force us into the flag. We'll set up and cover their likely staging areas and hit them first. If you feel nervous or weak, remember what they're doing to your friends right now."

Without waiting for agreement, I lean over and study the map, noting points for ambushes and avenues of attack while formulating a plan.

I wave my arms. "Everyone, get close. We don't have much time before the storm hits."

There are twenty-six others in addition to myself. After they crowd around the map, I explain the plan to maximize our heavily outnumbered force. My confidence soars as I detail a hit-and-run strategy because my strong suit is thinking while Syd's is brute strength. The positive energy infects the others and they stand straighter, with expressions of determination, ready to fight the great evil in this universe. When Bob cracks a joke in his southern twang, a few chuckles greet the punchline.

After I finish and everyone understands their roles, we jump into the boats, and avoiding the plants, head to our targets.

As the little eleven ship flotilla drives against the slow current, I picture myself as some sort of avenging angel come to this lethal, plant-infested hell to rid the universe of the composites. I focus on eliminating Syd and the thrills I've had at killing his kind until I'm ready to deal with Walt, Syd, Belle, Syrin, or anyone else I meet from the other side. This is the one instance where my actions will be absolutely justified.

However, despite my lack of fear and my anticipation for the righteousness of the coming battle, one thing nags at my core.

I can't get rid of a sinking feeling in the pit of my stomach.

———

After arriving at a bean-shaped island, I lie with four others on the boundary of the beach as the screams of the damned rise from the horizon and claw into the surrounding darkness.

My fingers tighten on my weapon while my companions shift on the hard sand.

The sheer number of composites and people corrupted by the blue liquid have somehow created a critical mass of evil among our enemies. That combined with the eerie glows of the fires flickering off the leaves of the deadly plants makes my vision of this being a demented version of hell look truer with each passing minute.

Hopefully, the avenging angel emerges triumphant.

Bob balls his hands and lifts his body.

Despite my firsthand knowledge of the sadistic techniques Syd and his people are using, I squeeze his shoulder, forcing him to remain in place.

"We wait."

Although his eyes are hard under the visor, he relents after a tense moment. "It raises my hackles."

While I want to cover my ears, my voice remains calm as I say to everyone, "We have to win the whole scenario, not one skirmish."

"I've been in enough scenarios where I'd thought I'd seen and heard it all," Bob replies.

It's good the distance has made the forms indistinct and my group can't see what Syd's people are doing to their friends. "Every battle has something different that you need to conquer."

"Is that how you reached nine sigmas?"

"One of the reasons."

"I'll remember that so I can get there too."

Noncommittally, I nod.

In spite of my warnings of the odds against us, Bob still foolishly believes he'll survive to ten sigmas. It's a strange quirk of human nature, but everyone thinks they own the winning lottery ticket. However, while I won't feed anyone's optimism, I won't kill it either.

Another scream, pitiful and so full of pain I can't tell if it's been released from a man or woman, knifes through us.

"Those people deserve better," Bob says. His back arches as he readies to break into an unbridled attack.

If I knew Syd was in this particular bunch, I'd probably join in the stupidity. "The five of us blindly charging would be a quick way to get killed. These people are the best, and they won't make mistakes in combat."

Still anxious, the group retreats from the brink.

"I just hate the waiting," Bob finally spits out.

Without responding, I return my attention to the silhouettes moving among the orange bonfires. Because of the disparity of forces, we need to stay at the effective limit of our assault rifles and can't safely get closer.

"Do you think the other teams are in place?" I ask Bob.

He replies with a tight-lipped nod.

"And all the retreat boats positioned?"

"They should be."

"If they aren't, this plan isn't going anywhere."

"These are good people and they'll do their jobs," he replies in a testy tone.

Since the overlords favor individuality over teamwork, there are never any communications devices. Large-scale coordination is restricted to line of sight or by messenger. *"Like in the times of Alexander the Great,"* a black thread chirps.

I've given them enough time.

With all the pieces apparently in position and no other reason for delay, I raise my rifle. Troubled by the sinking feeling still twisting my stomach, I pause and bring my armored hand under the visor to wipe my cheek.

"Be just like stirring up a hornet's nest. Let's send them all to hell," Bob says.

Be careful what you wish for.

As long as we kill Syd, I'll be satisfied. A samurai thread produces a strange idea. Wondering if Syd would accept a duel, only the two of us on a single island battling to the death, I debate rising and bellowing out an ancient challenge.

Almost instantly, I discard the stupid notion. Except for my personal animosity, killing Syd is only a small part of the equation. My deal with the overlords was to stop all the composites and end the program. Even if Syd accepts the challenge and I win—no mean feat— the rest will sweep over the remains of my team to victory and eventually the real world.

I take a long breath. Starting now or later isn't going to change the outcome. A three-round burst leaves my rifle. The others join in, the pops of their weapons ringing in my ears.

Two of the distant forms tumble and a thrill rises inside me. While I hope my prior self didn't have the same reaction to death, I rationalize that ending menageries of death row inmates is different from killing normal human beings.

The rest of the enemies disappear below the orange glows, and the tortured shrieks stop. Only two hits is a disappointing result, but against these opponents, I'm not sure what I was hoping to achieve.

As return fire showers sand around us, waves of gunfire rise from the nearby islands.

"Time to move. We're done here," I yell.

Bob resists.

He's still thinking of rescue or revenge, and both are bad decisions

"There's nothing we can do for them. We inflict maximum damage and leave. Keep your discipline."

His angry gaze lingers for another moment, then he nods and follows the others to the boat.

The firing from the other islands lasts too long, but without communications with the other groups, I can only hope they follow my instructions and get away with a minimum of casualties.

As our craft settles into the water, the screams begin anew, our enemies not allowing a few annoying gnats to interrupt their blood ceremony. They will come after us in their own due time.

It's unnerving, but I finally understand why the pit of my stomach is sinking. With every composite and blue liquid infected person arrayed against us, there isn't a viable strategy to beat them. They are too good and too many. The best we can hope for is to extract maximum casualties. We might even get lucky and catch Syd in a crossfire.

But in any outcome imaginable, we're going to lose and die horribly.

FIFTY-THREE

THE TORMENTED screams from the prisoners have faded, and now, the hornets are out in full force, except these insects carry modern assault weapons and have sociopathic personalities.

I rush up a gravelly incline as the low whine of an engine purrs from past the adjacent island. Behind a crest of plants, I dive next to Bob and the three others.

"They're coming," I say.

Bob grins as he sights his weapon up the long swath of water.

While watching thin coils of mist float in the distance, my companions breathe heavily from the stress of combat. However, despite their anxieties, we've been lucky, so far having only experienced a few close calls and some scratched armor; nobody is the worse for the wear.

Another minute passes before a tiny prow edges into view.

Faint, scattered gunfire arrives from a neighboring island.

As if sensing danger, the rubber craft stops beyond our effective range.

Bob curses.

I kneel, cutting loose with shots. The others join in.

Impacts spatter the water as the outboard engine swings to the side. The boat swivels and escapes into the mist, the sudden jerk spilling an enemy into the river.

"Stop shooting," I say, watching the bobbing figure struggle, the armor restricting just enough movement and adding just enough weight to make swimming impossible.

The pops of gunfire reverberate louder and more insistent.

"Let's go," I say.

"They might come back for that one," says a girl with a 2.65 score.

Knowing the opponents, I shake my head. "The shooting means they're coming down the other islands. We can't get cut off. Remember, against these guys, any mistake can get us killed."

When she glares, Bob adds, "Tammy, there'll be plenty to kill later."

As the faraway splashing stills, I lead my teammates toward a network of waist-high trenches crisscrossing the long island and select the one leading to our boat. Crouching and in single file between the walls of dirt, we manage a decent clip, but when we near the landing point, the spiders flitter over my nape. I stop.

"What's wrong?" Bob whispers.

Trusting my instincts, I reply, "We're in trouble." I point to the far side of the island. "We go to the reserve boat."

Not fully understanding, Bob follows with the others as I move into a leftward veering trench.

Shadows flicker near the shoreline on our right. "Damn, they're getting around us."

The statement sets off alarms. The others crunch on pebbles and scrape against plants as we scramble toward our escape.

"Noise discipline," I hiss.

Their motions quiet, but our pace noticeably slows.

Frustration boiling, and needing to stop the threat, I slow at a junction and wave everyone past. "No matter what, keep moving," I whisper to Bob.

As I slowly back after them, I keep my attention on the flank, picking out a single shadow sliding among a spiral of plants.

After studying the quick movements, I settle on a bonfire in the figure's path.

When it moves behind the flames for cover, I pull the trigger.

The three-round burst connects with armor.

Without waiting, I burn the rest of the magazine in a barrage of suppressing fire to make the enemy more cautious. Then, quickly reloading, I turn.

Ahead, three darkened forms jump at Bob and the others. The intermingled battle doesn't allow for a clean shot, so I leap out of the trench and sprint ahead.

After clearing some shiny leaves, I sling my rifle and leap between the dirt walls, yanking out my knife. As I fly past Bob, I slash at the person attacking him.

She throws up enough of a defense to block the strike, but the distraction tips the fight in his favor.

Not stopping, I plow into the next opponent, using my free hand to create enough of an opening to plunge my knife into her gut. Then instead of letting go, I jam my shoulder into her chest and push her into the next fight.

She laughs, trying to bite through my armor.

The final one stabs Tammy and then, leaving the knife in her, grabs at his pistol.

I hunch lower, and when he shoots, the bullets smack into my human shield, killing her. When his gun empties, I toss the body into him and charge. The unconventional tactic catches him by surprise, and I nail a side kick into his chest.

The large man flies into a wall.

I follow and pile drive my shoulder under his chin. Then flipping his visor up, I swivel and shove him face first into a plant. A pointy leaf disintegrates against the back of his helmet.

As his limp body spills down the wall, the passage quiets.

Bob has disposed of his opponent and while he helps up my other two dazed teammates, I retrieve my knife and check on Tammy.

She's dead.

Surprised the good luck lasted as long as it did, I say, "We've got a few seconds before they figure out what happened. Run."

Bob tugs my arm. "There's only three or four more. We can take them."

We probably can, but we can't afford a prolonged fight. "No, we stick with the plan."

After a last check of the landscape, I push myself from the trench and dash directly to the shore with everyone struggling to keep up.

As I near, a momentary fear shivers up my spine, but thankfully the reserve boat sits at the water's edge. When we reach it, I say to Bob, "It's here like you said it would be."

He winks as I shove the boat off the beach. "Everyone in."

After the others board, I force the rubber craft further from the riverbank and slide over the side tube.

Down an intersecting channel a couple of hundred meters away, one of the enemy boats lands near some bonfires.

A crossfire erupts from their front and across the channel.

"Get em," Bob says while the others cheer.

In a few seconds, the brutal firefight consumes the five enemies, the last twisting into a bonfire and releasing an orgy of angry orange sparks.

Bob announces with a smile, "We're finally whooping some ass."

Staying silent, I watch the water rush by as we head to the next defense position. Soon, we're going to run out of ground to give and we'll have to stand and fight.

Then, this shit-show will get worse.

A lot worse.

———

Razor leaves slice at my shin protection with each of my hurried steps. I dive over a row of prickly shrubs and land in a shallow trough.

Bullets follow, smacking through packed earth and exploding deadly plants.

As metallic debris rains over me, I press my face into the dirt.

More shots blast into a nearby fire.

I jerk sideways as hot ash spatters the area, spilling over my armor and seeping between the shoulder plates. I roll behind another shrub, grimacing from the pinpricks of heat stabbing my skin.

The gunfire hits a crescendo and then ebbs, a familiar pattern being replayed during the last few minutes.

True to my worst fears, we've run out of room to retreat and the battle has become a nightmare. Just like in the ninja scenario, the enemy is vicious, cunning, and ruthless—everything one could desire in elite combat assets.

I peek beyond the fading orange specks.

A shadow separates from the dim landscape.

Expending valuable ammunition, I fire behind the sprinting form, placing shots into dark patches that could hide lurking evils. Afterward, I hunch and scuttle to my right.

Sand sprays as Bob thumps next to me.

"Anyone left?" I ask.

He shakes his head. "They're not trying anything resembling strategy."

"They don't need any. Killing and torture—that's their goal."

"They're doing an outstanding job." A smirk appears under the crack in his visor. "I got two of those pricks."

As long as Syd is alive, I can't afford the levity. "Don't get too happy."

Bob lifts his visor. "In my younger days, I did some cruel things. I don't remember them, at least not most of them. I wanted to survive long enough to forget everything, but this makes up for it. I suppose."

This time when his stare lingers, seeking some sort of absolution, my anger rises. Walt killed his neighbor's dog and thought forgetting it would be the same as not doing it.

"Even if you forget, you can't undo what you've done. And what you do here will be worse and you'll never get rid of those memories."

When his eyes waver, I regret the harsh words. It's not his fault Walt betrayed me or Suri died. Bob's trying to become a better person. By being good or lucky, I've reached a nine sigma level, but that doesn't qualify me as a priest.

I turn my head to yellow dots winking across the other islands. A second later, faded pops fill the air. It's reassuring. "The team's fighting well. Much better than I had any right to expect."

Bob turns serious. "There's no stopping them."

Like the lulls in our battle, the distant flashes die as the remaining combatants conserve ammunition and seek more advantageous positions. "We're giving much more than we're getting."

"That won't last," he says with resignation. "We're not going to win, are we?"

Syd's people outnumber us more than four to one. They could attack with everything at once and we'd be done. But they're not. "No, we won't, but so long as we're alive, we keep fighting. Never forget that."

A bullet shatters a nearby plant. Bob ducks before I can see if my advice had any effect.

Silence follows. Another calm in the chaos. I peer beyond the shallow rise of our cover.

Distant forms shift positions under the bright moonlight.

I tap Bob on the shoulder. "There are five more. Probably going to try a flanking attack. Let's move."

"Maybe I'll kill enough of them to scrub that guilt stain off my conscience," he offers.

"You might, you might just do that," I reply, exaggerating his southern accent.

Nodding, he gives a grim smile, the expression of someone who has finally accepted his death.

Good.

After taking a last peek at the shadows crossing the long landmass, I lead him, mostly sliding and sometimes crawling, past the raised line of plants and into a shallow dimple at the edge of the beach.

Behind us, wisps of a thin fog from the coming storm crawl over the channel, while far across the waterway, our flag shimmers. Protecting the landing beach from the opposite side is a three-person team led by Odet and so far unengaged. Another good sign.

Bob freezes as a sexy voice drifts past. "Brin? Girl with the pretty red hair. Is that you hiding?"

Belle.

I lift my head and scan the darkness.

"They know you?" Bob whispers. "What the hell's going on?"

"Be quiet," I reply in too angry a tone.

Faint footsteps come from our right as a shadow darts between the cover of the shrubs. "Why so shy, Brin?"

They know I'm here because of Walt.

I should have killed him.

The deranged voice continues, "Syd is thrilled you're here for his send-off. He's coming for you. He's going to get what you promised before he leaves this universe. But he's not here now. Now, you're mine. All the wonderful suffering I have planned for you."

Despite my combat experiences, the hairs rise on my arms as I think of Belle between my thighs cutting my femoral nerves. I fight the urge to toss my grenades because I only have two of the precious commodities. Instead, I satisfy my fear and anger by snap firing over a small arc and wasting ammunition.

No wet crunches of bullets piercing armor and entering soft flesh come from the darkness.

"What are you doing?" Bob hisses.

Probably getting us killed.

I should know better than to allow my personal feelings to interfere with the scenario.

"But if nothing else, this battle is entirely personal," internal me states.

Turning to Bob, I stab my finger in the direction of my stalker. "Keep watch." Then I slide down the loose sand and onto the wasted shell casings. I'm too fixated on what's in front of me. The familiar spiders are crawling on my nape, and I'm missing something. The enemy is feral and animal smart. Everything happens for a reason.

Because it's a decoy.

I twist onto my back and fire at a leaping form. The bullet hits center mass, blowing a hole in his chest. The body flops out of sight as I switch to fully automatic and empty the magazine into a helmet rising over the crest of our shallow depression. Sand and blood spray everywhere.

Bob fires in the opposite direction.

Before I can reload, a massive outline blots out the full moon.

I toss my weapon at it and dive, tumbling onto the riverbank with bullets stitching the ground behind me.

From the side, Bob curses. Dark forms swirl in the dimness as he engages Belle in desperate hand-to-hand combat.

The firing stops.

Instantly, I'm on my feet and drawing my knife, I leap at the final two before they can reload.

The first, a smallish woman, yanks out her pistol, shouting, "She's got red hair. Kill her. Cut her up."

As the barrel swings toward me, I quick step inside her guard and launch my knife through her breastplate.

Groaning, she drops the gun and wraps her hands around the hilt.

Shocked by the unbridled hatred in her eyes, I hesitate as she falls and twists the knife from my grip.

A huge shadow flies at me, covering the night sky.

Surprised, I backpedal.

The second opponent, more giant than man, lands and charges with his raised knife glinting in the moonlight.

I execute a two-handed block and stop the blade.

A punch slams into my chest, denting the armor and knocking the air from my lungs.

I stagger but maintain the block on his knife hand.

He's unnaturally strong and lands another vicious blow.

Gasping from bruised ribs, I slip, trying to find purchase in the sand, then as his fist rises again, I twist to avoid the follow-up. The blow glances off my shoulder, but in my awkward position, I sink to a knee.

A groan comes from Bob. I can't help him.

My opponent stabs at my head.

I grab his wrist with both hands, stopping the point a centimeter from my helmet.

Leaning over me, the monster-sized man grunts as he uses his superior weight to drive me into the ground.

From the contorted stance, I resist with every bit of strength I can muster, but the knife tip hovers millimeters above my visor.

A cry of pain and a snap of cartilage come from the other fight. I have my own troubles.

Words float past me. "Kill the meat. Cleave the meat. Eat the meat."

The crazed chant is coming from my opponent.

Terror rising, I fire a punch into one of his thick legs.

Without the force of both my hands, the knife sinks, slicing the clear material of my visor, but with a desperate shove, I stop it short of my eye as the chanting rings louder in my ears.

I punch again, harder and nearer his knee, leaving a dent in his armor.

This time he grunts and shifts his body.

The change in his balance allows me to twist his wrist. His knife leaves a gash across the visor as I guide it past my face. He grimaces as I bring my punching hand back to break his grip.

The weapon falls into the sand. Although monstrous, he's no bald giant.

I pop up and drive an open palm into his chin, rattling his head and knocking his helmet askew.

With a snarl and blood dripping from his mouth, he clutches my shoulders and pushes forward, powered by an unnatural rage.

The blue liquid.

My legs buckle as I strain to hold my ground.

He relaxes his grip, chanting as he gathers strength for a final assault. When he shoves at my chest, I swivel. Tucking, I use his momentum to shoulder throw him into a circle of plants. His massive form smashes through the brittle leaves with loud crunches and flops into the water.

As he rises, I swoop over the plant stems and into the river, launching a hook that catches his temple and sends his helmet flying.

He staggers a few steps and then tumbles with a gigantic splash.

Trembling from the effort, I suck down a long breath to settle my nerves.

Rivulets of water pour down his armor when he turns over and sluggishly stands. Painted streaks of blood, black and oily in the moonlight, create a zigzag pattern around his dull, beady eyes. While he stares unnaturally, a blocky smile containing an odd gap between his huge front teeth appears on his face. He utters, "Meat."

I leap and jab his throat with armored knuckles. As he coughs, I brush past a feeble block and jump up. Latching onto his shoulders, I twist my legs and pull him down, slamming his unprotected head onto a plant.

What's behind his face splits into pieces.

While bits of skull and brain float away in dark streams of blood, the insanity of the blue liquid forms on my tongue. I spit and after taking another calming breath, kick his body into the water.

A gap in his armor snags on a broken plant stem, leaving his thick limbs waving in the slow current.

Although the spiders aren't dancing on my nape, I draw my pistol and sweep the moonlit terrain.

Everything has stilled, and, at least temporarily, the fighting is over.

I exit the channel and check for injuries. Besides being scratched, my armor has done its job protecting me from the dangerous flora. There are superficial wounds, a minor burn on my shoulder and several bruised ribs but nothing to impede my combat abilities.

Cackles float from above the beach.

Taking deliberate steps to gather myself, I put away my pistol, and after I ascend the slope, step to my first female victim.

Not recognizing her but wondering why she hated me, I let my gaze linger.

Blonde hair with frosted purple tips peeks from under her helmet, partially obscuring her large green eyes. A slight upturn makes her nose cute, while a perfect alabaster complexion and full lips complete her innocent but sexy look. Even amongst the perfectly fit people of the Ten Sigma Program, she's stunning and not someone to forget.

I scowl.

Who cares why she hated me?

Although not obvious, dabs of blood adorn the sides of her face. She's a mass murderer on a team of mass murderers and is probably one of the worst people who's ever existed. None of them deserve any mercy.

When I pull my knife from her chest, her eyes jitter with fury.

A scary moment passes before I blow out a disgusted sigh. It's only moonlight reflecting off her visor. There are enough terrifying things running around this scenario without factoring in the supernatural.

Here, death is final.

To show my disdain, I lift the visor and wipe the bloody knife on her face before sheathing it. Then I nab my assault rifle and add the magazines from the dead to my ammo belt. I don't find much; they've had a lengthy scenario too.

After finishing, I march toward the last combatants lying in the moonlit side of the shallow dimple.

Bob is gone. His face presses into the junction of his killer's thighs, his knife buried at the end of a long slit in her belly. Except for being clad in armor, they could pass for lovers in foreplay.

When I stand above the pair, the woman pulls off her helmet. Hair with red streaks cascade around her blood-painted face.

"Hello, Belle."

Her unblinking, dark eyes stare as she cackles again. "The master has many plans for you, Brin."

"You mean Syd."

"He has progressed far beyond a mere name." She coughs, and blood dribbles down her chin.

I eject the empty magazine from my weapon. As I reload, I tickle the knife extending from her abdomen with my boot.

A shriek of pain leaves her mouth, and then her eyes glaze as her mind wanders into fantasy. "So much fun. So much pleasure when he catches you."

"Too bad you won't be there."

She puckers her bloody lips. "Give us a kiss."

I fire into her chest.

After the last breath leaves her body, I head to the shore and step into the final retreat boat.

A disconcerting quiet hangs over the surrounding islands. That's a terrible sign.

Looping deep into the channel to avoid the plants, I set course for the last stand position.

FIFTY-FOUR

BEFORE THE BOAT touches dry land, I hop into the shallow water and drag it ashore. Something is occupying the enemy, and I don't intend to waste time.

Odet waves from the bluff. The position sits across a wide channel from the landing beach of our home island and is the last point Syd needs before assaulting the flag.

There's no immediate danger, but I sweep the area with my rifle as I trot to her.

She raises an eyebrow. "Bob?"

I lift my gashed visor. Spinning his death in the best way possible, I say, "He's gone, but he took a bunch of them with him."

"That's good."

The dark shapes of the other two team members run to us.

After motioning for everyone to stay low, I say to the grim-faced newcomers, "We didn't have a chance to meet personally. I'm Brin." Since we'll be dying together, I should at least learn their names.

Already knowing whom the nine sigma is, the two nod and lift their visors.

The nearer one, round-faced with inset eyes and barrel-chested armor, softly shakes my hand. "Blue."

It's the same as the unhelpful ally in the scenario with the seven sigma. Weirdly, not knowing her name causes more guilt within me than being the instrument of her death.

The other man, prominent-nosed, more a professor than a soldier, extends his hand and says his name.

"Jock?"

"No, Jack."

"Good to meet you," I say, grabbing his hand, relieved not to be haunted by ghosts from the past.

"What's the plan?" Jack asks.

Odet answers. "Kill as many as you can."

In the face of death, their calmness is a positive, and despite the odds, I grin.

Blue says, "They haven't tried the river, yet."

"They won't until they wipe out this position. They'll be coming from overland," I reply.

"Strategy doesn't appear to be their strong suit."

Shaking my head, I say, "It's not."

And they don't need it.

A shriek pierces the night.

We dive on the ground, readying our weapons.

Through the broken moonlight, a distant form runs toward us with wild, stumbling strides.

Suspicious, I peek at the flanks. Empty. If anything, this smacks of a rather obvious decoy making it unlikely this actually is a decoy. "Don't shoot," I tell the others.

The helmetless figure rambles closer, now clearly gimping from a leg wound and curiously not carrying any weapons.

"It's Cleo," Odet says.

Her good leg slams into a leaf and she tumbles, spilling her disheveled hair over her face. After rolling back onto her feet, she staggers more than runs the final steps to us.

Before she can hurt herself, I jump up and catch her. When she's firmly in my arms, I gently set her on the ground.

"Calm down," I say, brushing hair from her eyes. "What happened?"

Tears streak her cheeks. Her breaths come in broken gasps. "Coming. Coming," she says in a hoarse voice.

Odet marches over and squeezes Cleo's chin between armored fingers. "Tell us what happened."

Cleo looks past us, seeing a threat that isn't there.

When Odet moves to slap the distraught girl, I grab her hand. "That's enough."

With a scowl, Odet steps backward as Cleo fights back more tears.

"Cleo, I can't help unless I know what happened," I say in a sympathetic tone. "Cleo? Take a deep breath, we don't have a lot of time."

Her eyes focus on me. "There isn't any time!" she cries out. "You only have enough time to decide how you want to die."

"That's nonsense," Odet says. "Brin's over nine sigmas."

"They have a 9.99," Cleo retorts.

She met Syd.

Given that tidy fact, the panicked response is perfectly rational. "Start with him and go from there."

Her eyes glaze as she relives the nightmare. "We were captured. They tortured the others. Even with all the experience threads, I never imagined anything close to what they were doing. They made me watch while they—"

I don't need the details. "What happened when they finished?"

She shivers. "That 9.99."

"Syd."

"Yes, I think that's his name. After they finished, he came to me. He said to tell you he's coming for what was promised."

"I'm not afraid of him."

Her hands clutch my forearms. "You should be. He's unstoppable. And he'll win and when he does..." The final word trails into a sniffle.

"Keep going."

"He told me what he's going to do to you. To all of us. Worse than what happened to the others." She stops, her eyes wildly roaming over the landscape.

Odet interjects, "What things?"

The poor girl's body seems to shrink. "Terrible. I can't repeat them."

I try to imagine something ten times more gruesome than anything I can imagine.

What Syd would have done to me if Suri hadn't interceded.

"Get yourself together," I snap at the sniveling girl.

"That can't happen to me," Cleo says to nobody. Her hands quiver, shaking my arms. "This is your fault."

I struggle to pull away, but her grip is too tight.

"Don't you understand? He wants you, Brin. We're going to die horrible deaths for his pleasure because of you!"

This time, when Odet steps up with a raised hand, I do nothing. She delivers a solid slap to Cleo's cheek.

Cleo lets go of me and shockingly, grabs Odet's pistol and scoots backward, swinging it wildly back and forth between us.

I raise my hand to forestall any bad reactions and keep my assault rifle aimed at the ground. "Cleo, think about what you're doing. We aren't your enemies."

A twisted laugh pours from her lips. It can't be the blue liquid, but Syd's insanity has somehow infected her. With a crazed stare, she replies, "I'm your friend. I'll be doing everyone a favor by killing you."

"No, you won't. We still have a chance."

"You have no idea, Brin. None. He's saving the worst things for you," she says, pointing the gun directly at my chest.

I force myself to remain calm as she pulls back the hammer. Although only a 2.5 sigma, she has every black and red thread I have. At this distance, she can end my life with a simple pull of the trigger.

Odet points her rifle at Cleo. "Drop it."

One of the men hollers, "Movement. They're coming."

Everything is a shit-show.

I make one final plea. "Cleo, let's kill as many of them as possible. I'll make sure you don't fall into their hands. Let's go out fighting."

"Guys, what do we do?" Blue says with panic seeping into his tone.

Cleo looks at me with pity. Then she points the gun at her temple and pulls the trigger.

The silencer quiets the shot, and the only sounds are the tiny piece of lead cracking through her skull and the soft sighing of her body slumping onto the hard sand.

Assault rifles chatter.

I slam my visor closed and dive into cover.

The battle is on.

FIFTY-FIVE

Gunfire slings dirt over my helmet as I stare at Cleo's prone form. Beyond volunteering for the Ten Sigma Program, she didn't deserve this fate.

"Idle sympathy will get you killed," my internal voice warns.

I push my attention to the raging firefight.

Lit by the orange bonfires and intermittent moonlight, an oversized team of sixteen advances across the rippled landscape. As the dim, shifting figures dart between cover, their bullets hiss past, spraying sand, destroying rocks, and exploding the aloe vera-like flora with loud pops.

A close impact blows apart a nearby plant. Waves of sharp debris rattle over my armor.

Flinching, I push myself further into the ground. These foes are superbly talented—at least fours—and far superior to my teammates.

However, despite being outnumbered and outmatched, we have to stop the composite personas from getting through us. And I can't call upon my one-time dalliance with the taste of murder to help.

We are totally screwed.

Odet curses over the noise while Blue and Jack blaze away with their assault rifles.

"Save ammo," I yell.

A rational commander would use the cover of the attack to advance along the river and take our flag. Instinctively, I check the water. There's nothing but a thin mist curling over its surface.

Syd is sending just enough force to whittle away the rest of my less accomplished and less lucky peers without killing me.

He wants me alive.

I'll oblige him by killing as many of his people as possible. "Odet," I scream.

Hugging the ground, she turns her head.

The weight of fire is pushing us back. They're coming in roughly a straight line, intending to shrink our perimeter against the bluff where we'll be captured or drown in the channel. "Hold this position. No matter what."

She quickly nods before returning to the fight.

Cutting past the attacking flank to the riverbank presents the best opportunity to increase our odds. I keep low and push to the right. At the edge of the shallow crest, I stop and peek past the side.

Sharp impacts smack around me.

I jerk back as sand rattles against my armor.

Three of them have gathered to prevent exactly what I'm trying to do.

I return fire with quick shots. The spider cracks spreading from the gash in my visor make a clear line of sight impossible, but I can't remove it because I don't need one of the sharp leaves blinding an eye.

Between aiming and snapping off rounds, I switch positions but am constantly checked since I'm stuck in the death cage of flying lead like everyone else.

Odet gets lucky with a center-mass hit, the limp form of the attacker flopping onto a plant, but it's not even close to equalizing the disparity of numbers.

After a minute, the rate of fire slows to a trickle. Both sides are low on ammunition from the extended fighting, and when it runs out, our enemies will only need to march over and beat the snot out of us.

Since I started later, I have more. I toss a few magazines to Odet who passes the valuable commodities to Blue and Jack.

The breeze shifts and a feral keening scrapes into the shrouds of darkness.

As my stomach clenches into a knot, I look to Odet.

She hears it too. The shrill sounds grow louder, similar to a rebel yell, only a thousand times more frightening. I can't believe they're coming from human beings.

"What the hell is that?" Jack screams.

"Shut up and shoot," Odet replies. Despite the bravado of her words, everyone is near the breaking point.

"Pull back to the next defensive crest," I say. While halving our fighting area, the tactic will allow me to better control the others.

As they slither backward, I keep up a steady rate of protective fire.

An object floats from the night sky. Odet hollers, "Grenade."

While the others duck, I follow its trail. It's too big and floppy to be a grenade.

Blood spatters when it lands.

Surprised, I wipe dark droplets from my visor and grimace. The mushy shape is an internal organ, maybe a liver.

More gory things arc past the twinkling stars. A head impales itself on a nearby plant and splits open, pouring brains over the sharp leaves. A soft organ flops behind me. It's a penis.

Jack screams, "They're from our team. The prisoners."

Or at least parts of them. While disgust taints my thoughts, I appreciate their mastery of psychological warfare. "Stay calm," I shout to no one in particular.

Blue curses as more gore lands around him.

A bewildering instant passes before I recognize the next item that splats in front of my face. It's most of a vagina. As my hands curl into a ball, I curse, wishing for a bath in the worst possible way.

More grisly pieces rain. Hands, feet, hearts, other unidentifiable organs make gruesome impacts around and on us. I can't understand how they've managed to carry so many body parts and their weapons too.

A thrown penis hits Blue on the visor. As he wipes the mess away, his fear turns into fury. "Screw this!"

Before I can stop him, he rises and charges, his weapon flashing against the darkness. The audacity of his attack catches our tormentors by surprise, their reactions slow in switching from terrorizing us to actual combat.

Bullets smack around Blue with one blowing out a piece of his leg, but he keeps charging. Odet fires to support him, yelling incoherent words of encouragement. Past the enemy line, their gunfire shreds a dark silhouette in the process of throwing another organ.

The moment of confusion is an opportunity. I unclip my grenades and toss them at the three foes in front of me.

Panicked shouts come as the grenades explode, spraying metal along with dirt and plants over the area.

The flank is finally open.

As the fight rages, I rush to the right. Staying in cover but using precious seconds, I hug the ground, plowing over soft sand and pebbles as I hurry to the river bank. When my boots squish into damp ground, I peek over the embankment.

Blue screams in defiance from his knees as he bleeds from a half-dozen wounds and fires his pistol. Two prone forms lie near him.

Jack also is down to his pistol while Odet fires her rifle from next to him.

Twelve of the enemy remain, and my three teammates won't last long.

A bullet explodes Blue's head, and his body flops onto the ground.

I roll over the lip of the embankment. Using every wrinkle in the shallow terrain, I rush, rapidly closing the distance to my three opponents.

The disturbing wails of insanity increase in volume. As the horrible sounds hit an apex, they rise and charge at Odet and Jack.

Ignoring the chills running up my back, I straighten and fire at my closest enemy.

The cracked visor isn't an issue at this range. The bullet plows through his helmet, an instant kill.

Before his body hits the ground, I advance, shooting at the other two women guarding the side. The first falls as a bullet explodes her face against the inside of her visor while the second twists, receiving only a crease in her shoulder armor. Her pistol whirls in my direction and fires.

The bullets fly high as I sink to a knee and shoot her in the throat.

With her neck blown out, her head tilts at an odd angle while she crumples between a couple of plants and disappears into a crevasse.

Two of the charging enemy notice me and turn. When they aim their weapons, I dive into a ditch and run into a nasty surprise, folds of human skin holding human organs. While I cringe, my logical mind informs me that Syd's people used the freshly cut skin as carrying bags for the body parts of their victims.

I'm going to kill them all by myself.

Shaking from the discovery, I control my rage and pop up, shooting the first one through the visor.

There is a rat-tat-tat of impacts from a silenced pistol. They've run out of rifle ammunition.

I lunge to the side and fire into the second opponent, splashing huge red blossoms over his breastplate and then slam my last magazine into my rifle. Shooting quickly while dodging return fire, I manage to kill one more, although hitting anything else of value without hurting any of my teammates is impossible.

As my rifle clicks on empty, I dash into the melee and everything turns to chaos.

Odet has killed one and of the five remaining, one fights with Jack, two charge at her, and the other two, one thin, one stocky come at me.

I toss the rifle and pull out my knife, a more effective close weapon than a gun.

As the stocky woman aims her pistol, I duck and slice at her hand, keeping her between myself and her partner.

She curses something incomprehensible and takes a wild swing with her free hand.

I step up, and blocking the movement, thrust my knife into her elbow.

The gun falls and I twist and fling her into her partner who brushes her aside and shoots.

Rolling on the ground to dodge, I nab her pistol and kill both in rapid succession.

A click comes from behind.

I twirl, avoiding a bullet, then a kick slams into my side and I crash onto a plant, crushing its leaves with crinkly metallic pops and losing the pistol. My body stops tumbling near a bloody pile of organs. As my female attacker leaps, I grab the skin sack and toss it. The contents drench her in every vile kind of gore and blood.

Yanking out my pistol, I dive and fire into her crotch.

She bellows in madness as her legs give way.

A final shot silences her.

Odet grapples with a shadowy form while Jack is in big trouble.

I scramble to help him.

His bigger enemy knees him in the chest, crushing his breastplate and breaking ribs. As Jack crumples, his opponent grabs a plant leaf and stabs at his exposed throat.

Jack lets out a squeal.

I fire, the bullet plowing through helmet and skull. The large man's body jerks once then falls. Below him, Jack is dead, a ghastly expression on his face and blood dripping from his mouth.

When nothing else moves, silence settles over the battlefield. In many ways the stillness is more disconcerting than combat.

There is a groan.

I rush to Odet, who lies flat on the ground. A bloody form is nearby, a knife buried deep in his chest.

Kneeling next to the tough woman, I check for injuries. Nothing is obvious.

"Plant," she whispers in a hoarse voice. "Landed on a stupid plant. I can't feel my body."

Without touching her, I lean over to examine underneath her neck. When I raise my visor, I see blood trailing from a spike embedded between her helmet and shoulder armor. An unlucky break.

"You're paralyzed."

She blows out a huff. "Tell me something I don't know."

"I'll leave you here and finish the scenario."

"No," she says. "Don't leave me like this."

"When I win, you'll come back healthy."

"Liar. You're not winning."

I purse my lips. She's right.

When I bring up my pistol, she pleads, "Not in the face." Her watery eyes blink back tears. "I really thought I was going to reach ten sigmas."

Everyone thinks they have the winning lottery ticket.

"Do you have any memories left?"

"A few."

"Tell me the best one," I say, returning the pistol to its holster.

"I have four children. All girls, all brats."

"Happy memories."

"I'm getting there." Her eyes wander. "My oldest daughter married a bum. Good for nothing bum. When she got pregnant, he beat on her. But I got her out of there. Put him in the hospital too. A month later she gave birth to my beautiful grandson."

I lean closer. "Tell me about him."

"He had the most inquisitive stare and the cutest nose. Took after my husband. He always wanted a son. I had forgotten how wonderful children are." She cracks a half-smile as a tear leaks from the corner of her eye. "Those years watching him grow up were the best years of my life. I miss my girls; I was so mean to them."

She stops, gurgling her last breath.

Leaving her knife in her chest, I stand and wipe my cheek. To my disappointment, it's dry.

I wonder for a fleeting moment if I will be punished for killing another teammate before I shake it off. I have a bargain with the virtual overlords, and win or lose, this is my last scenario.

A smoky breeze blows past as I sweep my eyes over the scattered bodies. Beyond them, the entire map is quiet.

It's only me against Syd and his teammates. My people have fought well but even if they took two of Syd's for every one of them, that still leaves over forty enemies. Forty of the toughest and most evil individuals mankind has to offer. And that's not including Syd, who is the most formidable opponent in this or any other universe.

Cleo's words ring in my ears. *"He's reserving the worst things for you."*

Remembering the horrendous injuries Syd inflicted the last time we met, I tremble. Whatever happened to those people who were hacked into body parts awaits me. Only a lot worse. The type of sadistic torture only a mix of the worst parts of rapists and murderers could devise.

My fingers touch the pistol strapped to my thigh.

"You made a promise," says my internal voice.

The silence stretches.

"You are the avenging angel!"

I straighten. Now is the moment to be strong. I made a promise to stop Syd and his brethren, and I intend to keep it.

This is where I belong.

Although I'm in the all too familiar state of being alone, that's okay. Somehow my worst fears of loneliness have dissipated.

"Do the unexpected," my internal voice shouts.

As I look at the razor leaves sprouting from the plants and the shimmering water beyond, a plan comes together. Although not much, the proactive strategy offers my only chance of success.

I kneel and start pulling off Odet's armor. The pieces aren't designed to be removed and I have to waste extra seconds breaking some stubborn clasps. When I'm done, and after I retrieve the knife from her last kill, I board the boat and cross the channel to the home island. The world map is still etched into the sand and I step on it as I walk toward the flag.

My preparations require a few minutes and after finishing, I return to the beach. As my bare feet touch the shimmering water, I pause and enjoy the surrounding calm.

Across the way, orange glints flicker over the deadly plant leaves while speeding clouds obscuring the full moon run playful shadows over the broken masses of land. In the distance, thunder rumbles and lightning flashes from the dark wall of the approaching storm.

No more time to waste.

I step off the sand and plunge into the icy river.

Syd's coming.

FIFTY-SIX

AIR GUSHES as the sharp steel slices through the thick rubber segments, gutting the craft from stem to stern. My enemies tumble into the freezing water.

Satisfied by their drowning cries, I slide my knife into its sheath and angle myself to face against the gentle current. Using a modified breaststroke, my head barely breaching the water's surface, I swim toward my protecting position as the feeble sounds fade into silence, the newly dead joining their three other sets of teammates at the bottom.

Even as the frigid surroundings numb my skin, I keep my motions smooth and efficient. I'm not naked, but I've stripped to just my under-garments with my only weapons, the knife wrapped around my thigh and silenced pistol jammed into my bra. A single reload, which I hope not to use, forms a conspicuous bulge in the back of my panties.

I slice through a thin mist and swim closer to the curving river bank to save time.

An underwater plant scrapes against my bare leg. It's only a shallow cut, and although I twitch from the pain, I keep focused on controlling a growing nervousness from the coming confrontation with Syd.

A bolt of white forks in the distance, revealing ominous clouds with dark bellies, the vanguard of the approaching storm. When the stark illumination fades, only the broken radiance of the moon remains. A few moments later, faint thunder passes me, accompanied by a breeze laden with warm moisture. The storm, bringing chaos and uncertainty, will be here soon.

Something tickles my bare arm, and I yank out my knife. It's a helmet from one of my victims. I put the weapon away, admonishing my jumpiness.

The low hum of boat engines slides over the water.

My heart skips a beat. It shouldn't be possible for the enemy to have moved that quickly.

Shedding my disbelief, I increase the pace of my strokes and take inventory. Except for the minor wounds I've sustained, I'm functional, and that's a positive. The negatives are growing fatigue, a tiny supply of weapons, no protection against the inhospitable environment, and worst of all, having a host of merciless enemies.

"And a promise to survive, and you get to kill Syd and rid the universe of evil," internal me chimes.

I roll my eyes, not sure why its optimism no longer bothers me.

As I rush to the island, the hanging mist scatters to reveal two small crafts resting on the empty strip of beach.

Fine mud, littered with jagged pebbles, squishes under my feet as I hurry from the water. My freezing muscles want to shiver, but I relax to allow blood to flow to my extremities.

Time is short, and I focus inland. Although having a head start, my enemies advance cautiously and with surprising inexperience. I read them as lowly 2.5 sigmas in their first battle.

But regardless of their experience level, if they touch the flag, the scenario ends and Syd goes on to the real world. I force my freezing muscles to action, and in plodding steps, leave the beach and head toward the waiting rows of lethal plants.

While I keep my sight glued to my targets, the razor leaves take turns slicing my bare shins. While helpful in the water, the lack of armor is a massive detriment on land. I wince with each cut, and soon, everything below my knees is a crosshatch of gashes under a dripping layer of blood.

As a sharp sliver of plant spikes into my heel, a single form peals from the group and kneels in the dim light, scanning the flanks against attack.

Readying my knife, my bare feet stay silent as I rush to his blind spot. A quick back twist of my hand parts the flexible armor plates protecting the neck and head while the blade slips through the gap. Blood spurts over my fingers. Before he sags to the ground, I slide past, wiping the knife on my panties.

I advance further inland, my teeth grinding from the pain radiating from my sliced shins and wounded heel.

Before long, I locate another rearguard. This one narrows at the waist—a female. Even though the man in the broad-brimmed hat explained my fascination with her, I hope it's not the girl with the violet eyes.

Because of the evil flora, my hobbled strides take a more cautious tone as I alter my path into the wavy shadows cast from a nearby fire.

Suppressed gunfire rings in front. They're shredding the empty armor shells I've left defending the flag. Since the decoy was meant for Syd as a last line of defense, it's another setback for my plans.

"All plans die upon the initial contact with the enemy," a black thread announces.

With everyone's attention shifted to the gunfight, I hasten over the remaining distance. When I reach her, I use the same hand technique to create a weak spot in her armor.

Soundlessly, the girl dies, her body collapsing face first into the muck and to my relief, hiding the color of her eyes.

I follow the final eight with my anger increasing from each cut of the hateful vegetation. Besides the degradation of my abilities, I'm worried about the simmering rage of the blue liquid overcoming my sanity.

However, the armor has served its purpose, making my neophyte opponents fear ambush and become timid in their advance. And because I lack armor in such a hostile environment, they have no idea I could traverse the river without drowning and arrive directly behind them.

The advantage is almost worth the clawing pain.

After the fifteenth cut, the malevolence of the blue liquid surges and I tighten my jaw to stop from shrieking in rage.

Forcing calm into my mind, I re-sheath my knife and yank the pistol from my bra.

The popping sounds fade while smoke climbs from the tatters of the two sets of armor. The remaining combatants rise and advance.

I fire at the edge of effective range. In real Sergeant York style, I start with the rearmost opponent and work my way forward. Four of the shadowy figures crumple from shots into the back of the neck before I take cover behind a shallow ripple.

The others arrive at the shredded decoys, unaware. When they turn, I take out the one furthest from me and then the next with throat shots. The other two dive, and instead of firing at them, I shoot at where they're seeking cover. There are several sharp cracks from the bullets piercing the ceramic armor.

I pull the other magazine from my panties and reload but everything stays still.

As the leading edge of the storm crosses in front of the moon, lengthening shadows reach past my face and blanket the rest of the island. Beyond the smoky armor, the flag's pinpoints of light wave proudly in the rising breeze.

Raindrops touch my body.

Puzzled with the entire situation, I survey the battlefield as I stride to the prone forms.

Droplets splash in the pools of blood around their bodies. Surprisingly, their faces aren't painted and look familiar. After a moment, I realize they're AIs, and just like the girl with the violet eyes, I've killed them many times.

However, in the midst of all the composites, myself, and Syd, the finest warriors the virtual universe has to offer, the arrival of these AI neophytes is bewildering.

They never had a chance.

My bloody calf brushes against a curled leaf with thorny spikes.

I grab a rifle and smash the hated plant. As I fling the weapon into the next one, the irrational but wonderful darkness of murder seeps into my mind.

Angrily, I flick wet hair from my face then squeeze my lips between my thumb and forefinger. I won't let the stupid plants drive me over the edge.

Motor sounds arrive through a gust of wind.

Syd!

Adrenaline dumps into my bloodstream while the pit of my stomach drops. For all of my tactical acumen, and for all of his not caring about strategy, I'm cornered.

Nothing comes easy.

With no more tricks or allies, and because I have to defend the flag, which limits my mobility, I'm in deep trouble.

Cleo's words whisper in my mind. *"He's reserving the worst things for you."*

I'm going to die as Syd's final sacrifice in his journey to the real world.

The thought angers me. Syd isn't dead, and I made a promise to beat him.

My eyes dart across the barren landscape, searching for a solution. I can't surrender to the inevitable.

There isn't any way out.

Clenching my hands into fists, I swallow a pool of saliva and battle with my panicky desire for the murderous power of the blue liquid. Since it saved me from the bald giant, certainly it could help against Syd and his friends.

Blood trickles under my toes.

I glance downward, bringing myself back from the abyss.

Like me, each of the AIs carried into battle a standard load consisting of an assault rifle, a pistol with one reload, a combat knife, and two grenades.

But they just entered the fight and have barely expended any ammunition.

It makes no sense.

"Hey, Dummy, it has to make sense," internal me adds in a snarky voice.

"When did you decide sarcasm was fun?"

"You have plenty of optimism for us both; somebody has to be a realist."

I nibble on a nail. Arguing with internal me won't solve anything. Time is running out, but I need to reason through the problem.

For this to be my last scenario, the overlords needed to stack the odds against me. The jump from slightly more than nine to ten sigmas is staggering, and these novices provided the smallest fraction of the total. With the number of reinforcements joining Syd's side, it could have been done through many combinations.

And these AIs died so quickly.

The novice team was sent to resupply me.

"Yes, Dummy, they still have most of their ordnance."

I look upward to the sky, and thickening raindrops pelt my face. Behind the gigantic clouds of the storm and the nighttime blackness beyond hides the glorious blue dome. I imagine the man in the broad-brimmed hat looking downward.

My lips mouth a "Thank you."

I have a path to get home.

FIFTY-SEVEN

As the rain splatters mud over my bloody shins, I take a calming breath. I need to apply my experiences from every scenario along with the knowledge embedded in each thread and all my abilities to devise a workable strategy.

Although I'm not emerging unscathed, with a little luck and a lot of skill, I'll have a chance—albeit a slim one—of surviving.

And kill Syd too.

Despite my wounds and physical exhaustion, my energy surges at the prospect of one final fight. Surrendering to my senses, I notice the temperature, the worsening rain, the nuances of the wind, every frond protruding from the vegetation, and each variation in the terrain. Everything that will influence the coming battle.

Time is critical.

For each of my last eight kills, I drag the body into sight of the flag and prepare both grenades, pulling their pins and tucking them into whatever sturdy place like under a hand or arm that allows easy freedom while preventing the safety handle from releasing. After finishing, I glance longingly at their ceramic armor, but as I discovered with Odet, the protection isn't built to be removed, much less put back on a different person. Cursed plants or not, I'm winning or losing in my unclad state.

Ridding myself of weak thoughts, I jog to the two rear guards, and after appropriating their weapons, head toward the beach buoyed by confidence in the plan as well as the rifle slung across my chest and the four grenades and pistol crammed into my bra and panties.

When I arrive, a thick mist still hugs the channel in spite of the awful weather. I stake out an overwatch position nestled behind a waist-level rise in the terrain that offers a straightforward egress to the flag.

As I wait, brushing wet strands of hair from my eyes, the rain pours and lightning crashes onto nearby islands with loud cracks of thunder.

The storm is mine.

I relish in the water pelting my face and rushing down my body, my toes curling in the coarse mud, the hisses of the droplets extinguishing the fires, and the wind gusting across the landscape.

There is nowhere in the universe I would rather be.

Only moments pass before four boats emerge from the fog.

It's time!

Nineteen armor-clad soldiers jump onto the island in expert fashion. The least of them owns a five sigma score, and even in the awful conditions, they speedily clear the beach.

Then a single malevolent figure strides ashore. He screams loud enough to cut through the burgeoning storm. "Brin! Sweetie, are you ready for me?"

I grind my teeth, refusing to be intimidated.

Syd motions for his people to advance and scatter to the flanks.

Because I can't have them spread out, I stand and yell, "I'm right here Syd."

They stop. Syd yanks off his helmet, the rain instantly drenching his spiky hair and smearing his blood-painted face. As he flings it into the wild weather, he lets out a broad smile.

I send back an obscene gesture.

The heavens rip open. Waterfalls pour from the sky, joined by thick, incandescent strikes of lightning, which whiten out the land. The earth trembles from gigantic claps of thunder. And through everything, the wind shrieks.

Drenched and blinking from the streams of water cascading down my face, I steady myself against the brunt of the storm.

Several figures raise their rifles.

I yank the pin from a grenade and toss it onto the beach.

Everyone scatters.

The muffled explosion sends up a shower of sand that the violent winds and deluge of rain immediately erase.

In the confusion, I start a sniping battle with my appropriated rifle. Although my goal is funneling the advance into a narrow front by attacking their flanks, I would consider any incidental death or injury I cause a positive.

I flinch but keep shooting as suppressing fire sends stinging jets of water laced with sand and pebbles past my head. The magazine empties too quickly, and I toss the rifle. My bare feet slide in the worsening terrain as I turn, retreating for my next set of weapons.

A blast of wind slaps a sheet of rain over my face as I exit the overwatch position. Raising a hand over my eyes, I stagger toward the center of the island, catching more cuts from the plants on the gashes covering my shins. Although the pain is beyond terrible, I silently thank Mother Nature. Without the chaos, I would already be dead.

Forcing aside the distractions, my situational awareness uses the illumination from every type of lightning crossing under the black clouds as well as glimpses I catch from flashes of gunfire through the wind and rain to create a map of the battle. When the attack spreads too far to the sides, I fling a grenade to entice my enemies to stay together.

The grenades are gone by the time I get to the dead rearguard. I grab his rifle, and continuing my retreat, shoot at the fleeting forms through the gale. In the impossible conditions, I surprisingly hit one, the dark form jerking and dropping from sight.

A stray shot pops in front of me as I adjust my path to avoid a row of plants. The enemy is too close, and I hasten to my next objective, climbing up a slope, my fingers grasping at muddy rivulets and my feet sliding on the unsure ground.

Lightning crashes on a nearby mound, the concussion knocking me into the muck on the other side.

Ears ringing, I ignore a plant leaf hovering a millimeter from my nose and start crawling through a torrent of water rushing toward the beach. Occasionally, when cracks of lightning break the blackness, I lean up and shoot along the flanks until the second rifle runs empty.

After discarding it, I swivel and run for another weapon but promptly trip over an extinguished fire, the doused wood digging into the bloody meat around my shins. The wind whips away my angry curses as I rise and wipe mud from my face. With my feet struggling to find purchase in the glop, I stumble to the next set of arms.

A howling gust slaps fat raindrops across my body as more shots splatter the nearby ground with wet pops.

I disregard them, and shielding my eyes with both hands, I hunch and push forward.

"The enemy has the same problems too."

"There are almost twenty of them."

"And you were doing so well with my optimism."

A crack of thunder overwhelms my cry of frustration. I hate new internal me.

Crawling more than walking, I finally reach the woman I killed. When I flip her over, flashes of lightning expose her face.

Although it's not the girl with the violet eyes, I'm furious I even care. Grabbing her rifle, I shove her back into the mud and keep moving, all the while shooting at more targets of opportunity until the gun empties.

When I arrive at the main line of the AI dead, I nab another two rifles and extra ammo without disturbing the precious booby traps, which remain blessedly intact from the mayhem. To avoid the worst of the vicious weather and not present a prime target, I keep low, reverse crawling toward the flag with the rain pounding the hundred cuts running along my legs.

While the pain builds, I grit my teeth, forcing my thoughts from the distraction.

A bullet explodes a plant next to me. I recoil from whizzing metallic shards. A second afterward, other shots follow as the rest of Syd's team arrives.

Taking a quick survey through the bedlam, I notice the shooting originates from only a small arc. At least that part of my strategy is working.

I return fire, but for every round, ten rifles crack in response.

As the impacts shred everything nearby, pulverized rocks mix with jagged fragments of flora and join the torrents of rain splattering over me. Soon I'm covered in the foul mixture, with the sharp edges of the organic matter rubbing into the raw tissue of my exposed wounds.

On the bright side, while I'm not sure if I've hit anything, at least I haven't been hit either. However, it's a situation that can only end badly. I have to give ground before a lucky shot or flying piece of plant kills me.

Cradling my rifles above the mud, I slither backward, only stopping when I reach the flag—my last stand position.

Suddenly, the storm abates. The crashes of lightning stop, and the rumbles of thunder disappear. A moment later, the air stills while the torrential rain ebbs into a light shower.

I stare helplessly as moonlight fills the thinning clouds and casts a blue pall over the landscape.

"This is bad."

A torrent of bullets flies through the newly sedate surroundings. Nearby plants explode with sharp clacks while metallic pings reverberate off the flagpole.

Panic rising, I flatten, willing my body to shrink behind the scant remaining cover.

The enemy is just beginning. The level of firing rises to a crescendo, the staccato of pops, whistles, and pings from the projectiles smeared into a long note of death, inching ever closer to my position. As I push lower, my fingers clawing at the ground, a bullet scorches the back of my thigh, leaving an angry furrow of pain. Another clips my hair while more ricochets spatter mud over me.

My fear explodes and closing my eyes, I twist my face and launch a scream into the muck.

As dirty water bubbles into my nose and sludge smears my lips, bullets leave streaks of sizzling air crisscrossing my back.

My body trembles as I lose control. Although we don't need to pee, the utter helplessness consuming my insides threatens to empty my bladder. I clench my lower half while mixed curses of frustration at my impotence, rage at the overlords, and fury at my enemies pour from my mouth.

Time stretches into eternity as I try to slither further into the mushy ground, cowering and waiting for the end. My competing thoughts merge into a storm of incoherence, hating the situation and wanting to lash out and leap into any foolhardy action that might change the predicament.

At the height of my hysteria, just as I'm ready to stand and perish in a hail of lead, a soothing image of Suri enters my mind. Others follow, Bob, Odet, poor Cleo, the boy in the icy cabin, and my original teammates, Rick, Jock, and Ally. All are victims of Syd and his kind. The composites are the enemy, and I need to punish them for their crimes.

The sliver of calm guides me from the brink.

Moments afterward, the fusillade subsides.

Shedding my surprise of remaining amongst the living, I peek past the base of the flag. My enemies have advanced into the line of the dead AI soldiers.

I swing a rifle up, and with a prayer to the great blue dome, fire into each of the booby traps.

The dead jerk from my flawless shooting, releasing their presents.

I hug the earth, thanking the seven sigma for teaching me the shooting the hidden grenade trick.

Seconds later, explosions rip through my enemies. Gore, blood, and weapons intertwine with splatters of mud and tumble through the lingering rain.

Before the final scraps hit the ground, I grab the fresh rifle and stuff an extra two magazines into the front of my panties. Then, letting wrath cleanse the last trepidations from my mind, I focus on my enemies and transform into an avenging angel, rushing past the flag and hurdling the gleaming remains of a despicable plant.

I'm going to kill every last evil one of them.

A dark shadow on the flank runs. I fire a three-round burst and the malevolent thing falls. Holding his head, a huge man stands and explodes into gore when I empty the magazine into his torso.

As I reload and advance, metal shards from broken leaves stick into the soles of my feet. The new torture is inconsequential in the face of my mission. Grimacing, I charge past the remains of the fallen AI soldiers and leap beyond the shallow ridge. I land in the midst of my enemies. A few of them I recognize from the scenario where Suri died. My glee surges.

One, two, three of the vile forms crawling in the muck go down to sharp cracks from my rifle.

Another fiend pokes his head above a mound. As my shot rips through his helmet, I stifle a giggle.

A bullet smashes a nearby plant into metallic flakes.

No time to get sloppy.

Dark against the dim moonlight, his visor shattered, the tallest of Syd's team advances, trying to wipe blood from his eyes while blindly shooting his firearm.

As rounds fly past, I fire, my shot slamming through the cracks of the visor and plowing into the top of his lewd mouth. His long body flops, crushing the broken stems of a plant, and awkwardly rolls out of sight.

I take a quick survey. Although I haven't seen Syd, I can't worry. I need to execute as many composites in as little time as possible.

Rushing ahead, I splash through a puddle and charge up the next rise, seeking more targets. As I slide to the opposite side, I sink into gooey mud with water rising past my ankles.

A thin streak of lightning branching between distant clouds illuminates the scene.

Jackpot!

On its knees, a disheveled creature cradles its bloody head. Another demonic construct staggers about in confusion, tugging to free his pistol. I kill both. In the muck to my left, a brew of malevolence pretending to be a woman writhes with a shattered leg, laughing.

None of them deserves any mercy, and I empty my weapon into her face.

Although not from the blue liquid, a wave of ecstasy washes over me from killing so many of the composites.

I yank the last magazine from my panties and shove it into the rifle.

A clink comes from behind me. I twist and duck, but a bullet clips my shoulder and knocks me backward. I return fire. As I hit the ground, spiky leaves shred my bicep, and my face twists in agony.

My assailant falls, one of the wave of my bullets catching his throat, but another rises in his place. Instead of flinging myself away from the awful plant, I continue rolling to get to cover. Screams of misery cascade past my clenched teeth as the points stab into my shoulder and the edges slice my back.

I pull the trigger, but the crippled muscles in my left arm won't function properly. The projectiles fly skyward while the magazine empties. More leaves hack at my thighs as I discard the useless weapon and tumble into an adjoining gully.

My opponent moves slower than expected. A white flash shows half his helmet torn away.

Over the paralyzing pain, I will my legs to push me upright, and with my good arm, yank the pistol from my bra. I fire twice.

As he flops into the darkness, an iron grip seizes my hand, forcing me to drop the gun.

I turn to face Syd.

FIFTY-EIGHT

"Did you really think a stupid little trick would harm me?" Syd says before backhanding me across the cheek.

As my face explodes in pain, I twist to avoid one of the plants and splash into a deep puddle.

Before I can stand, he's on me. Grabbing two fistfuls of sopping hair, he drags me through the water and to my feet.

I pull out my knife with my working arm and swipe at his head.

He delivers a sword strike, the flat of his hand slamming into my wrist, and the knife flies into the darkness. An instant later, his armored fist drives into my bare stomach.

Gasping, I keel over, but he yanks me up and plants a full, wet, disgusting kiss on my lips.

With a snarl, I bite and draw blood from his lip. When he pulls away, I spit the vile taste into his malicious grin.

As the drizzle washes it off, I ignore his laughter and stare into the swirling hatred of his eyes, gauging the malice of the composite traits in an effort to gain some advantage from my knowledge of his inner workings.

The desperate thoughts produce nothing.

How can anyone beat so many forms of evil?

"Hello," purrs a female voice. Boots sloshing through the muck, Syrin emerges from the gloom. When she reaches us, she rips off her helmet and tosses it aside. To my annoyance, besides a bruise on her scalp, she otherwise appears intact.

While I struggle against Syd's grip, her hand trails down my injured arm. I wince as her fingers dig into my cuts.

Although the diminishing rain streaks the blood, she paints a circle pattern on her forehead and cheeks. Then stepping back, she draws her knife. "This will be fun."

Hardly able to stand on my shredded legs, I clench my jaw. I won't scream for her enjoyment.

"Only a few cuts," Syd says. "I still need the rest of her body."

An evil grin crosses Syrin's narrow face as the blade plays under my eye. "Let's blind her—"

Syd finishes the sentence. "But then, she couldn't see what we're doing."

Syrin shakes her head and then says with joy, "Oh! I have something much better."

Shuddering, I brace myself for what's coming.

It's not what I expect. Syrin's head bursts with bits of flesh and bone spattering over Syd and myself.

Aiming a pistol, a thin figure without a helmet runs at us. Before I can see the details of his face, I recognize Walt's running style.

Syd pushes me in front of him as a human shield.

Shooting my legs around his knees and twisting, I drop and knock him off balance.

He flops into the mud, rolling to his side, as more shots splash around him.

I lash out with a kick to his knee.

Even though he grunts, my wounded leg can't generate enough power to do any real damage, but before he strikes back, more impacts force him to dive away.

Walt runs out of ammunition. Syd pops up and with blazing speed, attacks before the teen reloads.

Knowing Walt is inferior to Syd in every aspect of combat, I shakily rise and head to the dark forms struggling in the dim blue light.

After knocking the gun from Walt's hand, Syd takes his time, relishing in inflicting punishment on his teammate. Ex-teammate, I remind myself.

Slowed by the mud and hobbling from my wounds, too many seconds pass before I arrive at the fight. Walt's armor is dented in half a dozen places and he has a hyperextended knee and elbow.

I launch a stomp kick at Syd, but he's too quick and grabs my leg.

Knife in hand, Walt jumps to my aid. Syd tosses me aside.

Helpless, I tumble down a slope between a couple of shattered plants and land in the muck near Syrin's fallen form. After scrambling the final distance, I tug at her pistol with my working hand, but the damn thing is stuck under her body and won't come out.

Syd twists the knife from Walt's grasp and stabs him, leaving the blade buried deep in his lower ribs. "You little cretin. After everything I've done to help you, this is how you repay me?"

Defenseless, Walt whimpers.

Syd slaps him and grabs his hand, snapping one finger then another. The teen cries out, feeding Syd's sadistic pleasures.

When another finger breaks, giggles erupt from Walt's mouth. A tormented cackle follows. His free hand reaches to his back and yanks out a plant frond hidden under his armor. He stabs at Syd's face.

At the last instant, Syd sees the threat, his hand rising and deflecting the metallic leaf. But the point catches his left eye and slices into his forehead. Half-blinded, he bellows in a mixture of rage and pain.

Syrin's pistol finally comes free, but before I can shoot, Syd ducks and escapes into the dim landscape.

Walt collapses as Syd's howls pour from the darkness.

Keeping watch with the pistol ready, I stand and stumble to my wounded friend.

As I approach, he rolls and sits up with a groan. "My back is on fire," he says, ignoring his broken fingers and the knife embedded somewhere in his liver.

"How did you manage to run and keep a straight face with that thing under your armor?"

With a sigh, he flicks the bloody leaf into a nearby puddle. "I have a high threshold for pain."

The statement almost brings a smile, but I stop myself because his high tolerance is entirely because of his vicious upbringing.

"Walt, you can't betray your own team."

He raises his mangled hand. "Let me speak. I can't control the blue liquid for much longer. Syd was only supposed to end the scenario by killing Suri, nothing else. When they tortured you, I cut Suri free and gave her the knife." His eyes fill with tears. "I loved her, but I couldn't bear the thought of you going all the way back to zero. I didn't betray her for myself. You're tired, Brin, and you wouldn't have made it back."

I disagree with the last point but don't argue.

The teen sinks into the mud, his strength spent. "I was never making it out of here. But I needed to do something good before my end."

The only person not thinking he owns the winning lottery ticket.

"You did, Walt. You saved me." After kneeling next to him, I whisper, "We have to move."

Walt's eyes focus. "The blue liquid's calling. Kill me before I can't take it any longer."

"Syd's still out there. We have to kill him." I neglect to mention I won't have another friend dead by my hand.

Because we can't linger, I jam my shoulder into his armpit and wrap my healthy arm around him.

"Brin, no."

He reaches for the protruding knife handle.

I stop him. "Don't pull that out. We don't have anything to stop the flow of blood."

"For you to win, I have to die."

"That's not happening. Keep awake, I'll hide you and think of something."

Of what, I have no idea.

I rise, pushing him to his feet. Although he's light, my slashed legs and pitted feet can barely hold him upright.

The nearby landscape offers no clues to Syd's whereabouts. Besides the soft patter of rain, I detect only silence. My exhaustion and wounds from the long battle have destroyed my situational awareness.

A different opponent would head to the flag, but Syd wants a final goodbye. Even half-blind, he's extremely dangerous, and somewhere in the darkness, he's circling, waiting for his opportunity.

"He wants to die. Leave him," my internal voice pleads while my black threads and common sense echo the same sentiment. And that's what I should do. Given the many dark patches across the terrain, even with my terrible wounds, I would have half a chance with the pistol.

But leaving Walt to perish would make me no better than Syd.

A cone of moonlight spears through the patchy clouds.

Which means big trouble.

Moving faster, we stagger through puddles and muck with loud splashes as I look for a safe place to hide him.

Walt speaks, his voice distant. "I don't remember, but I think a lot of bad things happened in my life. It's helped me so far to handle my feelings, but I can't take the pain anymore. The blue liquid's winning. Kill me."

"Stop talking about death. We'll find a way."

He groans from agony. "Listen. I was never reaching ten sigmas. It's okay, Brin. Let me die doing the right thing. Finish it."

Before I utter a retort, a bullet spears into my back and punches out of my side. A scream leaps from my mouth, and my pistol flies into a puddle. I lose my grip on the teen as my insides seep out.

Bang! Another round smacks into my ribs, adding another layer to the pain overwhelming my senses.

"Do something. Syd's winning."

My legs buckle, and my knees sink into soft sludge.

Walt doesn't fall but looms over me, his gray eyes black in the dim moonlight, a victim of the blue liquid. His lips draw back into a snarl. Then his bared teeth rush toward my neck.

I flinch.

At the last instant, he swivels, and pouring out demented giggles, rushes at Syd.

Two shots slam into his chest. Walt staggers another step then crumples.

I twist my aching body and crawl to him. Every movement is torture, but using my good arm, I roll him onto his back.

He gazes skyward with a lifeless stare.

Unlike everyone else, Walt understood he wasn't getting out of this universe. Not that he even wanted to return to the real world. But at least he survived past his memories, letting him have a sense of peace before his end.

I gently close his eyes to give him some form of absolution.

Not bothering to mask his approach, Syd steps toward me. Blood runs from a gouge slicing through his left eye while the right one doesn't blink.

Only the drizzle, the pitter-patter of its light drops falling onto the sopping ground, separates me from the perfect killer as he slowly raises his pistol and aims between my eyes.

Syd is the crown jewel of the composites and the future of the Ten Sigma Program.

Letting death take me would be so simple...

But the agony, the exhaustion, everything, it's all irrelevant compared to my promise of never giving up.

I want to be here.

On my knees, long on pain and short of ideas, I straighten and face my enemy.

His lips widen into a gloating smile.

Flexing the fingers of my good arm, which is the only thing my body still has working, I desperately search for a nonexistent solution.

All my weapons are gone, and my unbeatable foe stands five steps away, knowing every dirty trick I do. If I were healthy and equally armed, I'm not sure I could beat him. But now, even if my hacked-up legs could cover the distance without my death, my bullet wounds and dangling arm ensure that in close combat, he would destroy me.

There's no way to win, but I can't let myself be defeated.

As Syd cocks the pistol's hammer for the final shot, he glances to Walt's body.

Surprised by the depth of my feelings for the teen, I say, "You know, after his memories faded, he really was a decent person."

Syd snorts. "I never understood what I saw in him." He pauses, laughing. "Come to think of it, I don't understand what I ever saw in you!"

I smirk, clutching at the slim hope that's been offered. With a raspy voice, I reply, "It's because part of your being is taken from the scientist who brought me here. He's in love with me. You're in love with me."

His good eye makes a long blink. The gun barrel wavers and he hesitates, his competing traits embroiled in battle.

In a single desperate motion, I rise and yanking the knife from Walt's body, fling it at him.

Moonlight glints off the blade before it drives into the soft flesh of his throat with a wet thud.

Stunned, Syd's arm drops while a mixture of denial, rage, and fear erase his confident expression. A shallow cough spills blood down his chin.

After a long moment, the strength of his malice overcomes the horrible wound and a mask of hatred settles over his face.

Barely able to stand, and holding my hand over the leaking holes in my abdomen, I meet his malevolent stare and force myself to remain upright, engaging him in a contest of willpower.

The first to fall will be killed by the other.

His gun rises.

Groaning in disbelief, I will my heavy legs to move, but I only have the strength to take one plodding step at him.

However, Syd's injuries have taken their toll too and as he tries to aim, his arm shakes and his legs falter. Blood spurts down his breastplate, and although the hateful gaze from his working eye never leaves me, his weakening body collapses in a slow motion twist.

Before he hits the ground, the gun jerks, and he fires in a final act of spite.

The bullet slams into my chest.

Mortally wounded, my body flops backward and into a shallow puddle, drenching me with mud and water.

FIFTY-NINE

My eyes open as my lungs labor to draw thin sucking breaths. Bubbles leak from a hole in my chest.

I'm dying.

A feeble moan pours from my mouth as I raise my shoulders.

Syd lies on his back a few steps past Walt, the knife buried in his throat. Accompanied by anemic gurgles, the breastplate of his armor slowly rises and falls.

It's my final contest in the virtual world, the race to live a little longer than Syd. I give a hard stare, willing him to die and for the golden end of the scenario static to take me.

Nothing happens.

Spent from the effort, my head sinks into the mud. From the prone position, the last remnants of the storm land on my face, the tiny droplets appearing to curve from the infinite distance to the moonlight crusted clouds.

Lying beyond but invisible is the great blue dome. And farther still, past the edge of this universe, lies the real world and my true home.

A wet cough spills from my lips as more fluid trickles into my lungs.

Distant thunder echoes, but I can't see the lightning. While the outer circle of my vision darkens, the pattering of water dims until they are only fuzzy taps on my skin. The fiery pain crisscrossing my body subsides.

It is bitterly cold.

I'm not sure if this ends in victory or death, but no matter the outcome, my time in the virtual universe is done. I've withstood everything the overlords have hurled at me and kept my humanity.

Inside, there is only a peculiar emptiness. Without understanding the reason, I know my internal voice is gone, a final casualty during the climactic battle with Syd. It's only fair because, with all my friends dead, I deserve to die alone.

Walt was right. I'm tired and never would have made it from zero back to become a ten sigma. At least not as myself.

Besides the teen, I think of Suri. Of cute Ally and big Jock. Ramrod-straight Sergeant Rick, the ever-suspicious Vela, Carol with the beautiful hair, and even sneaky Simon. I miss my original team.

More faces join them. My last teammates, Bob and Odet. Terrified Cleo. The boy who died in the cabin. The other innumerable people fighting with me during the scenarios.

Also, those who fell by my hand in battle, especially the nameless seven sigma who had the two children, Melody and Melissa.

I'm sorry we couldn't have been on the same side.

And finally, the man in the broad-brimmed hat under the black cloak.

Wetness covers my eyes.

All the AIs, composites, and real people who have helped to shape what I've become.

And Syd and his creator, the witch avatar too. Even the evil desires of the blue liquid which allowed me to defeat the bald giant.

But for all the hate, violence, and death of this universe, it's the love of my friends, Walt and Suri, and even the small sliver of humanity within Syd, that has carried me this far.

As I say a silent *"Thank You,"* the dark cloud of the blue liquid fades from my mind.

The last tingles on my skin disappear and my body goes numb. The air flowing into my lungs dwindles into a trickle.

There isn't much time left.

As I fight the tightening circle of black, I direct my attention inward to the green threads containing my past.

Without looking at my old name, I skip the file header. Inside are reams of words. I jump over them and into the pictures.

A young girl with violet eyes stares back at me. The caption says her name is Darla. The next thread has an older couple, my parents. Another contains a strawberry blonde with a mischievous grin, my sister Emily.

I search faster, finding friends, lovers, and images of my home amid other wonderful bits from my forgotten life.

A picture of a man in a faded bomber jacket stops me. His name is Nick, and he is my husband. Clean shaven, he wears a wide, reassuring smile. The musky scent of old, crinkly leather washes through my mind.

With memories of everything I've done and everyone I've met, I will never be alone.

A petite redhead wearing specialty walking shoes stands in the center of the next picture. It's my real self, with the label "Mary."

When I reread the word, it feels comfortable and right.

My name is Mary.

This is my life and these people are my loved ones.

A surge of strength lifts my spirits. My dying lungs fill with blessed air. My vision clears as I gain a precious minute in my race to outlive Syd. Moments later, another wonderful breath pushes me further from death. A third follows.

It's my last one.

As my body stills, I focus on the love of my husband and family, as well as my close friends from both the real world and virtual universe.

My heart thumps wildly then slows from the lack of oxygen.

A few beats later, it stops.

Without a pulse, without breath, everything ebbs into an unnatural stillness.

Death is near, and as I calmly watch the remaining circle of my vision collapse, I ready myself for his icy touch.

My final moments pass too quickly, but just before the universe fades to black, golden stars sparkle through the clouds.

SIXTY

Misty curls drift in vast surroundings. A myriad of dots float in the far distance. My body is indistinct, and everything nearby is blurry.

Is this death?

A huge being sidles next to me.

"Finally, you fulfilled your potential and won," says a familiar voice.

I'm not dead.

"No," the voice deadpans. "You're not."

"You said I would never see you again." The snarky answer once again feels righter than anything else I could utter to the man in the broad-brimmed hat.

The substance around me wobbles, being, I imagine, the equivalent of an eye roll for this strange place.

"I said you would never see me again. Given that my form here is invisible, I would suggest that once again, the words were truthful."

His amusement arrives before his snicker rumbles through my fuzzy form. Somehow, without the skin and tissue of a body, emotions are easier to read.

"That's very perceptive, but thoughts can be read too."

Great.

"It allows for easier communications, your sarcasm notwithstanding."

This is where I went after I grabbed the leprechaun. Where I would have gone if the witch hadn't interceded and I had continued to follow Syd under the building. And somehow, this location is even more familiar than that.

"What is this?" I say with my nonexistent arms trying to gesture at everything.

"Your current body is somewhat limited in perceiving what is truly around you. But consider this our combination control station and workshop, where we indoctrinate those from the real world, create those from the virtual universe, and construct the sanctuaries and scenarios."

With the last words, my attention shifts to the tiny dots of the maps in the distance, the sanctuaries and scenarios of the program in its never-ending quest to produce another ten sigma individual.

"The home of the virtual overlords," I say.

"We're not overlords," he replies in a contrite tone. "Nothing so grandiose. We're simply the scientists who run the program. But this place should feel special for you."

"Oh?"

"This is where you first entered this universe and where we placed the threads inside your being. Also, where the idealized body you took so long to grow into was designed."

I focus extra hard on the location he indicates. Using a drop of imagination, I see tangles of black and red threads whirling around spinning scraps of golden material.

More entrants into the program.

My lack of sentimentality for my warrior origin doesn't surprise me.

"Those people don't know what they're in for," I reply.

"They all volunteered because something about their life was unbearable. This is their second chance."

A slim one.

"A slim chance is better than no chance. You are proof of that."

"That doesn't make it right."

He pauses. "Because of your success as the first person to graduate from the program, we have decided that humans will no longer have to fight humans in the scenarios."

I remember the seven sigma whose children were named Melody and Melissa. At least nobody else will have to kill another person in this crazy universe.

"It doesn't seem like enough," I say.

Politely, he replies, "Take that as a victory. The nature of the program is necessary, and the basic parameters need to remain the same. You can't change it nor should you try."

He's right.

As much as I abhor the scenarios, their essence is something beyond my ability to alter.

"And you called me back here for one last goodbye?"

"No."

"No?"

"No, she did."

"Hello," the voice of the witch says from my other side. "I wished to offer my congratulations. I didn't believe you had any way to prevail against those odds. You surprised me. Although, from the results of this program, I should have known never to be surprised at the human ability to overcome any obstacle."

The words are honest and match her emotions. "You promised you'd end the composites."

"We shall, and you are here to witness the payment."

The surroundings vibrate and more of the gigantic presences materialize. These seem chastised, their brooding attention centered on my being, which I find strangely satisfying. After a moment, I recognize their familiar taints belong to the leprechaun and the other harassing avatars. Just like the man in the broad-brimmed hat using Haiku as a skin, they used other avatars to do the same.

But outside of the software constructs, the malcontents seem more like juvenile and socially awkward scientists rather than anything malevolent.

The witch says, "Don't you gentlemen and lady have something to say?"

Their disdain washes over me as they speak. "You have won. We will destroy the reservoirs holding the traits we use in the composites. This experiment will never be started again."

Not in the least frightened, I prod them. "And?"

"There is nothing further to say."

"How about an apology?"

"That was not part of the agreement."

They're just petulant obnoxious twerps.

"We can hear your thoughts."

Good.

Before things get testier, the witch says, "Carry out your part of the bargain."

The medium shimmers, leaving me with only the witch and the man in the broad-brimmed hat as companions.

"The loss of their toys will hurt more than they let on," she explains.

"They set up a scenario to get my friend Suri killed and to drive me insane."

"Perhaps you will approve of our next program, which I promise they will hate. Because of how well you and your first team did— beyond anything statistically possible—we are revamping the AIs with the desirable traits of your teammates."

"Can you bring them back too?"

"No. Death is final here."

I'm saddened.

"Please don't be sad," she says. "One day, perhaps you will meet another ten sigma from this program who seems familiar. That individual will have parts of your friends inside his or her makeup."

The statement improves my mood.

Sighs of dissipating anger intermixed with the tinkles of breaking glass roll past us.

"Those are the death sounds of the composite traits," the witch says. "Curiously, I feel a bit uplifted without them in this universe."

And true to her word, even over the distance, the sorrow of loss emanating from the other scientists washes over us. I almost have pity for them. Almost.

"Don't judge them too hard, the real world has changed, and I'm afraid for the worst. They did have the best of intentions."

The road to hell is paved with good intentions.

"That it is," she says. "Well, I'd better be off to supervise the petulant, obnoxious twerps and make sure they complete this task."

I really like her.

Her indistinct form brightens into a smile.

"The fondness is mutual. Please do the program justice when you leave."

As she vanishes, like my first unwelcome foray into this place, my body trembles from the lack of internal organs.

The man in the broad-brimmed hat says, "It's time to begin your next journey."

"Wait, what's your name?"

"That is unimportant."

"After everything I've been through, you won't answer this one thing?"

"What do you think it is?"

"Alowishus?"

A chuckle reverberates through the medium. "That name is better than the real one."

"Is this an issue you had with your family?"

"One of them."

"I can't believe you won't tell me this one itsy-bitsy thing."

"Instead of my name, I'll answer the last question you asked before the final scenario."

"What?"

"It was important for you and Syd to be teammates, so he could get to know you and see you as more than a mere enemy to kill."

"Are you saying you set the whole thing up?"

"Don't give me too much credit. I gave you, the human with the greatest potential, a chance to prove herself worthy and beat him. For war, he was truly the most desirable mix of human qualities, but for peace, the absolute worst. He and his ilk were abominations that needed to be made extinct."

"Is that why you gave me the perfect body? To get him interested?"

His amusement bubbles around me. "Perhaps, but let's stay with the original reason. You received the body I thought your potential deserved."

This is the clearest answer I've gotten from him.

Starving for oxygen, my body shivers, but I have one more question. "What do you think I'll be doing next? The witch said things were really bad, but it can't be worse than this last scenario, right?"

"I don't know, but whatever the situation is, the world needs you and I'm sure you'll do well. Just as long as you don't revert to your old self."

Even without a face, I give him my worst "Only a Mother Could Love" expression.

The medium quakes with his laughter.

I sense him doing the equivalent of the leave motion as he says, "This time I promise we shall never meet again in any form."

"Why? What about the real world?"

"When we first met in your cottage, I was dying. My consciousness only resides here."

"Can't you go back?"

"I would never survive the final test, crossing the threshold into a new body."

"Test?"

No answer comes.

Survive?

———

The last ten sigma challenge begins when I materialize inside a freezing sea of dim blue light. Like the workshop of the scientists, the medium is not quite a gas and not quite a liquid.

Far below my feet, the glowing sphere of the blue dome recedes, leaving only stifling darkness.

Not knowing what to do, I shiver from the isolation.

Pinpricks of light aligned in a ten-by-ten lattice appear in the distance.

As I propel myself toward them, one by one, the tiny dots wink from existence. I move faster while my heart races, and my anxieties increase with each passing second.

Soon, only three sparks remain, then two, then one.

However, instead of fading, the last flares to life, radiating a welcome warmth.

I swim for its embrace. But with each stroke, my need for oxygen rises and my mind dizzies. My fears spike into a panic, and I quicken my pace.

When I finally get close enough to touch it, a thick material covered by a layer of frost blocks my path.

The final test.

My fists pound at the unyielding obstacle while my screams make no sound. Black rings surround my vision as unconsciousness threatens to overcome me.

Letting myself sink into the cold, I gather my strength. Then I ascend with powerful strokes and fire my fist at the barrier. The tough surface reverberates but does not yield.

I will not die.

With more force, I send a harsher blow, the impact ripping the skin on my hand. The wound doesn't matter, nothing does except for winning this final battle.

My fists smash repeatedly into the surface, bruising my knuckles and shooting waves of pain up my arms.

A crack forms and heat pulses into the surroundings.

I double my efforts, sending my throbbing hands again and again at the opaque substance. More fractures spread from the opening, but my waning strength can't sustain the furious pace.

Completely spent, my body sinks into the depths. As the life-giving beacon recedes, my muscles tremble as my consciousness fades.

A pair of violet eyes stares at me. When I focus, they don't belong to my recurring AI nightmare but to a young child, my niece Darla. Some of what I was still exists, and with the green threads, I have the instrument to get my life back. My family is on the other side of that barrier.

I made a promise to return.

My eyes pop open, and with renewed determination, I use a last surge of energy and launch myself upward. As my salvation grows against the murkiness, I kick harder and raise my fists over my head. One final time, I slam into the frosty surface, and this time, it shatters.

When my fingers touch the light, life and strength flood into my being. For a glorious moment, I savor the amazing sensation, and then as my essence flows through the gap, my awareness splinters.

SIXTY-ONE

CONSCIOUSNESS RETURNS to my being when warm air forces its way into my lungs. The tingly sensations of static crawling over my skin fade after another blessed breath.

I have a body!

Something flat lies beneath me, and pain claws inside my skull.

Grimacing, I open my eyes to harsh fluorescent light pouring from the ceiling. My eyelids want to squeeze shut, but I resort to squinting as the first step in orienting myself in my new situation.

When my headache clears enough for coherent thought, I have no idea what I am supposed to do.

But it's definitely not lying on a cold surface.

I tilt my head. A coffin of clear polymer surrounds me. The papery material of a hospital gown covering my body rustles as I push the lid off and rise into a sitting position. After a moment to let some dizziness subside, I twist myself over the rim of the container and jump onto a tiled floor.

As I land, something tugs at my head. I raise my hand and run my fingertips over a snug strip of metal. Thin wires connect it to a familiar contraption, a glassy sphere topped by a golden ring. Which means...

I'm back in the real world.

Thick red hair cascades in front of my face and over my shoulders after I pull the headband off and toss it aside. Wrapping my arms around myself and shivering with goosebumps from excitement, I take a minute to appreciate every nitty-gritty detail of my new existence. Unexpectedly, the vitality of being live flesh and blood is far more vivid than anything in the virtual universe.

And I've kept the promise I made so long ago.

Before I can check through the green threads or get too overjoyed, a muffled explosion travels through the walls and rattles the overhead lights. Glass tinkles behind me while traces of smoke enter my nose.

As muddled thoughts pour through my mind, I chew on a thumbnail, enjoying its salty taste, and ready myself for the next challenge.

But, regardless of what's coming, it's only incidental to my true purpose.

My family is somewhere in this world, and I'm going to find them.

Mary's journey continues in
Ten Sigma
- Renegade -

ABOUT THE AUTHOR

A. W. Wang is an enthusiast for studying military history and enjoys reading all genres, especially science fiction and fantasy. In his adolescent years, he exercised his mind by playing strategy games and his body by running around a soccer field.

He really should have shown Course 21 more love.

After letting his small amount of talent in computer programming hijack his post-college years, his life's journey has taken him back to his first true dream - writing science fiction and fantasy stories.

Besides the usual forms of mundane entertainment, his scant time outside of writing is spent going on ocean cruises and entertaining the cat, whom he is (of course) allergic to.

www.awwangauthor.com

facebook.com/awwang.writes
twitter.com/awwangauthor
instagram.com/awwang_writes

Manufactured by Amazon.ca
Bolton, ON

27897791R00245